Branwell Bron

By the same author

Adult poetry

Amphitheatre
Steel Wings
Solving Atlantis
Selected Poems

Children's poetry

The Imaginator

Anthologies

An Enduring Flame
Poetry in the Parks

Novels

The Other Concerto
Wordsworth in Chains
Wordsworth's Women

Novellas

Jupiter & Passage to Osiris: Two Supernatural Novellas

Non-fiction

Introducing Information Technology
Journeys

To the memory of my Mother

Branwell Brontë's Creation

Published by Methuen 2017

First published in Great Britain in 2007
by Forrest Text

Reissued in 2011 by Skylark Books

This revised edition published in 2017 by
Methuen
Orchard House, Railway Street
Slingsby, York YO62 4AN

Copyright © 2007, 2011, 2017 Wendy Louise Bardsley
The moral right of the author has been asserted

This is a novel.
While many of the people and events are real,
the characterization and story are from the
imagination of the author.

All rights reserved
Without limiting the right under copyright
reserved above, no part of this publication may be
reproduced, stored in or introduced into a retrieval system,
or transmitted, in any form or by any means
(electronic, mechanical, photocopying, recording or otherwise),
without the prior written permission of both
the copyright owner and the above publisher of this book.

A CIP catalogue record for this book is available
from the British Library

ISBN: 978 0 413 777843

www.methuen.co.uk

Typeset by SX Composing DTP, Rayleigh Essex SS6 7EF
Printed in Great Britain by CPI Group (UK) Ltd,
Croydon, Surrey CR0 4YY

Every reasonable effort has been made to acknowledge the sources of information
used in this novel and to contact copyright holders of material reproduced.
However, if any have been inadvertently overlooked the publisher would be
glad to hear from copyright holders and to make good in future editions
any errors or omissions brought to their attention.

Branwell Brontë's *Creation*

Wendy Louise Bardsley

Methuen

1

In 1839, Edgar Allen Poe's blood-curdling story, The Fall of the House of Usher, was published: the terrible tale of a young man's slide into insanity; Mendelssohn conducted the first performance of Schubert's Symphony, The Great; and the Swiss Physicist, Carl August Steinheil, built the first electric clock.

The parson at Haworth Parsonage had heard about that electric phenomenon, and wondered at it in amazement as he wound up the old grandfather clock on the stairs. Patrick Brontë liked winding up the clock, it grounded him for the night. Habits were important, he reflected, they helped you organise your day. The parsonage was a comfortable, elegant building he thought; built in 1779, just two years younger than himself, he felt an affinity with it. The front faced the graveyard and the church tower while the back looked out towards moorland, in close communion with the elements.

Approached by Main Street, a formidable climb, Haworth village does not encourage visitors. The sick and elderly struggle with the hill. Horses labour with their cargoes. At the top of the hill stands the Church of St Michael and All Angels, where Patrick delivers his sermons, carries out weddings and funerals, and hopes to impart consolation and grace to his flock. The little village has a cold, damp climate, and in better times has thrived on the business of wool. Water pours down from the hills, in thrall to its history, servicing the mills on the river. Handloom weavers have reason to brood and lose sleep.

It is a chill December evening. Inside the parsonage all is neat and clean. Two people sit by a vigorous fire in the parlour. Their conversation is intense, punctuated by sharp, nettled comments, only matched by their deep unspoken love. Such is often the way with families. To protect that love they must enter the other's pain, and by striving with them, become them. This is an illusory power, old, old as the moors, gentle or lethal as the rain.

'Hold still!' cried Charlotte. 'I must look!' Branwell moaned and gritted his teeth. Blood still oozed from the wound on his eyebrow. She dabbed it with a soft, damp cloth. She was angry. Branwell enjoyed his boxing, but the parson's son, twenty-two years of age, fighting in the street? She squeezed the cloth into a bowl of warm water, watching the blood spread out like a pink summer cloud, oddly quite beautiful. What was happening to her brother? He couldn't hold down a job, and whatever interested him one minute bored him the next.

Branwell winced. 'Ouch, Charlotte! Not so rough if you please. – I got in an argument with someone from Bradford.'

Charlotte watched him intently as he fidgeted about, putting his hands in and out of his pockets by turns. He could never stay still for long. She knew how frustrated he got when he sat about writing or painting. He liked to be active. Even when writing their stories as children he had raced ahead without punctuating, even without breathing sometimes, no wonder he was subject to fits. The shadows in the room drew close about them. The moment somehow disturbed her, it was too like a scene from the past. The imagined life was so much a part of her now, that there were days she couldn't sort truth from fiction in her head. She knew Branwell was the same. 'Why did you have to fight?' she moaned, glancing at the doorway, hoping no-one came in. 'Couldn't you just have talked?'

'Ah, the man riled me,' Branwell growled. He worked his hands together tensely. 'He insulted Father. What was I expected to do?'

'What did he say?' Charlotte sat down, observing him carefully. The wound had stopped bleeding. Outside gusts of wind tore at the windows suddenly then quietened as fast. Throughout that day, she had feared for Branwell's mood. He would hate it at Broughton-in-Furness. He would despise teaching. Her brother would rather be free as a bird, winging his way above the cliffs, alighting on rocks as he might, more like Emily's hawk than a human being.

Branwell shrugged. He didn't want to be questioned. She could see his look. He would either go sullen or burst into one of his rages. He spoke quietly, though vehemently. 'We were talking about the church rate and the new ideas for the parish. It got quite heated. The new vicar of Bradford, Dr Scoresby, is stirring up yet more trouble. Aye, if they split the parish into smaller districts Papa will certainly suffer, and I doubt Dr Scoresby would bat an eyelid.'

Charlotte sighed exasperated. The last few years had been deeply exhausting for their father, there was so much unrest in the area. Dissenters wanted the church rates abolished and education for non-Anglicans. Chartists were campaigning for suffrage and a ten-hour working day, and wanted education for workers. Education for all was a matter of great importance. The religious amongst the Chartists joined forces with the dissenters, their father could spot them in an instant. Charlotte had seen him throw back his shoulders and glare in their faces as they'd pushed towards him, aggressively shouting their cause. At such times he would turn on his heel, stride fast up the hill and thrust open the door of the parsonage, to dash off yet another letter to the *Leeds Intelligencer*. She was worried, too, about his eyes. They were failing. Branwell was nodding off to sleep. 'So how did you reply?' she asked, badgering him again. 'That's if you spoke at all, and didn't just grapple.'

'My reply, dear sister, was not for the ears of women,' Branwell said drowsily. He yawned and kicked off his boots.

'Don't be ridiculous. Tell me what you said, all of it, right from the start!' She sat up straight, her thin, strong body taut with purpose. 'It is only I who ask you. It will go no further. Now out with it!'

Branwell's eyes remained closed. His skin, Charlotte thought, looked worryingly pale. Due, she decided, to the lack of sleep he'd suffered lately. She picked up a candle and went to look at him more carefully. He did not stir. She feared for the way he involved himself in their father's troubles. There were violent people in the area. In truth, Branwell cared little for religion. The problems of the poor, however, were never far from his mind. He would talk passionately for hours in the parish about the evils of unemployment, and how the rising cost of grain was starving the poor.

Literature though, Charlotte reflected hopefully, was thriving, and there was a growing audience for newspapers. While poetry had only ever had a few devotees, there was increasing interest in the novel. Great writers, poets, musicians and artists were everywhere. She gazed about the room at the pictures, the books, all avidly read by Branwell, and thought of the cottage piano he played so well next door. He too longed for greatness. And the seed of greatness was within him. But he would not give it a chance to grow and become whatever it might be. She knew his highs. And she knew his lows, like now. Tomorrow he would be in misery. She felt such highs and lows herself, but she wasn't overwhelmed like he was by the constant need to succeed. The male in the family, he must become his father's dream. How would he do it? His mind was far too wayward. He wanted to succeed in so many ways at once, and he could not give his attention to anything for long.

He also wanted to help his father with his work. She had seen it in his eyes. And it came out sometimes in outbursts of pent up feeling when he knew their father was weary. Then she saw the weariness in his eyes too, and a kind of hopeless sadness because he could not find his father's son in his being. And so he would assume it, walking beside him on the streets of Haworth, talking to the poor and listening to their needs. It racked their father's nerves when a man lost his work and was unable to feed his family. And Charlotte knew of her father's private concerns; the parsonage was only their home while he lived, when he died they'd be rendered homeless. Branwell's failings he experienced as a kind of haplessness; sooner or later he would succeed.

Her brother was a man of so many parts, he didn't know who he was. His face, she mused, could sometimes look so kind and good, other times she feared it. Then there could be a stubbornness in his features, as if he might travel whatever path he desired, regardless of where it led. The result was this, a peculiar anguished emptiness, where he sat in moody silence as if he had left himself behind. What would become of him? She could hear his deep little moans, those strange rumbling groans he made that sounded as if they came from the throat of the thunder. He started suddenly: 'Charlotte! Charlotte, what's happening?' He sat up quickly. 'Ah, now I remember. Well, it's done with. Blood has been drawn.'

'Aye, yours from the looks of it,' she shrugged, turning away restlessly.

'Not just mine,' he asserted, straightening. 'I gave him a bloody nose. And a black eye too, I'll wager, for morning.' Branwell spoke in the high pitched tone he used when excited. Most of the time his voice had a warm, musical quality, Charlotte liked to hear. He stood up slowly and went to lean on the fireplace, gazing at the flames.

'Anyway, at least Papa has Mr Weightman to help him,' Charlotte said, more cheerful. 'Papa tells me he will make a very fine curate. – He was here at the parsonage earlier.' She frowned at the fire. 'I hope he didn't see you fighting.'

'Weightman?' laughed Branwell. 'I doubt a bit of a scrap would bother Weightman.'

Charlotte felt tired, but there was work to do, and she needed to settle Branwell before going to bed. She spoke thoughtfully. 'The Reverend Dr Scoresby is a fine scientist, I believe. And an Arctic explorer to boot. Oh, so many accomplishments! He is out to score the bull's eye in everything ... But he is not too able with politics.' Branwell was tapping out a tune with his fingers on the mantelpiece. She shook her head. 'I can't believe you've been fighting in the street. A man of your age and standing.' She went on talking, describing how it would be gossiped about in the village, how awful it would be for their father. She built up scenes, illustrating them with heated talk, embroidering them, working herself into a state. 'And you're drunk,' she said finally.

'Ah, you noticed.' He smiled wryly and returned to his chair.

'It turns you into a fool,' she said firmly.

'Shush,' he urged, putting out his palm. 'You're shouting. – Is Father in the kitchen? What's he doing?' He tilted his ear to the door, where he could hear movement.

'He's stitching another pocket on his coat for his pistol.' Their father slept with a loaded pistol by his bedside at night, which he discharged each morning through his bedroom window so the powder didn't spoil. 'However you creep about, Papa will certainly find you. He'll see that wound in a second and he'll want some answers.'

'So he will,' said Branwell, suddenly assuming a thick Irish accent from his father's roots. He folded his arms and blew out exhaustedly. Apart from the odd sound in the kitchen and the tick of the clock on the stairs, the parsonage was silent. 'I'll tell him I slipped on the hill. There has been a fall of snow.'

'Anne and Emily are upstairs doing some writing. What are you going to tell them? They might come down.'

'Oh, I doubt Anne will even mention it, and Emily will probably laugh.'

'You make your sisters sound heartless,' she replied crossly. She picked up the bowl from the floor where she'd placed it and stared at the water intently.

'Do I?' said Branwell, giving her a curious look. 'That's not what I meant. I'm sorry. As a matter of fact their hearts are mighty, Charlotte. Bigger than yours, for certain. Why, yours has shrunk to the size of a button lately.'

'That's a cruel thing to say,' she murmured. 'My heart is as big as ever it was. It is simply afraid ...'

'*Afraid?*' gasped Branwell, swinging on her. He met her eyes, his own fierce and staring. 'Never let your heart be fearful! A fearful heart is a worthless heart – do you hear?'

Charlotte continued to contemplate the water in the bowl abstractedly. 'So what will you tell them?'

'Oh, I'll think of something,' he sighed. He searched her face quickly with his eyes. 'I'm good at inventing, remember?' More tenderly, and with a softer voice, he said, 'You of all people know that.' 'There's a lot of work to be done at the parsonage now Tabby has left us,' Charlotte said flatly. 'We're relying too heavily on Martha. – Why, she is barely grown up.' Charlotte felt a sudden familiar panic. She continued, talking quickly. 'We are sewing like mad to prepare your clothes for the Lakes. And a fine tutor you'll make too, behaving like this.' Branwell replied with silence. She stood for a moment thinking then took the bowl to the kitchen.

Within seconds she was back. 'Papa's gone upstairs,' she said quietly. 'Thank goodness.'

'Ah, he'll have heard it all,' Branwell sniffed. 'The old man misses nothing.'

Charlotte looked downwards. There always seemed to be a domestic drama happening. More often than not, their father ignored it and got on with his work. She would sometimes gaze out of the window and look to the hills, to the wide freedom of the moors and the sky, and think how binding it was to be human, to be answerable for all you did and said, to be forced to tame your thinking, your actions . . .

A hushed December stillness pervaded the rooms of the house. Branwell sat by the fire, his head resting on the back of the chair, his bright carroty hair sticking to his face. Charlotte watched him thoughtfully. The light from a candle fell on his heavy eyelids. His face looked grand and stately, just as a great Pharaoh's might at rest in his tomb. Her brother could have been grand like that. There was something quite lofty about him. He strode the streets of Haworth like a prince. But his passions were waiting at every turn of corner. They would always catch him out. They would use him as surely as the seasons used the moor. All he could do was endure them. 'I hope you will try to make a go of it in Broughton-in-Furness,' she said tentatively. 'You might just land on your feet.'

He heaved a sigh and opened his eyes slowly, turning to her. 'My dear Charlotte, a bit of teaching is hardly likely to kill me, and it's a lot less dull than painting portraits.' He lowered his voice to a whisper. 'Listen . . .'

He sat up straight and put his hands on his knees. 'I outstripped the lot of you ages ago in learning, so please don't treat me like an idiot.'

She frowned, confused. 'It's not just the teaching. It's more than that. You have a fine intellect, Branwell. I am fully aware of that . . .' She could hear him breathing shakily, deeply emotional. 'But you never see anything through . . .'

They were both silent for a moment.

'You are not as clever as Maria was . . .' she said suddenly, in a rush. Her brow creased as she realised the power of her words. How awful it was that the words you would rather not say came out, while the ones you would rather have said stayed silent. 'None of us is,' she added softly. Quickly changing the subject, she said, 'Mr Weightman told us that when the horses are approaching the top of the hill they can scarce get their breath. I have often noticed it myself.' Branwell might easily hit back at her by talking about her lack of success with the Sidgewick children recently. She was hardly the model governess, though the children were little villains.

'Aye, it's true,' said Branwell, deep in thought. 'It takes strong horses to pull a coach up that hill.'

'Yes, poor creatures,' Charlotte frowned. She could see Branwell was preoccupied. She knew she'd upset him.

'That wretched school, Charlotte! What a dreadful place it was.' He grimaced. 'Those freezing rooms and scarcely a morsel to eat. If only Father had known. Our poor, poor sisters, dying at eleven and ten!'

Charlotte noted the pain in his voice as he spoke. When he spoke of the Clergy Daughters' School at Cowan Bridge it seemed his soul collapsed. He carried on talking in a low, shaky voice. 'A place of execution, that's what it was. Maria and Elizabeth came back here to die, they were so worn down.'

'I shouldn't have made you think of it,' Charlotte whispered.

'Sometimes, at night,' Branwell continued quietly, 'I can hear Maria coughing. – No, really I can. When Father is winding up the clock, that's when I hear her.' He pointed to the doorway. 'I halt right there. I hear her here in this room.'

'Nonsense,' said Charlotte shuddering. She rubbed her arms then took the poker to the fire.

All of a sudden Branwell cried out, 'If ye suffer hunger or thirst for my sake, happy are ye!' He stared at the flames in anger. 'Die! Die! wretched children, and by so doing become immortal!'

'In the name of God, Branwell!' Charlotte pleaded.

'Oh yes, everything in the name of God,' Branwell said scornfully. He went to the window to look out. 'What is the matter with the wind tonight? It howls like a wolf.'

'I suppose it will please itself how it howls,' she replied flatly, piling coals on the fire and restoring the flames. 'The wind is its own master. The moor is in want of life. All that is left is the wind.'

'The snow's still there,' Branwell said thoughtfully. He frowned. 'There is scarcely a moon tonight. The moor is so dark, only the snow lights it.' He continued talking in slow, melancholy tones, then turned to her, suddenly excited. 'Do you remember how it was, years ago, when we ran in the heather, careless as hares, and Emily knew each flower, each tree, the colour of the sky in all seasons? And you never complained when your shoes were hurting, all to save Father money.'

Charlotte pressed her lips tightly together. It hurt her to talk about the past.

'Do you remember when I took you to The Rydings? – Oh, what a day! I missed you so much while you were there. I loved that house with its forked tree bitten in two by lightning, and that dark mysterious rookery with its mad, shrieking birds!' He looked down at his hands. His knuckles were sore and some of the skin had come off on one of his hands. He touched it gently with a finger.

'You should think before you act,' she said, watching him.

'You're never going to let me forget this, are you?' he sighed. He met her eyes slowly. Suddenly, with a quick change of thought, he burst into laughter, stamping about the floor. Dust fell from his trousers. Then he stood still, gazing at her, his red hair limp about his face, his clothes dirty and torn. 'Put away that sewing, Charlotte.'

'A fine wardrobe you'll have if I do,' she replied, stitching even faster. 'Why can't I sew?'

Branwell went to her and kissed the top of her head. 'I hate to see you wasting your time, that's why.'

'Well, you are the expert on wasting time,' said Charlotte drily. 'You wasted enough of it in Bradford.'

'Ah, portrait painting was never for me. I can't screw a drop of passion out of it, however I try.' He turned away.

'Sometimes, that's how it is,' Charlotte said quietly. 'We must forget passion, and work.'

He turned back to her and smiled. 'Charlotte, Charlotte, you need to enter the music sometimes. Take your place in whatever it has to offer, symphony or cacophony. It's unnerving, I know, but . . .'

Charlotte gave a low little laugh. 'And aren't you the lucky one eh, having us close our ears to your pandemonium, our eyes to your abominations. Aye, you're lucky all right.' She gazed for a moment at his bruised and swollen face, his muddy attire. 'Don't you think you should tidy yourself up?'

'Tidy myself up?' he said abstractedly. He gazed down at his trousers. 'Yes, I suppose you're right.'

2

'Damn it! –Where is my pen? – I must write to Brown.' Branwell searched about his desk. – 'Ah, there you are . . . Now my ink . . .' He sat, thoughtful, biting his lip. So what shall I tell the Old Knave of Trumps . . .

Branwell knew he wouldn't fool Brown for a second. The sexton at Haworth, his old friend, knew him too well. He would have to tell him the whole truth about what he was up to in the Lakes and how he had fared so far. He sat pondering by the open window, his pen in his hand, a blank sheet of paper before him. He had taken lodgings at High Syke House, a farmhouse in Broughton, where he lived with Edward Fish, a surgeon, his kind wife Anne and their children. John was twelve, Harriet was nine, and lovely Margaret was eighteen.

This Fish fellow is something of a drunken liability, Branwell mused, scribbling a lively cartoon at the top of the page. He drinks till he's dizzy, and him a surgeon at that! He wouldn't have felt too happy about being in his care. – But oh, what a comely daughter! He would have to tell Brown about her!

He gazed outside through the open window, drawing the fresh, sweet air into his lungs. The breeze from the valley tasted good, and the views across the sands were splendid. Broughton-in-Furness on the river Duddon estuary had once been a thriving place for handloom weaving. Robert Postlethwaite, his new middle-aged employer, was a rich landowner with an air of aloofness about him, which sometimes put Branwell on edge. He revealed very little of his character. He gave commands; he gave them once, for good. Branwell had come to tutor William and John, his sons. But he doubted he would teach them much. A pair of lusty young bulls aged eleven and ten, they would rather bang their heads on a gate than learn. Broughton House had been built by

Postlethwaite's father for his family to live in. It didn't take long for Branwell to get there from his lodgings.

He felt full of strange emotions. Could it be true that he felt relaxed and even a tiny bit happy? He glanced around the room. The rooms at High Syke House weren't large, but he had managed to organise his things. His books were neatly arranged on the bookshelf, his papers tidily in the drawer. The mahogany furniture was strong and of excellent quality. The drawers were deep and slid easily in and out. And his bed was soft and yielding. A comfortable bed was vital. Immediately, he had pressed his hands into the mattress to see how it was. His dreams had been more like nightmares lately, filled with vile visitations, a rhythmical succession of dancing demons coming up close to his face and disturbing his sleep.

It was a mild March day with scarcely a cloud in sight. He was getting to know the land. I will try to describe how lovely it is to Brown, he decided. Perhaps he will pay me a visit. The heavy worries that had previously weighed on his mind seemed far away. Yes, it was quite a victory. Might he become someone different here, a very different Branwell, who was decent, reliable and honest?

The midday sun shone through the window lighting up the white of the paper before him. No sounds were perceptible about him. At times like this a flood of ideas would often rush through his mind and sometimes he felt as if he glowed. Past joys would enter his thoughts. He had known such exultations often in boyhood. Despite the loss of his sisters and his mother, he had known great happiness through his stories. Best of his creations was Percy! Percy, Earl of Northangerland, a handsome, selfish rogue, who did not care whose heart he broke and whose ultimate purpose in life was to simply have pleasure! How he had loved Percy! But a chance had been afforded him now to redeem Percy. Though at heart he wondered if he could, or if Percy would allow it.

He dipped his pen in the ink, then wrote the name of the addressee:

John Brown, Sexton of Haworth, Master of the Three Graces Lodge. 13 March 1840.'

He wrote on swiftly, words pouring from his pen. He knew the effect his letter would have on Brown, how it would cheer him up. It would bring a quicker pace to his step, a louder voice to his laughter. His pen worked on. He would not limit the strength of his feeling, it would have full flow! – But I must tell him to blot out the red! Oh yes, he must always blot out the red!

He concentrated on describing how he had fooled his employers so easily. They thought him quite a gentleman. He was a gentleman, of course. Or at least he intended to be, henceforth. – 'Oh! death and damnation,' he laughed to himself. 'A very pretty daughter indeed!'

'... If you saw me now, you would not know me, and you would laugh to hear the character the people give me. Oh, the falsehood and hypocrisy of this world! ... Well, what am I? That is, what do they think I am? A most calm, sedate, sober, abstemious, patient, mild-hearted, virtuous, gentlemanly philosopher, – the picture of good works, and the treasure house of righteous thoughts. –- Cards are shuffled under the table-cloth, glasses are thrust into the cupboard, if I enter the room. I take neither spirits, wine nor malt liquors, I dress in black and smile like a saint or martyr. Everybody says "what a good young Gentleman is Mr Postlethwaite's tutor! ..."'

He stopped for a moment, thoughtful. Yes, it was true, he could put on a very good act. He'd had plenty of practise at the Black Bull, acting out characters, using a variety of accents, and watching as they guffawed with laughter at his stories. He knew how they needed to watch him, how important his presence was, how he could make them feel bigger than they were, extend their imagination! Oh, how his friends needed him! – Even when he failed. For he often failed. There were times he felt tired and weary. Then his figure was bent as he walked round the village, and his spirit would tangle into itself like the brambles did in the winter. He was churlish and miserable then; he was not himself; he was lost. He braced himself and wrote on.

'... I am getting as fat as Prince William at Springhead and as godly as his friend Parson Winterbotham – my hand shakes no longer. I ride to the banker's at Ulverston with Mr Postlewaithe and sit drinking tea and talking scandal with old ladies – as to the young ones! – I have one sitting by me just now – fair-faced, blue eyes, dark haired sweet eighteen – she little thinks the devil is so near her!' Apart from the sound of his pen scratching the paper, the room was silent. *'... Keep to thy teetotalism, old squire, till I return; that will mend that old body of yours, till I come back, when we will have a puff & a stiffener.'* He signed off with a flourish, *'The Philosopher.'*

He smiled as he folded the letter. Where would Brown be now, he wondered, at that very minute? What was he doing?

Sitting in the graveyard at Haworth, John Brown looked at his index finger. It was bruised and swollen. Wasn't it over a week? It ought to have been getting better. But at least he could straighten it out. He had given it a nasty crack with his hammer while chiselling a gravestone. It was very painful. He worked it backwards and forwards. It would have to function at half its capacity however, there was nothing else for it, there was work to be done and money to be made that week. Gripping his hammer he banged on his chisel, shaping out the last '*A*' in the name '*MARTHA*', the name of the apothecary's wife who had died earlier that week. Why was A so difficult to carve, he wondered. The rest of the name was fine. He doubted anyone could chisel *'In Loving Memory'* faster than he could, and with such a perfect finish.

It was just as well he was fast; it was hard keeping up with the deaths, and it often made him unhappy when several children died in a row, all from the same family. He took a rag from his pocket and wiped his brow. He was missing Branwell. He was always a good bit of fun. It hadn't been the same since he'd left. It was an odd letter he'd sent . . . The first part hinted at a new kind of Brontë. Though the second reinforced the Branwell Brontë he knew. 'On my life!' he laughed, his teeth glinting in the sunlight. 'Brontë will never change, however he tries. He will always be creating a demon or two to torment himself with!'

He turned his face to the sun, letting it bathe his features. A mild March wind moaned down from the moors, cold on his ears. He knew it well. Sometimes it whistled round his chisel as if in song. Then he would play a game with his hammer, listening to it as it whirled round the gravestones, knowing which way it came and how it would sound, and making his chisel dance to its tune. A sexton in Haworth had scarcely a minute to spare. He'd a grave to dig and must finish his carving soon, or his day's work wouldn't be done. – And he hadn't blotted out the red on Branwell's letter . . . He shrugged his shoulders. He was glad he was only the son of a sexton and not the son of a parson. He couldn't help thinking he'd probably have been a rebel himself if Patrick Brontë had been his father. He wondered how Branwell stayed sane. He sat thoughtful for a moment. He wasn't as spiritual as he'd like to have been, he decided guiltily. When your arms ached from the digging of graves and the carving of gravestones, there wasn't a lot of energy left for praying. He recalled the start of Branwell's letter, opened earlier that day.

'If you saw me now, you would not know me, and you would laugh to hear the character the people give me . . .'

Brown smiled. He doubted Branwell could keep up the act for long. He was bound to be discovered soon, by himself first, most probably. He glanced about the graveyard. You couldn't put a foot between the graves. And he wished the housewives didn't dry their washing on the gravestones, covering his beautiful carvings. It didn't seem fair. He thought about the bowl of currants Charlotte had brought to the graveyard for him last year from their bush. He had never known currants so sweet. The currants kept coming. But the dead life laid in the ground had gone for good, and it hurt him to see the parson's face when he must bury the children, often before their parents. There were times he'd seen his lips twitching when he'd buried a mother with her baby. Brown wondered if it made him think of his own wife dying so young when their children were tiny. Oh, what a terrible time.

The man is full of suffering, Brown thought sadly. He could see the parsonage across the graves, its grey outline like a bold sturdy reminder of virtue and prayer. All those gloomy words he must read from bibles, thought Brown, all those weary sermons he must give from the pulpit. Branwell must swim on the froth of feigned happiness, Brown decided, drawn from drink and laughter. It was how he survived. He felt in his pocket and pulled out a long black bootlace. He slid the leather through his fingers. It felt cold and damp. It was Branwell's bootlace from the time he'd removed his boots at the pub for a jig. He'd keep it in his pocket till next time he saw him. 'I must rally my strength,' he told himself wearily, 'and tear this tiredness from my bones!'

3

'Eva Carter told me where ye were,' said Violet Draper, pulling on her shawl. 'What did ye go for?' It was one of those evenings in Haworth that sounded hollow, as if the whole world were far away, lost to the little melancholy town and its problems. Joe Draper fastened the collar of his coat and quickened his pace. It was raining.

'Yer up to summat again, that's what it is,' said Violet. 'All that rantin' an' ravin' they do. I knew ye'd gone tuh t' trouble. Ye'll naiver listen to me will ye?' Her husband's eyes glittered in the darkness. She stopped for a moment and turned to him. 'I hope there won't be trouble at t' parson's meetin' tomorrow in t' schoolroom. Young Branwell's away in t' Lake District teachin'.' Branwell Brontë was a strong support to his father against the dissenters, though he always tried to be fair. 'Oh, t' world's comin' to an end wi' all this,' Violet muttered. The men in Haworth rushed off to gatherings all too frequently lately. And they didn't mind travelling either, sometimes they journeyed all night to join others like-minded. 'There'll only be Reverend Weightman there. An' he'll not be as spirited as Branwell.' The villagers thought Weightman all kindness, even while arguing he always stayed calm and gentle. Which was more than you could say for Branwell and the parson; there were times Violet thought they might raise the roof with their anger.

'Ah, Weightman's no milksop. Ye should hear him man to man,' said her husband, noting the hole in the toe of his boot. He shook his foot. Water trickled out of the sole.

'You an' yer man to man,' shrugged Violet. 'I don't know . . .' And she didn't. It was all so disturbing, and her arthritis was bad that week. The men were relentless in their cause. Much as Violet Draper bickered with her husband, he was determined to join the others whenever he could. Every corner was haunted by something sinister. Secrets were whispered. It was deadly serious business. 'So who will it be tomorrow?' she wailed. 'Georgie Walters wor found stone dead in t' street last night. Upon my sowl, how terrible for t' childer round here! A mighty bump he had on his head an' all. – Did ye know about that?'

'Aye, I knew,' her husband said gruffly. 'A fatal slip on t' cobbles, probably. Them cobbles are slippery at night.'

'Not half as slippery as some o' t' lies I'm hearin',' Violet asserted. They set off walking again carefully. 'He were fightin' wi' Branwell, him, a bit back. He were bloody-minded tuh t' parson an' Branwell, that lad.'

'So what are ye sayin'?' said her husband. He laughed quietly. 'Ye dunna need t' worry about t' parson then if he's got his assassins about!'

'I'm not sayin' owt,' said Violet sighing.

'I wudna put it past Branwell,' her husband said thoughtfully. 'He's a temper as black an' oily as t' peat bog when it's up. An' he's noan feard o' t' Lord like his father.'

'Branwell Brontë? Nah, it couldn't a' been Branwell,' said Violet, looking up at him shocked. 'He's away. An' anyhow, t' parson has far worse enemies than Georgie Walters. It's summat to do wi' thievin', more like. I scarce know where it's safe round here of a night anymore.' She glanced round the bleak little street.

'Well, there's no-one'll rob ye, lass, ye've nowt worth robbin'.'

'Bah! An' whose fault's that then?' she said, shaking the rain from her greying hair. Her husband gave her a long sideways look. 'See, yer startin' again,' he growled. 'That's what I mean. You women are allus complainin' there's nowt t' feed kids wi', then ye grumble when yer menfolk start fightin'.'

Instead of answering him, Violet Draper linked her husband's arm as they went up the road. Some of the women were just as determined as the men to make themselves felt, and just as aggressive. There were meetings amongst the womenfolk too, but Violet didn't attend them. With seven children to feed and manage, she scarcely had time to think. Each day she prayed and hoped. *'Vengeance is mine! saith the Lord,'* she would murmur when anger rose up in her blood. It was a small, damp cottage they lived in. There was little money to heat it, and often little to eat, and the Drapers loathed charity, but she kept on hoping and praying.

Her husband heaved a sigh of relief as she squeezed his arm. It was enough to feel as vexed as he did without falling out with his wife. They were both thoughtful for a while. Branwell Brontë was missed in the village. In the Black Bull Inn, just before he'd left, Joe Draper had heard him talking with the sexton: "The police are far too violent with the crowds. The whole thing's out of control!" He'd spoken his words in the grand manner the villagers had grown accustomed to when Branwell Brontë talked politics. He talked like an Army Commander. Joe Draper had noted young Brontë's confusion that night, his smooth brow tightening with passion, his eagerness to find a solution. He'd been struggling to get his facts right. But facts weren't always what they seemed, Joe Draper reflected. And as you grew older, solutions were harder to come by. Brontë's intensity had brought tears to his eyes as he'd listened, the proud young shape of his bony face silhouetted in the candle lit corner. Trouble was never a welcome visitor anywhere, but straightforward talking was all too easily ignored.

'How can they call it progress when we can't feed our families?' Joe said bitterly. They were alone in the dark street. Cold rain trickled down his neck as he spoke. 'Machines are doin' our work and robbin' us o' money, an' t' Corn Laws are robbin' us o' bread!'

'Are ye afraid?' Violet asked, stopping again and facing him slowly. Her round eyes stared at him worriedly.

Her husband frowned at the floor. 'Are you?' he asked her back.

For a moment or two they were both still and silent. Violet wondered what would happen. Would little Rachel still be alive next month? She was very weak. Would Walter run away from home again, just so there was one less mouth to feed in the family? 'What have ye done with yer cap?' she asked him. 'Have ye lost it?' He took it out of his pocket and put it on his head.

4

It was almost April. Time had passed so fast. Branwell was happy in Broughton. Though he wasn't succeeding in what he had come to do. He was failing to teach the Postlethwaite boys, and he felt resentful about it, for he had tried. But just as he'd feared, the boys could not be taught; they were too unruly. He had given it his best shot; he could do no more. It was, however, unsettling. At moments when all was lost, he turned again to his writing, which seemed, of course, a sensible thing to do.

Margaret sat in his room by the window, looking out. 'Will you listen to a poem?' he asked her tentatively. She faced him slowly and nodded. Swallowing his pride, for she hadn't shown the slightest interest when he had read to her before, he took it out of the drawer. She came to him and stood by his side as he held it, though her eyes were more curious than eager. Margaret, he felt, was totally perplexed as to why he should want to write poetry. But he'd see how things went.

It was a warm spring afternoon. The bird songs were loud in the garden. The trees had burst into blossom, their potent scents wandering the room. For a moment or two he stared at the poem in silence. He could never find the right mood for poetry with Margaret. She confused him with her lack of response. He lifted his face and met her eyes. Her smile was more than friendly. He knew she would like him to kiss her. He'd been playing games with Margaret, he knew. He'd been flirting, he couldn't deny it. But he knew he could never love her. She could not give him the kind of gladness he needed from a woman, a kind of intensity he believed there might be. She inflamed him sometimes with desire. But he did not really want her in the proper way, and was often embarrassed when his charms affected her as they did. She was very easily charmed. Also, he'd perceived, she might be difficult if crossed.

She was a proud and clever woman; it was just that she didn't appear to like poetry very much.

The house was still today. Mrs Fish lay ill in bed with a cold. Fish was out on business. He could hear John and Harriet through the window, running about in the garden, generally ruining the flower beds and climbing the trees. They too, it seemed, were ill disposed to education. He was glad in a way that he was tutoring the Postlethwaite boys and not them; he suspected they might be even more of a problem. Were there any children anywhere, he wondered, who actually wanted to learn? Margaret talked a lot with her father and had a broad understanding of world events and politics. But she avoided talking about the arts. He wasn't sure why that was, and wondered about it. He thought it might be him. She knew he had been a painter. And she knew he would like to be a writer, especially a poet. But it seemed she was averse to talking about it. He couldn't help thinking she had probably been warned away from his creative inclinations, and instructed to ward him off them. For it was true they might devour him. As much as his writing was his master it was out to undo him. It would not let him be. He must always be writing, or else dreaming.

'Go and sit down,' he said. 'Close your eyes if you must. But please try to listen, Margaret.' He was serious now. It jarred on his nerves when he lost himself in a poem while her thoughts were elsewhere. He'd vowed to himself he would never read to her again. Yet here he was, asking her to hear his work, begging her even.

It was a new development, this reading out loud of his poetry to strangers, and it was vital to him that he did it. He was actually attempting to come out of hiding, and was anxious. Didn't she realise how privileged she was? He had always signed his poetry *'Northangerland'*, before, never *'Branwell Brontë'*. Branwell Brontë was at last daring to take ownership. It was such a vital moment. He had submitted himself to the nullification of Percy, to the fragile emergence of himself.

He sighed. Margaret's expression was frustrated and woeful, not at all what he wanted to see. Excitement, pleasure, even admiration if possible was what he wanted. He knew she would rather be held than listen to his poetry. He gazed at her for a moment, wondering if she could ever feel as he did. Did she have any inkling of how it was?

'Alright, I'm waiting,' she said quietly, composing herself like a polite, obedient child. 'I'll listen just as you wish. I promise to try.'

He shook his head. She shouldn't have to try, he thought irritably.

It should happen naturally or it's not going to happen at all! He gazed at the page again, wondering if he should put the poem away. He felt his poetry disappointed her. And it probably did. He couldn't get away from the serious deep-felt issues he needed to explore, the feelings he'd known as a child, looking out on the graveyard, watching the sexton day after day digging graves, witnessing the horrible deaths of his sisters, hearing his father's sermons, and Tabby's stories about withered, abandoned ghosts. However he tried to create jubilant poems they would somehow crawl into the darkest depths of his mind. That's where his poetry lived, down in the dungeons of hell. No, they were not the issues Wordsworth explored, and certainly not those of Byron. Though he suspected that's what she wanted, the sort of poetry Byron would have written, poems about love and passion; poems about her. He could never have loved her, he reasoned, the essential ingredients were missing. Though he didn't know what they were, it was just a perception. Her eyes, he saw, were vague and distant as she watched him. Seeing she was waiting, he began to read, slowly, carefully and with feeling, *Percy's Last Sonnet*.

> 'Cease, Mourner, cease thy sorrowing o'er the Dead
> For, if their Life be lost its Toils are o'er
> And Woe and want shall visit them no more
> Nor ever slept they in an earthly bed
> Such sleep as that which lulls them dreamless laid
> In the lone chambers of the eternal shore
> Where sacred silence seals each guarded door.
> Oh! Turn from tears for these thy bended head
> And mourn the "Dead Alive" whose pleasure flies
> And Life departs before their death has come;
> Who lose the Earth from their benighted eyes,
> Yet see no Heaven gleam through the rayless gloom.
> These only feel the worm that never dies
> The Quenchless fire the "Horrors" of a Tomb!'

Suddenly the room went silent. Margaret's head was bowed. It was a moving poem; at least for him. But had it moved Margaret? She raised her eyes, and he saw she looked deeply unhappy. She blinked and looked downwards again. 'So what did you think?' he asked awkwardly. She turned her face towards the window again.

'Your poems are always so sad,' she said. Her voice trembled as she spoke. 'It's hard to hear such pain.'

Well, he thought, it was only what he'd expected. It hurt him though that the poem had upset her. It was a joyous poem in truth, the release of Percy from his mind, the freedom of Percy's spirit, and his own. Didn't she realise how important that was?

There was a long silence. He sighed. At least she'd been honest. Margaret, of course, Branwell knew, could never have understood where Percy lived, how difficult it was to banish him. How could she? She didn't know who Percy was, who he had been. She could not feel him as he could, deep in his soul. She would simply see the poem as a poem about death, a sad poem about mortality.

'I shouldn't make you listen,' he said. Margaret was sobbing softly. He stood for a moment, baffled, amazed that his poetry had upset her so badly. He brought himself, with a shudder to the understanding of this, to the honest understanding that she could not share the deepest feelings of his heart. And yet it was poetry. It was genuine feeling, genuine emotion transformed into poetry! He went to his desk and gazed down at his writings. He might have read her poems that were less intense. Though he knew he wouldn't. It was over.

'Your words confuse me. They are always so full of suffering,' she said, covering her face with her hands.

'It's a poem, Margaret,' he said shakily. 'It expresses things deep inside me.' He frowned thoughtfully.

'I ought to be more sympathetic,' she sighed, drying her eyes with her handkerchief. 'You have known deep pain. I have never known such feelings myself. I . . .'

'No,' Branwell murmured. 'I suppose that's true.' He folded the poem and put it back in the drawer. 'It's a very important poem,' he said, turning to her again. 'But you wouldn't have known.'

He observed her carefully, up and down, wondering why he should have thought she could join him in his poem, in that deep, churning part of himself that was longing to be free. She was a lovely woman in a soft silk dress, sitting by the window, the sun on her hair, a beautiful woman, looking to him for love. He met her eyes slowly. He was surprised at his own stupidity in reading it, in going against his common sense, his decision. He assumed it was desperation. He was feverishly seeking feedback now for his work. 'It's about Percy,' he whispered.

'Percy?' she asked, frowning and curious. 'Who's Percy?'

Branwell ignored her question. How could he ever have talked to Margaret about Percy? The poem derived from the Angrian writings of his childhood, he could never have talked to her about those. He sighed. He had thought the poem had done with Percy. But it seemed he was alive and well. It wasn't as easy as that. Percy would never be vanquished!

'Oh, Branwell,' Margaret said wretchedly. 'I am so sorry. What do you want me to say?'

He paced the room wringing his hands. His poetry had to be good. First class! Good enough for Hartley Coleridge to hear! That sick feeling of despair entered him again, that terrible sense of having failed. 'You mustn't say anything unless it comes from your heart,' he said wearily.

'I don't mean to hurt you,' she moaned. 'I can tell I have ...'

'It doesn't matter,' said Branwell, sighing. The wind stirred the curtain at the open window blowing his papers off the desk. He rushed to retrieve them from the floor, ordering them neatly, each page sacred. 'There are things ...' he murmured, 'that can only be said in poetry.' He was coming to the end of his patience with Margaret. Her lack of response brought a kind of terror to him. He was never prepared for her look. He feared to recite her poetry from Wordsworth or Byron, for what if she went into raptures over it? How would he cope? He could never have suffered the comparison. She sat in the chair, almost without stirring, as if waiting for further instruction. The air was charged with anger now, Branwell's anger. 'I think you should go,' he said quietly.

Margaret's skin tightened on her brow. 'That's not how it was before,' she pleaded. 'Just weeks ago, remember. Then you wanted me to stay ...'

'Is that so?' he said distantly. He swallowed and moistened his lips. The scent of Margaret's perfume was strong in the air. He was coming to dislike it lately. She moved about on the chair, the silk of her dress sighing about her.

'You are very unkind,' she protested. 'Let me hear it again. I'll listen to it better. I promise!'

Branwell shook his head. 'The moment has gone. You've killed it.'

'You are far too cruel,' she retorted bitterly. 'You judge me too fiercely!'

'You are just as you are, Margaret,' he said, taking a deep breath. 'I judge you as you judge me. Did you not hear what you said just now? I have dared to speak the words of my soul, and they upset you.'

Margaret rose slowly and went to the door. Branwell's thoughts were moving away from her now. She'd return tomorrow, he knew, she would come to him like she always did. He rubbed his face tiredly. There were times he felt furious with himself. He expected too much of people, of himself, of the world. When he was in full swing he was happy, content and in tune with life. But at times like this a darkness descended upon him; it crept through his bones; it enthralled him.

I am the foolish one, not Margaret, he decided firmly. I should never have asked her to listen. Poetry, of course, was often hard to interpret. Just like music, it was only for the elect. It hurt him though that she could not feel his words. Her lithe body was beautiful, the bones of her face were wonderfully outlined, her blue eyes bright with mystery. And yet she could not join him in his soul. In spite of all she was, she could not enter his spirit.

Yet Milly could, he reflected. He had seen it in her face. And the way she had grasped his hand when he'd finished reading. Whenever he read to Milly, she kept her eyes fixed on him as if clinging to every syllable, sweet, beautiful Milly, who couldn't even read. Was it any wonder he was harsh with Margaret, who could? He heard her open the door behind him and let herself out. He heard her footsteps on the stairs.

Then came the sound of the other ... A sound that froze his blood. He heard the sound of the hooves again, coming at him from somewhere deep in his mind. He could hear the weight of the devil's bulk thundering towards him, searching for him, searching for Branwell Brontë!

5

'Albert seems honest and courageous,' said Branwell to Brown. 'And that's important.' They were sitting in The Old King's Head, the grand 17th century inn opposite Broughton House where Postlethwaite lived. Branwell looked up from his drawing and glanced about. The young Queen Victoria had married her German cousin, Albert, that February and people were still celebrating. 'I think they are a perfect match.' He screwed up his eyes and traced the detail of Milly's nose with his pencil, the gentle angle of her cheek bones.

'Let's hope so,' said Brown, lifting his drink from the table.

'Careful,' warned Branwell, moving his drawings to a safer place, then focusing on Milly again as she went round the room. He loved to draw the sensual lines of her face, the softness of her mouth, her deeply soulful eyes. He shaded her hair then swiftly, skilfully, sharpened her eyes to laughter. This was but one of many drawings he had done of Milly. He loved her every feature, her every movement.

But he knew his feelings were wrong, and wrestled with them daily. She was a simple, uneducated girl. And she was mute. Whatever she felt she freed in sounds from her throat; sounds, not words; sounds like Branwell had heard in the wind and the sea, sometimes soft and gentle, other times passionate and angry. There was a misty down on her skin, most obvious now when her bare arms shone in the sunlight. He could not capture it in pencil, only in feeling.

He finished the drawing, knowing again that pang of love that bewildered him. He was apprehensive about it. He did not want to flirt with Milly then abandon her, as he had sometimes done with women. He wanted to have her forever. But how? She belonged to a different world. Could the two worlds ever unite? Or could they only meet when he held her, in those brief moments of bliss heaven had allowed them?

Brown was talking about Queen Victoria again, but Branwell wasn't listening. Brown had arrived that morning from Haworth and was to stay till the following day. Branwell had requested his company. He had wanted him to meet Milly. In spite of his resolve to teach the boys, weary that afternoon of their noise, he'd gone to find Brown at the inn earlier than arranged. 'I wish our young queen well,' said Branwell, taking a drink from his glass. 'She may be young, but she's wise. A person doesn't get wiser because they get older. If wisdom is there at all, it is there from the start.'

'Indeed,' said Brown, pursing his lips and thinking about it. Though older than Branwell, he knew he was certainly no wiser. He was always making mistakes; he sometimes tumbled over them. But watching his young friend now, observing how he felt about the barmaid, he wondered if Branwell's wisdom might have deserted him. The girl was exquisite to look at, and her manner was lovely. But the two of them together? No, it could never be. His eyes wandered over Branwell's form. His thick red hair glistened. He looked fresh and strong. His black coat fitted finely on his sturdy body. He watched him, silent and intent, rubbing his thumb on the pencilled hair, making it look more real. It was quite magical the way he could turn his talents from one thing to another.

'Well, the Poor Law has been reformed,' said Branwell, his eyes distant and serious. 'For what the reforms are worth. But we've a long way to go before we've beaten starvation and crime.'

'How right you are, sir,' said a man at a nearby table. 'We might have to wait a bit longer for that!'

But these were stimulating times for Branwell. The magazines were full of exciting developments. Art, science and politics were busier than ever. The French instrument maker, A.F. Debain had constructed the first *harmonium orgue expressif*, of enormous interest to musicians like himself. Thinkers and word-smiths like Dickens, Thackeray and Wordsworth were alive and well. And there was great enthusiasm for the uniform penny postage, soon to be introduced, and a great boon for writers. In the meantime, he was trying to educate the Postlethwaite boys as best he could, though increasingly distracted by their boisterous and wayward behaviour, and his own desire to write, talk, and think. The boys were learning very little. The fellows at The Old King's Head were learning more. At High Syke House, Margaret was forever on his trail, which made it increasingly difficult for him to see Milly. And see her he must. He constantly needed to be with her, and there was never sufficient time. It had all happened so quickly, almost like something lying in wait to surprise him. And it had. He must see her eyes searching for him, whenever he entered the inn. He must run his hands through her hair. They could scarcely wait for when they could be together. When out walking, his eyes were peeled, searching for secret places. There was the hollowed hill by the river, and a place near the rocks by the old perished oak, where the stream ran deep.

Milly was small with beautifully rounded limbs and long chestnut hair. He would watch the clock as she finished cleaning the tables and tidied up the bar. She was highly sought after by the men. Though her air was one of pride and dignity and they had learned to keep their distance. Milly kept to herself. But with him, Branwell reflected fondly, there had been an instant attraction. She had smiled at him in an oddly familiar way, as if she had met her fate. And from the moment of setting eyes on her he had fallen helplessly in love.

But it was hard to accommodate the feeling. He had never known it before. He wanted to tell how he felt to someone, and had finally written to Brown. He had needed him to come to meet her, to see her for himself, to say what he thought about it all. There was no nonsense about it. Milly was a serious concern. He couldn't tell his family at the parsonage. – What a barmaid? A girl without any learning, living in a humble cottage with her uncle and scarcely a copper between them?

Earlier that day in his room at High Syke House, he'd confided everything to Brown. And in his usual composed manner, Brown had listened. He had taken him to meet her that morning in a place on the way to the inn. And she'd greeted Brown with a smile and a kiss, and the little embraces she gave when she felt emotional. Brown had warmed to her instantly. And Branwell had known right there and then that he'd given his approval. For he needed Brown's approval. He had so far failed in all he had ever tried to do. But he had not tried with this; this falling in love had been of its own volition. The impulse was right from his heart.

Milly's family had been spinners of woollen yarn, working from home. But the factory system had ruined them. Now her parents were dead, and she lived with her middle-aged uncle in a cottage at the foot of the hill. Branwell loved Milly's kind of woman, the poor girl, who had nothing at all but her work and beauty. She was quite the opposite of the women he'd created in his stories with Charlotte, women with wealth and position, without a single concern for anyone but themselves. They'd enjoyed creating such people; it was an escape from the poverty and disease that abounded where they lived.

Milly was bright and healthy, her skin dewy and fresh. Branwell saw her as a sort of biblical character. His Percy would never have had the least interest in Milly. He would see her life as a life without riches, without books, without music, without any cultivated aesthetic sense at all. And yet her soul was big, like a God given entity. She was living proof of what beauty really was; innocent, solemn beauty, that took ennoblement simply from itself.

The afternoon light came in, picking out the strands of red in her hair that merged gently with the brown. She was cleaning the tables by the door. For a minute or two he watched her, till she turned and smiled. The earnestness in her eyes revealed how she felt. It would be another half hour before she finished her work. Then he would walk her back to her cottage. Or if the weather was mild they might walk on further.

Today it was warm. The days were becoming longer and the flowers were blooming in the hedgerows and on the hills. The trees were bursting with soft new green. Branwell's fervid love for her would give him no peace. He needed her like the dry earth needs the rain. Sometimes she robbed him of sleep. He would feel his body reaching out for her, reaching out of itself.

All his thoughts were of Milly. He wanted to write poetry about her. But he wondered if words could ever describe how he felt; the way it was when he held her, the feel of her body against his own, the smoothness of her skin. It was all so wonderfully good. And she made no conditions for their love. She would let him sit and make sketches of her whenever they went out walking. Then she would bathe her feet in the stream, or else sit in the ferns and plait her hair. He watched her as she went about the room working, placing her hand on her forehead when she was tired, her soft beautiful lips smiling if she caught his eye. She was a woman with great strength of character, firmly rooted in her life, in the subtle moods of the land about her. She knew its flora and scents intimately, just as his sisters did at Haworth. Though she could not communicate through words, only through her eyes, gestures and sounds. But he understood her language, just as he knew the tongues of the wind and the rain.

It was almost five o'clock. She had come to the end of her work.

He watched her as she pulled on her cloak, a thin coarse cloth, and fastened it about her neck. He would like to have bought her something prettier and had offered her money. Though he'd seen she'd been hurt and offended. He would not suffer her to feel like that again. But she'd accept his food gratefully. If they went out on a picnic, they would sometimes eat by the water and lie in the grass. She would take back home whatever food was left over.

'I shall have to be heading back,' said Brown, rising from his chair and rousing Branwell from his thoughts. He was staying at a nearby farmhouse, and would leave for Haworth next morning. He nodded at Milly and she waved him off through the door. Minutes passed. Presently, she looked at Branwell again, and gave him the look he had waited for; the look that meant he should leave. He rose and went out. She would follow him, in the usual way, at a distance, knowing which way he had gone.

He made his way round a corner and down the hill. Hearing her footsteps he let her catch up. She joined him quickly, taking hold of his hand, leading him through the ferns and wild flowers.

'I thought you might take forever,' he jested. 'Would you make mirrors of the tables?'

She leaned towards him, resting her head on his arm, making the strange little sounds he had grown to love. Then she squeezed his hand in her palms, and pressed her lips to his cheek.

'You have to finish things properly, I suppose,' he said, suddenly thoughtful. 'I suffer worst when you're coming to the end of your work. The last few minutes are unbearable.' He talked on in a kind of intoxication, the sounds of the early evening closing around them. She put out the flat of her hand before him as he reached to try to hold her.

'Whatever you like,' he laughed, seeing she wanted to walk on further before embracing. How good it was to be with her like this, to feel the release of the tension within him, to just let it go!

'Oooosh,' she went, stopping for a moment. She lodged her foot on a rock, lifting her skirts slightly to tie her bootlace. When she had tied it, she turned to him, grasping his hand and putting it to her lips. Her look was one of innocent, total love.

'What a beautiful witch you are!' he whispered. She turned her face to the sky and laughed. It always made her laugh when he called her a witch. Her laughter was rich and strong, and came from her throat with its own individual sound as everyone's did. Her movements filled him with delight. She did not move as others did, but more in a sort of union with the things about her, like blossoms did in the breeze, or the gentle movement of cotton grass on the moors. And it was all so comforting for him, quite distinct from the sadness he so often knew. There were times when he felt unworthy of her. But he was aware of something inside himself, longing to be free, a kind of richness he knew he had yet to give.

They had reached the place where the stream grew deep and became a small pool. Lying together in the cool ferns, it was as if they were at the centre of a great rich fruit, at its very core. At times like this he did not need to speak. Apart from the bird songs and the sound of water lapping against the bank, everywhere was silent. The pale blue sky was still. He kissed the soft white skin on her arms and her neck. He could feel her breath gently throbbing on his cheek. He kissed her mouth, and she began to undo the strings of her smock, effortlessly, easily, revealing her firm smooth breasts. He saw she was crying a little, though she smiled through her tears.

'I mustn't, Milly,' he said, pulling away. But she drew him on. 'Milly,' he whispered. *'I daren't.'*

Still she pulled him down then threw her arms above her head, the sunlight shining on her beauty. He could not stop his mind from moving ahead, forcing him forward. He wanted their love to come alive, to reach its highest peak, to find its resolution like a piece of beautiful music.

He gasped and drew away from her again. It could not happen! And yet it seemed so cruel that they could not have each other, just as they wanted, right then. She frowned, cross at his confusion. It was all so simple for her; she was not captured as he was. He turned from her, face down in the ferns, his back towards her. But the quick pain of heavy slaps on his back brought him to his senses.

He shook his head, awakening again to his existence in time and space. Now she was standing before him, pulling down her smock. The soft cream coloured cloth fell to the ground, revealing her short white petticoat beneath. She bent and put out her hand. He took it, drawing her towards him. She lay beside him again. And she offered her neck with a gentle, almost tragic movement, like a doe at the moment of death surrendering to the tiger. He kissed her long and tenderly then took off his shirt, only to draw away again at the shock feel of his naked chest on her breasts.

He sat for a moment lost, running his hands down the muscles of his arms, looking at them in wonder, finding his flesh so fully, painfully alive. She was making loving murmurs, hurt and neglected. It was a strange flaming moment, as if enclosed in light. She stood up slowly, and he watched in wonder as she removed the rest of her clothes. Then she stretched out her hands before him. He could not move, though his flesh quickened with desire.

As if with sudden decision, she ran to the pool, and in a speedy, supple movement dived in the water. He got up quickly and followed, watching her swim, sleek, silver as a fish. Then all of a sudden, nothing. Not even a ripple of water.

'Milly! Milly!' he cried frantically. 'Where are you?' A terrible fear came over him. He waited for several moments, watching anxiously. Till an arm thrust up from the pool, waving slowly. Then another. And then her face, openly laughing and gasping. He stripped off his clothes and swam to her. Reaching her they clung together embracing.

Together they swam to the bank and fell on the grass. She held him tightly and kissed him, laughing and smiling in her effortless, shimmering way. His lips wandered the gentle curves of her wet, gleaming body. Only the moment mattered; not before, not after, just now. Again and again he flooded her with his being. Till they both lay still, gazing at the sky, gradually becoming aware of themselves again.

They lay together for a while then dressed and walked on, listening to the voices of birds, the whisper of grasses. A warm wind murmured round his ears. Was it the wind that wailed past his ears on the moors at Haworth? Could it make the very same cry, that weary tormented cry that had wailed portents since time began? He did not want to know what it said about Milly.

6

After Brown had left for Haworth next morning, Branwell felt lost. He sat thinking in his room. He needed his friend just now. Brown had an indefinable quality that made him feel good; he made him feel strong. And he had understood perfectly about Milly. In an odd way Brown and Milly were a bit alike. Brown was a quiet man, and unlike himself, didn't have the least need of an audience; there was a certain steadiness in him, he was solid and composed. Sometimes Branwell wished he were more like Brown, his life would certainly have been easier. How good it would be to be silent and calm, he thought, like him. How many times had he raged at his sisters, even his father, and deeply regretted his words? Footsteps on the stairs just then, announced Margaret.

'Come in!' he called, even before she had knocked. For a moment or two he breathed uneasily, he didn't want to see her today. In fact, he didn't want to see her at all. What does she want from me, he wondered irritably. If it was love then he could not give it; it belonged elsewhere.

Talking to Margaret made him irritable and they inevitably argued. Strangely, when he had read her the poem about saying goodbye to Percy, he had said goodbye to her. They hadn't spent a lot of time together since then. Their encounters had been simply over dinner, or in the garden when he'd been reading, or like now when she came to his room. He wondered how long she could maintain the falsity of acting as if they were friends. For they were not. He had sadly come to dislike her. And he also suspected she followed him. That, he could not forgive. He wondered if she knew about Milly. The thought disturbed him. As she entered the room, he wasn't sure what to do next. How could he tell her that they'd no longer anything to say to each other, that he didn't want her to bother him? She would no doubt question him in that bold way of hers, shaking her sun hat restlessly if he did not answer.

Today he had much to attend to. He must prepare his lessons for the boys. He had letters to write to Haworth. And he longed to see Milly. He had thought about finding other lodgings. But he liked High Syke House and had settled there now. And Fish's wife ignored him in just the right way. But he'd flirted with Margaret inappropriately, and had led her on. He knew what he'd done, and he deeply regretted it now. For she appeared to have fallen in love with him.

He was writing when she walked across the room, his back towards her. He did not turn from his desk. He knew how she'd be, standing behind him looking at him with that steely stare of hers. He turned to her slowly. She gazed at him unhappily, touching the ribbon trimming around the sleeves of her dress. 'A beautiful silk,' she said.

'Yes,' he murmured. 'A very nice shade of purple.' They were silent a moment. He folded his arms and gazed at the shining ribbon, screwing up his eyes. 'The term purple, is derived from the Greek word *"porphura"*, he said imperiously, 'the name of a dye manufactured in Classical antiquity from the mucus-secretion of the gland of a marine snail.'

She met his eyes coldly. He didn't know what she wanted from him. It was frustration he experienced with Margaret, pure frustration. She sat down elegantly on a chair, and held his gaze for a moment. He frowned and looked away. A kiss or two is hardly a proposal of marriage, he thought anxiously. Why does she look at me like that? He turned to his desk again, resting his chin on his hands.

'Margaret,' he said quietly, over his shoulder. 'I am not sure why you are here?' He turned to her again, slowly. Her cheeks were red with emotion.

'I see I am not welcome,' she said, her forehead tightening with anger. She glanced at his desk and frowned. 'You are writing poetry.'

Branwell sighed. He wasn't writing poetry, though he would like to have tried that morning; he was feeling inspired. There was so much bitterness in her tone nowadays, he thought. He didn't want to hurt her. But he could not give what she required. Her back was towards the open window. Her long dark curls swayed a little in the breeze. Light gusts of wind played with the collar of her dress. Her skin lit by the sunlight, she looked quite enchanting. Yes, Margaret was certainly beautiful. Someone could love her undoubtedly, but it wouldn't be him.

`I believe you have had a visitor from Haworth,' she said, searching his face. 'Someone saw you at the inn.'

He remained seated at his desk, observing her mood, trying not to show how startled he was. What did she know about Brown? Did she actually know about Milly? 'Ah, you have spies, Margaret,' he said playfully. 'I can see I shall have to be careful.' His mind ran on worriedly. What did she *really* know?

'One of the Postlethwaite boys saw you entering the inn together. The man is a friend, I believe.'

Branwell smiled and looked downwards. 'Good, good. The Postlethwaite boy learns something then. I'm glad.' He put down his pen and stood up, pacing the room thoughtfully, biting his lip and thinking quickly. 'I have almost reached the point of forgetting to teach them. They are so . . .'

'– It is always others who are at fault,' Margaret interrupted curtly. 'I am at fault because I do not respond to your poetry. And yet you refuse to instruct me. The Postlethwaite boys are at fault because they cannot learn from you. What foolish people we are!' She made to rise, as if she were about to leave.

Branwell glanced at her, raising his eyebrows, she was angry again, and her anger might be dangerous. He had come to terms with it now, the fact that whatever he read to her did not touch her. His work meant nothing to Margaret. Nothing. But he hadn't expected her to watch him as she did, and criticise him. A melancholy note from the breeze came in through the window, whistling on the pane. She faced him again. Tears had formed in her eyes. It hurt him to see them.

'Why do you . . . Why do you treat me so badly?' she faltered.

'Do I treat you badly, Margaret?' he said, looking astonished. 'My dear, I do not intend it. I am sorry.' He frowned. 'Sometimes it hurts me too when we don't get on.' His voice filled with emotion. There was silence again for a moment. 'Oh, I have had all this at the parsonage with Charlotte,' he said suddenly, throwing out his hands and turning from her. 'She must always be arguing with me.' He turned back to her, covering his face with his hands. 'I'm sorry, Margaret. I really am. If I hurt people, I'm sorry. I like you. I do. I have enjoyed your company. But I can't . . .'

'You can't bear anyone to disagree with you,' she said quietly, catching her breath. She spoke firmly, her head bent low.

He turned to her, with a curious, perplexed look. How odd it was that they couldn't get through to each other. It was good to disagree; of course it was, to try to see things plainly. But that wasn't how it was with them. By some unaccountable force it seemed their words were torn to shreds in the very air they breathed. It made them vexed with each other so they weren't even friends. Why did it happen, he wondered. He tried to think of a reason. Perhaps it was because she loved him.

His mind moved on quickly. It was one of those days. He wanted to write, and needed to think. Days like this, his thoughts sped on too urgently. He would need to lie down. Sometimes he shook uncontrollably; thoughts, ideas, feelings came to him, too many, too fast. It reminded him of a wood that had been forsaken, where the trees had grown into each other, and the ivy grew up round the branches, each thing in its turn dying for the other.

Margaret seized on the silence. 'You are remembering your spite yesterday, the way you wouldn't come walking out as you'd promised. – But you intended to see your friend instead.'

'I wasn't sure he'd arrive,' Branwell said quietly. He observed her face carefully, wondering over and over, what she might know about Milly. It was actually true what he'd said. He hadn't expected Brown to be so prompt; the roads were unreliable, as was the weather. He was glad Brown had met Milly, and that they'd liked each other. What had happened was good, new and invigorating. 'Oh, don't look so gloomy, Margaret,' he said, trying to be kind. He waited for her to speak, but she remained silent. 'See,' he said, pointing to the window, 'there is the sun again. You could go for a walk right now.' He glanced at the sky and frowned. 'I suspect it will rain later.'

'I don't want to walk on my own,' she said sullenly. 'What is the use of that?' A Cabbage White butterfly came in through the window, settling on the rim of her hat. She batted it off and it flew out.

'A lot of use, I'd have thought . . .' Branwell murmured, turning back to his writing. She stood in silence, contemplating the garden through the window. 'Anyway,' he said finally. 'I shall have to get on. I've lessons to prepare for the boys.' He sighed and threw back his hair. 'I can at least attempt to teach them, though I fear it is a lost cause.'

'You are the lost cause,' she said flatly, beneath her breath.

He turned to her and frowned. *A lost cause?* Is that what he was? He sighed. It was probably true. Though he hoped it wasn't. He shrugged. She was standing before him now, playing with her fingers like a child, nervous of him, confused. 'What will you do this evening?' she asked unhappily.

'I don't know,' he said. 'I'm not sure.' But he did know what he would do that evening, he intended to go to see Milly at her uncle's cottage. He glanced at the clock. He would have to get on with his work. He met Margaret's eyes; they were sad and lonely. But he could not give her any comfort.

The scene in the room looked calm enough; the light was bright from the window, the place was neat, but their minds were in disarray. And he feared that look of hers. He wondered what she might do if she knew about Milly and it got to the parsonage. He chilled at the thought. They would never have approved of Milly at the parsonage. A quick pulse of fear went through him. Would he ever succeed in pleasing his family? Could he ever rise to the greatness his sisters required of him? He could never be a Wordsworth or a Shakespeare ... He caught his breath. He could give of himself enough, in spoken words, in laughter, even in inspiration perhaps, to others. But what was he, really? Charlotte thought he was lazy. Emily thought him a genius; how could he satisfy her dreams? And Anne, dear Anne ... oh, that fragile softness of hers, that vulnerability! Could he ever be strong enough for Anne? And his father ... A sudden weakness came over him. He turned to his desk and rested his head in his hands. Margaret had left.

He gazed down at the page in front of him. It had nothing to do with the Postlethwaite boys at all. He'd been trying to compose a letter to Hartley Coleridge. 'I am writing to the son of Samuel Taylor Coleridge,' he said to himself. 'The nephew of Robert Southey, the Poet Laureate. It has to be right!' He recalled some lines he had once written to Wordsworth a few years earlier.

'... Surely in this day when there is not a writing poet worth a sixpence the field must be open if a better man can step forward ...'

He shivered at the recollection. Did he really write that to Wordsworth? What must the man have thought? But he was younger then, a careless, urgent, even reckless Branwell! He drew a breath. Slowly, carefully, he took his pen to the paper.

'Sir, It is with much reluctance that I venture to request, for the perusal of the following lines, a portion of the time of one upon whom I can have no claim, and should not dare to intrude; but ... I could not resist my longing to ask a man from whose judgement there would be little hope of appeal. Since my childhood I have been wont to devote the hours I could spare from other and

very different employments to efforts at literary composition, always keeping the results to myself, nor have they in more than two or three instances been seen by any other. But I am about to enter active life, and prudence tells me not to waste the time which must make my independence; yet sir, I love writing too well to fling aside the practice of it without an effort to ascertain whether I could turn it to account . . .'

He wrote on bravely, pleading his case politely. Finishing the letter he enclosed a poem and a couple of translations from Horace. That done, he went in a drawer and brought out the lessons he was preparing for the Postlethwaite boys.

7

It was almost nine o'clock as he made his way down the hill towards Michael's cottage. No-one appeared to be about. It was a damp April evening. Early April had been warm, and almost like summer, though despite the sun in the daytime the cold had returned in the evenings and with it the rain.

He had eaten silently at the table at High Syke House. Robert Fish was away that week; only the mother and children had joined him at supper. He had felt uncomfortable throughout. He could tell that something had been said. Over the meal, Margaret had determined not to look at him. She had also stayed silent. He'd scarcely been able to contain himself, and had eaten little. What he did with his life was his own business, he reflected angrily, glancing behind him frustratedly. It pained him to keep thinking he was followed.

It was a still sweet lane where Milly lived, lots of pleasant smelling blossoms, a silent calmness, one or two cottages huddled together one side of the road, the other side soft hillside and a medley of trees. The people who lived there were poor, though they were proud and dignified he'd thought, watching them as they'd come and gone from their homes. He walked on quickly familiarising himself with the new environment that would soon, he hoped, become an important part of his life.

He felt quietly confident tonight about him and Milly; their relationship was sure to flourish. But he hadn't met Uncle Michael yet and felt slightly uneasy about that. As he neared the cottage, he wondered what she might have told him in her own charming way, where she used her hands and her smiles, and scribbled down shapes and drawings. Her drawings often intrigued him; she would make them wherever she might, even in the spills on top of the tables at the inn.

He arrived suddenly at the door. Bracing himself, he knocked. He stood about in the damp silence, waiting, contemplating the gritty earth at his feet. What if Michael answered, what would they say to each other?

The sound of the door opening unnerved him a little. He breathed in deeply, watching it widen. A tall, middle-aged man with gentle, searching eyes, stood in the doorway. His clothes were made from a rough tan coloured cloth, his shirt was open at the neck and a string, loose at the waist, tied his trousers. His sleeves were rolled to the elbow displaying strong forearms, one arm resting on the door, the other by his side.

'So you are Branwell!' he laughed. 'I wasn't sure when you were coming, Milly had forgotten the time.' Michael Langton shook Branwell's hand and asked him inside.

'It's good to meet you, Michael,' Branwell returned, though a little nervous. A lively fire burned in the grate. The atmosphere was warm and cosy. Branwell smiled at Milly. He saw she was drying dishes from their evening meal, putting them on shelves.

'Here, give me your coat,' said Michael. 'Come and sit down.' They moved to the fire.

The room, though neat and comfortable, was sparsely furnished. Here and there handmade cushions softened the wooden furniture. The floor was flagstones, clean and shining, glistening with the light from the fire. Shadows from lighted candles flickered round the room, small wooden carvings stood on the mantelpiece, rude and unpolished, though made with care and spirit – a horse, a bird, a tiny spindle that matched the real one in the corner, a testimony to a life gone by.

Branwell had dreaded this moment. He wanted Michael to accept him, and hopefully like him. Milly came to the fire and sat down quietly at the hearth. He saw her serious look. The importance of what was happening shone in her eyes.

'I'm glad you came,' said Michael.

He was a big, powerful man, though his voice was a little shaky, Branwell thought, and he didn't seem well. He lowered himself into a chair by the fire and gazed at Branwell, looking him over genially. Branwell could hear him breathing heavily, it seemed he too was tense.

'Milly tells me you're a painter as well as a poet,' said Michael. His tone was excited though slow. 'I do a bit o' painting myself. Nothing grand, mind, just one or two scenes from the hills.'

Branwell stretched out his legs and leaned back in the chair. He had felt fatigued that day, not knowing which way to turn, worried about whether he could continue teaching at the Postlethwaite's, how his father was coping at Haworth, and how the meeting would go with Michael. He was glad he had sent the letter to Hartley Coleridge. Now he must wait.

'I taught myself,' said Michael. 'I'd draw on drystone walls at first with charcoal. Then I got to mixing colours with Milly and trying them out on wood.'

Milly stroked Michael's fingers then tapped on his palm. Branwell watched. There was so much intimacy between them. Michael patted her cheek and smiled. 'She wants me to show you the paints,' he said. 'There's every hue of every season beneath that table!' He dragged out a box.

Lifting the lid, he removed a damp cloth, placed across the colours. Branwell gazed inside, amazed at the contents. The colours were in small wooden dishes. Fifteen different shades danced in the candlelight. 'I make them from whatever I can find on the hills,' said Michael, animated. 'The cloth must be allus kept damp, so they don't dry out. Now and again I might mix a bit of water in. I like to vary the greens. – See! I've spring, summer, autumn and winter in there! You can take your pick. Milly has a knack for knowing what'll mix. You must see them in daylight though. Aye, t' daylight brings them to life.'

Branwell took them from the box one at a time, observing them carefully, holding them close to a candle, stirring them with his finger, deeply impressed.

'Milly brings plants an' clays from the hills to keep 'em topped up,' said Michael, watching Branwell's expression. 'The sulphur-yellow is my pride.'

'I'm sure,' Branwell murmured. 'You have made it well.' The sulphur-yellow glistened in the dish, a difficult colour to achieve. He stirred it with his finger, a thick, full tone. Yes, so much richer in daylight. He knew a lot about the making of paints but he had never seen anything like these. They were quite spectacular.

'I carved the dishes myself,' said Michael proudly, touching the wood. His tone was low and measured, filled with his own wonder. – 'Were you going to make us some tea, Milly?' he said, addressing her as she sat on the rug by the fire. Milly went off to fill a kettle. 'Matthew Parker, the woodcutter, brings me the wood,' Michael added with a sniff. 'He can cut it straighter than I can.'

'Oh?' said Branwell, still engrossed in the paints. 'Matthew Parker? Who's he?'

Michael fixed his lips firmly together, as if he should say no more. 'Now let me show you my paintings . . .' he said, frowning. 'They're in the cupboard over here . . .' He went to a cupboard and opened the door, looking in on a dozen or so paintings made on sheets of wood. The wood was thin and light, the paintings set apart by small pieces of stone.

Branwell examined them carefully. 'They're good,' he said, curious and attentive. The images were carefully accomplished, though with a rush of familiar feeling he noted the colours were fading. 'I have often thought about painting on wood, myself,' he said. It was almost a natural impulse, he thought, for an artist to paint on wood. He had talked about it with other painters he knew. He fixed his eyes on the pictures, carefully examining them one by one. He felt great admiration for Michael. He had made an extraordinary effort. The paintings were of Broughton-in-Furness, places he'd visited with Milly. There was a picture of the river Duddon, seen from the top of the hill in summer, flowers covering the banks. He tried to imagine what the pictures would look like in daylight, when the colours could spring from the wood.

'Tell me, Michael,' he said, preoccupied. 'Who is Matthew Parker? – A woodcutter, did you say?' The candlelight flashed on the little dishes so that the hues reached out from their wetness dancing and glistening. He could hear Milly making the tea in the kitchen. She'd return to them soon. 'Does he live locally?'

'Aye, he lives locally,' said Michael, faltering a little. 'He's a friend of Milly's. They've known each other since childhood. Though Matthew's a year or two older.' He rubbed his forehead and frowned. Going to his chair he sat down slowly, staring at the fire. 'It's getting awkward though now.'

'What is?' asked Branwell. He returned the pictures to the cupboard, placing the pieces of stone carefully between them.

Michael looked at him worriedly. 'Well, it's hard on the lad. He wants to marry her, you see.'

Branwell's mind worked quickly. He had come to see Milly as his own, imagining her living a solitary existence, apart from her life with her uncle and her work at the inn. Because of this, he'd created a dream world around her in which he thought they were safe. Now he felt threatened. 'He wants to *marry* her?' said Branwell, smiling and feigning nonchalance. Who was this man, who had suddenly entered his mind, his life, his happiness? 'Did he say so?'

'Oh, a time or two,' said Michael scratching his head. 'Now and then he might pay us a visit, though he doesn't stay long. He lives across the road on the hill, in the old tumbledown cottage. His parents lived there before. But there's only Matthew now. He's a quiet sort; always out on the hills working. You'll not find him drinking at the inn.'

Branwell leaned against the wall and folded his arms. 'I see . . .' His head was swimming with thoughts. His blood pounded fast through his body. He must pace his breathing. Nothing is ever as good or as bad as it seems, he reasoned. 'I can see there are things I must learn,' he laughed quietly.

'Ah, dunna worry about it, lad,' said Michael with a sigh. 'You must leave it to fate.'

Branwell was now in torment. Milly was young and would do whatever she wanted. What if Matthew Parker was also her lover? His face paled at the thought. He recalled the first time he'd kissed her, that gentle evening on the hills. At first he had been afraid. He remembered the smell of her hair that night, the panic he had felt in his chest, the fear of losing himself to a woman for the very first time, the wrench of his soul from his body as he gave her his love. Somehow, in a magical way, for a brief time, he'd felt like something else, not a person at all, like something ethereal instead. He had lost himself in spirit. All that mattered in those moments had been their love. Had all that changed? He could scarcely think for the speed with which the thoughts devoured him. Milly brought in the tea.

He smiled at her as she put down the tray, content and happy. She had tied back her hair in a ribbon. He felt oddly distant from her now, wondering about Matthew Parker. This man had a history. How many times had he visited the cottage? How often did she see him? He gazed about the room. He had only just made acquaintance with the cottage himself. Though he did not feel like a stranger. There was a grace in the house and he'd entered it. He held her gaze for a moment. Matthew Parker was nowhere to be seen in her eyes. They drank their tea. Images entered his mind. He wondered what it was like times past when Milly's parents had lived there and they'd all been together. There was a smell of sweetness in the house coming from tiny flowers she had gathered from the hills, in jugs about the room. She got up slowly from the floor and went to her uncle. Putting her arms around his neck, she kissed his cheek. Michael stroked her arm and made gestures with his hands. Milly made gestures back. Branwell had yet to discover more of her sounds. There were more exchanges between them, sounds Branwell had never heard, a sacred almost unearthly language. Glancing down he saw his footprints on the shining flagstones. He'd been pacing about for a while as he often did when disturbed, though he had not noticed.

'What happened to Milly's parents?' he asked, sitting down in the chair again and trying to relax. His eyes had lighted on the spindle in the corner. Milly's face was tense, her bright blue eyes fixed on them both by turns. Deep in thought, Michael poked at the fire. 'You don't have to tell me if it's painful,' said Branwell, suddenly apologetic. Milly had lowered her face. 'I know how hard it is to talk of the dead. It's just that I wondered about them. – They told me up at the inn.'

'Aye, they would . . .' said Michael, gravely. 'They died from consumption i' this house.' He touched Milly's hand and continued. 'It were a wicked winter. There were little to eat and little i' the way of money. We must sweat blood to keep goin'! – There were demons flyin' about us!' He waved his hand in the air. 'You could see 'em flyin' all over! – Me and Milly were spared.'

'Demons, yes,' Branwell murmured, looking at Milly. He drew her close. 'The demons are always waiting.'

'Burnt 'em up i' the wick o' the candles wi' the moths!' Michael laughed. 'Saw 'em out wi' the shadows!' He was suddenly silent again, absorbed in the past.

They sat quietly for a while. Wind rattled at the windows. It had started to rain heavily. Michael continued. 'They took my Elizabeth too, that winter. I came to live here with Milly. We've managed a life of sorts. – My back's been bad and sometimes I've a pain in my chest. I do what I can.' He put more logs on the fire. Flames fled up the chimney. 'So will you read us a poem then?' he said, changing the subject. He braced himself and attempted a smile. 'Milly's been telling me what you write. She says you write poems about storms. – The storms o' the mind too!'

'I do indeed,' Branwell laughed, trying to become more cheerful. He wondered how Milly had explained his poetry to Michael. They enjoyed a mysterious communication. A rolled up piece of paper poked out of his pocket. She drew it out and smiled, making the sounds she made when she wanted him to read.

'It's a sonnet to Black Comb,' said Branwell, watching as she handed it to Michael excitedly, straightening it out. 'The mountain that's over the estuary. You will know it of course.'

'Oh, I do, I do,' said Michael seriously. 'I know it well.' He screwed up his eyes, eagerly scanning the page. 'I'll not be able to read it, though,' he laughed. 'I never learned reading.' He chuckled as he gazed at the writing. His eyes sparkled with interest. 'Our Milly told me about it.' He returned the poem to Branwell quickly. 'Will you read it to us?'

Branwell stood silent, happily surprised. 'Of course,' he said, though oddly a little shakily. 'I sort of intended it.'

'Milly knows her poetry from my brother,' said Michael, relaxing into thought. 'Arthur knew all his poetry by heart. He often liked to recite it. It's a terrible thing he died as young as he did.' He leaned towards Branwell. 'Well, read it, my boy! Come on! You are to be listened to, aren't you?'

Branwell looked at Milly, sitting quietly by the fire, her cream smock glistening, her small beautiful body full of life. Michael leaned back waiting. 'I don't know why my hand is trembling,' said Branwell. He laughed nervously. His mind was whirling with thoughts of Matthew Parker and the unseen life he had yet to learn of that the man shared with Milly. For a few moments he'd forgotten everything – Haworth, his sisters, his father, even himself. All he could think of was Matthew Parker and Milly. Another demon had discovered him.

'We're ready,' said Michael. Branwell cleared his throat and began.

'Far off, and half revealed, 'mid shade and light,
Blackcomb half smiles, half frowns; his mighty form
Scarce bending in to peace; – more formed to fight
A thousand years of struggles with a storm
Than bask one hour, subdued by sunshine warm
To bright and breezeless rest; yet even his height
Towers not o'er this world's sympathies – he smiles,
While many a human heart to pleasure's wiles
Can bear to bend, and still forget to rise;
As though he, huge and heath clad, on our sight
Again rejoices in his stormy skies,
Man loses vigour in unstable joys.
Thus tempests find Blackcomb invincible,
While we are lost, who should know life so well!'

He lifted his face and met their eyes. What did Michael think? Had he understood the poem? Had he seen Black Comb the way he had seen it himself, an eternal invincible power that didn't grow weary or suffer as he did, but rejoiced instead in the elements and its own grandeur?

'I've had such thoughts myself about that mountain,' said Michael with a sigh. 'Though I couldn't have said them like that.' And he told Branwell of the way the sight of the mountain had given him comfort in times of grief, the peace it gave him to think of its mighty height, reaching out of the miseries of life into somewhere else in the skies.

Branwell stood gazing at the flagstones, wondering why he had suddenly lost composure, why he had felt so nervous about reading the poem. He presumed it must be his feelings for Milly, and the fear of losing her. 'Thank you,' he said. He felt quite humbled. Michael had listened and had shown discernment and pleasure. He could ask no more than that. He straightened and felt much better. Reading his work always made him feel better. Milly put her arm around her uncle's shoulder and stroked his cheek. Branwell returned the poem to his pocket. 'I'm glad you enjoyed it,' he said. 'You must tell me which poems you know. Perhaps you will recite me something?' He met Milly's eyes and smiled then reached for his coat. He must make the journey up the hill to High Syke House.

The roof was noisy with rain. There would have to be a break in it soon, he thought; he would sit for a while and wait. He told Michael about his family at the parsonage, how his sisters also wrote poetry, how his father had written it also. His father, the parson, was very busy just now, he said. Ill health had caused many deaths. The political situation was very unstable and tiring. Milly sat still, listening.

The rain drew to a halt, and Michael went to the door to look out. The road shone with wetness, the trees hung limp, their branches bent, their leaves heavy with rain. Moonlight lit the path to the top of the hill. Branwell walked out on the still, glittering evening. After a couple of yards, he turned. They were both standing in the doorway. – And just for a moment he saw the figure of a man watching by a tree. On a second glance he had gone.

8

Crazed with anticipation, Branwell went out on the hills to think. He put his hand in his pocket. –Yes, it was still there! His fingers grasped the fresh, crisp paper, warming it next to his thigh. He had actually received a letter from Hartley Coleridge! He flung back the front of his coat and clasped his hands in the small of his back. How awesome he felt today, how stately! He wouldn't be a Byron or a Wordsworth, but he would certainly be a Branwell Brontë! Hartley Coleridge had decreed it.

He laughed quietly to himself. He couldn't get over it. He had actually managed to impress him! 'It's unbelievable,' he said to himself, his joy mingling with that of the bird-songs about him. 'Quite unbelievable!' He thrust back his shoulders and lengthened his stride. 'Perhaps it will happen after all. Maybe I'll be rich and famous! – Oh, the things I shall buy for Milly! What a house we shall live in! What a horse and carriage she . . .' He stopped suddenly, gazing at the grass at his feet. He was getting carried away. Hartley Coleridge had simply invited him to talk, no more, no less. Anyhow, it was a start, and a fine start too.

It was coming to the end of April. A soft warm breeze blew through his hair. It felt good on his face. People were out walking, enjoying the spring weather. An abundance of wild flowers had burst into bloom. Buttercups were most prevalent; a dazzling carpet of yellow at his feet that looked as if the sun had fallen from the sky. I must manage this carefully, he decided, running his hand round his chin thoughtfully. He recalled a lesson from Aristotle: Don't be too bold. Don't be too timid. Hit the mean. – Yes, I must keep it in proportion. Handle it properly and all will be well. Arrogance and genius are jealous bedfellows, he reflected. Wordsworth was never puffed up; he carried his genius with a self-respecting pride, an independent dignity. Branwell nodded at passers by as Wordsworth might, greeting them with polite condescension, practising greatness. Yes, he would be proud and self-determined.

He needed this august support. Coleridge would now afford him the link between the physical and the spiritual life. He could now begin to consider them in a mature framework, discuss them with a famous poet think about such matters carefully. He could talk to his father with a dignified, worthy countenance. There was a spiritual life, of course. Despite being often dejected, his father believed in it. He would like to believe in it himself if he could. There were so many issues he wanted to discuss with Hartley.

I would like my life to be something quite special, he told himself. I want it to be like Milly's. I want to be at one with my world, not apart from it as I have always been, as if out on a limb. Like a conductor conducts his orchestra, I shall conduct my words, and make of them such a symphony! Oh, what a sound there will be! What poetry I shall write, what novels ... All I have needed is someone with knowledge and position to see my potential. Hartley Coleridge is my answer!

He wondered what Charlotte would think of Coleridge's letter when he told her. On second thoughts, he decided not to tell her at all. She would only be jealous and spoil it. He wished it were not so, but it was more than likely. Or worse than that, she would write to Coleridge herself. And if his reply were unfavourable then she would probably be rude. There wasn't a single line he could reach that Charlotte wouldn't try to step over. And she would elbow him out too, if she could. Charlotte had the advantage of forgetting her mistakes, or somehow managing to hide them from herself, or else oddly making them his.

Though perhaps it is true, he reflected. Maybe her errors are mine. In their youthful writings he'd goaded her, taunted her even, made her think more outrageously, more brutally than she might otherwise have done. He would set her a scene, provide her with the opening lines, and she would then take over. – Oh, how she loved to take over. How beautifully she performed. He could create in her any kind of being he wanted, and she hadn't a clue he did it. But it brought an energy to her life, an extra force to her blood.

He would write to Brown forthwith. Yes, Brown would certainly be delighted. It was good to have a friend like Brown, someone who cared what you did, understood your frustrations and aspirations. Brown didn't talk about aspirations. He simply got on with his life. And yet for all that, he was always eager to know what was happening with people, and thrilled if they had some luck. Brown believed most success was down to luck. You might struggle and strive for what you wanted, he'd say, but without luck on your side, you had nowt.

Branwell breathed in deeply and turned his face to the sky it was almost cloudless. An unusual sky for April he thought, so white and still. Oh yes, he smiled; he could always give Charlotte an excellent run for her money. He walked on deep in thought. He would like to have told her about Hartley Coleridge though. It was a shame he couldn't. In earlier times, when they were different people and the world of childhood had allowed them a freedom that adults could never have, then he could have told her anything.

'Think what touches your heart, Branwell, and work from that,' she would tell him when they were writing together. 'And try to have something strange and mysterious in your story.'

'Or else something disgraceful,' he would whisper in her ear. 'Or even cruel and wicked!' Then she would fold her arms and pucker her forehead, and go storming off to Emily to abuse him, delivering her a pack of wrongs he had done that day, and inventing a lot of them too. Charlotte was brave though, he reasoned. If she lived in a world of dreams, she could also face reality if she must. She was a complex woman and an admirable sister. He loved her dearly, as he loved all his family. Though he and Charlotte had something special between them; they shared the same tap root. Sometimes it made him catch his breath.

A blue haze of hills glittered before him. He'd been gone from the Postlethwaites for just over an hour. The boys, as ever, had refused to pay attention to their lesson. He had never been very good when it came to asserting himself; he was rather more of a friend, and ended up reading them poetry, or else just letting them draw. Or worse than that, getting into conversations with them about all and sundry, and finding he'd wasted an hour discussing anything other than their lesson. There were days he arranged to see them and they were nowhere in sight, and if Postlethwaite was out then their mother didn't care too much what they were up to. So he didn't care either and went off to write.

He quickened his pace; he ought to have been back by now. Postlethwaite was coming home early that day. If he found him out, there'd be trouble. A couple of yards ahead he saw two figures emerging out of the light. It was Michael and Milly. Milly came running with her basket.

'What a surprise!' he laughed. The basket contained an assortment of plants from the hills. She put it on the ground and kissed him. 'Michael, good morning!' said Branwell as he joined them. Michael frowned and nodded. There was a look of worry in his eyes. Both Michael and Milly were preoccupied. He looked from Milly to Michael and back. 'What is it?' he asked, filled with a thousand fears.

'Listen . . .' Michael began. He got down and made himself comfortable then plucked at the grass. 'There's something I . . .'

'You're angry?' said Branwell, getting down beside him.

'Nay, I'm not angry,' said Michael quietly, though turning away. 'I've been overlooking things, that's what it is.'

Branwell didn't respond for a minute; he was thinking quickly. What had Michael overlooked? Was it something to do with his work with the Postlethwaites? He knew he'd been slack. Word got round very quickly in Broughton-in-Furness, especially if Margaret had been talking. He put out his hand and drew Milly down to the grass. She winced briefly as he put his arm around her shoulder. Her skin felt hot. Her arms were red from the sun. Michael sat looking ahead, still pulling at the grass. Something had obviously disturbed him, and his mood was strange. It was a mood Branwell wasn't familiar with, a sort of tenseness and anger he couldn't quite fathom, mixed with an odd kind of tenderness. 'You appear to be worried about something,' said Branwell. 'Do let me know what it is.'

'Aye, I'm worried,' said Michael quietly. Milly gazed downwards, her fresh white smock floating about her like a cloud.

'I hope you're not ill,' Branwell said to Michael. He knew he suffered with his breathing once the blossoms were out. He wondered for a minute if something had happened at the parsonage.

Had Brown been over? He had a sudden feeling of dread.

'No, I'm not ill,' Michael said, shaking his head. 'A little bit down, but not ill. There's summat that's a bit of a worry though, and ye'll have to know what it is.' They sat for some minutes in silence. 'Ye've come to a pretty pass.' He shook his head and sighed.

'Have I?' Branwell frowned. He waited with bated breath.

Michael gazed at him, searching for words. 'Milly's with child,' he said, breathing in deeply. He looked at Branwell and frowned. 'An' I'll not conceal what I think. – Ye've disappointed me, boy!'

The thin sound of church bells came from the distance. Branwell met Milly's gaze. She shook her head confusedly and shivered slightly, biting her lip worriedly. Branwell drew her into his arms and held her close, kissing her hair, kissing her cheeks, closing his eyes with joy. They were all silent a moment. There were no words for any of them just then.

'Oh, don't be disappointed, Michael,' Branwell said finally, his eyes shining. 'It's wonderful! It's beautiful! I'm in love with Milly, and I'm determined to make her happy!' He talked on hurriedly in a frenzy of feeling. Nothing seemed to matter just now except this. He, Branwell Brontë, would be a father! His eyes were moist with tears. Milly's face flushed with emotion, she kissed his cheek.

Michael listened, gazing up at the sky as Branwell went on. 'She can't be working at the inn much longer,' Michael said. 'I shall have to help her with the little 'un an' all . . .'

'Oh not at all, that is my responsibility,' Branwell asserted, standing and brushing down his clothes. 'I shall take care of Milly.' He spoke with authority now, in a tone of annoyance that Michael should dare to dismiss him.

'Will ye?' said Michael looking up, and nodding his head thoughtfully. 'Not if Postlethwaite has owt to do wi' it. It seems he must keep an eye on yer every movement. – What if he shows ye the gate?'

'Bide with me, Michael,' said Branwell, glancing about. A certain young lady, Branwell suspected, had been talking. 'You needn't worry. Postlethwaite isn't important. I am now on the verge of . . .' He stopped abruptly. He would probably see Hartley Coleridge for about fifteen minutes, and that would be that. He sighed and threw out his hands. 'Who else will believe in a man if he doesn't believe in himself?' he declared sadly.

'Aye, you're right,' said Michael. 'But seeing is believing in my book. And I don't see much that's good about you, boy just now.'

'Oh, but you will, you will . . .' Branwell said resolvedly. True enough, there wasn't much good about him at present, he couldn't deny it. But it wasn't how he wanted it to be. He stood for a moment perplexed. How could he become successful with his writing, fulfil his family's expectations, and at the same time earn money for Milly and his baby? Tension mounted within him. Michael stood up.

Milly stood up and clutched on to Branwell's arm, looking at him worriedly. Between the three of them there was a kind of unity now. They were all uneasy, standing about in silence. Branwell braced himself, determined. He would work for Milly. He would make the magic happen. Wasn't he the chief genie? Couldn't he always do it? Of course, he could, and he would. The whole of his mind filled with the wonderful joy that so often found him in his moments of despair; the joy that told him anything, anything at all was possible! Just as the trees bore fruit, he too would have his time. He had earthed himself in Milly. She would bear their child. Fame would come to him on the wings of song! What could go wrong? He was happy.

His thoughts moved on speedily to practical matters. Milly would present a total stranger to his family at the parsonage. She could not read. She could not write. She could not speak. But they would see how sensitive she was, how caring, how she could feel more deeply than ordinary people. This moment was like no other. Milly was pregnant with his child. His blood would pass on through Milly. His whole body tingled. He felt more alive than ever, as if some seraph were passing a message through his bones! Milly locked her fingers in his own, making those special sounds she made when she loved him best. He saw her breasts swell in her smock as she breathed in deeply, her face serious, suddenly different. In her eyes he saw the mother she would be. She stroked his arm and met his eyes then held his face in her hands and kissed his lips. She took his hand and pressed it against her belly. Branwell's throat tightened with emotion. She rested her head on his chest. He felt so absorbed in the moment, so lost in its joy. Michael picked up her basket and set foot on the path. Soon he was lost in the distance.

9

'The earliest wish I ever knew
Was woman's kind regard to win;
I felt it long e'er passion grew.
E'er such a wish could be no sin.
And still it lasts; – the yearning ache
No cure has found, no comfort known:
If she did love, 'twas for my sake,
She could not love me for her own.'

Branwell read the poem again. He was puzzled. Was it a poem about lost love? Who was Hartley Coleridge talking about? Perhaps there might be a moment when he could ask him. He closed the book and put it into his pocket. His eyes ached from trying to read while travelling. He had wanted the poetry fresh in his mind; he'd like to have recited a couple of lines when he got there. The coach wheels jangled on the stony road, an odd erratic fanfare.

It was May Day. Just another half a mile and it would happen; he'd be face to face with Hartley Coleridge. He rubbed his eyes. He was gradually coming down to earth. All the way there he'd been dreaming, carried away on the poems, glancing about at the beautiful scenery and enjoying the sunshine. He gazed at Rydal Water, what a charming lake it was, small and moody, he thought. The water glittered like ice. The grass on the banks was a rich new tender green. Clumps of wild flowers curved and twisted in the lifts and folds of the hills, while clusters of dark green trees herded round the lake. It was a bright clear day.

Branwell felt full of hope. His employers had been kind when he'd asked for a couple of days' leave. Their generosity had surprised him. And nothing untoward had been mentioned as regards his teaching.

Postlethwaite knows I'll make up for it later, Branwell decided. He had no way of knowing what would happen with Hartley Coleridge. Perhaps he would invite him to stay, otherwise he'd stop at an inn.

Yes, the Postlethwaites had certainly been generous. Though he'd actually lied about his reason for wanting the leave, and had pretended his father had requested him urgently. He felt quite bad about that. Ah well, he reasoned, rubbing his nose, a visit to Nab Cottage is a good enough reason to lie. He doubted his father would worry too much if he confessed; he was far more likely to be fascinated by his tale. It was a pity he couldn't have told him the story, or even asked Brown to tell him. But it was all too risky. His father though, would have given him some tips as to how he ought to behave; he was good at managing important people, it was a vital part of his job and he did it well. Branwell didn't know what he would say when he got there, his confidence was flagging by the minute.

Turning the bend a thin white mist hovered over the lake. Rydal Water was tranquil and calm just now, encompassed by a gentle embrace of hills. It was a warm, sleepy afternoon. How much more inspired I'd have been living here by a lake, he reasoned, than at Haworth surrounded by graves. What can you learn from the dead, and the wind howling from the moors? Here by this lake all is alive and vibrant!

Considerably older than himself, Branwell wasn't sure how to address Hartley Coleridge. The son of Samuel Taylor Coleridge and the nephew of Robert Southey, he would hardly be easy to talk to. With such gargantuan spectres about him he was bound to be slightly peculiar. He supposed he might be cautious and reserved, though his letter had been friendly enough. What giants have shared his life! Branwell shivered. There were all sorts of tales about them. Though they were probably mainly fictitious. Some said Hartley had been driven insane when his parents split up and he'd gone to live with Robert Southey. And having failed to gain the Newdigate Prize at Oxford had made him even more morose. Yes, the man had certainly been through it. And he'd lost an Oriel Fellowship too, through drunkenness. Branwell remembered he had been a literary journalist for a while in London before publishing his poems. Eventually, he had taken a job as a teacher at Ambleside, though it seemed that the school too, had lost its way. Yes, Hartley had quite a history. Branwell sighed; he knew too well the frustrations of teaching when the mind was eager for invention.

Anyhow, at least he's been successful with his writing, Branwell reflected with gladness, and wasn't that what mattered in the end? Since coming to live in the Lake District, Hartley had been a kind of recluse.

All the more reason to feel privileged today, Branwell reasoned, I doubt he has many visitors. He sat deep in thought. He hankered after success himself. And because of Milly and the pregnancy, he needed it more than ever. How it warmed him to think of Milly. He felt she was with him constantly now, connected to him straight as a ray of light. He'd apologised to her for leaving her to come to see Hartley, and he'd tried to explain how it was. She had shown enthusiasm for his visit, though he doubted she understood; it was just a matter of fact to her, though she accepted it with grace. 'I must get my poems recognised,' he had said, which is all he could think of at the time. 'This man can help me.'

That's what he hoped for eventually. How wonderful it must be to hold a book of your poetry in your hand, he thought, to see your name on the cover! He wondered if Brown had got his letter. He hadn't felt good, opening up as he had to him, while staying silent with his family. He'd asked Brown if he would visit him again when he returned to Broughton, since it was hardly likely he could manage to see him in Haworth; he would need to make up for the time he'd lost with the boys. And he must spend some time with Milly.

As the coach clattered on he mused on how it might be when the baby arrived, then wondered anxiously if the child might be mute like Milly. How would they cope? He loved Milly with a passion, just as she was, but he hoped his child could speak. He had never asked Milly about her muteness, and had presumed it was there since birth, or had somehow happened in childhood. On leaving her that day, her eyes had been languid, and she'd looked quite pale. She'd waved him off with a smile, but what a wrench it had been to leave her.

He drew himself up and sighed. A now familiar worry entered his mind. He still didn't know how often Parker was at the cottage, or the nature of Milly's relationship with him. It concerned him that she had bent her head when he'd mentioned him. Once, just once, he had seen them walking on the hills together, but just as he was catching them up, Parker had left her and gone into a copse of trees. Matthew Parker walked with a determined stride. He was a strong looking man of medium height, dark, surly and sinister, a man who lived in the shadows. Just then the coachman pulled on the reins, the horses snorted and rattled their harnesses. They were almost there.

10

'In Xanadu did Kubla Khan
A stately pleasure-dome decree:
Where Alph, the sacred river, ran
Through caverns measureless to man
Down to a sunless sea.
So twice five miles of fertile ground
With walls and towers were girdled round:
And there were gardens bright with sinuous rills,
Where blossomed many an incense-bearing tree;
And here were forests ancient as the hills,
Enfolding sunny spots of greenery . . .'

Hartley Coleridge was on his hands and knees, searching the floor. 'Where's that piece of paper?' he moaned, interrupting the trance-like flow of poetry he'd found himself uttering, "*. . . composed, in a sort of Reverie brought on by two grains of opium taken to check a dysentery,*'" his father had said. And there was more of it too, much, much more that had somehow got lost in his head. What his father had written already went on forever. And the words were sort of hypnotic. What of the words he had lost? What did they say and where had they gone? What marvellous art lay dying behind the doors of perception? And why, Hartley wondered, sitting on the floor and leaning his back against the wall, could we not reach it? What is happening in the human brain, he asked himself, that we need to break down doors so ferociously to get to the best of its art? He had thought about it a lot. He had tried certain 'experiments' himself, yet he had to admit he feared them. He would talk to Brontë about that.

But first of all he must find that page of notes he'd made, important points to bring up at their meeting – where could it be? Branwell's work was good, the man had talent and inspiration, he might go far.

He crawled about on the floor searching beneath the chairs and his desk, crawling between the multitude of scattered books. Yes, he'd enjoyed what Brontë had sent him. His translations were excellent. And he'd liked that letter too. 'I think I understand him,' he said to the floor. 'He's a struggling, desperate fellow who feels somehow captured in his head.' When creativity ravaged your veins it was hard to get through the day.

He got up and sat by his desk, pondering on what might have happened to his notes. Sometimes things disappeared, right into thin air. Oh, he was certain. 'He'll be here shortly,' he murmured. 'He'll probably want something to eat.' He had no housekeeper that day, and would have to do everything himself. He went through to the kitchen.

Nab Cottage was an interesting sort of house, he pondered. Though he sometimes felt the rooms changed shape, and would walk into the kitchen, he thought, only to find himself outside instead. Or else think he was coming into the dining room when he was actually entering the kitchen. A lot of the time he must stop and think by a doorway before going through, fearing what he might find. He often heard whispering sounds in the house, voices reciting his father's poems; there were times it went on for hours, then he would scream at them and bid them silence, banging his fists on the walls until they went away.

One of the whisperers had stolen his notes, he decided. It was hard work dodging their antics. The dead were more of a plague than the living, he mused, taking cheeses from a cupboard and putting them on to a board. He brought out some crusty bread. 'Now where is that butter?' he murmured. He searched in another cupboard. He'd some good firm apples he'd bought that week and some excellent wine. Would Brontë want red or white?

He went into the dining room and put the food on the table. The room was a riot of frantic, dappled light. 'I should tidy up some of these books,' he muttered, glancing about. 'I am a clever navigator of things on my floor, but not knowing his way about, Brontë might trip.' He didn't want him to fall on his face, well, not until they'd had a drink or two he chuckled.

He gazed around the room. He loved his books. And he loved the cottage too, even with its ghostly whisperings and lonely shadows. With its nice furnishings and the fire crackling with logs in the evening it was a cosy place to live in.

He went to look through the window. Brontë was nowhere in sight. In fact the place was deserted. He scratched his head. He was having one of his morbidly sensitive days, imagining he was ill, that all sorts of things were wrong with him, that he was being tormented by ghosts, that he was totally unequal to anything he might try to do. He'd attempted a couple of poems that week, but he wasn't happy with them. He thought he might try them on Brontë; though each time he'd read them that morning he hadn't liked them, he had constantly wanted to change things, unable to capture the true essence of what he had wanted to say. But that's how it is, he reasoned, a poet can never totally capture the essence of a poem. It was impossible to hold the pure jewel in your hand.

The opening verse of Kubla Khan kept going round in his head. 'And so much was lost of all that,' he murmured curiously. How much art was lost to the world, he wondered. And did it actually matter? Perhaps there was another world happening, a wonderful world of art and creation existing in the mind which humans could only access occasionally. Or was the mind just a doorway, a sort of channel?

Today he felt like a great plodding bear finding his way about his house, his limbs heavy with tiredness, for he had stayed up late many evenings that week trying to write, though little of value had come to him. I must lose some weight, he thought, feeling his thickening girth. I can't sit about all day and night eating and drinking like I do without taking some exercise. He glanced again through the window. A man with bright red hair strode down his path. Of average height and certainly with something of an Irish look, it had to be Branwell Brontë.

Opening the door, he saw that Branwell was pacing about nervously.

'Hartley Coleridge, sir?' Branwell faltered. His busy, excited eyes, surveyed Hartley Coleridge quickly. He was quite different from what he'd thought; his dark hair was untidy, his shirt was stained on the front, and his trousers were grubby. Though his eyes were alert, there were dark circles beneath them.

Hartley stood looking at Branwell for a moment; he too, was surprised. 'Branwell Brontë! Well you don't square up with the sickly fellow you pretend to be in that letter!' he laughed. 'Were you looking for sympathy or something? – Come in.'

Branwell stepped into the house and shook his hand. Coleridge spoke with deep lengthened vowels, in a sing-song voice. Branwell gave him a quick smile then looked downwards. 'Well, I might have been,' he said meekly. 'I can see you know all the tricks.'

Hartley Coleridge smiled wryly, 'Only because I've played them myself! – Here, give me your coat and that bag. Go and sit down by the fire. I've prepared us some food.'

Branwell unbuttoned his coat and handed it across. Hartley hung it by the door. There was a large jug in the corner filled with flowers; their sweet scents wandered the air. 'You look busy,' said Branwell glancing about. He saw the books piled around the floor and filling up his desk. 'I'm not disturbing you am I?'

'Disturbing me from what?' said Hartley. He frowned through the sunlight. 'Do sit down.' They sat opposite each other by the fire on deep comfy chairs. 'I was getting on with the business of doing nothing,' Hartley laughed.

For a long moment Branwell watched him, trying to take him in.

'You have the cool stare of an orang-outang,' Hartley said, giving him the very same look. Leaning forward, he pulled a strand of Branwell's hair. 'All this red hair hanging about your person!'

'Oh, I am not cool, sir,' said Branwell taken aback. 'Mark my words. – Well, at least not normally. It is only your kindness allows it.' Branwell smiled awkwardly. He felt oddly at one with Hartley, as if he knew him already, as if there were nothing he could hide. Hartley went on to ask him about his journey. Branwell replied by telling him how much he had liked the lake, and how much more he would like to have lived by Rydal Water as he did, instead of on the bleak Yorkshire moors.

'It's all relative of course,' said Hartley, folding his arms. 'You sort of get used to the general ambience of a place. Though I think I'll be staying put.' He was thoughtful for a moment. 'Don't underestimate the passion you gain from that bleak moorland, my man; it is there in your writing.'

Branwell gazed at him seriously. 'I sometimes think I have nothing to write about but misery.'

Hartley pursed his lips. 'That's how writers are,' he said frowning. 'We write because we are unhappy. We hope it will make things better.'

'Yes,' Branwell murmured.

'We must write also to celebrate happiness when we can,' Hartley added, though tiredly.

Branwell continued to stare at Hartley curiously. He felt that he could have asked him anything; he could have told him anything too. His mind leapt back to the poems he had read on the way. He could hear their rhythms still going round in his head. There was music in Hartley's work, beautiful music, just as there was in his father's. He wondered what inspirations he might find for himself here in his cottage. He glanced about, wondering what masterpieces Hartley had yet to create. Hartley Coleridge was a published writer, a successful man. Success justified everything, failure made it all seem ridiculous.

Hartley closed his eyes and screwed up his face. 'My father's poems will never leave me alone . . .' he groaned.

'Oh,' said Branwell. 'Why is that?'

Hartley tapped the sides of his head. 'They go round and round in here! – My father, you know, enjoyed certain states. Oh, the mind and the need to dream! He was always on a quest for the dream. Though he rarely finished his poems. He was often miserable. – The psychic energy is stolen when the spirit is depressed. That's when we have to replenish ourselves if we can.' He leaned forward opening his eyes widely. 'I too have unhealthy proclivities,' he whispered. He narrowed his eyes watching Branwell steadily.

'You mean drinking?' Branwell said cautiously.

Hartley remained silent.

'I miss my music at Haworth,' Branwell added quickly.

'Ah, through music we are sanctified!' said Hartley in an affected grandiose manner. 'We are cleansed!'

'Well, for a while at least,' said Branwell awkwardly.

'Yes,' Hartley murmured. 'We are alone in the mess, the earth is quite indifferent to our sufferings, it does not love us as we think, it is all wrapped up in itself.'

They were both thoughtful. 'There have been a lot of bumble bees about this spring,' said Branwell.

'Yes,' said Hartley. 'I noticed. Something to do with these diamond days I suspect. – I found one dead in that metal thing over there.' He pointed to an old metal vase by the door. 'Must have got stuck in the bottom. Insects can be so stupid. Imagine you had a pair of wings and you didn't use them; how stupid.'

Branwell glanced at the vase.

'Oh, it has gone now,' Hartley said with a sigh. 'I threw it out in the garden. – Ah, that is the vessel in which I store my grief,' he said gravely. 'You can go and look if you wish . . . It is empty. My grief is invisible of course. – Unless I weep.'

'Weep?' said Branwell surprised. Did Hartley Coleridge weep?

'Sometimes I weep,' said Hartley quietly. He swelled his chest with a deep intake of breath and was silent for a moment. He waved a finger. 'We have to be careful,' he said. 'We must try to manage our miseries, or they will manage us.'

Branwell shuddered.

'Ah, yes,' sighed Hartley. 'The metaphysics of perception ... What a conundrum. My father would have stolen a star from the night if he could, just to have its light for himself. Sometimes we seek the impossible.'

'I know,' said Branwell thinking about his own flights of fancy, the impossibilities he envisaged, the disappointments he had suffered. His eyes focused on the metal vase again; there was a sheet of paper sticking out, he could just see the edge. 'You said the vase was empty,' he said pointing. 'There appears to be something inside it.'

'Ah, so there does!' laughed Hartley leaning to look. He went across. 'The whisperers have sent them back ...' He read the page quickly. 'Though it doesn't matter now. I had made some notes for you, things I intended to say. Though we rarely say what we intend to say, or even what we think, eh?' He glanced at them again, then screwed them up and tossed them on the fire. The flames devoured them quickly. 'Come,' he said, beckoning Branwell to the table. 'Come and eat.'

Branwell went to the table and sat down. Hartley cut into the blocks of cheese and sliced the apples. The apples were red and shining. He asked Branwell which wine he wanted to drink. Hartley poured red wine into two large glasses. 'Cheers!' they said, smiling.

They drank for a moment quietly watching the fire. Then Hartley passed him the cheeses and bread. The bread smelt wholesome and fresh. 'Baked by a woman down the hill,' he said. 'The best bread in the Lakes!' Again they were silent, eating. 'I feel I know so much about you,' said Hartley, looking at Branwell curiously. 'You have told me so many things in your letter. And your work, of course, is revealing.'

'Yes,' said Branwell. 'I imagine it is. We forget how revealing our work is. We lay our souls on the page without knowing what we do, they are there for all to see.'

'But if the soul can be seen through the writing then the writer has won, don't you think?' said Hartley, taking a drink of his wine.

'It's quite unnerving though,' said Branwell.

'But that's what it's all about,' said Hartley. 'To dare to see yourself in your work, to see the many dimensions of your mind, the power, the horror, the joy! – Doesn't anyone listen to you at home?'

Branwell's eyebrows rose at the strange question. He was silent for a moment. 'Not very much,' he smiled. 'Unless I'm creating a fuss.' He changed his position on the chair. 'Father's busy, of course. And my sisters. Well, you know how it is with women.' He wondered a lot about his family, what they were doing, what they were eating, and how they were feeling. There was always an ache inside him when he wasn't with them, a sort of illness and fear. He felt split into pieces sometimes, as if a part of him were there with Anne at Thorp Green, or perhaps with Emily and Charlotte, or his father and aunt at the parsonage. Now he ached deeply for Milly and his unborn child. He ached for them most.

Hartley watched Branwell with the face of a man who had forgotten himself for a while, deeply intrigued by the other.

'I have three sisters,' said Branwell. 'I know that women can do amazing, miraculous things.' He broke off a chunk of bread and spread it with butter. 'I know their frustrations too. My sisters, you see, are as capable of genius as any man might be. – My sister Charlotte for instance . . .'

'Ah, your sister Charlotte,' said Hartley, shaking his head. 'I have heard of Charlotte's aspirations.'

Branwell gazed at him surprised. He had wondered if Charlotte's letter to Southey had been talked of. Though they hardly thought themselves worthy of mention by the mighty. 'Women,' Branwell began. 'Well, they put things off. They have to. There are always chores to be done, things to be dealt with that might to the world seem trivial, but are nevertheless important to the matter of living. And as for my sisters, they must always think about having to earn a living. We are not well off at the parsonage. And the house is only Father's, of course, while he lives.'

'Too true,' said Hartley with a sigh. 'Always a problem for a parson. And I feel for your sisters. Procrastination is the thief of time! Your sisters must write when they can.' He gazed at space, preoccupied for a moment. 'I'm not as disciplined as I'd like to be, myself, there are days I can write and days I can't, but I can't tell one from the other as some writers can. My moods are my masters I'm afraid.'

The afternoon light crossed the room in long thin lines, falling on the table, the glassware, the gleaming silver knives. Branwell saw that Hartley's hands trembled a little as he drank. It did not seem like nervousness, but more like something caused by his own sensitivities; a deep felt fear of himself possibly, that he too understood. The air throbbed with energy. There were so many things they needed to say to each other, so much knowledge to impart, so much friendship to be built. They talked about Wordsworth and his relationship with Hartley's father, Samuel; how they had walked with Wordsworth's sister, Dorothy, from Nether Stowey to Dulverton together in the autumn of 1797, planning the *Rime of the Ancient Mariner* that day.

'My father, you know,' Hartley said wistfully, 'was sometimes sore as a boil while writing a poem. He was often distressed when creating. But he would not cease from his quest. Kubla Khan was a psychological curiosity, he said, written after taking opium. Written, you understand, in an abstract state of mind.' He laughed loudly. 'You will need such a mind to interpret it too! – I tell you that poem is a mystery!'

He filled up Branwell's glass again and laid more logs on the fire. They talked on further, discussing Wordsworth, then Sarah Hutchinson who his father had fallen in love with, the sister of Wordsworth's wife. They talked about his father and Byron, comparing their work then went on to discuss metaphysics and the development of science and technology. Branwell told Hartley of the problems that beset his father in Haworth, how the growth of the factories had resulted in poverty for many of his father's parishioners.

'A man must have work!' said Hartley vehemently. 'It is natural to work; the whole of nature is at work.' He glanced at the window. 'See how busy the countryside is out there, the blossoms spring out from the trees, the birds emerge from their eggs, the grass shoots up from the earth.'

'We must always have something to aspire to,' Branwell said. And he wondered about it as he said it. He could never aspire to be a teacher; he needed to create. Just as a tree must suck from the earth to create its blossom, so he must draw from inside himself to create his writing. He delivered his art constantly, through laughter; joy, even sometimes through suffering. Now he knew he must write. 'You are lucky,' he said to Hartley, meeting his eyes. 'You are the son of a great poet.'

'And you are the son of a saver of souls,' Hartley said with gravity.

'I am not so sure we can save the souls of others,' said Branwell, frowning. 'It's hard enough saving our own.' He felt guilty that he had lost his belief in God, and wondered if it had really happened at all, or if it might be in a kind of sulk instead. 'God has done little, if anything, for us at the parsonage,' he said bitterly. And when he'd looked out from the window at the countless graves in the graveyard, he had sometimes thought God had forgotten them all in Haworth.

Hartley kept his eyes on him for a while but did not speak. Branwell tore at a piece of bread. 'Have you ever been in love?' Branwell said quietly.

'A horrifying state to be in!' Hartley sniffed, bracing himself quickly. Branwell recalled the poem he had read on the way, perhaps this was the moment to speak of it. Strange creaking sounds came from the ceiling.

'Squirrels,' said Hartley glancing up. 'But you will know the answer to your question from my poetry, surely . . .'

Branwell nodded embarrassed.

'Well then,' said Hartley. 'And you?' He stared at Branwell intensely.

'I am in love,' said Branwell. His voice trembled a little at the fragility of what he had said. 'Her name is Milly. She lives in Broughton. She works as a barmaid at the inn.'

'Milly,' said Hartley moving in close. 'And is this private?'

Branwell swallowed more wine. 'Yes, I suppose it is. But I shall have to reveal it soon.'

'Hmmm,' said Hartley. 'And does she write poetry?'

'Milly, write poetry?' said Branwell, feeling bewildered. Something in him told him she would if she could, that the impulse was certainly there in her, even the talent, but it was somehow captured; it found its freedom in him. 'Milly can't write at all. She sort of scribbles. She can't even read.' He picked at crumbs on his plate. How good it was to talk about Milly like this with Hartley who seemed so genuinely interested. And he realised how he had needed to discuss her with someone. He could certainly talk to Brown about her, but Brown only saw him as the boy from Haworth, the parson's son. Hartley saw him as the man he wanted to be, the lover, a father even in time. 'But she certainly enjoys poetry,' Branwell continued. 'She feels it.'

'And you glean all this from what she tells you?' Hartley said dubiously.

Branwell gazed at him thoughtfully. 'Well, yes in a way . . . Though Milly is mute. She says it all with her eyes and her gestures. She tells me things with her fingers on my palms, and . . .'

'It sounds incredible,' Hartley murmured, changing his position on the chair and staring at Branwell. 'Forgive me, my man. But how can you know what she thinks? – I mean, really?'

'I have sisters,' said Branwell smiling. 'They don't always tell me what they think. But I know what they think anyway, much more than if they said it in words. There is nothing like watching the movement of bodies and what people say with their eyes, I am quite an expert at it, it is far more revealing than talk.' He straightened up, and took a drink from his wine, then continued. Hartley listened carefully. 'Just as our deepest feelings come through our writings – yours and mine,' said Branwell. 'Milly's come through her eyes and her body. – She has such a notion of colour too.' He talked on quickly. 'Her uncle paints pictures. Milly makes the paints from what she finds on the hills. She knows the plants and clays that make up the colours. I'm amazed at her skill.'

'Her song is as complex as the nightingale's!' Hartley cried, clapping his hands in the air. 'And you must hear it as you will. The girl has your love, I can see.' He went to the window and looked out. 'The water has many moods,' he said solemnly. 'It is almost human. Some days it seems excited, other times sad.'

'Milly is pregnant with my child,' said Branwell, suddenly deeply emotional. His words floated on the dusty air of the room. As they left his throat they felt strange and unfamiliar. Hartley went back to his seat by the fire. Branwell gazed at him waiting. There was a long silence. He met Hartley's eyes.

'And so you will be a father,' said Hartley, quietly. He clasped his hands in his lap, looking at Branwell with a concerned, serious expression.

'Yes,' said Branwell. 'I can hardly believe it's happening.' And the truth of it all came to him again, though from such a different perspective, here at Nab Cottage by Rydal Water with a blackbird singing outside, and Hartley Coleridge gazing at him so kindly. 'I haven't told anyone at the parsonage yet,' he murmured. 'They don't know anything about her.'

'It will all work out in time,' said Hartley. 'These things usually do.'

The atmosphere seemed to have suddenly changed. They were both solemn for a moment. A kind of urgency prevailed. Hartley got up from his chair. He went to a drawer and brought out Branwell's letter, and the work he had sent him to look at. Pushing back the cheese board and plates, he laid the papers on the table. 'Do you want to talk about this?' he asked. Branwell nodded. It seemed like a good idea.

11

For most of the way back to Broughton, Branwell sat quietly singing. He was in such a jubilant mood. What a tale he could have told Charlotte. Over the last two days he'd made an excellent bond with Hartley. He felt he could visit him now whenever he liked; it was exactly what he had hoped for. And he must write! He must set his talent free, free from Percy, free for himself! It was simply a matter of applying his energies sensibly. He glanced about at the changing scenery, always so different returning. His mind was alive and active. He was bursting with ideas, as if a new person looked out on the world about him. He had real business to catch up with now. First of all he must sort things out with Milly. He would marry her. He must impress on his family now, the importance of what he had. He stopped singing and focused his thoughts. How could his family ever think, for a single minute, that what had happened with Milly was anything but wonderful? It was all so amazingly good, somehow apart from the blind random events that were normally his life. Other people's lives had order, he reflected; or at least a kind of order, his own was chaotic, full of little sabotages like psychological explosions.

It was late afternoon when he arrived at High Syke House. His bag felt heavier than before. Though all it contained that was extra were a couple of books he'd managed to cadge off Hartley. The door at the front of the house was open. He went inside. As he put his foot on the stairs, Mrs Fish poked her head round the door of the parlour. 'I hope your visit was successful!' she called. Her voice was shrill; not at all her normal delivery.

'Ah, yes, Mrs Fish, it certainly was!' he said, slightly taken aback. Her manner was cold and formal. 'I shall tell you about it at supper.' He looked thoughtfully at the stairs. He would have to invent something quickly. The grandfather clock ticked loudly in the hall. He had never known the house so silent.

'Well, if it isn't John!' he said turning, as the boy ran into the house. The child was normally friendly; today he was sullen. He went to stand by his mother. Mrs Fish put her arm around his shoulder and stroked the back of his hair. He gazed at Branwell strangely. 'May I have a bottle of wine, Mrs Fish, for my room, please?' Branwell asked. 'Red if you have it.' He lifted his bag again. The tension in the air was almost palpable. He would be glad to get behind the door of his room and think.

'Margaret isn't here!' Mrs Fish called out, as he reached the top of the stairs. He turned. The child beside her gazed at him contemptuously. 'She's gone with her father and Harriet to Kendal. They won't be back until tomorrow.' The boy looked up at his mother triumphantly.

'Oh, what a shame,' said Branwell. 'I was looking forward to chatting with her over supper.' Mrs Fish gave him a slow derisory look, and said no more. Deciding on a different tack, he put his hands on his hips and smiled at the boy. 'You've been doing your lessons in the garden, have you?' he said genially.

'No,' said the boy flatly.

'That's none of your concern,' said Mrs Fish. 'We must each attend to our own shop.'

'That's it, Mrs Fish,' Branwell said with a loud sigh. He stood for a moment deep in thought. Margaret rarely went off with Fish. If she needed to see her father away from the house, something was definitely astir. She has probably discovered that I didn't go home at all, he decided, and intends to tell him about it. There were bound to be people from Haworth who stopped by at the inn. If she found anything out, she would no doubt tell her mother, who in turn would tell Mrs Postlethwaite. – And what else would she say, he wondered. Would she say he'd treated her badly; that he'd encouraged her then cast her aside? Perhaps he had. But other men came to see her, anyway at their house. The boy and his mother gazed at him in stony silence. He feared the worst.

'We'll see you at supper,' said Mrs Fish, turning back to the parlour. 'Usual time.'

'Thank you,' said Branwell, standing about in the doorway of his room confounded. He sat for a while on his bed thinking. There came a knock on the door.

'Your wine,' said Mrs Fish coolly, handing him a bottle of red.
He took it from her and thanked her. 'I'll pay for it later,' he said.
'You certainly will,' said Mrs Fish, going downstairs.

Departing from the house later that evening, Branwell felt deeply relieved. What a terrible meal it had been. The vegetables hadn't been cooked properly. But the food was always inferior when Fish was away. If Margaret was away, too, then it was worse. He passed the tall grand houses with their wealthy, successful inhabitants, and crossed to the cottages on the hill. In the last few days the mosses on the walls had changed to a darker green and had somehow settled. The birds had silenced for the evening.

He walked on eagerly, thinking about seeing Milly again, and longing to hold her. As sure as the child grew inside her, she too lived within him. The taste of her returned to his tongue, the feel of her skin returned again to his fingers. The wild roses had burst into bloom on the lane. They trembled with soft pinkness, their bright yellow centres glistening with dew. He breathed in their fragrance. It was perfectly clear to him now what he must do. First of all he would ask Milly to marry him. Then he would talk to Michael. After that he would talk to his family at the parsonage. He dare not allow the thought of losing his work to enter his mind; he must cling to his new found strength. Glancing about, he saw that the road was empty of people. There was an eerie stillness in the air. A dog dashed out and yapped at his feet then ran off. – All of a sudden, a man called out from behind him, speaking in a rough local accent. 'Get back where ye come from! – We dunna want your sort round 'ere!'

Branwell turned slowly, and fixed his eyes on Parker! He knew instinctively who it was. Parker's eyes were dark and cold, his hair black as a raven's plumage, curling on his shoulders. He had square, weighty features. 'I haven't a clue who you are,' Branwell said, straightening up. He knew so little about Parker, though he envied his relationship with Milly, which seemed like a timeless, brooding thing, unbending as steel.

'No,' said Parker, coming closer. 'But I know who *you* are. And I wish she'd never set eyes on yer.' He glared at Branwell with the face of a fiend, his shirt sleeves rolled to the elbow, exposing powerful arms.

'Well, as a matter of fact . . .' Branwell said grandly. 'I am quite entitled to her. – If we are talking about the same woman, that is.' He gazed at Parker's work worn boots, his shabby clothes. He had a short growth of beard, black and curled as his hair. He looked slightly older than Branwell had thought. There was great strength in his body. Branwell had a sudden vision of Parker, lunging at machinery, hammering it to pieces just as he sawed down the trees on the hills. His arms were made for labour. And he knew that Parker was jealous of him. He wanted Milly for himself; Michael had said so. 'I am going to see the woman I love,' Branwell said calmly. 'You and I have nothing at all to say to each other.' He brushed his lapels with his hands and frowned. His blood raced with anger. As the minutes passed he discovered in himself a profound hatred for Parker, even a foul intention. However he chose to stand and display his strength, if he angered him any further, he would silence him with his fist!

Parker laughed loudly. Branwell felt confronted by a demon; a real live demon! What right did he have to behave like this? By what authority? Though the answer was there in his person. Parker had his own authority; an uncanny singular power, no doubt due to his intimacy with the region, his familiarity with the trees and hills.

'The likes of you should be weighted down and cast i' the river!' Parker said hoarsely.

Branwell laughed, though a little anxiously. He had heard at the inn of corpses dragged from the Duddon with stones in their pockets. 'My poor man,' he said. 'You are not going to murder me are you? – What, here on this lonely lane? Someone is bound to find out.'

'Get back to yer own hills! The child'll be better off without ye,' said Parker grimly.

Branwell stared at him boldly. So Parker knew about the pregnancy! He felt a surge of venomous jealousy. Parker moved in, even closer. He lunged forward, grasping the front of Branwell's coat, clenching his fist round the cloth. They were both silent for a moment, breathing heavily. Branwell locked his eyes into Parker's, their deep uncanny soul like a great unfathomable fissure in the moor. His veins tingled with anger. 'Unhand me, man!' he shouted. 'I'm an excellent boxer, and I'll have you know I punch well above my weight! – I tell you now, it's an idiot who takes me on!' With all the strength he could muster, he pushed Parker away. Parker stumbled and fell backwards on the ground. Wiping his hands slowly together, Branwell waited while Parker got to his feet. 'Get out of my way,' he said coolly. 'I must pass.'

Parker spat on the ground before him then raised his face to the night. 'Fool! – Fool!' he cried. 'Ye don't even know 'er! An' ye never will!' He spoke with an accustomed pride, knocking the earth from his clothes. For a moment or two he continued to laugh quietly. Branwell passed him and strode down the hill. After about fifty yards he turned. Parker was nowhere in sight.

12

When he arrived at the cottage, Milly seemed more emotional than usual, concerned about whether he would continue to work for Postlethwaite and stay in the Lakes. Apart from a little morning sickness, she appeared to have been quite well. Michael was quiet and thoughtful, and didn't inquire about the alleged visit to Haworth. Branwell felt relieved. He'd like to have mentioned what had happened with Parker though earlier, and ask a few questions. Michael sat staring at space for a while then went out for a stroll. The air outside was warm and sweet after a fall of light rain.

Milly didn't question things much. What happened happened, and she dealt with it as it came. Just as easily though, if she felt like staying with Michael in the cottage, to bring up the baby there with Matthew Parker coming and going as he wanted then that's what she'd do. Their lives were so simple and free.

His role as a tutor was fading fast from his mind. After his visit to Hartley Coleridge, he had a great urgency to write. Yet he must keep on earning money! He had every inspiration to write. He wanted to write poetry. He wanted to write a novel. But when would he do it? Already he could see the slight raise beneath Milly's smock. And her breasts were bigger. She was changing. He was in a quandary. He wanted her to live at the parsonage, but what would he do for work? Come what may, he decided, he must keep his job with Postlethwaite. If Postlethwaite showed him the gate, as Michael had put it, then he would need to find work elsewhere, and it wouldn't be easy. He racked his brains for an answer.

Milly was mixing paints that evening for Michael. There were two pots left to be done. She sat now at the table, her hair pinned up, her neck elegant as a swan's. She had so much tenderness and grace in her, he thought, a certain poise in which he could come to rest. She came to the end of her work, and put the paints in the box under the table. He went to her and kissed her. She drew her fingers through his own and clasped them hard, then turned his palm towards her, working her fingers around it, making those little movements that spoke of love.

'Will you marry me, Milly?' he said softly. 'You know how I love you.'

She held his gaze bewildered, then turned from him quickly. 'Please?' he said smiling, and a little nervous. He turned her to him again and cupped her face in his hands. She remained quite still, her eyes confused and afraid. He shuddered slightly, taken aback. It was so removed from what he'd hoped for; it made him afraid. 'I'm sorry if I've upset you with what I've said,' he faltered, looking downwards. 'I love you so much, you see, and I long to be with you. – I resolve to work hard for you, Milly. – Oh, I know I bungle things. It's not that I'm neglectful of my duties . . .' He threw out his arms hopelessly. 'It's just that it all goes wrong.' He laughed nervously. 'Oh, Milly. – Above all else, I must be with you!' He shook his head and recovered himself. The incident with Parker was still on his mind. What did he mean, *"You don't even know her..."*? What more was there to learn about Milly? She had given herself body and soul. He shrugged; Parker was talking nonsense.

Branwell had brought her a block of soap as a gift; a bird with outstretched wings. The almost living power of it had captured his attention, and he'd thought she might like to have it. She brought it from the table, holding it in her hands, smoothing her fingers slowly across its thin, delicate feathers. Her mood was strange and dark. Her skin shone in the thin light from the candles. He wanted her so much, yet he felt he could not reach her. A kind of gulf had grown between them in the last few days. How had it happened? 'What is it?' he asked wretchedly. He waited.

She frowned, fingering the bird, shaking her head slowly. There was a suffering in her he could not read. He felt she was somewhere else, far away, in a place where he did not belong. He went to a chair and sat down, covering his face with his hands. The noiselessness of her rejection, the total silence in the room hurt him deeply. 'You do love me, don't you?' he said quietly, collecting himself. She knew of his devotion to her. It was true, he came from a different class, he was the son of a parson, a 'gentleman'. He lived in Haworth, a considerable way from Broughton. But wasn't she carrying his child? And weren't they in love? He wanted Milly for his wife, and he thought she wanted him too. 'There isn't anyone else, is there?' he asked her softly. He lifted his eyes. His throat dried with emotion. Just then it seemed the tenderness they shared, the oneness he thought they knew, had drifted away.

She came to him, and pressed her fingers on his mouth. Tears fell down her cheeks. He gazed at her perplexed. He sat looking in her face as she stood before him, a bold, strong woman who knew her own mind. Or at least he had thought so.

'I had hoped, once we were married . . .' he continued, hesitantly, 'that you might come and live at the parsonage. – Oh, I know you'd rather be in Broughton with Michael, where you know people . . . But I'm sure you'd like us eventually. The villagers would make you welcome, and . . .'

He broke off quickly. What was he saying? He didn't have any work in Haworth. Milly had never been there. His family didn't know she existed. He swallowed hard. He had so much to do. He must think quickly, and make some decisions. He felt so frustrated. Milly stared at the fire. 'I don't want Matthew Parker coming to this cottage,' he said firmly, and with a sudden finality that surprised him.

And so the words had come. But there was something there between Milly and Parker that plagued him mercilessly, even horrified him; a past he could never know, and perhaps a present too. He clenched his fists on the arms of the chair. Moments passed in silence. She stood very still by the fire, gripping the bird.

'I know he's your friend . . .' Branwell continued, though even more awkwardly. This wasn't how he wanted to talk to her, but Parker had a hold on her he loathed. He must break it once and for all! He saw she was trembling slightly. He heard a sound like the snapping of a twig, and saw to his alarm, she had wilfully broken a wing from the bird. With a fast, determined movement, she threw it on to the fire, where it sizzled and perished in the flames. Next she broke off the other and did the same.

'Milly! – What are you doing?' he cried. For a moment or two she gazed down sadly on the wingless bird in her hands then lifted it up in her palms. He watched in awe. She put the remains of the bird carefully, almost ceremoniously, down on the table. Then she went to a cupboard and brought out a cardboard box. Taking it to a chair, she sat staring at it, sobbing softly. Slowly she took off the lid.

A musky scent of the hills issued from inside. He saw the box held leaves and pine cones. From beneath them she drew out a doll. The delicately crafted creature had been carefully worked together in yellow, shining straw, expertly woven to make a smooth firm head, glistening hair, arms, body, legs and a neatly made skirt. The doll was slender and faceless. As she held it in her hands it gleamed in the firelight, hard, strong and firmly bound together; as bound as the sun itself. Making sounds that he didn't understand, she ran her fingers over the little straw skirt and down its limbs, then held it close and caressed it. It looked so new and yellow. She was all alone with the doll, excluding him. She put it back in the box. Digging her fingers deep down in the leaves, she brought out another, this time larger, and with short cropped hair and trousers. For a moment or two she held it close to her face, rocking backwards and forwards as if in a trance.

Branwell hated the dolls; he hated the sense of isolation they gave him, the identity they gave to her. After a couple of minutes, she laid the doll back in the box with the other, and took it to the cupboard. Returning to him, she knelt by the fire on the hearth rug.

'I just want you to be happy,' he sighed. His emotions were tangling up again in the way that was hard to manage. He had said the wrong things. He had done the wrong things. And he must suffer. 'You must live with Michael, here at the cottage, if you want,' he said, his words tumbling about them. 'But the baby is growing. You will have to stop working soon, and . . .' He prayed inwardly that he'd keep his post with Postlethwaite.

She met his eyes and gazed at him gently. He wondered why she had broken the wings off the bird, why she should be so angry. He wondered too at the significance of the dolls, why she had wept, and the part Parker might play in it all. Never before had he hated a man so much! She pulled the slides from her hair, so that it dropped loosely on her shoulders. Outside, darkness had crept up to the window. She put out her arms and drew him towards her. He must celebrate his return to her now. It was time.

13

Since his recent visit to Milly, and the ominous encounter with Matthew Parker, Branwell was determined to succeed. By hook or by crook, he must keep his post with Postlethwaite! He was making his way to Broughton House with the lessons he'd prepared for the boys earlier that day. He had just reached the yew trees. As he was opening the gate, he saw that the door to the house was opening too. Postlethwaite came striding out. Reading the expression on his face, Branwell decided there was no way fate would be kind. Postlethwaite's footsteps on the stone path were heavy and determined. Branwell stood firm and smiled. He asked over Postlethwaite's health and that of his family.

Postlethwaite stood with his hands clasped behind his back, staring at the ground. 'We are all very well, thank you,' he said drily. Lifting his eyes, he glanced over Branwell thoughtfully.

There was a look of sad resignation in his face, Branwell thought. It didn't bode well. He tightened his nerves in readiness, waiting, hoping, though he knew what was coming. Postlethwaite was about to dismiss him. Now his mind was in turmoil. He filled with horror at the thought of telling Michael and Milly, telling his family at the parsonage . . .

'Your father was glad to see you, I take it?'

'Well, yes,' said Branwell, smiling weakly. 'And of all the peculiar things, the oddest was finding everything in perfect order. I had reason to believe my father might be ill, you see. He's had problems with his eyesight. I was able to help him however . . .'

'Yes,' said Postlethwaite, nodding. 'I am sure you have helped him immensely.'

Branwell braced himself. Would this awful discourse continue here on the path? Did Mrs Postlethwaite despise him? The children, he felt, had at least a little affection for him.

Postlethwaite paced the path for a while then spoke again. 'You will find what I have to say rather unpleasant,' he said with a cough. 'I would prefer not to say it at all, of course.' He glanced about the garden, at the trees, the flowers, the sky.

Branwell feigned ignorance and raised his eyebrows at Postlethwaite.

'It's a pity we have come to this,' said Postlethwaite looking down his nose.

Branwell put the boys' lessons on the wall. He stood very still, clasping his hands before him. Postlethwaite's words attacked him like an army of knives.

'You haven't been about much, have you?' Postlethwaite said. 'I mean, my boys know who you are, of course, and you can sketch an excellent falcon ... But you haven't been really teaching them a lot have you?' Postlethwaite rubbed his nose.

Branwell strained his eyes, to see if the boys were watching from upstairs. His mind worked quickly. Margaret Fish had probably told Postlethwaite he hadn't been to Haworth at all, that he had gone elsewhere. In her own clever way she would have found out.

'Now I put it to you, Branwell,' Postlethwaite continued, lowering his voice, and in a not unkind tone. 'Is it right that I pay you good money to let my boys away to the village to talk with the barber about railways?'

'Railways?' said Branwell, fixing his eyes on him curiously. 'What does the barber know about railways?'

'What doesn't he know about railways?' Postlethwaite replied, gazing thoughtfully at the sky. 'Railways will lead us to the future! My boys are railway mad! But I think you know what I am getting at here, don't you?'

Branwell waited.

'I have long held the suspicion that you are happier at the inn than with us. I think I am correct? – Why my boys could rival Bewick's Birds for the number of drawings they've made. I have not employed you to teach them to draw birds! – From time to time perhaps they might draw a bird or two, but ...'

'Mr Postlethwaite,' Branwell protested, 'I have done my best. I'm sorry to have to tell you, but the boys are very poor learners. They will not listen.'

'Are you suggesting my boys are dull?' Postlethwaite said, swelling his chest. 'It is up to their tutor to make them listen. Where is your discipline?'

Postlethwaite's condemnatory tone horrified Branwell. He fell silent. But it was all unfortunately true. He did like going to The Old King's Head, if only to talk with the locals. And he enjoyed a drink; it helped him relax.

'The truth of the matter is,' Postlethwaite continued, 'I am giving you notice.'

Neither of them spoke for a moment. Branwell sat down on the wall.

'I have talked this over with my wife,' said Postlethwaite gravely. 'We are very sorry.'

'And the boys?' Branwell asked painfully.

'Well, boys will be boys, of course. They like drawing birds.' Postlethwaite smiled sardonically.

'Yes,' said Branwell, gazing at the yellow flowers swaying by the wall.

'People gossip around here,' said Postlethwaite. 'You have been talked about.'

'By a certain young lady, I'll wager,' said Branwell through his teeth.

'We will not name names,' Postlethwaite said. 'We know what's been happening. – Or more to the point, what hasn't been happening. I can't just provide you with money for nothing. You must work like the rest of us!'

Branwell heard a rustle in the thicket behind him. The boys sprang out chortling with laughter then ran into the house.

'I'll be hanged if I know how to manage them!' Postlethwaite muttered, watching them.

'Me neither,' said Branwell, pulling himself together. Ah well, he thought, matters might have been worse. He had heard Postlethwaite sorting out business with people. He was hardly easy to deal with when it came to money. And he hadn't asked for anything back. Branwell saw he was sweating on his upper lip. Postlethwaite probably admired his father, the parson, Branwell decided, and only with difficulty had he done what he'd had to do.

'I have someone else coming to tutor them soon,' Postlethwaite said.

Branwell stared at him for a moment; it looked like it was all sorted out. He stood about anxious. Postlethwaite turned towards the door. 'You have till the end of June,' he said over his shoulder. 'You may have the rest of today to yourself.' He began to whistle a tune and the boys came out to join him, chattering regardless. 'Mr Brontë is leaving us soon,' he told them. 'You are having another tutor for summer. I've cancelled your lessons for today.'

This was the way things were in the Postlethwaite household. The tutor had been dismissed. It was just another event in their lives. But Branwell knew it might destroy him.

14

Aspirations? Oh, I have plenty of those! Branwell told himself, as he went down the hill for a deeply uncomfortable talk with Michael; without resources though, aspirations were ineffectual.

It was almost the end of June, a warm languid evening. What would he say, he wondered anxiously, as he closed on the cottage. He'd declare, certainly, what had happened with Postlethwaite wasn't entirely his fault, that the boys were impossible to teach, that his intentions towards Milly had never been anything but honourable. And that he'd return to Broughton as soon as he had found some work. He screwed up his eyes against the bright evening sunlight. What a calm evening it was, so different from what was going on in his head. He heaved a sigh. He had given Milly his drawings to take care of. She'd taken them with pride and pleasure.

Now though, as he opened the door, Michael's manner was cool. He shook his head. 'I knew it'd happen. I said so to Milly.'

Branwell bit tensely on his lip. Milly was seated on a chair by the fire, her back towards him. She did not turn. She had obviously given Michael the news.

'I'm very sorry,' Branwell began, with a heavy spirit. He removed his coat, but stayed standing where he was. He didn't know what to do. Did Michael want him to leave? Did Milly? She'd appeared thoughtful, earlier that day when he'd told her. Now, it seemed, she ignored him. He could have chilled to death, the air felt so cold. There was a horrible moodiness about her; she sat so still. And there was little he could say for certain that would make things better. They both had a right to feel upset. But he hadn't anticipated this. He felt like a shorn lamb in a bitter wind.

Milly put wood on the fire; it crackled and spluttered. He talked on quickly, relieved to be breaking the silence, relieved to deliver his story, the tale of how he had tried so hard with the boys, of their impossible behaviour, of their lack of attention, of his heartfelt aspirations to become a poet. And of the way Hartley Coleridge had received him and given him hope.

'Ah, dunna start on about poetry, boy! – Shame on ye!' Michael cried. 'Go sit ye dahn. I shall have to go out for a bit, afowr I seh summat I'm sorry fer.' He put on his coat and hat and stormed out of the door.

Branwell stood lost in the silence then took a seat by Milly in the charming familiar cottage he had come to love. He watched her as she gazed at the fire; shame raging his blood; a lonely, frantic hideous thing trying to hide. They sat for some time in silence. She continued staring at the fire, her eyes troubled, her fingers working nervously together in her lap. She looked so lovely in her soft blue smock. He wanted so much to embrace her.

'Milly?' he said quietly. 'I shall come to visit you regularly. I shall think of you every moment of every day. – And I shall try hard to find work.' She was sobbing quietly. He wanted to reach for her hand, but he feared she'd reject him. 'Please don't cry,' he pleaded. His voice was strained, almost to a whisper. 'When things are bad, you have to remember they get better. They do if you try.'

She turned to him, her large liquid eyes searching his face. Then she turned back to the hearth, shaking her head confusedly and pointing. He followed the line of her finger. His eyes fell on some charred papers by her feet. He bent in closer. In a moment of terrible recognition he saw what they were. He reached down for what remained of his drawings, catching his breath. 'All of them?' he whispered horrified. The brittle, burnt paper fell through his fingers. His voice broke with emotion. 'But why?'

Rising from her chair, she came to him, kneeling before him shaking. He felt he might die with sadness. How could she do such a thing? They weren't just drawings, they were more than that. Surely she knew? Why would she want to destroy them? For a long time she rested her head in his lap. He stroked her hair, deeply disturbed and hurting.

Michael returned, removing his boots by the door. He walked slowly towards them then sat in a chair, fixing his eyes on the charcoaled remains in the hearth. He stayed silent for a while. 'Matthew did it,' he said finally. 'It were done in anger. He came earlier. He had an argument with Milly.'

Branwell gazed at space, lost in a kind of stupor, only half hearing his words. *'An argument with Milly?'* he said, suddenly alert, searching his face incredulously. 'What sort of argument?' And he wondered again, strangely, what sort of communication had happened between them.

Michael scratched his head. 'Oh, it were bitter, bitter! May God deliver us from any demons as were listenin'. Aye, it were bitter!'

'He abused her?'

Milly's eyes remained closed. She did not move.

'She were beatin' his chest and slappin' his face,' Michael said shakily. 'But he burnt her pictures. I sent him off. He upset her.'

Milly got up and ran to her bedroom. Branwell stood and straightened, then paced the floor for a while, angry, finally returning to his chair. 'I'll cut his throat if I find him!' he said, glaring at the fire. 'Oh, I will, I promise you!'

Michael shrank back. They were both silent again.

'I must go,' said Branwell, pulling on his coat.

'Where to?' asked Michael fearfully.

'To find him!' said Branwell. He left the cottage and strode across the road, making his way up the path towards Parker's house. Finding his way through the blackberry bushes, he went through the ferns and elderberry trees bending towards him wearily in the growing dusk. He pushed them aside. He felt as if he were a furnace, such was the blaze in his blood.

Further ahead he could hear the rasp of a saw. He closed in on Parker, dropping back for a moment, trying to gather himself together, observing his furious energy, his mouth set and certain, his jet black hair covering his devilish eyes. He was full of purpose, so mechanically directed; he went through a log as if he were slicing bread.

Branwell moved forward. Striding over a bank of slippery clay, he stepped on firmer ground then stood still for a moment. Parker stopped, then continued. 'They were only images on paper!' Branwell called, above the sound of the sawing. 'You can never destroy our love!' Arms folded, he stared at Parker madly. The sound of the sawing sang out loud in the air. Parker shifted his position and sniffed, then started again. 'You might burn them!' Branwell continued, even louder. 'You might send them out on the wind. But you can never destroy what's in our hearts!'

Parker stopped again and gazed at the sky. 'Yer hearts?' he laughed. 'Ye dunna know what her heart's made o', ye fool!' His eyes shone with a deep, uncanny blackness. 'Ye shoulda known better than mek drawin's o' t' girl like that. Ye've brought her down. – Ah, get on yer way, will ye. Some of us 'ave work t' attend tuh.' He turned again to his sawing, careless of Branwell's presence.

'You fiend!' Branwell sneered. 'I know your type!' He wanted to run at him, savage him even. He glanced at Parker's house. 'Why, you'd lock her up in that miserable hell hole if you could, wouldn't you? You'd keep her prisoner!' He waited for Parker to turn, to bare his teeth. He wanted it. He was a practised boxer; he knew he could tire him out, and in doing so give him a hiding.

Parker stood thoughtful for a moment then turned, his eyebrows knitted together, his lip curled contemptuously. He flung down his saw and faced Branwell like a warrior. They stood for a moment looking at each other, their eyes filled with hatred.

'I don't care if I kill you!' cried Branwell. He lunged forward, thrusting his fist in Parker's face. Parker reeled backwards and fell on the logs, so that they scattered down the hillside, tossing and tumbling. The sweet scent of damp sawdust rose about them.

Parker scrambled up quickly. 'Ah, go an' draw yer pictures, man!' he growled. 'Go an' draw yer pictures. But ye munna draw pictures o' her like that, or I wunna be answerable for me actions!' He pulled down the sleeves of his rough cotton shirt and straightened his hair.

Branwell went for him again, landing him yet another blow, this time on his brow. That too sent him reeling. Branwell stood firmly before him. 'Come on - do your worst!' he shouted. 'I doubt you will land a single blow on this pretty chin of mine!'

Every cell in Branwell's body was marshalled for battle. His whole will rose within him. Parker got up and came at him again. 'Oh yes, quite close!' cried Branwell, with mock laughter. 'But not close enough. – I warned you!'

Parker punched out again, and again, his fists clenched tightly, though only the hollow air received his blows. Gasping heavily and wiping blood from his mouth, he finally bent over, falling to his knees on the grass. 'It's not what Milly wants, all this,' he said, breathlessly. 'I know 'er better than you do.'

Branwell braced himself, watching him. He hated Parker. He loathed him. And he couldn't understand him.

'Nah, it's not what Milly wants,' Parker repeated.

'You started this,' said Branwell, trying to catch his breath. Parker lay back on the ground, gazing up at the sky. Branwell wondered why he hadn't fought harder. He hadn't used the best of his strength. He lay still as a dead man, his face spattered with blood, his lip bleeding heavily, though in a strange way not the least broken or humbled. Branwell shuddered. And it wasn't true either. He had never known Parker's type. Not ever. Except in nightmare. As he went down the hill he glanced back several times. Parker had returned to his house. Had anything important happened that evening, or had nothing happened at all?

15

Branwell left Broughton-in-Furness filled with foreboding. What a wicked few weeks it had been; the boys paying less attention than ever and Mrs Postlethwaite constantly watching him. For most of the suppers at High Syke House, Margaret had been absent from the table. She undoubtedly had her admirers; from time to time, he'd spotted them arriving at the house, but they didn't stay long. She generally took them walking out in the garden. Whenever she'd needed to speak to him, she'd done so coolly, without once meeting his eyes. Once or twice she'd annoyed him with her lack of civility, but the annoyance hadn't lasted long. The damage had been done. That was the end of that. And in any case he'd had too many other things to think about; he was glad of her reserve.

He hadn't seen Matthew Parker again after the fight by his house, and he hadn't mentioned it to Milly or Michael; and he hadn't spoken about the drawings. Milly got on with her work at the inn as usual, and cleverly contrived to dissuade him from talking about Haworth. He'd determined to be brave and take her, but she'd refused to listen, putting her palms on his mouth if he spoke, even in front of Michael. He knew he couldn't broach it with Michael. They both had made the decision. She would not visit the parsonage. If he wanted to be by her side, then it would have to be there in Broughton. The power in her face and emotions when he brought it up, the charm of her movements and gestures, left nothing to be said.

And he'd tried to be sensitive to her desires. But he didn't have any money and he had nowhere to live. The cottage was tiny. There wasn't room for them all. And the baby was coming. He wondered how he'd support her now without work. And the disgrace he felt, which was of his own making, lay heavy in his mind. He'd told his friends at The Old King's Head, who had gazed at him perplexed. Had he truly known what his imaginings would do, his wanderings, his living in his head, he would certainly have done things differently.

Or would he, he wondered as he walked down the path to the parsonage? Here he was, the same old Branwell, the same old dreary failure walking to the door.

'I've an odd feeling we've been here before,' said his father, standing in the doorway. His eyes lingered on Branwell with sadness and concern.

'I'm sorry, Father,' said Branwell, entering the house.

'You're never going to learn, are you?' said the parson, shaking his head.

Branwell threw out his hands and sighed.

'Ah, nothing is as gloomy as all that,' said the parson, inviting him into the kitchen where he was brewing some tea. There was a long silence. Branwell stood by his father, his bags in the hall. He unbuttoned his coat. 'You have vexed me, of course, with this,' said his father flatly. 'I have to say, you are quick at it, you know, this getting bored of your work.' He pressed his lips firmly together and stirred the tea in the pot. 'Let's go and sit down.'

'I'm very sorry...' Branwell said again, following him into the parlour.

'Ah, don't dishearten me further by begging forgiveness...' said his father to the walls.

'I don't ask forgiveness for my failure to teach, Father,' Branwell asserted. 'It's as much the fault of the boys as mine. But I ask you to forgive me for – well, for being as I am.'

Patrick put his hands round the teapot and gazed at space. 'And so I do,' he said in a broad Irish accent. 'How can I not? You are my son.'

'I can never measure up to ...' Branwell began miserably.

'Oh, stop this measuring business,' Patrick said, pouring the tea. 'How can the day measure its light, or the night its darkness? I too have faults, my son. Relax. Your sisters will be back with your aunt, shortly. None of us is perfect. Don't punish yourself about this, you will find something else. The good Lord will help you.'

They were both silent a while.

'You went to see Hartley Coleridge, I believe,' said Patrick with interest.

'Yes,' said Branwell. He'd been forced to write to them and tell them the truth of what had happened. His father had dismissed the indiscretion. He doubted Charlotte would be as generous. 'He was very impressed with my work.'

'I'm sure he was,' said the parson. He settled back in the chair, surveying Branwell, deeply unhappy that fate should decree that he should make his son feel inadequate.

'He encouraged me to work on Horace's Odes. I've sent him some more translations. I offered to share the profits if they were published.'

Patrick Brontë frowned quickly. 'Oh, you shouldn't have done that.'

'Why not?' Branwell said, suddenly alarmed.

'Nothing to do with the money, simply the pride. A man of his background won't want to talk about money.'

'I suppose not,' Branwell sighed. 'Anyway, it's done. But I added a comment to say that I wasn't being impudent, simply inexperienced if anything. Hartley understands all that. We are much alike.'

'Aye,' sighed Patrick. 'By all accounts, you are.

'Branwell went into his pocket. 'I have his letter.' He handed it across. Patrick took it attentively, his eyes widening. He found his spectacles and drew the writing close to his face, reading slowly.

'. . . I smile to think that so small an asteroid as myself should have satellites . . . Howbeit, you are – without exception – the only young Poet in whom I could find merit enough to comment without flattery – on stuff worth finding fault with, I think I told you how much I was struck with the power and energy of the lines you sent before I had the pleasure of seeing you. Your translation of Horace is a work of much greater promise, and though I do not counsel a publication of the whole – I think many odes might appear with very little alteration. Your versification is often masterly - and you have shown skill in great variety of measures. There is a racy English in your language which is rarely to be found in the original – that is to say –untranslated, and certainly untranslateable effusions of many of our juveniles . . .'

Patrick sat thinking about it. 'It is true, what he says,' he said finally.

'True?'

'But of course, you're a brilliant young man. You only need to keep trying. You will reach your goal in the end.'

'But why is it so hard?' said Branwell, resting his head in his hands.

'But why does it have to be easy?' said his father, folding his arms. Branwell returned the letter to his pocket. 'Better look after that,' said Patrick, nodding towards it.

'I know I could do such wonderful things,' said Branwell, clasping his fist in his hand. 'They are there in my mind, longing to be born ...' His father was pouring more tea. He offered Branwell some cake. They ate for a moment in silence.

'God is essentially creative,' Patrick said solemnly. 'He has bestowed that creativity on us. We may use it for good or ill. Even the heavens are not without faults. Comets come at us out of the blue. They too lose their way. We are often dismayed.'

'I shall have to go back to Broughton,' Branwell said, the great flood of Milly entering his mind. The heavy weight of her pregnancy filled his being. 'You see, there's a ...' But the words wouldn't come. He was as mute as Milly just then.

His silence brought a strange glance from his father. 'So why do you need to go back?' he asked curiously, biting his cake. He knew his son. He waited

'There are things I must do,' Branwell replied troubled. They were both silent again.

The silence was broken suddenly by the sound of his sisters coming up the path with his aunt.

'So what news do you bring us, Branwell?' cried Charlotte, rushing in. 'Something bright and cheery, I hope.' There was a sharp edge of sarcasm in her tone. Each of them kissed him.

'Good heavens!' laughed Aunt Branwell. 'Mrs Fish has certainly been feeding you up. How padded your chest has become, and look at the plumpness in your cheeks!' She pinched his cheek and patted his arm. Emily stood by silent, looking at him with her strange, though familiar look.

'Take off your coats and bonnets and come and have some tea,' said the parson.

Emily was holding a bunch of wild flowers from the moor, yellow celandines, bluebells and lilac bistorts. She took them into the kitchen then brought them out in a vase.

Who are these people about me? Branwell wondered, as if suddenly detached from himself. They are all bathed in light. My sisters, my aunt, my father, myself ... none of us is real. I doubt they see who I am. They make of me what they will. And I make of myself what I want. I am always trying to lift myself from the perpetual shadow of reality! He glanced at the wild flowers, fresh from the moor, so pretty on top of the table. What is my destiny, he wondered fearfully. I am as much subject to fate, as the toy soldiers of my childhood were to the lives we gave them!

He wondered for a moment how Anne was faring at Thorp Green, where she had gone to work as a governess in May with the Robinson family. She would no doubt be coping fine. In her normal dutiful way, she would grin and bear it. He hoped the Robinsons were kind. The house was set in the middle of a big estate, with servants in attendance. Anne wouldn't want for food and warmth, so that was something. But those were only the physical things, Branwell reasoned. She would pine for her creativity as the rest of them did. 'I must remove my bags from the hall,' he said, over the voice of his aunt, who was talking about potatoes. He left them and went to his room, where he washed, then returned to the parlour. His father went out into Haworth.

'I think I shall take a nap,' said Aunt Branwell, coming to embrace him. 'I'll talk to you later.' Charlotte re-arranged the little flowers in the vase. 'Mary Taylor is coming to visit us,' she said, over her shoulder.

Branwell looked up. 'Mary?'

'Yes, very soon. I expect her to stay for the week.'

'The week?' he murmured. Mary Taylor, Charlotte's friend, was certainly pleasurable company. And a beautiful woman too. She might have cheered him, though he wouldn't be cheered by her now. There was Milly to think of. And he needed to have a serious talk with his family. When would he do it? He must find a way of letting them know what had happened in Broughton, and prepare them for the future. Whatever the future held . . . At present he had no idea. 'What's Weightman up to?' he asked, by way of changing the subject. William Weightman, his father's curate had caused something of a stir in the Brontë household. He had sent his sisters a Valentine card in February. It was rumoured Anne was in love with him. 'And the church-rates? What's happened there?'

Emily gave a little humph, but stayed characteristically silent. She rarely said what she thought; more often than not she committed her thoughts to paper, or they stayed in her head.

'Oh, nothing's changed,' Charlotte sighed, sitting down. 'The dissenters are still at it.'

'Pests!' Branwell hissed.

'We had a meeting in the Schoolroom in March . . .' Charlotte said with a smile. 'Oh, it was awful. Papa was in the chair, and the Reverends Mr Collins and Mr Weightman were there as supporters. There was almost a fight. The dissenters can be so aggressive. Oh, what a to-do!' She laughed. 'The newspapers have it we are quite a curiosity out here. They couldn't believe that intellects like ours could be found on the boggy moors.'

Branwell sat back in his chair and smiled. It was good to be home, hearing all the news. He wondered about Willie Weightman. It was obvious from Charlotte's letters she had a strong attachment to him. Weightman, it seemed, had touched the hearts of his sisters.

'I shall have to get round to helping with supper shortly,' Emily said, close by. 'How have you been? – Or is that something you would rather forget?'

Branwell lowered his face to his hands in his lap. 'I'm disgraced again, dear sister,' he said quietly. 'What shame I bring you.' He sighed loudly. 'Yet I am always so welcome in this house. – Why, even Aunt doesn't scold me. Not one of you judges me.'

'Judging can grow quite tiresome,' Charlotte yawned.

'Perhaps people judge from false premises,' Emily retorted defensively. 'Teaching is much too dull for Branwell. I couldn't have stood it for a week with those Postlethwaites, let alone months.'

'Anne does very well,' said Charlotte, thoughtfully. 'I have to admit, she's strong.' Charlotte looked downwards; she wasn't working herself just now and felt guilty. Emily hated anything that took her from the moors, and was also at home. Only Anne was out working.

'I shall soon find employment . . .' said Branwell, wrinkling his forehead. 'I intend to keep looking.' Here was a moment when he might have confided his worries to his sisters. But he sat immersed in thought instead; the words wouldn't come. Emily and Charlotte gazed at him curiously, wondering at his mood. He glanced up, first at Emily then at Charlotte.

'What is it?' asked Emily.

'Oh, we know what Branwell will say,' said Charlotte wearily.

'I doubt you do,' said Branwell, frowning. Charlotte's manner was one he knew only too well; anxious and frustrated. She was as much frustrated with herself, he thought, as she was with him. And while she liked to think otherwise, she could no more settle.

'I'd like to hear more about Hartley Coleridge,' said Charlotte, her eyes lighting up. 'How was your conversation?'

Branwell settled to tell them the story, then passed them the letter. Emily and Charlotte read it together with pleasure.

'I might just write to him myself . . .' said Charlotte, suddenly deep in thought.

Emily and Branwell held each other's gaze. Charlotte was bound to be disappointed. She'd been practically dismissed by Southey. Why should Hartley Coleridge be any different? Wouldn't she just be categorised again as a foolish woman allowing herself to dream, when she ought to have been doing womanly things like sewing and baking bread?

'Hartley Coleridge imagines he really is somebody,' Charlotte said haughtily. 'All because he's had a bit of help from his relatives. – Robert Southey for an uncle, Samuel Taylor Coleridge for a father. How can he fail?'

'He's an excellent poet,' Branwell protested firmly.

'Bah!' said Charlotte, handing him back the letter.

'His work speaks for itself,' said Branwell quietly.

'We three,' Charlotte continued adamantly, glancing at Branwell and Emily, 'are every bit as good as he is. He is simply more fortunate, that's all.' She wrung her hands irritably.

'I don't think you should write to him,' said Branwell. 'Not so soon after I have.'

'What will you send him?' Emily murmured, knowing it was inevitable.

'I don't know,' Charlotte said thoughtfully. 'I have one or two pieces.'

'I would rather you didn't send anything,' Branwell groaned.

'Well, you have simply beaten me to it,' Charlotte replied dismissively. 'I'd intended to write to him earlier this year, I haven't had time.'

All three were silent for a while. Emily got up and went to the kitchen. Charlotte went upstairs. Branwell sat pondering in the chair. Would there ever be a moment when he could tell his family about Milly?

16

It might just as well have been winter; the parsonage had such a chill about it that morning. Mary Taylor couldn't have felt very cheerful as she went through the silent rooms. The happy, carefree conversations that normally went on in the house had gone. Both Charlotte and Mary were miserable.

It was almost certainly Branwell's aloofness that had caused it, Charlotte thought. He hadn't been at all himself with Mary, she told Emily at breakfast that day. Emily argued he was preoccupied; he'd relax when he'd found employment. He'd talked about working for the railways, she added, though quietly. Charlotte exploded with laughter. Mary Taylor looked vacantly at the air. But the railways were up and coming, said Emily forcefully, and there was work to be had that would undoubtedly interest men. It was certainly better than moping about in the parsonage.

'Then let him do it,' Charlotte smiled wryly. 'He'll no doubt set the parsonage on fire with his fervour.' She couldn't think of anything duller, she added incredulously.

'Talking of fires,' said Emily with a slight shudder. 'I think I might light one. The weather is cold for summer. Do we have any kindling?'

'I filled the box,' murmured Charlotte.

On her arrival, Mary had brought sunshine with her smile, but the sun had disappeared since then. Branwell had scarcely acknowledged her, and Emily had been silent as ever. Aunt Branwell had stayed in her room, and their father had been out in the village a lot, working. It wasn't at all the holiday Charlotte had envisaged for Mary; they both felt tense.

'I'll light the fire,' said Emily, making to rise. 'Then I must do some writing.'

'We'll take a walk on the moor,' said Charlotte to Mary. 'It's a little blowy, but fresh.'

Through the window, on her way upstairs, Emily saw that Branwell was still with Brown in the graveyard. He'd been talking for almost an hour. What did he have to say that was so important?

'Well, you're certainly in a fix,' said Brown, listening to Branwell's tale. Though he could never see Branwell as a teacher; he would strain like a hound on a leash. 'Surely you knew that Milly would never come here. Girls like her are very parochial. They like to stay where they are. They know their neighbours, not just the people, they know the trees, the ground they walk on, the flowers on the hills. You say yourself how familiar she is with what all that.'

'I know,' said Branwell pensively, sitting down on a gravestone.

Brown carried on digging. 'It's getting to you this, isn't it?' he said, leaning on his spade. 'Especially that Parker business. Though it's hard to see how a fellow like you can be troubled by such a simpleton.'

'There's something very peculiar about him ...' Branwell said, gazing at the clouds. 'I can't work him out. And I don't know what his relationship is with Milly ...'

Brown peered at him through a mop of dark brown hair. He brushed it back with his hand. 'You should tell your family about this. The longer you leave it, the harder it'll get. Well, at least tell your father.'

'But how can I?' said Branwell desperately. 'Charlotte's friend is staying with us now. There is never the right moment.' He looked down into the damp grave. It all looked innocent enough, shining beetles scuttling about with abandon, worms wending their way.

Brown was studying his spade. 'Aye, it's a bit of a mess. You need to find work and quick. You can't do anything till you've got some money in your pocket.'

'I have one or two plans ...' Branwell said quietly. He wondered what Milly was up to in Broughton; it had been four days. 'I shall have to see Milly soon, though,' he said anxiously. 'I love her, John. I need her!'

They were both silent for a moment.

'I knocked him down, you know. – Did I tell you? I knocked him down twice.' Branwell put his tongue in his cheek and thought about it. 'Yes, I gave him a hiding.' He sighed deeply. 'I'm not sure it mattered though much. He's sort of unreal. Yes, a very definite demon.'

'Why did you fight him?' Brown asked, digging hard and tossing earth from the grave.

'He threw my drawings on the fire. Those sketches I'd made of Milly. I could have killed him for that. – Have you any idea what they meant to me? What they meant to us both?'

'But why did she let him see them?'

Branwell frowned thoughtfully. 'I don't know, John; it puzzles me. They were private between us, special. It hurts that she let him see them, wanted it even, perhaps. As if he had the right . . .'

Brown carried on digging quietly. Branwell talked on. 'It disturbed her though that he'd put them on the fire. She had raked them out. Half of the images were saved, though they were lost from what they had been; holes burned through her beautiful face and arms, and . . . They crumbled to pieces in my fingers.'

It was a cold, cheerless morning. There were few people out. Brown pulled up his collar and continued his work, talking to Branwell through a series of deep breaths, broken by fitful coughs. 'So you went to find him.'

'Yes. And I fought him too. But he wouldn't fight back. Well, not properly. He let me hit him and hit him. It was almost like beating my fists into a tree. I beat him till his face was bloody, but it made no difference. Nothing will change, I know.'

They were thoughtful again for a while. Apart from the sound of Brown's spade slicing the earth, the graveyard was still.

'There's a sort of malevolence in him,' Branwell continued, almost in a whisper. He thought of the straw dolls, cold, horrible, shining things. 'Parker has made those dolls, you know.'

'Dolls?' said Brown stopping his digging again. 'You didn't tell me anything about dolls.'

'Didn't I? – She keeps two dolls in a box. They're supposed to be male and female. They're made from straw. She's sort of captivated by them. He made them, I know it.' He went on talking, telling Brown how the dolls obsessed her, how she treasured them.

Brown smiled. 'Ah, they're nought but a couple of dolls.'

'No they're not. They're more than that,' Branwell insisted. 'I want rid of them!'

'Now then,' said Brown, gazing at Branwell concernedly. 'You'll not do that if they're precious to her.'

'I hate that they're precious!' The marks of Branwell's footprints were all over the damp clay. And he was still pacing.

'You're getting this out of proportion,' said Brown. 'She's probably had them since childhood. Women do that kind of thing.' He sighed. 'I've never seen you like this. Where's the fun in you nowadays? That melancholy of yours'll be the death of you if you let it! The girl has a couple of dolls, that's all. – Do you want to go see her tomorrow? I'll join you, if you like.'

'Oh would you, John?' Branwell said eagerly.

'Aye, I could do with a break. And the carving's done for a bit.'

'The pregnancy's started to show,' Branwell said suddenly happier. 'There's a sort of swelling. It makes me feel strange.'

'I expect it does,' said Brown thoughtfully. 'Will you still try to get her to come to live here with us?'

Branwell breathed in deeply. 'Oh, I daren't even speak about that. The very idea of moving from Broughton disturbs her. And it's sort of as if she's all right, as if there's a providence there that makes her feel safe. It's not just Michael, not just the land, it's . . .'

'You shouldn't be thinking what you're thinking,' said Brown firmly.

'But I imagine it. I imagine him going to see her at the cottage. I imagine him looking after her. In fact, I think he's always looked after her.' Branwell was breathing fast as he spoke. 'I hate even thinking of it, John. But I have to because . . .'

'But how do you know where you'll be when she has the baby?' Brown said worriedly. 'You must get some work. Where are you going to find it? It might be a good way off.'

'Surely there is work close by?' Branwell stood wringing his hands. 'There has to be something. – Anyway, I'm determined she won't live at his house!'

'Why would she want to live there?' asked Brown, surprised.

'Because he will ask her. – Not even that, he will *take* her. – It must not happen! It can't!' The tone in his voice was hopeless. His music, his odes, his poetry were lost to him now. Nothing would come to his aid.

'We'll pay her a visit tomorrow,' said Brown. 'We can talk on the way.'

17

But Branwell and Brown spoke very little on the way. Neither of them felt relaxed and the journey seemed endless. Stopping at an inn for the night, they'd sat silently eating and drinking before retiring to bed.

Brown, however, looked strong and confident, Branwell thought. He'd put on his best clothes, as if he were going on an errand of great importance. Which of course, he was; he would try to add credence to Branwell's argument that Haworth was a good place to live, a place where Milly would feel welcome. He was coming to see how she was, and to meet her uncle. And he was coming as their friend. Branwell was quite decisive now. He would discuss it all with his family soon. Wherever he had to work, Milly and the baby would live with his people at the parsonage; she would be right in the heart of his life.

'Do you want to be first to get out?' Brown asked, as they arrived at The Old King's Head. 'There are bound to be some who are curious.'

There was a screeching sound as the wheels scraped the pavement. The coach drew up. The horses snorted and gasped, catching their breath.

'Oh, for sure, they'll be curious,' said Branwell. 'I expect I'm the talk of the inn. Postlethwaite is highly respected here. I am bound to have riled the locals.'

It was late afternoon. There were few people about, though inside the inn was full. 'Will you be staying?' asked the barman.

Branwell nodded. 'Myself and the gentleman here.'

They found their rooms then went down to eat. Afterwards, they made their way to the cottage. The voices in The Old King's Head, Branwell thought, had somehow sounded unfamiliar. He had felt people were avoiding him with their eyes. He shrank from the place now and no longer felt welcome.

All the way from Haworth, he'd felt guilty. He had told his father that he and Brown were going to see a man about a headstone; a piece of marble, Brown had said, something he fancied carving. Poor old Brown, Branwell reflected sadly, he was getting good at inventing. Branwell had listened amazed, as Brown had delivered his story; he had almost believed it himself. All the time his father's eyes had been fixed on his friend knowingly, but he would never have stooped to inquire.

Branwell had had a bad few days at the parsonage. He hadn't wanted to be rude to Mary Taylor, and he wished he'd been able to explain his reserve to his family, but he couldn't have told them the truth with Mary in the house. It would be hard enough telling them later. He sat clenching his fists. 'I shall throw him out if he's there! – Just watch me!' he cried.

'Try to stay calm,' said Brown, touching his sleeve. The door of the cottage opened.

'My very good friend, John Brown!' said Branwell to Michael. 'I have brought him to meet you.'

Brown shook Michael's hand. 'Pleased to make your acquaintance,' he said cordially.

Michael appeared embarrassed and taken aback by their arrival. The lane was empty, the stone walls lit by moonlight. 'You've come at an awkward time,' he said uneasily.

'We're staying at the The Old King's Head,' Branwell said, wondering why they were having to stand outside. He tried to look through the doorway.

'Milly's out walking,' said Michael, glancing at Brown and Branwell by turns, and obviously lost for words.

'Alone?' Branwell frowned, with a little impatience.

'You mustn't upset her,' said Michael. 'She's been thinking.'

'Thinking about what?' said Branwell irritably.

'Look – you'd better come in,' said Michael, opening the door further.

Branwell felt there was little welcome in his words. He felt as if there were a conspiracy against him; Michael, Parker and Milly were all against him. 'I have no intention of losing her,' he said vehemently. He folded his arms and braced himself. 'Milly belongs to me.'

Michael sat down and gazed at the fire. 'Oh, no, my boy, she doesn't belong to anybody,' he said quietly, `except herself.'

'She loves me,' Branwell protested. 'She's carrying my child . . .'

'Love plays tricks,' Michael said to the flames, offering them seats by the fire. 'You must allus keep track of what it's up to. You've got yourself into something bigger than you know.'

There was a moment's silence.

'What do you mean?' asked Branwell, leaning towards him. 'Why are you saying such things?'

'I canna see what good it'll do if I don't,' said Michael with a sigh.

'Please explain,' said Branwell frustratedly. 'What have I got myself into that is bigger than I know?'

Michael sat quietly, shaking his head. Brown's eyes wandered the room; he was quite perplexed.

By degrees, Branwell grew calmer. 'I see my gift has arrived,' he said, glancing at the table, noting the parcel of food he'd sent earlier that week. 'It has cakes and pies in it; I thought you might like them.'

'It came this morning. Milly will see to it later,' said Michael. He did not take his eyes from the fire as he spoke.

'Has she been gone for long?' Branwell asked searchingly.

'A couple of hours,' said Michael. 'I expect her back soon.'

The cottage was comfortable and tidy. There was a jug on the table brimming with flowers that grew by the walls on the lane. But Branwell didn't feel comfortable, and the delicate flowers offered no peace of mind. He felt Michael was hiding something, something that might hurt him to hear. There was a sort of barrier between them now when it came to questions.

Michael's eyes were hard. Branwell was surprised by his coldness, and it seemed Brown was too, for he sat in silence. Branwell had a battle on now. He wanted Milly badly. She had gone to Parker's cottage. Oh, he was certain! He wanted to bring her back, to banish Parker from her life. But he knew he daren't. He feared in his heart she would hate him for it if he did. But at least he might meet her, coming back on the lane. 'I want to go out,' he said suddenly, turning to Brown. He rose from the chair and went to the door. Brown got up and followed.

The lane was dark. They walked on quickly past the walls and trees then stopped. 'There,' said Branwell. He pointed up to the old cottage on the hill. 'That's where she'll be. There's a path at the back of the trees.'

Brown looked at his frenzied face; there was no doubting the fight going on in his blood, his lips were white and he was breathing heavily. Brown had no idea what he had in mind, but he feared his look. They made their way through the dense vegetation till they came to the house.

'The door's open,' said Brown, beckoning him closer. 'There's a man and a woman talking. They're quarrelling, I think.' They moved to a place behind the hawthorns, straining to listen, but the words were lost.

'All this mystery,' Branwell murmured. He stood baffled, resenting this world more and more by the second, this world he could not speak of and didn't understand. He fell to his knees on the grass. Strangely, instinctively, he felt there was something he'd lost, something vital, like an organ he couldn't live without. He wanted to scream. But the scream raged inside him, till he felt Brown's hand on his arm and returned to his senses.

18

Not knowing where else to search, Branwell and Brown had returned to Michael's cottage. It was getting late when Milly arrived back home, and it alarmed Branwell that she'd returned in the darkness alone. He and Brown were looking at Michael's paintings. The room fell silent as she entered. She stood very still by the door, surprised and frowning. It was an awkward moment for them all.

'They came earlier,' said Michael, putting his paintings in the cupboard. 'They went to find you.'

Beneath her bonnet, Branwell saw she was brooding. She untied the strings slowly. 'It's good to see you,' he said quietly. She closed the door, deep in thought and disturbed. Turning back she collected herself and took off her cloak. Then she came to him at a slow pace and embraced him, less warmly though than he wanted. She glanced at Brown and smiled. Branwell took her hand. 'I had to come over,' he said. Her skin felt cold.

'Don't be too hard on him,' said Brown, hanging his head. 'He's been fair falling apart. If he hadn't come to see you, he'd have pined away like an animal lost on the moor.'

'John wanted to meet me,' said Michael, relaxing a little and in an easier voice than before. 'Branwell felt we should make each other's acquaintance.'

Branwell thought Michael looked tired. His hair hung about his face raggedly; greyer it seemed. There were shadows under his eyes. His movements were slower.

'And I came to see Milly, too,' Brown added quickly. After a further exchange of words, he and Michael fell to talking quietly. Milly sat down on the hearth rug. Branwell stood by, still puzzled as to where she had been and whom she'd been out with. 'I'll return to the inn right now, if you want,' he said finally. 'I can see we shouldn't be here.' He drew a breath and straightened. 'We've arranged a coach for morning.'

She raised her face, and he saw to his surprise, that her eyes had filled with tears. 'I won't steal you away,' he said gently, kneeling beside her. 'If you want to stay here in Broughton with Michael, then so be it.' He met her eyes; there was a waywardness there he knew, an allure that was all her own; something he feared. He did not feel he could touch her. 'And in any case,' he said, taking a deep breath, and suddenly thoughtful. 'I need to find work.' He wondered why he felt he dare not touch her, dare not kiss her! 'Have I not told you, over and over, how I love you?' he whispered. 'Have I not asked you to marry me?'

'Don't labour it, boy,' said Michael coming from the shadows. His eyes were kind. There was a hurt tone in his voice.

Milly met Branwell's eyes and rested her head on his chest. Branwell felt a surge of relief. 'Walk out with me,' he begged, kissing her hair and holding her tightly in his arms. He took her to her cloak and bonnet by the door, taking it from where she had hung it. It was dark outside, but the evening was warm and sweet. He tied the strings of her bonnet, and pulled her cloak around her shoulders, then they stepped out on to the lane.

'Come and sit over here,' said Michael, beckoning Brown to the fire. 'I'll get us a drink.' He found a bottle of elderberry wine and filled two glasses. 'Home brewed, of course,' said Michael. 'Once the berries are ready, Milly and Matthew collect them. – So what's going on in Haworth?'

Brown reflected as they drank. 'Few things change,' he said with a sigh. 'The dissenters are still very busy.' He frowned, silent for a moment. 'The Reverend Brontë is often put to the test.' Brown braced himself and spoke with annoyance. 'Some of them try him too far.'

'No-one round here would dare do wrong to a parson,' said Michael with a questioning look. He sat thoughtful for a moment, pursing his lips. 'I'm not one as visits the church much. An' Milly's not one for prayin', but we always respect a parson.'

'Reverend Brontë is an excellent man,' said Brown, more cheerfully. 'He doesn't spend a lot of time praying, himself; he gets things done. Children are working far too long in the factories. He is very unhappy about that. And he'd like them to have more schooling. The villagers are poor, but they help each other as they can.'

'How long has he been in Haworth?' asked Michael, listening with interest.

'A long time now.' The sorrows and cares of Haworth came to Brown again through his thoughts; the way he had seen the parson grow graver and serious, more passionate about reforms. Reverend Brontë's energies were always awake; he rarely rested. 'His children were tiny when he came. They lost their mother soon after. They were left in darkness. We all felt sorry for the parson. It was as if he'd forgotten how to smile. Six little children without a mother. His sister-in-law came to help them from Cornwall. She brought the light in her hands.' He dropped his voice. 'And she stayed.'

'She sounds like a fine woman,' said Michael.

'Yes, they were bad days. She helped manage the house and bring up the children. She sang to them and told them stories. They are a warm, caring family.'

'Branwell has a passion for Milly,' Michael murmured.

'Well, yes . . .' said Brown hesitantly, surprised by his words. 'He loves her.' He gazed at Michael uneasily.

'It would be far better if he didn't,' Michael said flatly. Brown searched Michael's face. Michael spoke shakily. 'If there's owt you can do to stop him loving her, then do it. It'll come to no good.' He locked his eyes into Brown's.

They were both silent for a moment.

Brown shook his head. 'I could never do that,' he said, his voice a whisper. 'They will soon have a child. And does she not love him too?'

'His family don't know about the baby, do they?' Michael said quickly, and in a tone of despair. 'No. That tells me a lot.'

'It tells me . . .' Brown began, 'that they are all very busy, that the parson has much to attend to, that the girls are looking for work, just as Branwell is. I can assure you, Michael, Branwell is an honourable man, a kind man, a . . .'

Pleading Branwell's cause, Brown felt suddenly tired. There was a sense of hopelessness about it. His throat was dry. He swallowed and stared at Michael, whose face was determined as he spoke.

'And where will he find this work? And will he stick at it if he gets it? – Nah, his writing's his master. Milly would always come second.'

'I doubt it would be as you say, Michael,' said Brown more spiritedly.

'Ah, but you doubt,' said Michael shaking his head. 'No, she'll be happier with us.'

'*Us,*' Brown repeated, shakily. He was beginning to feel what Branwell felt, to understand that there might be more to Milly than he had first thought.

'She has friends . . .'

'I see,' said Brown, knitting his eyebrows. He glanced round the cottage, recalling the dolls Branwell had talked about; the way he had loathed them. 'There are some dolls, I believe . . .'

'Dolls? – What dolls?'

'She has shown Branwell some dolls. She keeps them in a box.'

Michael bent further towards him. 'She showed him the straw dolls?' He spoke loudly, as if Brown had uttered a curse.

'Are they a keepsake from her childhood?' Brown asked, daring to continue. He did not intend to trifle over it; he wanted the truth.

Michael leaned back in his chair and sighed at the ceiling. 'Oh, they're more than a keepsake. Matthew made them. You must never talk about the dolls, not to Milly. Not if you've any sense.'

'Perhaps I shouldn't have told you,' said Brown, worriedly.

'A girl might love her childhood toys,' said Michael. 'That's understandable. But the dolls are more than that. He made them for her twelfth birthday. She had just turned into a woman.'

Brown stayed silent; it was obvious that something very important was being said.

'After giving birth to Milly, my sister fell ill.' Michael continued, in a slow, measured tone. 'The child was often alone. She was such a silent little thing, mekin' her funny sounds, shapin' words wi' her fingers. My brother recited her poems; that's when she seemed most happy. She loved all that. And Matthew would always come to see her . . .'

'*Matthew?*'

'He was here right from the start; from the very first day she was born.'

Brown sat deep in thought. He felt a shiver pass over his skin. This will end in sorrow for Branwell, he thought. The door opened. Branwell and Milly walked in.

19

The July weather had been perfect. Work went on in the parsonage just as before. The floors were spotlessly clean. Meals were prepared at exactly the right time. The parson wound up the grandfather clock as he always did when retiring to bed. And at regular intervals Branwell went to see Milly. August continued much the same.

'And so I must give you money to find work!' the parson exclaimed to Branwell that morning in his study. 'A fine way to do business, this is.' He went to a drawer and brought out some cash, handing it to Branwell, who put it into his pocket with a sigh.

Patrick Brontë wondered sometimes if his children thought he had a pot of gold hidden somewhere, fallen right out of heaven. Oh, how he wished it were true. Only by the sweat of his brow could he make ends meet. They had no idea what a battle it had been, frugally struggling through Cambridge, then going into the clergy, where the pay was hardly generous, and the house was only on loan. He winced at the thought of that. What would happen to his children if he died? Where would they live? It was a constant worry. He didn't want to push them into work they hated, but he'd have slept more soundly if they could each have been independent.

'I am about to surprise you, Father,' said Branwell. 'I shall soon have money of my own.' He'd been busily scouring the newspapers, and had asked people to let him know of any employment they thought might suit him. And it seemed work was in the offing. He was succeeding with Michael and Milly also and had gained their loyalty and affection. Michael was making a cradle for the baby, and to celebrate her pregnancy, he had carved a wooden bangle for Milly. Since Parker had burned his drawings, and they'd had the fight near his house, he appeared to have gone into hiding. Branwell had disclosed his interest in the railways to

Michael and his hopes of a job, and Michael had been encouraging. For the time being, Branwell noted, Charlotte was happy at home with Emily and their father, and was getting on with her writing. Seeking work wasn't something she thought about much. For him though, it was urgent. He must earn money to support Milly and the baby. It was sheer torture for them being away from each other. Each time he left her, she ran after him up the lane for a last embrace. The vulnerable, childlike fear she sometimes showed worried him deeply.

'A job with the railways?' said the parson curiously. 'Well, it's certainly different...' He frowned and gazed at his son. It had never really registered that Branwell might actually be serious; he had often talked about the railways. But his son talked about all sorts of things. He might have travelled to Timbuktoo as an explorer. He might have done anything. 'I wonder if you'll be warm enough in the winter?' Patrick murmured.

'Warm enough?' Branwell frowned.

'They'll have you sitting in a shack you know, some dark little hut on a hillside. You'll have to wrap up.'

Branwell stood in front of his father helpless. He had wanted him to be proud. Now it seemed they were past all that. All that mattered was employment. Apart from the two of them the house was empty. Ought he to tell him about Milly? Did he have the courage? But it was all so far away ... like something in one of his stories ... not belonging to the real world at all. How strange it was having Milly in Broughton pregnant with his child, while he was here, talking to his father about taking a job with the railways. It was quite absurd. Nothing fitted together. He also owed money. He needed drink. And there were times when he needed laudanum to help with his headaches. 'I hope you don't feel humiliated, Father,' he said, bending his head. He knew how Charlotte felt about what he was doing. She'd made no secret of her contempt. 'The railways are an amazing engineering achievement. I'd like to be involved in some small way if I can.'

'To be sure,' said his father, deep in thought. A new railway was to link Leeds with Manchester. There was certainly work there.

'Charlotte is being disagreeable about it,' said Branwell irritably. 'There is no need for her sarcasm.'

'What? – Is she being sarcastic?' said the parson glancing about. 'Oh, I'll not have that. Where is she?'

'It isn't important. It's just that she's written a letter to her friend, and she's mentioned it. She's left it on the table downstairs. But I'd rather you didn't see it. Please don't look. I wish I hadn't looked at it myself.'

'Would Charlotte do such a thing?' said the parson incredulously.

'Oh, yes! I've disappointed her, you see. She would rather I were a Byron or a Shakespeare, than a mere railway clerk.'

The parson took a deep breath. 'Never mind all that. You are quite right, Branwell, the railways are a wonderful achievement. No more bumping about in coaches, eh? No more getting soaked through. – Well, not in the future, anyway. Alleluya! to the railways!'

'Yes,' said Branwell. But something churned painfully inside him. What a great sacrifice time was. Who knew what it might have contained. He tried to think well of the idea. He wasn't as strong as he knew he could be when writing; an essential self was missing. But he'd make the best of whatever was on offer and be thankful. He saw vividly his child, with a totally different life from his own, travelling the country from city to city on the railways, having experiences he couldn't even dream.

'I can't do it,' he murmured in despair, as he walked away from his father and went to his room. He stretched himself on his bed, his hands clasped behind his head, and looked at the ceiling. For several minutes he felt delirious. He felt a loathing for himself, for what he'd become. He tried not to think of anything, to clear his mind of the clutter. But the whistling sands of desolation found him instead.

20

Assistant-clerk-in-charge at Sowerby Bridge station was hardly an exciting occupation, Branwell reflected as he sat working at his desk. But at least he was earning money. He steeled himself against the sick, demented feeling he sometimes had balancing the figures. And he could never be sure he'd got them right. He rushed head first into it, as if charging an opposing army. The enormous mental effort made him feel dizzy.

September came, and the leaves turned red and gold. October came and they fell. Time went by in a noisy confusion of speed, oil smells and tension. Friends came to congratulate him on his new found work. He smiled and laughed. But it wasn't himself smiling; it was a crazed soul he'd adopted for the time being. His real self haunted him constantly in a kind of frenzy. He harboured the hope that he might find lodgings near his work eventually, large enough for Milly and the baby. He would ask her to come to live with him when the time was right. It was a hope he clung to daily. He went to see her in Broughton whenever he could and took gifts and provisions. It thrilled him to watch her make clothes for the baby, and to see how well she was keeping. A brand new voice would soon be heard in an old, old weary world!

His secret life was still a secret from his family. Throughout the whole of the last two months, Brown, Charlotte said, had become "strangely reserved", and she'd wondered if something was bothering him. Brown could be trusted to stay silent, Branwell reflected, as he went up the parsonage steps, but he had better not overdo it. I shall tell them about Milly this weekend, he thought, resolvedly; I'm determined.

They were all at home.

'I've come for the weekend, if you'll have me,' he said, entering the parlour with a smile.

'Branwell!' his father said cheerily. 'What a nice surprise! So tell us what you are up to.'

Emily, Anne and Charlotte were writing at the table. They each got up and embraced him. Emily went to bring tea and cakes. He had at last found the time he was looking for, a time when they were all together, calm and reasonably content.

'Well, why did you decide to come home?' asked Charlotte. 'What's wrong?'

Branwell raised his eyebrows. Nothing was actually wrong. His job was tolerable, Milly was well, and it seemed the family was fine. 'Well, thank you, Charlotte,' he said. 'You are always after finding a mote in my eye, aren't you?'

Aunt Branwell came into the room. Her skin was flushed from an earlier walk in the village. 'How good to see you, Branwell!' She kissed his cheek. 'So now you are a man of numbers!'

'Am I?' he replied, looking a little alarmed.

'Well, I hope so,' said Aunt Branwell, smiling. 'My dear nephew, if you are not a man of numbers by now, then you had soon better be. – Are you making the necessary effort?'

Branwell unbuttoned his coat and hung it up, then walked back to them thoughtfully. 'Well, dear Aunt, I can reckon up in my head quite fast nowadays. I find I am doing it without thinking. All the way here as I walked I have added up numbers. A useful thing to be doing, don't you think?'

Charlotte sighed and leaned back, watching him. 'What's the matter? What have you come to tell us?'

His father looked at him straight. For a few seconds they were silent.

Branwell looked at Charlotte. 'So how's Willie Weightman?' he asked, putting his elbows on the table and resting his chin on his hands.

'I haven't seen him today,' said Charlotte, relaxing. Her face resumed the softness it had shown earlier. Anne glanced at her and frowned.

Branwell saw that Anne too was captured by his father's curate. What a charmer Weightman was! Emily brought in the tea. 'Tea! Perfect!' said Branwell. 'No-one can brew a pot of tea like Emily.' 'Well, come on then,' Aunt Branwell said. 'Tell us what's happening in Halifax. – Bands of robbers, no doubt. Oh, you have to be careful in Halifax!'

'Aunt Branwell! What terrible jokes you make!' Branwell laughed. 'You are quite wrong. I have met some interesting people there. There is a lot going on in Halifax. Their musical performances are splendid.'

Charlotte sighed irritably. She couldn't find any work, she said, and neither could she write. 'Nothing but rubbish comes from my pen these days,' she grumbled.

Aunt Branwell searched out Branwell's eyes with her own. 'It's bilberry pie for supper,' she said. 'What do you think?'

'I think it sounds delicious,' he said eagerly. 'I could eat it right now.'

'Well, you shan't,' said Charlotte. 'It's for supper. You always think you can eat the food before mealtimes.'

Emily glanced at Branwell and smiled. After a while his sisters went out into the village. Aunt Branwell went off to sew.

Alone with his father, Branwell talked on quickly telling him anything and everything. His father sat listening carefully, hanging on his every word. He loved his son with a passion. Had he been able to do it, he would have given him the moon. He had feared though, that he might find the work too dreary and monotonous, if he had not done so already. 'Tell me about this music then, at Halifax,' he said finally. 'How does it compare with ours?'

'Oh, you needn't feel threatened, Father,' Branwell smiled. 'The musical performances in Haworth take a lot of beating. But the music in Halifax is good. Come over some time and hear it.'

'I certainly will,' said Patrick. 'But I haven't any time just now. There's something going round in the village. I must keep an eye on my flock.' His father heaved a sigh. Branwell thought he looked pale. Sometimes his father didn't know where to turn. There were weeks when it seemed the whole village fell ill.

After the supper and the wonderful bilberry pie, Branwell sat alone with his father by the fire. The parson put down his book. 'Charlotte is right, you know,' he said quietly. 'You haven't come simply to see us, have you? There's something you want to tell us.' His father gazed at him straight. 'To blazes with worrying,' he said. 'Whatever it is, if you've something to say, then say it.'

'Father,' said Branwell, falteringly. 'I am in full possession of myself. I am happy. Why must I always have problems? Will you allow me not to have problems for a while?' He drew a breath. 'Come to Halifax, and see how I do. – You *will* come, won't you?' He was trying his utmost not to allow the words to burst from his lips that wanted to come. He was filled with suppressed emotion. It was still the wrong time. The whole scenario was wrong. Just as Milly's pregnancy grew bigger, his secret life grew bigger, and even more secret. 'I'm fine, Father,' he said, trying to reassure him. 'I would let you know if I wasn't.'

Patrick gave him a nod then got up from his chair. 'I think I shall follow the others to bed, I'm tired.'

'Goodnight,' said Branwell softly. The fire had burned low and the room was cooling. His father wound up the clock, then made his way to his room. Branwell rested his head on the back of the chair and closed his eyes. It was painfully obvious now; his two worlds were definitely apart.

He had almost fallen asleep, when a knock came on the door. It was quite definitely Brown's. What could he possibly want at this hour of night?

'Come!' cried Brown, breathless in the doorway. 'Hurry!'

'Come where?' Branwell asked anxiously, glancing down the path. Everywhere was dark and silent. 'I can't just leave the parsonage like that. They are all in bed.'

'You must, Branwell! You must!'

Branwell threw on his coat. 'But what's the matter? Why such a panic?'

Brown looked to the garden gate and pointed. 'Michael's down at the church. Someone brought me from my house. Milly's started with the baby.'

'But it isn't time,' Branwell moaned, as they ran down the hill. 'She'll not be alone, surely?'

Brown gave him a sideways, fearful look.

Branwell ran faster, gritting his teeth, filled with despair. He could just see the coach waiting at the top of Main Street. 'I should have been there!' he shouted. 'My very heart is in the hands of that fiend! – There is harm in this, real harm!'

21

The journey to Broughton seemed endless. Travelling through the night, Branwell and Michael felt tense. And again they travelled, all through the following day, stopping just briefly for refreshment. It was as well the weather was kind and the horses were strong. Branwell saw Michael clasped his hands as they journeyed, almost as if he were praying. 'I had to fetch ye myself,' he said. 'There's nobody else could do it.' It was almost three a.m. The coach clattered down the hill as they reached Broughton, a loud noise on the otherwise silent lane. 'It hurt me to leave her.'

'You did well,' Branwell said tiredly. They had scarcely spoken throughout the journey; now they were almost there, but the fear of what he might find plagued Branwell relentlessly. He gazed out of the coach. Everything glittered. The tops of the cottages, the windows, the crisp leaves on the trees all shone in the moonlight. It was a beautiful silent night. The earthy scent of autumn was thick in the air.

'It's difficult to know how I'm placed nowadays,' Michael murmured. 'I suppose Milly is none o' my business any more. Yet I still feel responsible for her.'

'I'm sorry you feel like that,' said Branwell. 'It's not how I want it, of course. I am hoping matters will be much improved next year. I have prospects, Michael. You'll see.'

'I'll leave ye to go on your own when we get down the hill,' said Michael. 'Ye know where to find her.'

The night was still. Wild shadows flitted about the trees. The light seemed struggling for dawn. 'Thank you,' said Branwell, his voice soft in the darkness. The large bones of Michael's face were outlined in the moonlight, still and strong.

'Ye'll let me know how she is though, won't ye. If I'm needed, ye know where I am.'

The coach came to a sudden halt and they both climbed out. Michael went into his cottage. Branwell crossed over the road.

The infinite power of creativity is a wonderful thing, Branwell thought, as he made his way along the winding path up the hill. But the finite power of reality prevails in the end! Here he was, striding towards Parker's house to see his own beloved Milly! All his strength, every fibre of his being was with him now. Michael had told him nothing of how she was, and he'd feared to inquire. The silence had said it all.

Reaching the house, he saw that plumes of smoke rose from the chimney. The windows were lit by candlelight. The door, this time, was closed, the dark, solid weight of it ominous in the shadows. He tried the handle and the door slid inward easily, though it creaked on its hinges. The smell of candle-wax met him as he entered the dimly lit room. There was a fusty odour of stale flowers in the air.

His footsteps sounded loud and unfamiliar as he walked across the stone floor. He felt as if intense activity had taken place earlier in the house. It's energy was still in the air. He blinked hard, trying to focus his eyes. A strong fire burned in the grate. There was a table and four chairs in the middle of the room. A sideboard stood by the wall with lighted candles on top of it. Apart from the crackle of the fire, the whole house was silent.

Walking on further, he could see that candles lighted one of the rooms. Slowly, he made his way across. The room, like the other, was dim, but he could see that a man sat by a bed, silent and still.

Parker sat slightly bent over. He did not raise his head as Branwell entered, though he must have heard him. Branwell's eyes rapidly moved to the bed, where Milly lay pale as a ghost.

'Milly! Oh, Milly!' he cried rushing to kneel by the bed. Her eyes were sad and there were tears on her cheeks. He kissed her fingers then comforted her silently with caresses. 'Milly. I ought to have been here. I am so sorry.' He slid his hand across the top of the bedclothes to where the swelling of the pregnancy had been. The sheets lay flat on her body. And he saw to his horror one of them held splashes of blood.

'She wanted ye,' Parker said quietly, his head still bent. 'Ye've been a long time comin'.'

'I came as fast as I could,' Branwell said, despising him and wondering why he didn't leave them. Then he saw to his horror that at the other side of the bed, Milly was clasping his hand. The sight of her features so wasted and worn were unbearable to him. And the fact that she needed

Parker's comfort confounded him. 'Did you get a doctor?' he asked him, mistrustfully. He gazed at Milly and stroked her brow. She was sobbing softly.

'No doctor,' said Parker flatly. 'We dunna have doctors round 'ere.'

Branwell glanced around the room. He couldn't see the baby anywhere. Worse was the silence. He watched Parker rise from his chair and go towards the fire next door, which he piled high with logs. His big bulk by the lighted candles sent shadows racing across the walls. 'Have you suffered much pain?' Branwell asked her, tidying her hair, which was matted against her cheeks. She squeezed his hand gently, making sounds that were hard to understand, though they expressed turbulence in her. 'It's dark in here,' he frowned, peering about. 'Far too dark.'

'It's light enough,' called Parker, returning to the bedroom. 'There's nowt ye'll be wanting to see as'll give ye much gladness.'

'Where's my baby?' Branwell asked finally, steeling himself. It sickened him that he must ask Parker such a question.

'Here, i' this house,' said Parker stiffly. He hesitated then sat down in a chair. His voice came low. 'It were me who delivered it.'

The bulk of him, the thick dull weight of his arms, the flatness and power in his manner were appalling to Branwell. Branwell was in a panic. He knew that country folk often delivered their own children. There were rarely enough doctors to go round and it was difficult travelling.

In the tired silence he listened anxiously to what Parker had to say. – 'It were an awkward labour. The child cried but once. I couldna save her. She were 'ere too soon. She wunna ready.'

'Her?' said Branwell shakily. He froze at Parker's words. The long pregnancy was suddenly a living thing. Yet so soon dead. He held on to Milly's hand. She still sobbed softly. He shrank away from himself in a kind of guilty misery at the knowledge that his baby was dead. His little daughter was dead! But where was she now? He didn't dare think just then what Parker had done with her.

'She lived but minutes,' said Parker, in a low unfeeling tone. 'I've laid her out i' there. I've swaddled her.' He nodded to a second bedroom.

Leaving Milly, Branwell took a lighted candle from the dresser next door. Just for an instant as he did so, the candlelight flickered on the wooden bangle Michael had made for Milly, which lay on the top. It was a beautiful shining thing. What it represented now though, made him wince. Struggling to calm his nerves he went to the second bedroom. The door was open. Through it he saw the pitch-black nothingness of night.

Cautious and fearful, he stepped quietly into the darkness. Such light the candle offered was thin and vaporous, disappearing then glowing again as if searching. Compared to the rest of the house, the room smelt oddly fresh, with a peculiar scent of spring. The air was light and clean. He moved the candle around the room, peering about, though he dared not imagine what he searched for. A linen box stood in a corner. On top of it he made out a tiny bundle of what looked like some wrapped up linen. Branwell's heart pounded. He stumbled closer then stood for a moment trembling, weak with sadness. The candle shook in his hand. He could not cope with the feelings that flooded his mind; they burst from his skin in sweat. He steadied himself against the wall.

After several agonising moments, he moved in further. It was just a tiny bundle ... A tiny, tiny bundle ... Some wrapped up bread perhaps ... Yes, people kept bread wrapped up like that in Haworth ... He gripped the candle, bending over to look.

For a moment he felt as if his body had turned to stone. He feared to look any further, yet his fingers went before him, touching and opening the cloth. A sweet and gentle fragrance issued from inside. Little by little he parted the cloth, till his fingers touched the bony head of his child! Just now he didn't want to see, only to feel! The soft tenderness of her lips kissed the tips of his fingers. He ran them across the fragile tiny nose and the soft closed eyes. The top of the head was covered in what felt like cotton grass. Moving forward, he dared to look closer.

'What a pretty little face she has,' he murmured, surprise mingling with his tears. And he saw with a rush of joy, that the hair was red as his own, a bold redness, startling against the waxen creamy skin. Strange moans came from his throat. He unwrapped the cloth further, revealing the tiny arms, the delicate fingers. Oh, such soft new nails, glistening like something from the sea. The little child was so perfect and clean, her skin so new and tender. She was such a splendid baby. He put down the candle and sank to his knees. For a few moments he wept.

'There's nowt ye can do for her now,' said Parker gruffly, suddenly there in the doorway.

'Get out! – Damn you!' Branwell cried, without turning. He felt Parker did not belong to this world of Milly and his child, yet he'd fixed himself firmly within it. His presence was abhorrent to Branwell;

it tainted the very air. Parker sighed loudly and turned away. Branwell continued to kneel by his child, stroking her face, kissing her cold white cheek. He put his finger in her baby hand, and though she was dead it seemed to him she grasped it. Presently, carefully and tenderly, he wrapped her back in the cloth and returned to Milly.

Parker sat just as before, by her side. 'You've had fair enough time with Milly and my child,' said Branwell firmly. The way Milly accepted Parker, even wanted him near, confused and upset him. 'I'd like to talk to her alone,' he said, his voice trembling with anger.

Parker sniffed and frowned. 'I'll get ye some broth,' he told her. He left them and went to the fire.

Milly clung tightly to Branwell's fingers. He felt cold and emptied of strength, as if he had died himself with his child, as if he must somehow breathe himself back into being. 'She's a lovely baby, Milly,' he whispered. 'I'm so sorry . . .' They were both tearful. He put his cheek on her own, and felt the wet of her sadness against his skin. 'Milly . . .' he said through his tears. He saw she waited.

An air of hopelessness pervaded the room. She tried to raise herself up, but he urged her to rest. 'Milly,' he continued, shakily, 'we have lost our child. I can only attempt to know your suffering. And as for mine, I might scream forever, and it wouldn't show half of what I feel. But we can help each other. We shall have more children. We have plenty of time. I am doing well with my work. I can find us somewhere to live that is away from all this.'

He kissed her cool hands. The place was mysteriously silent, like a silence he had never known before. Again, she was waiting. 'Milly, might I . . . Might I . . .' he faltered. 'Might I bury our baby at Haworth?' The words felt strange as he said them. How many times had he heard of babies dying in Haworth? How many mothers had he comforted with his father? Yet now when it came up close, it was all so different; it was right there in his blood.

Haworth village was indeed a place for the dead. His father's graveyard was overflowing. But he wouldn't bury her there, he said. He would find somewhere he loved on the moors instead. 'If Michael could make her a coffin, then I could return to Broughton in a day or so to collect her. – Oh, let me bury her at Haworth, Milly. John will dig us the grave. And Weightman will give her his blessing. They are both wonderful men.' His voice cracked and faltered as he spoke. The words were so new and fragile, yet so cruel and final in content. He watched her face intensely, and felt a sudden surge of relief as she nodded, touching his face tenderly. He would have to return to Haworth now, he said, though he'd prefer to have remained by her side. He must keep his job with the railway company or he'd have nothing at all to offer her. He hoped Michael would take her back to the cottage, he said. There were so many questions he wanted to ask that remained unanswered in his mind. But he would not ask them now.

A dark, wretched nervous energy had entered him. None of this was what he'd hoped for. It was far removed from his plans. But his imagination was fertile. He would imagine their baby's life. He would imagine her joy at seeing the setting sun and the changing seasons, her profound pleasure at listening to the music of the masters, at feeling the power of the words of great writers ... He would create a life for his child right there in his mind, as only he could. And he would somehow make it real for him and Milly. The baby would live in their hearts.

'She needs to eat,' said Parker. 'Then she must sleep.' He helped her sit up then brought her the broth and some bread on a tray. He broke the bread and put it into her mouth.

Branwell watched shrinking away, lost in an agony of fear. His thoughts raced on. Was it the end? Would she stay in this house with Parker for ever? Was that the truth? Would she live with Parker for the rest of her life, forsaking him, as if he had never existed? She looked so comfortable with him, so at ease. His heart felt like a leaden weight in his chest. 'I'll go now, Milly,' he murmured. 'But I'll soon be back.' She opened her mouth for Parker's spoon, and he fed her the broth, slowly, tenderly, unusually, hideously gentle.

Getting up from his chair, Branwell stood for a moment abstracted. From the open door, a beam of silver light heralded the dawn. The whole universe seemed to be reaching out to him, calling him into its loneliness. He felt bereft and powerless. He would call at Michael's cottage before going for a carriage. He would ask him about the coffin. Then he would return to Haworth, fast as he could. And he would search out Brown and Weightman.

22

It was mid afternoon on a Tuesday, when Branwell walked into the parsonage. He'd been gone for almost four days. Charlotte came from the kitchen to greet him. She was eager to talk, but he felt tired and needed to think. Her eyes lingered on him curiously. 'Someone came from the railway,' she said, tentatively. Branwell knew he had obviously disturbed them by hurrying off as he had without leaving a message. 'They'd expected you in work today, but it seems you weren't there.'

'My dear Charlotte,' he said, wearily, 'they are quite right, I wasn't.' He went to the parlour. Finding a chair, he sat down with a thump. All he wanted to do was sleep. He felt dirty and unkempt. Charlotte went in after him, followed by their father. They both sat down and stared at him worriedly. It was a rare thing for Branwell to ignore his father, though today he did. He could not meet his eyes. Had he done so he would have wanted to divulge the terrible secrets of his heart right there and then, which he dare not do. His emotions felt knotted inside him. Would he always bring nothing but pain to his family like this?

'There wasn't a lot we could tell them,' Charlotte said, frowning. 'You just disappeared.'

Branwell lifted his face. Charlotte gazed at him, her eyes widening. He knew how he looked. The pain of the last few days rushed through his mind. To his surprise her usual scornful manner was absent. Had she ridiculed him, however, he wouldn't have cared. Nothing could be worse than the dark horror that engulfed him. His father shifted about in his chair, still watching him.

'You ought to have left us a note,' his father said in his strong parson's voice. 'Why, for all we knew you might have been lying murdered somewhere. –There are one or two dissenters who ...'

'*Murdered?*' Branwell interjected wearily. His voice fell to a murmur. 'Perhaps I was.'

Charlotte braced herself and laughed. 'Aye, and you a ghost and all walking in here so grim. You look awful.'

'I'm sure I do,' he sighed. He gazed at space and shivered, as the intimacy of his home entered him again with its loud, questioning voices, its long observant stares, its pointing fingers. Though he needed to be here just now, whatever its pains. The sight of his little dead girl haunted his mind; the gentle whiteness of her waxen skin, her long curled lashes, her soft red hair, so very red, even by the light of the candle. He hoped Milly would be well. Michael would probably be at Parker's cottage right now. He'd told him all that had happened before returning to Haworth. Michael, it seemed, had a way with Parker. He didn't trust Parker himself. He was harsh as a winter's wind.

'You've been drinking, haven't you?' Charlotte shrugged.

'How wrong you are,' said Branwell grandly, with a sigh. 'If only it were true. I should feel much better than this.'

Charlotte bit her lip. 'Why are your boots so dirty?' she asked, scowling.

Branwell looked down. His boots were filled with mud from the hill leading to Parker's house. Though the mud on his boots was as nothing compared to the muddiness in his mind. He felt detached from himself, detached from everything about him, detached from his life. He grew cold at the thought of bringing the little coffin back home, and wondered what he would say to Brown, how he would tell him, what he would say to Weightman. Though he knew Weightman wouldn't judge him, and would keep his secret. Branwell didn't care for the clergy, but Weightman was different. He was out of his own heart. And out of his father's heart too. Out of any man's heart that beat with love and passion. He wasn't sanctimonious and shallow like a lot of them were, which Branwell considered every bit as bad as being worldly. He was genuine, honest and vulnerable.

'I've work to attend to in the kitchen,' said Charlotte. 'I have to help Emily.'

Branwell sat with his father for a while in silence.

'I think there's a tale to be told, don't you?' said the parson. 'You look like you've been through hell.'

Branwell sighed. His eyes were closed; he had almost fallen asleep. 'There are far worse places than hell, Father, as you know.' He straightened and opened his eyes, looking at his father. He knew he couldn't find the words just now to express how he felt. Neither could he find the energy. It was all emotion. And he didn't know himself what it all added up to. He couldn't understand why Milly had been at Parker's anyway, unless she'd been there already. And the way she'd so easily accepted what had happened confused him. But there were no rights or wrongs with Milly, there was simply life. Or else death. She took them both in her stride. In that she was just like Parker. They had seemed so alike at his house, so certain of each other, it had almost torn him in two. What hurt him most was the way she had so much faith in Parker. He knew she didn't have faith like that in him. But he loved her with all his heart. And now, it seemed, he was in trouble with the railway company. One way or another, whatever he tried to do somehow fell apart.

'Well,' said his father, 'there's something afoot, that's obvious. And it's not that I want you to tell me for myself. It's more that I'd like to help you. The parsonage is your home, Branwell. You are always welcome here.' The parson threw out his palms. 'You know where I am if you need me.'

Branwell could hear a slight tremor in his father's voice as he spoke, as if he too were tired, as if he were suddenly older. He watched his father's hands, strong, large and veined, working together. 'I must ask your forgiveness, yet again,' said Branwell unhappily.

Patrick Brontë looked at his son, at the once careless and hopeful features, now filled with confusion and despair. 'Whatever it is you've done, you must ask forgiveness of God, not me,' he said solemnly. He bent his head. 'I could do with some of that forgiveness myself. It's a wonder the Lord has enough to go round at times.'

Branwell watched his father, who sat head bent and thoughtful. His father never had a single idea without he didn't pull it to pieces first to find out what is was made of. No matter how bold the authority, he would challenge it if he must. In an odd way he felt his father might know everything about him already, as he knew all things.

'I must work,' said Patrick finally. 'I've a letter to write to the *Leeds Intelligencer* before bedtime.' He got up to go to his study. Reaching the door, he turned. 'You intend to be at the railway I take it tomorrow?'

'It's impossible, Father,' said Branwell flatly. 'I have something to attend to. It is going to take some time.'

'So what must we say if they're here again making enquiries?'

Branwell hesitated. He braced himself. 'I ought to tell you ...' he began.

'No, no,' said Patrick putting out the flat of his hand. 'Just as soon as you're able. I suspect that fellow will show his face though tomorrow. I'll sort something out. – I hope you know what you're doing.'

Branwell sat bewildered for a while. As a matter of fact, he hadn't a clue what he was doing. He didn't even know where he was going either, or if he would have a job by the end of the week. But somehow it didn't matter. Something had died inside him. He would never be the same again. He forced himself up from the chair. Even moving his legs felt strange. He felt like a shell of himself; like a dead man walking. He forced his body along the hall. Then to the door. Then down the path to the graveyard.

'John! – John! How can I tell you what's happened?' he cried. He collapsed down on a gravestone beside him, covering his face with his hands.

Brown gazed at him afraid. He put down his tools. 'Start when you're ready,' he said. He stood beside him, listening to the wind from the moor.

'My life conspires against me, John,' Branwell moaned, lifting his face. 'No matter what I do it gets me!' Feverishly, he told him the tale, making violent exclamations against Parker, loud assertions that the man was indeed a devil, had cast a spell on Milly, had even done worse. His high-pitched voice cut through the air, breaking and crashing on the gravestones, crashing against the dry stone walls; a lost, lonely misery. The baby's death was a mystery, he said. Though she was early, surely she might have lived? She had simply given up the ghost. And now he must bring her to Haworth for her burial. He was no fool, he asserted, he knew what had happened. The moment would come for his revenge!

All the time Brown kept gazing at the sky. It was a terrible tale to hear. And it seemed to come from the depth of Branwell's being. His eyes moistened as he listened. 'I'm sorry for all of you,' he said, his voice breaking with feeling. Branwell looked like a cornered, terrified animal. His arms clasped around his knees, he rocked backwards and forwards moaning. 'But we can fight it together,' said Brown. 'I'll help you through it.'

'You're always so good to me, John. – Parker has killed my child, of course,' Branwell whispered hatefully.

'Steady on,' said Brown. 'It's not going to do you any good, thinking like that.' He cast his hand around the graveyard. 'Babies die, Branwell. This graveyard is full of babies.' Brown saw that Branwell's eyes were heavy with tortured thoughts.

'I know, I know,' said Branwell glancing about. 'Oh, but how tiny she is! Such a tiny, beautiful thing. – You will dig her grave for me, won't you, John? You must dig it deep. You needn't dig wide, but I want her buried deep . . .'

'I'll dig to the centre of the earth if you want,' said Brown.

Branwell gave a shuddering sigh.

For several minutes they were silent.

Brown took his rag from his pocket and wiped his brow. 'The autumn sunlight is bright,' he said squinting.

'Yes, a wonderful yellow,' said Branwell wistfully. 'A special kind of yellow that Milly likes to make. – I'm amazed at the colours she can make, you know.'

'You told me about that before,' Brown said, frowning.

'Yes, I probably did,' Branwell said wearily. He despised Parker, the forcefulness of the man, the stubborn power of his being. 'My baby's grave, you will dig it deep for me John, won't you?'

'Aye, of course I will. Show me where and I'll dig it as deep as you like.'

Branwell nodded. 'No-one must know about this,' he said urgently. 'This much is mine. Milly has allowed me this!'

'So where shall I dig?' said Brown. 'There's a place near Ponden Kirk,' Branwell said hurriedly. 'I know the exact spot. I've spoken to Michael about the coffin. He's doing the carpentry right now.'

'And how are you going to get the baby up here?' said Brown.

I shall go for her myself, tomorrow,' Branwell said. 'Can you get me a coach?'

'Aye,' said Brown, frowning. It was very short notice. 'I'll manage something.' His eyes rested on Branwell again concernedly. 'A man's been snooping from the railway. What will you do about that?'

'I know about him,' said Branwell, trying to think quickly. 'But there's nothing I can do. I must bring the baby to Haworth.'

'I'll go and fetch her myself if you like,' Brown offered.

Branwell shook his head. 'No, no. I shall go to Broughton in the morning and arrive back here the day after. I'll tell you where the grave is to be then we'll bury her at night. I must see if Weightman's available. This is our secret, John. I shan't tell the family yet.'

Brown looked into his face, there was something else ...

Branwell cleared his throat. 'There's something I don't understand,' he said, screwing up his face. 'I need to tell you about it. You see ... I need to investigate something.'

'Investigate?' Brown listened attentively.

'I wanted to ask Michael about it, but there was never the right moment.' Branwell could feel the blood rushing through his head, wave upon wave as he spoke. 'Do you remember the time we went looking for Milly?'

'Yes,' said Brown, waiting.

'We went to Parker's house ...' Branwell continued. 'Do you remember the woman's voice? – Oh, I shall never forget that voice. It's the sweetest I ever heard.' He tapped the sides of his head. 'I have kept it safe in my mind.'

'Did you ever find out who she was?'

'Yes, I think I did,' said Branwell, sighing deeply. 'In that dreadful dawn light as I left Parker's cottage, I heard it again ...'

Brown waited in suspense.

'It was Milly,' Branwell whispered, looking downwards.

'Are you sure?' said Brown, surprised and incredulous. 'Yes,' said Branwell, gloomily. 'She talks to Parker. That's twice I've heard her now. I stopped to listen, but I couldn't bear it. I had to come away. It was like ... It was like discovering that you might grow young again, and no-one had ever told you. Or might somehow re-live the wonderful moments you have lost. That's how it was. It was just like something unreal. And yet it was real, John; far too real to endure.'

'She talks to Parker, but she doesn't talk to you?' Brown whispered, disturbed and thoughtful.

Branwell nodded. 'I don't want to harass her about it. And the way things are, I couldn't ask Michael. In any case, he rarely talks about Parker, and Milly draws away if I mention him. But I've scarcely been able to bear it, John. I ought to have returned and asked her outright, but how could I?'

'It's as well you didn't,' said Brown quietly. 'It could have been disastrous. I've heard of a kind of mutism where the sufferer can only talk to one or two people ... Sometimes just one.'

Branwell frowned. 'Just one person?'

'Yes, someone who's sort of chosen. It's an accepted medical condition, something that happens to the mind. You can't do anything about it. And you haven't to harass the sufferer, or they might run away, or even kill themselves, they say. It's something strong and unbending. Once it's fixed it's final.'

Branwell put his hands to the sides of his head, as if to stop himself thinking, and gazed at the sky. 'It wasn't just her beautiful voice that chilled me,' he murmured, 'the fact that I'd never heard it, the fact that she might talk to Parker and not to me ... It wasn't just that ... What hurt most was the sound of the wholesomeness in it, the togetherness she had with him. She has never shared that kind of union with me. I doubt she could.'

Brown could feel Branwell's pain as if it were his own. 'And will she never talk to me?' Branwell implored him.

'Not so far as I know,' said Brown. 'You must ask your father about it, he'll know more than I do.'

Branwell shook his head. 'Not yet. – Oh, what does she have with Parker that she can't have with me?'

'Her childhood,' said Brown with a sigh. 'That's what those dolls are about.'

Branwell curled his lip in contempt. 'Do you think I shall let him have her as easily as that, all because of some dolls she has kept from her childhood?'

Brown watched him as he wrung his hands nervously. Suddenly to his horror, Branwell raised his arms to the sky and screamed. The scream came louder. And louder. Brown's eyes moved across the gravestones, fast to the parsonage. Back in the parsonage, the parson heard it in torment. Charlotte heard it from the parlour. Aunt Branwell heard it from her room. Emily in the kitchen, stared into an open drawer and forgot what it was she wanted.

23

Charlotte watched Emily kneading the dough for the bread that morning. She put so much effort into it, Charlotte thought, her dark lashes bent towards it, her bold features still and determined.

Over the last few days the house had been strangely silent. Emily and Charlotte had kept themselves busy, while trying to reassure their father all would be well, for he was more disturbed than ever about Branwell now. They too were worried. It was hardly likely that things would be well at all. They waited with bated breath for the next catastrophe. It was plain Branwell hadn't told their father where he'd been. And they hadn't inquired of him either. Whatever the situation, it was obviously raw and sensitive. Charlotte had never seen her brother so pale. That morning he'd gone off into the village to meet William Weightman, though he hadn't said why. 'I wonder what it's all about?' she said to Emily.

Emily stood thoughtful. What was happening to Branwell, she wondered, that had caused him to act so carelessly? He had compromised himself with the railway company too. And now this business with Weightman . . . 'Like Papa says,' she replied. 'He'll talk to us when he's ready.'

'Some consolation,' sighed Charlotte. 'I get so worried about him. I've written nothing for days. – Have you written anything yourself?' She poked a finger in the dough.

The clock on the stairs ticked on, louder it seemed today.

'I might have,' said Emily. She hated the way Charlotte pried. 'You mustn't go searching,' she warned. 'You know how I feel about that.'

'But I like to know what you're writing,' said Charlotte earnestly. 'I feel I don't lose you then. You always forget us when you write.'

'No more than you do,' said Emily.

'But I get so annoyed with him,' Charlotte went on, returning to Branwell. 'So, sort of desperate. You see ... It's as if my energy is somehow connected to his. I feel his distress here, deep in my body.' She laid the flat of her hands on her stomach. 'It's as if he lives in me somewhere. I get physically sick when I'm worrying about him. I need to know he's all right. I need to ...'

'You need to release him,' said Emily quietly.

Charlotte's eyes flashed. 'What do you mean?'

'You are never friendly with him these days. You're always hurting him, trying to control him, trying to ...'

'*Me,* hurting *him?*' Charlotte gasped. 'It's Branwell hurts us. See how he behaves.'

'How he behaves is his own concern,' Emily said drily. 'You must allow him to have his misery. It is his, not yours. He's actually stronger than you think. He battles with his problems.'

'There is nothing strong about battling with problems you have created for yourself,' said Charlotte smugly.

Their father was at home that morning working in his study. He had shot his pistol through the window, he had eaten breakfast and he'd been out for a stroll round the parish, now he was preparing a sermon.

'Don't!' said Emily seeing that Charlotte was tapping her fingers on the dough. 'It will rise in its own good time. You are so impatient.'

Charlotte regarded her sister carefully. Emily was younger than she was by a couple of years. Yet in a way she was ageless. Her graceful, elegant figure, her straight, dignified manner, was in perfect keeping with a steeliness in her; an inflexible certainty of purpose. Her heart beat fast at Emily's words, but she didn't want to argue. Emily said what she thought, regardless of anyone's feelings. Anne was kind and vulnerable and quite the opposite. How am I thought of myself, she wondered. I set myself such high standards. And oh, how it hurts to fall below them! I close my eyes and ears. I close my mind.

But she did not allow the same freedom to Branwell, and she knew this guiltily. But she wouldn't let go of her constant drive to improve him, to make him into what he could be, what their mother would have hoped for, their dead sisters, the world! Branwell was a man, and a lot was expected of him, yes. And rightly so. Didn't he have all the chances? He must not throw them away! And he must not awaken the sleeping leviathans who were all too eager to devour him. 'We'll probably get that man again from the railway today,' she said with a sigh. 'Oh, what a palaver!'

They both fell silent for a while.

'A coach arrived by the inn, apparently, late Saturday night,' Charlotte said eventually. 'It brought a stranger. There was no manservant with him, they say. He was hanging about by the church.'

'Someone looking for Papa, probably,' said Emily. 'There was all that fuss about the parish clerk's suicide in Keighley.'

'To avoid his debts, no doubt,' Charlotte shrugged. 'A man of dubious habits, they say.'

'They say a lot,' Emily said quietly.

They could hear Aunt Branwell rustling along the landing, going to her room. She shut the door behind her. 'I'll not put up with that railway fellow again, Emily,' said Charlotte. 'You can do the talking this time. I'm weary sick of Branwell, myself.'

'It doesn't mean the man gets answers because he asks questions,' said Emily dismissively. 'I shan't say a word. Anyway, I think Papa's got something worked out.'

'He knows no more than we do.'

'Never mind, he'll know what to say.'

Waiting outside the Black Bull Inn in Haworth, Branwell felt intense relief as Weightman came striding towards him.

'My dear Branwell,' he said, breathless from hurrying. 'I'm sorry I'm late. What's the matter?' He gave Branwell a firm handshake, and regarded him thoughtfully.

Branwell breathed more easily now. He had washed and changed and was trying to pull himself together.

'I have just been with a bag of coal to the Bamford family and a couple of loaves,' said Weightman. 'You know how they're suffering. No food, no warmth. It's a terrible business when a man loses his work.'

'Well, yes,' said Branwell staring at the ground. Weightman's handshake was always firm and strong. His hands were always warm, even his sisters had said so.

'You are in some bother?' said Weightman, patting him on the back, and directing him towards the moor. 'John Brown told me. – Let's walk.'

'I can't help it,' groaned Branwell. 'Bother is my middle name, according to Charlotte.'

Weightman turned to him and smiled. He was a strong, upright man, who strode steadily with a good measured pace. They put their feet on the moor, now beginning to harden and brown. The smell of it was rich and sweet. The chill in the air had sent much of the bird life away and had silenced many of the animals. Everywhere was still and calm. 'Bother is quite contagious,' said Weightman with a laugh. 'There's a lot of it about. It actually keeps me in work, you know.' He laughed again. 'As does sin of course!'

They walked on talking of Haworth, talking about the dissenters, the poverty of some of the parishioners and what might be done to help them. From time to time Weightman glanced sideways at Branwell, waiting for the moment when he was ready to reveal his plight. Had he bungled it on the railways, he wondered. Or was it worse? They stood now on the ridge of a hill and looked about, breathing the cool, fresh air into their lungs. 'How grand it is out here,' said Weightman. 'On days like this it is such a joy to be alive!'

Branwell watched Weightman's soft brown hair blowing in the wind. He had so much freedom in his spirit, Branwell thought. There was something larger than life about him. He glowed. 'I'm in agony,' Branwell murmured. They sat down on a flat rock face.

'But why?' asked Weightman looking at him. Weightman's eyes glittered in the sunlight, his skin tightened in readiness.

'It has beaten me,' said Branwell, miserably.

Weightman waited.

'My existence, I mean,' Branwell continued. 'It has beaten me. It has always tried to, ever since the day I was born, and now it has triumphed.'

Weightman fixed his eyes on Branwell's face. 'You may think what you like,' he said, folding his arms. 'But we are never beaten. Not if we keep on fighting. I have no idea what it is you are going to tell me, but I'm sure we can work it out. — I cannot, will not, listen to doom and gloom! God is forever with us, Branwell. We must seek His strength.'

'I want you to do something for me . . .' Branwell began.

'But of course — anything,' said Weightman. 'Are you in a hurry for this?'

'I'm afraid I am,' said Branwell.

Weightman raised his eyebrows. After a moment's silence he spoke again. 'So what do you want me to do?'

Branwell gazed at the strong, able bodied man, his bright, sincere eyes, the man who would perform the burial service for his baby. In a couple of days she would lie in the moor by Ponden Kirk, the old crag. It would all be over. But it wouldn't, he realised bitterly. It would never be over now. Milly would always be there in Broughton with

Parker. Would she live with Parker for good? It was all too painful to contemplate. He bent his head. 'I'm grateful for your time,' he said. His heart beat hard as he thought of how he might tell Weightman what had happened; how he had loved the mute girl, Milly in Broughton so deeply, how she had borne him a child, how the child had died so quickly after birth, his perfect beautiful child. He felt like a careless fool. And yet it wasn't like that at all. Everything that had happened with Milly had been so splendid and good. 'You see I need you to . . .' Branwell swallowed deeply.

'Come on,' urged Weightman gently. 'Let it out.' He spoke softly, with tenderness. There was so much empathy in his tone, Branwell felt he might weep. The story was ready to deliver itself from the dark, stiffening place where it lived in his mind.

'Please be at peace,' said Weightman, leaning towards him. 'We are out here, free on the moor, nothing but rock and wildlife for company. On with the business of secrets! – It is a secret you are about to tell me, isn't it? From the state of your nerves, I should think so.'

'I have a baby,' Branwell said finally. For a moment there was silence. It seemed the whole moor listened.

Weightman's eyes grew thoughtful. 'A baby?' He smiled warmly. 'Yours?' He put his head to one side, looking at Branwell curiously.

Branwell nodded. 'The woman lives in Broughton. She's a barmaid at The Old King's Head.'

'I see,' said Weightman, observing him carefully. 'You want me to do a Christening, is that what it is?

'I want you to do a burial,' said Branwell slowly, lowering his voice to a murmur. 'My baby is dead.'

It seemed the words as he spoke them couldn't possibly be true.

They were far too harsh and brutal. There was a long silence.

'I'm so sorry, Branwell,' said Weightman, putting his arm round his shoulder. 'I had no idea . . .'

'No-one knows anything yet. Apart from Brown that is, and you . . . I haven't told Father, and I haven't told my sisters or my Aunt.'

'But the woman in Broughton?' Weightman began. He opened his eyes widely, he was thinking fast. 'She must come to Haworth. We must . . .'

'She doesn't want to,' said Branwell with a sigh. 'I've asked her. There's another man, you see, who I think she prefers.' The words tore into him as he spoke.

Weightman looked bewildered. 'But the child was yours?'

'Of course,' Branwell nodded, recalling the bright red hair, the tiny nose he had thought looked so like Charlotte's.

'How warm it is this morning,' he said unbuttoning his coat. He felt afraid as he sat with Weightman, talking like this about his baby, discussing plans for her funeral, discussing Milly and Parker; talking about the truth. 'He's a woodcutter who lives in Broughton. They've been friends all her life. She wants to be with him. – She needs him . . .'

'My poor Branwell,' Weightman said in his warm, sympathetic way. 'You've had quite a rough time, haven't you?'

Branwell told him how Milly was mute but could somehow talk to Parker. He told him what Brown had explained to him about the condition. Weightman too had heard of it, though he had never met a sufferer, he said. He seemed perplexed. After a few more minutes they got up and walked.

It was an hour later when they arrived back in Haworth. 'And you're going to Broughton today?' Weightman asked, as they stood by the gate of the parsonage.

'In half an hour,' said Branwell. 'I hope to be back tomorrow at dusk.'

'I must part from you now,' said Weightman, 'But I'll see you by Ponden Kirk, as promised, at the time we've arranged.' He turned and went the other way.

24

It was raining heavily when the coachman entered Broughton. A cold wind blew from the hills. The tall trees, their leaves now falling, hung pitifully over, as if bending their heads in sadness. Branwell amazed himself, however, with his own fortitude as the coach went down the hill. Even now, even though his child was dead, he was eager to see the tiny coffin that contained her, to know she was safe within it, and might finally rest at Haworth in his beloved moorland. And he longed to know how Milly was faring. Would she see him? Oh, how he hoped she would see him!

'She isn't here. She's still up the hill,' Michael said gravely, as he opened the door. They went inside. Branwell's heart sank, though her health was his main concern, he could deal with the rest later. 'Is she well?' he asked. 'It doesn't really matter where she is. I just need to know she is well.'

'She's recovering nicely,' said Michael sniffing. Branwell saw there were piles of wood on the floor. 'I've been trying to sort out this wood,' Michael continued. 'It takes up a lot o' space, but it allus comes in. I can guarantee, if I get rid o' it, I'm likely to need it.'

'Will she see me?' Branwell asked anxiously. Michael stared at space. 'I must see her, Michael!' he protested. 'Listen to me, will you? I can't return to Haworth without seeing her! You do realise that, surely?'

Michael remained silent. Branwell watched him brushing the cobwebs off the pieces of wood, sorting it into tidy stacks. He wanted to ask him so many questions, though he doubted Michael would answer them. 'I spoke your name an' she started a shiverin' fit,' Michael said sadly. 'I should put her out o' your mind, boy. It's finished.'

'Finished?' said Branwell incredulously. 'What do you mean, finished?' He stood perplexed, searching his mind for something to relieve his hatred of Parker, his intense jealousy. He didn't want to force himself on Milly. But couldn't he just see her? Didn't he have a right? He was annoyed with Michael, who carried on dusting the wood regardless.

'She'd rather you left her alone,' said Michael finally.

'But she isn't alone, is she?' Branwell said angrily. 'And she wants to see me, I know it! She loves me. Why are you standing between us?'

Michael sat down and rested his head in his hands. 'It's not me who's keeping ye apart, boy. Ye must accept things for what they are, not what ye imagine.'

'But I know the truth!' Branwell said vehemently, pacing the floor. 'You will do her damage with this. You will both do her damage!'

'I can't explain,' said Michael, furrowing his brow. 'All I can ask, is that ye let her be. – It isn't me as wants it like this, it's her.'

They sat in silence for some minutes.

'I took the coffin and showed her,' he continued. 'She were tremblin' in every bone as she held that baby.'

Branwell gazed at him as if he were seeing a stranger. There was a heartlessness now in Michael, even a ruthlessness, something cold and remote. He continued talking in a slow, abstracted way. 'I put the babe in her coffin the minute I'd made it, so the demons couldn't find her and spirit her away from heaven.' He glanced across the room. 'She's there i' that corner.'

Branwell looked into the dim corner, making out the shape of the coffin; a small little boxlike thing, almost in darkness. He went across. It shone in the light of the candle, carefully, richly made, tinier than he'd imagined.

'She's safe inside it,' Michael whispered, close on his heels. 'It's some o' my best timber. Neither time nor worm can touch it.' He stroked his chin thoughtfully. 'It's hard sawin' oak, but I worked all night.'

Branwell slid his palm along the shining wood. His heart felt tender. 'You've made it beautifully,' he murmured. 'Thank you.'

With tears in his eyes, Michael shook Branwell's hand. 'Now go and get that coachman from the inn! And be off with the angel quick!'

As he ventured through the door, Branwell glanced across the road. Dare he visit that wretched house, just one last time? He was filled with so many feelings; he couldn't sort them out in his head. How could Milly be so cruel? Did she really just want him to bury their child on the moor and forget her; for them both to forget each other, their dead baby all that was left of their love?

'Hurry!' said Michael, pushing him on.

Branwell mustered all the strength he could find and turned his eyes from the hillside. He walked up the hill as if dreaming, his head bent towards the ground, his whole body gripped with naked suffering. He turned his mind to the task in hand. He must get back to Haworth with the coffin. Then he would find Brown. When night-time came they would walk on the moor and meet Weightman.

25

1841 had arrived quickly, and appeared to be racing on. Patrick Brontë was filled with gladness that the spring had started on the moor, and wondered what the new year held for his family.

'Impossible, impossible,' he muttered, pondering on how he would get through his duties that day. He could hardly keep up with the marriages, births and deaths, the constant reassurances he needed to give to his parishioners, the general cordiality he must always assume regardless of his personal pains. There were days he felt his strength sequestered by some dark mysterious force that no amount of praying could recover. He could only await its return. It was a drizzly March day.

He looked ahead, his eyes searching for the Ratchford's cottage at the bottom of the hill. It was early morning; there were few people about. Now that he'd lost his wife to consumption, the apothecary was having to bring up his children alone, all five of them girls. He didn't understand girls, he'd said. Patrick knew what it was like to have girls about the house without a mother. And there was always a worry with girls. You had to get them married. And a father was always concerned about who they might marry, for what if the man made them miserable? Men could be such rogues. – Why even parsons could be cheats! There was one he knew whose name he didn't want to think of. He had cheated on his wife shamelessly and had caused her immense distress. His wife had been to the parsonage, weeping about it. Not that his daughters had been shocked; they were wise, cautious women. He doubted they'd ever make fools of themselves with a man like that; they were far too shrewd.

He blew out into the air; the hill was almost as hard going down as coming up. But he had to see Ratchford this morning, he hadn't looked well yesterday. There was a lot of sickness in the village. The pain of his own loss still lay heavy in his mind, and the faces of his little children as they'd stood around his wife's deathbed still haunted him. Gordon Ratchford wasn't without a bob or two, luckily, so at least he'd get by. Not so with some of his parishioners, who didn't know where to turn, and finally turned to him, as if he knew of a quick pathway to God who could put everything right. Unemployment was ubiquitous, like a foul, wicked disease. History had it now, that just like invaders from a foreign land, hell bent on destruction, men had invaded the mills, smashing up machinery and attempting to destroy the future. But the future would have its day, Patrick reflected. It couldn't be stopped. He recalled a song the Luddites had sung to their hammer Enoch:

'Great Enoch still shall lead the van.
Stop him who dare! Stop him who can!
Press forward every gallant man
With hatchet, pike and gun!
Oh, the cropper lads for me,
The gallant lads for me,
Who with lusty stroke
The shear frames broke,
The cropper lads for me.'

Yes, it was a resolute song. He fell to wondering how Branwell was faring at Sowerby Bridge station. It was difficult to tell how he felt about his life nowadays; he'd become so distant. He had aggravated the people at the railway one or two times too many, but with a little jiggery pokery, things had been sorted out. But it worried Patrick that he still hadn't told him what had actually taken place last autumn. He knew it was still on his mind. He'd become unusually silent and morose, a very different person than the family knew him to be. Though he'd been through times like that himself, he reflected. There were occasions at Cambridge, when he'd gone into his shell for months. There were those who had said he was difficult, and they were probably right. He'd been the same with beautiful women; only expressing himself through writing, mainly through poetry, the words flying ecstatically off his pen, and landing, he hoped, like sunlight. In truth, they were often put off!

But not Maria. Never dear Maria. Could he dare to think of her now, just for a moment? He tenderly, cautiously, opened the box where she lived in his mind. How thrilled she'd been on the birth of Branwell.

How lovingly she'd held him in her arms. Was she watching them now, he wondered. Could her spirit divide itself to be with each of them, all at the same time? Was it possible? He gazed at the clouds. What secrets did the heavens hold? He wished he knew. He would read his Bible sometimes till his eyes were bursting with pain. He would listen carefully to the sounds of prayer, his ear tuned to the joyful whispers of the light about him, even to the voices of darkness, hoping for revelations.

The rain had drawn to a halt. He unbuttoned the top of his coat. The day was becoming warmer. There were understandings between people, Patrick reflected, that could never be expressed in words. Feelings were bigger than words. He slowed his pace, wanting to finish his thoughts before arriving at the apothecary's house. Three of his parishioners came out of a cottage and called to him. He quickly bade them good morning.

He knew that Branwell's silence bothered his daughters. There had been a time of absolute horrible distance in him on that strange night when he'd returned last year after his odd disappearance. It was almost like a little death. With all his heart he longed for his son to tell him about it, though he knew he couldn't ply him with questions. Not one of them who lived beneath the parsonage roof dared question him. They had gone through the darkness of winter in silence, would the spring offer any answers?

His mind turned to thinking about Charlotte, a governess now with the White family in Rawdon. The children were quite a handful. And she was often asked to take care of the baby too. He wondered how she was coping. He shook his head and woke from his musings. He had work to do and must stay on his toes. His son's image kept on returning to his thoughts; his pale, drawn features, his anguished eyes. He could not rid them from his mind. Nor could he banish his fears. As surely as the clock ticked on the stairs in the parsonage, Branwell would walk through the door again, helpless, lost and fatigued. There were times his thoughts made him wretched. Couldn't life give his son just a few cheerful moments? Just a few? And if not, why? Branwell had worked so hard. He had always paid attention to his studies. He was brilliant and witty and musical. He deserved much better than the shoddy existence meted out to him. As he'd fired his pistol through the open window that morning, he hadn't been able to contain himself: 'It will not do for a parson to be angry with his God!' And it wouldn't either.

He raised his face to the growing sunlight, feeling its warmth on his cheeks, and breathed the morning air deep into his lungs. He must write again to the *Leeds Intelligencer*, he decided. The dissenters wouldn't be happy till they'd got their way. They were out to destroy the established church, and he feared it might happen. There had to be a determined opposition. He would have to begin at the beginning, think about how the unrest had started, imagine the people's fears, how doctrines had become entangled. And he mustn't forget the role of poverty in it all, the evils of unemployment, the struggle with the spirit! When he had finished at the Ratchford's, he would go right home. He would not do his normal circuit today. He passed a group of children who had come out to play, and gave them a cheerful grin. A parson must always have a smile on his face, he told himself. If the parson didn't smile, who would?

26

Violet Draper saw that her husband's head was bent as he walked; partly, she thought, so he didn't have to look at people passing. He was being impolite to the neighbours and she didn't like it. He'd made no answer when she'd asked him about the smuggling. She'd heard it was happening at Robin Hood's Bay, and his name had been mentioned in the inn. It had set her on edge. 'Ye'll be hanged if they catch ye,' she murmured. He'd been missing three days with one or two others from Haworth. Sometimes her husband was wise and thoughtful, other times just plain stupid.

'I've nowt to do wi' t' smugglin',' he grunted. 'So let me be.'

She shook her head. 'Well, I'm glad,' she said, after a moment's thought.

Joe lifted his head and faced her. 'Ye munna worry, I'll not be bringin' ye disgrace.'

'Nay, I wunna suggestin' that,' she replied awkwardly.

They were taking a walk on the moor, watching the children playing as they went, leaping the streams and enjoying the open space. All her children were healthy, despite adversities, and that was a blessing. And it was spring. The spring weather always made Violet want to sing.

And sing she did for a moment, dancing about and holding her skirts, so that her husband's heart burst with love for her, and he hated himself that he could not provide for his children in the way he wanted. 'Ye'll none be so happy later in t' week,' he said firmly, 'when there's nowt i' t' cupboard again. I munna e'en pinch a rabbit up 'ere or someone'll shoot me for it!'

'Are ye sure?' she said frowning. 'What, just fer pinchin' a rabbit?'

Joe Draper shook his head. 'I dunna know owt any more. There's that many laws, I canna keep up wi' 'em.'

They walked on, listening to the ecstatic bird songs, enjoying the busy light, the flushed sky, the dignity of the natural world about them; it entered into their souls and made them feel better. Sometimes Violet had wondered about the dead, what it was like to be in heaven, or perhaps in hell. She didn't think a lot about hell; it was far too much like earth sometimes. But it was blasphemy to think like that, she told herself, so she put the thoughts from her mind. But she wanted to believe something proper, and have a God who was there in her kitchen, seeing the empty cupboards and the empty grate and caring, not sitting in some fancy church. She wasn't sure she'd be good enough for heaven. It bothered her, that. What if she just went nowhere at all and simply drifted about like the mist, or else changed into something awful after she'd died? What terrible thoughts came into her mind sometimes.

'There were a coachman up here t' other night,' she said. 'Did ye hear about that? A stranger were walkin' about in t' village. Nobody knew who he were. He didna 'ave a manservant wi' him.'

'Aye?' said Joe surprised. 'Nay, I naiver heard owt about that.'

'Late at night, it were,' Violet added quickly. 'Rattled down t' 'ill like a fall o' stones from Peniston Crag, they seh, it were goin' that fast.'

'It were probably a phantom,' Joe said smiling.

Violet stopped in her tracks. 'Well, Joe Draper, are ye turnin' into a lunatic then? I've heard about phantom dogs, but ne'er phantom coaches.'

'Oh aye. Talk about phantom dogs, ye munna walk on t' moor at night, lass, or t' Gytrash'll 'ave ye.'

'Be quiet, man, ye'll frighten t' childer!' Violet whispered.

Joe Draper went on laughing. 'Breathed out from t' wickedness o' Haworth. Glowin' red eyes, red as t' sun of a hot summer evenin', tail as big as a tree. – An' webbed feet an' all.'

'Well, I daresay I could outrun the thing, if it's just as ye seh,' said Violet with a shrug.

'Aye, but it can change itsen as it suits,' her husband warned, cocking his eyes.

'Might be a corpse i' disguise,' Violet said shakily, glancing about. The air seemed suddenly cold.

Joe Draper lowered his voice to a whisper. 'Some poor sowl saw it last year. Them big red eyes stared him full i' t' face. He were shrivelled to a currant i' seconds.'

Violet looked suddenly scared and called in the children.

'Ah, dunna be bothered about t' Gytrash lass, it's nowt but imagination,' he said, with a laugh. 'Them elephants though are summat else. They look like summat from t' beginnin' o' time, they do.'

'Aye, an' as big as a hundred men, they seh. An they can teach 'em tricks too. How can they teach 'em tricks if they're as big as that?'

'They're clever, that's why, like t' parson's family, they've got brains. Ye can teach 'em owt ye want and they'll learn how t' do it.'

'A brain's for thinkin' wi',' said Violet flatly. 'There's nowt clever about just doin' what yer towd. An' a bet they make 'em suffer an' all. I dunna agree wi' them circuses. Ye shouldna take t' animals from t' wild like that. It's mekin 'em just like us.'

Joe looked hard at his wife. Is that what she thought? Did people just perform tricks for tit bits, or instead of a lash? Was life just a circus? The children ran about playing again. He was a simple working man. Or at least he had been. His work still lingered in his soul as something he must do. Always, while he performed it, he thought about his family. When he was tired, he'd thought about his children at home, and had found new energy. Or he'd thought about Violet's smile. He had offered himself to the world bravely, offered his strength and his manhood, attempting to surmount all obstacles. Now though, with the loss of his work, he felt he'd lost something precious. He could not save his children or his family from their fate, and it fevered him what that fate might be. So many times when his children had been hungry he'd tried to explain why they couldn't have bread, why they couldn't be warm, but they sat perplexed. It was hopeless. Today Reverend Weightman had brought them food in a basket, and they'd clustered about him, hugging and kissing him like a father. Just now, for a while, his wife and children were happy. His wife stopped and bent to the grass. She grasped a daisy, then another, then another, until she had made a posy, which she thrust at him shyly. 'Ah, dunna be givin' me flowers, lass,' he smiled, pushing them away. She thrust them back with a frown. And he carried them all the way home.

27

'*Cogito, ergo sum*. I think, therefore I am!' Branwell murmured, gazing outside at the trees. He was scribbling down notes from Descartes. He lowered his eyes and read on.

'... *Having given the matter careful attention, I am convinced that existence can no more be taken away from the divine essence than the magnitude of its three angles taken together being equal to two right angles can be taken away from the essence of a triangle, or that the idea of a valley can be taken away from the idea of a mountain.*'

Closing his eyes, he tried to think more clearly. He would like to have believed in a higher reality. Oh, how it would comfort him right now! So many questions went through his mind. He felt tired. The effort he put into his work at the station was enormous. But it was dull. He might have been lugging a ton of coal up Main Street.

He perceived an emptiness about him, a sinister kind of emptiness in which he felt he didn't exist at all. He would like to have talked to his father about Descartes and missed their long conversations. His father often astonished him with his knowledge. He would fly from idea to idea in search of truth. Though he was often confused. When he saw his father praying, he felt strangely excluded. He couldn't understand who he prayed to, or why he did it. And it sometimes disturbed him that the strongest of men, his father, could fall on his knees to a God who didn't seem to listen.

Branwell, just now, was enjoying the study of demons, the look in their eye, the muscular structure of their dark, unhealthy being. He imagined their stealth, their evil ways, their invisible movements about him. He had drawn an excellent demon that morning. It had almost leapt off the page. A cold tremor had passed down his spine as he'd finished it, noting particularly the evil glare in its eyes ... The eyes were undeniably Parker's. He had always known that the devil would one day break into flesh and jump right into his life. Parker had done just that. It had finally happened.

Branwell had been back to Broughton on several occasions, only to have Michael turn him away from the cottage. Milly, he'd said, must be left in peace to live out her life with Parker, just as she wanted. He'd begged Branwell not to harass her. Branwell couldn't understand how he could say such things, treating him like a stranger, like someone he wanted to forget. Was that what those people did, he wondered, allow you into their lives as if they loved you, then forget you just like a dream? He wondered if that's what he'd been for Milly, just a dream; a toy she had played with for a while. How many times had he tried to will her to come to him, for Michael to bring her late at night in a coach. There was a mighty void inside him now. His soul had left him. It was out wandering somewhere, searching. Each day he waited, longing for it to return, hoping it would bring him a message. He was in a kind of madness, a still, waiting madness. The very air felt full of hopelessness about him.

He glanced outside and saw in a flash the light of Milly blending with that of the tree opposite his window ... Yes, yes, it was her. It was Milly! 'Oh, cruel Mistress Fate!' he cried. 'How I despise you!'

He remembered how it had been last autumn when they'd buried the little coffin by Ponden Kirk. Oh, what a sweet ceremony! The moss had been soft and lit by moonlight as Brown had struck it with his spade. And it was almost as if the rocks about them had spoken gently, as if the wind might never roar again, and had settled at strange angles around the cliffs, moaning gently and kindly. Brown had dug until sweating, deeper and deeper. Branwell recalled the smell of the earth as he'd climbed down into it for Brown to deliver him the coffin. He recalled the strength of the men's hands as they'd pulled him out. Weightman had shovelled back the earth ... He put his hands to his ears, shutting out the sound of the train rushing by, clanging out its cumbersome song. Soon there would be another. Then another.

The cool air of the late afternoon wafted through the window, bathing his face. He remembered Milly and the spring, the way she would run through the bluebells, their great, passionate love. How quickly time moved on. How wickedly happiness taunted you with its memory.

Well, at least his baby was safe. And her burial place was secret. Not even Milly knew where the child was hidden, for he feared Parker might discover it, then dig her up in some evil, malicious vendetta. All was safe with Brown and Weightman, he could trust them till the end of time.

He could taste the salt of his tears as they fell down his cheeks. However he tried, he could not stop the pain.

March turned into April. Branwell was sitting with Brown in the Black Bull Inn.

'Quite an achievement!' laughed Brown.

Amazingly, despite everything, Branwell had been given a promotion. He was now at Luddenden Foot station as Clerk-in-charge.

'Though I'm not surprised,' said Brown. 'You always put your back into things when you must.' Brown hoped Branwell might forget the business in Broughton now, and try to get on with his life. Through the open doorway the warm smell of wild flowers came in from the moor.

'My sisters want to open a school,' Branwell said thoughtfully. 'Mad idea, don't you think?' He saw Brown's look. 'No, it's true. They often discuss it. But I doubt it will happen, there's a lot of . . .' He stopped, then sighed. 'I sometimes wonder if Milly might think of me, John.'

Brown stayed silent. No, nothing was any different. It was just as Branwell had feared. Milly had gone to live with Parker, had loved Parker all along, was connected to Parker in an uncanny and disturbing way. Branwell brooded constantly over losing her to Parker. He wanted her. His personality was disintegrating. There were days he was lucid, other days he seemed crazy. A new year was well on its way, and a new season had begun. So Milly too would change, and grow into someone different; a different being than the girl Branwell had known and loved. It was a bitter pill to swallow, but swallow it Branwell must. And he would try to make sure he did. 'So there's a new project on the horizon is there?' Brown said brightly. 'A school, eh?'

'Oh, it's not going to happen,' said Branwell shaking his head for certainty. 'Not now Mary Taylor is touring the continent. It has whetted Charlotte's appetite. She'll get the money off Aunt, but she'll not be using it for a school. She'll use it to go abroad with. Oh, she will, she will! I can't see Charlotte spending her life in a school.'

'You've got to hand it to her. She's always looking forward.' Brown smiled.

'Yes, she is,' Branwell sighed. 'It's one of her strengths. Charlotte forgets things that hurt her too. A remarkable quality ... You might destroy yourself though, a little at a time that way. In order to keep ourselves whole we must suffer our pains.'

Brown raised his eyebrows. Branwell certainly suffered. He felt slightly alarmed at the distance that seemed to have developed lately between Branwell and his family. He knew Branwell well, but the others he didn't understand. 'So you think she'll be going abroad then, do you?'

'I don't know exactly what they're up to,' Branwell mused. 'But one way or another they'll spend Aunt's money and get what they want. What a dance we lead her, poor soul.' He smiled tenderly at the thought of his aunt's naivety. They could tell her anything and she believed it. 'It might be a good idea for them to tour the continent,' Branwell pondered.

'What, all three of them?' Brown brushed dust from his sleeves. He was still wearing his working pants and the boots he donned in the graveyard. Branwell had just turned up, and he'd brought him to the inn for a drink. Brown had seen the girls grow up. He couldn't imagine any of them leaving the country.

'It'll probably just be Charlotte and Emily,' said Branwell, frowning at the thought. `Charlotte won't go alone. She'll try to take Emily for company.'

'I doubt Emily would go,' said Brown thoughtfully. 'She'd be back like a homing pigeon in less than a month. She doesn't like leaving the parsonage.'

'I know,' Branwell yawned. Sleep had escaped him totally that week. He had wandered his lodgings like a sleep-walker, and had wondered if he would ever sleep again, or instead live in a kind of dreamy wakefulness where nothing seemed real. 'Emily cares little for the world,' he said. 'She has so many worlds in her head that are far more exciting.' He gazed at his long strong fingers, at the large callous on his middle finger where he'd rested his pen throughout so much furious writing. 'Look at that,' he laughed, pointing to it. 'I used to be a writer once. In the dim and distant past, of course.' He touched it tenderly. What had happened to his writing? How had it all slipped away? It felt like a betrayal. All that noise, all that laughter? Gone. 'Yes,' he murmured, 'Charlotte has a toughness about her. I doubt she will last at the White's though. She's trying hard to destroy what she might have achieved.'

Brown watched him as he talked. 'How is she doing that?'

'By criticising everything. By making it all seem worse than it is, just to get away.'

Their conversation was suddenly broken by the sound of a fiddler who had entered the inn and had gone to play in a corner. They both listened for a while. 'She hates teaching,' Branwell said, returning to their talk about Charlotte. 'And she's paid such miserable money at the White's. What sensible person would work as a governess for a pathetic £20 a year? Anne is paid double at Thorp Green. And she doesn't want for a thing. Why, that house is a veritable treasure trove!'

'But is she happy?'

'She rarely complains about anything, so you wouldn't know.' Branwell braced himself, proud of his sister's strength. 'Anne is a sort of angel,' he smiled.

'If they go ahead with this school, they might make a lot of money,' said Brown cheerfully.

'It's only an idea,' said Branwell.

'Who knows what will happen?' said Brown hopefully.

Branwell pursed his lips. 'Who knows anything. Life is all about strategy. You must catch it out in its tricks. I am not very good at that. I feel so weak, as if nothing is worth the effort.'

'What, not even your writing?' Brown said worriedly. Branwell was silent. Brown knew in that moment that he would not stay with the railways. And he wondered if something terrible might happen to Branwell, something he could not help him with, that might even kill him.

Branwell placed his palms on his chest. 'I want to work from my heart. I want to work from my feelings. They are dying for fear of living.' His eyes searched Brown's confusedly. 'I keep on killing them. Did you ever hear of such a thing? If you kill your feelings, then you are no longer human, you are just a machine ... That's how I feel, as if I am just a machine ... I need some laudanum, John. Can you lend me some money?'

Brown looked at him calmly, and saw his desperation. It was a large room they sat in, full of noisy, happy voices.

'I'm not sleeping. I'm constantly shaking,' Branwell said nervously. 'Look at my hands!' He thrust them out before him. Brown saw they were trembling. 'I've been sending money to Milly. – Oh, and groceries and gifts.'

'And do they get there?' Brown murmured.

'I don't know,' said Branwell thinly. 'I hope so.'

'I sent some stuff to Bradford last month,' said Brown with a sniff.

'They never received it.' He leaned back in his chair and folded his arms. 'Things can be intercepted.'

'I need to send her things,' said Branwell in a rush of feeling. He rested his hand firmly on his friend's arm. 'I want to, John. She gave me such joy. Joy is all we humans can know of heaven.'

Brown gazed at him in silence.

'A few more months of this torture and I might be through,' Branwell murmured.

'I may as well say it,' Brown said flatly. 'It's going to take longer than that.'

28

Patrick Brontë was searching for something to inspire him for his Sunday sermon. He leafed thoughtfully through the pages of his Bible and scratched down some notes. He needed more paper to write on, and paper was hard to come by. He blinked hard. His eyes were worse today. And his study felt chilly. One of these days he would have to do something about it; the room could be cold in the early morning. He gazed down at the page. His sermon wasn't what he'd hoped for, but it would have to do. 'Perhaps I could learn how to hypnotise them!' he laughed to himself. He had read that day about a surgeon who had recently discovered something he called, 'hypnosis'. You could put people under a sort of spell, he'd said; make them do anything you wanted. How intriguing, thought Patrick, I could try that out on the dissenters! He doubted the claim's credibility, but it had certainly been a good read. He wondered if Branwell had seen it. He would have to remember to ask him.

He looked outside. It had just turned eight in the morning .He could hear Brown coughing in the graveyard. His chest was bad again today. The man is carving too many gravestones, Patrick decided. The grit got into his lungs and made him unwell. Last time they'd talked, he'd been quite short of breath. He would have a word with Weightman about it later. He wondered again about Branwell and how he was doing. He'd have to go visit him soon. And so he earned more than Willie did he? It took some thinking about, that did. Serving the railways paid better than serving the Lord! But of all the surprises, Branwell had had a promotion, and he was proud of that. Weightman would be glad for him too. He'd taken to Branwell like a brother. Branwell talked to Willie a lot, more than he talked to him in fact, he reflected, rubbing his nose and wondering. Had he nothing more to impart to his son that was useful? Had he grown too old? The front door opened. Eliza had returned from her walk.

'Nobody about?' she whispered, peering round the door.

'Nobody but me,' said Patrick, glancing about playfully.

'Oh, the cloth in these skirts!' she grumbled. 'It gets so damp at the bottom.' Her cheeks were red from the breeze. 'I walked too far. You forget how steep that hill is.'

'We all forget,' said Patrick. He saw she was looking preoccupied.

'I've been wondering,' she said, a little ceremoniously. 'The children must think I'm a fool. – I sometimes talk like a fool, I know. I sometimes think like a fool. And I sometimes act like a fool. But I promise you, Patrick, in no way am I a fool!'

'Ah, you boss me about too much for that,' he laughed. 'No fool dare boss me about.' He leaned in closer towards her. 'In any case, the fool and the genius are often in cahoots with each other!' He smiled. Eliza Branwell, just then looked beautiful, her dark eyes thoughtful, her skirt spread heavy about her, a thin damp dew softening the silk round the hem. 'You sound so cross. All this talk about foolishness. What are you trying to say?'

'Oh, I'm not cross,' she assured him. 'I'm not cross with anyone. Our girls are clever women. They don't let me down.'

Patrick saw her features filled with pleasure as she spoke. 'I could see it in Charlotte's face,' she smiled. 'Not a single thought did she betray with her eyes, but I saw it in her brow. You know that little twitch she has when she's up to her tricks.'

'Aye, I know it,' Patrick laughed. He put his hands on his knees. 'So what's going on?'

'Oh, will you stop all this nonsense!' she said, looking at him, her great intelligent eyes glistening. Patrick held her gaze. 'This money she wants for that visit to the school in Brussels. Oh, what a to-do! I wish she had told me straight.'

Patrick sat silent, watching her. He liked it when she talked like this; excited, animated, alive. Whatever Charlotte was up to, Eliza was all for it, that was for apparent. 'What do you mean?' he said, frowning curiously.

'I wish she had said exactly why she wants the money!' said Eliza, as if spelling out the words. 'I knew she would hate it with the White's. – Oh, that baby! – If she wants my money for a visit to Belgium. – Ostensibly to learn about schools, then I really don't mind. But I wish it were her own idea . . .'

'And isn't it?' said Patrick, listening carefully and frowning.

'No, of course it isn't. She's copying Mary Taylor. Not what I expect of her at all.'

'I see,' Patrick sighed. 'So you don't believe she is going to Belgium for experience?'

'Do you?' said Eliza, pouncing on his words.

Patrick threw out his palms.

'Upon my soul,' said Eliza. 'Are we both saying Charlotte is a fraud? Let one of us believe her at least.'

'We might both half-believe her,' the parson laughed. 'And a half plus a half equals one!'

Eliza stamped her feet and laughed. 'You mustn't make me laugh,' she said breathlessly. 'I'm feeling a little bit faint from the walk up the hill.'

'Well, I don't know,' said Patrick. 'A walk in the bracing air is supposed to restore you, so it is, not make you faint! You are doing things the wrong way round.'

'My poor dears, they are excellent women,' she said, thoughtful again. 'I would like them to go abroad for a while, it would do them good.'

'And it would do Branwell bad to think about it,' Patrick murmured. 'All on his own in that hut.'

'Oh, my poor, beautiful, nephew,' she suddenly moaned. 'I hope he's all right. Is he really unhappy? I can't bear it if he is. Does he have any friends of his own intellectual standing there, or are they all dozy as sheep?'

Patrick spoke slowly and carefully. This is how Eliza was; one minute strong, another minute fragile as porcelain. 'He has fine friends, Eliza. Remarkable friends, I believe; railway engineers, musicians, artists ... He still sees Leyland, the sculptor. An excellent acquaintance.'

'So long as he doesn't go telling them about his frailties,' she said flatly. 'There are those who would fire them back at him like bullets.' Drawing her skirts about her she rose from the chair. 'Look, I must go. I'm stopping you from writing your sermon. Why, Haworth would go to rack and ruin without your sermons!'

The day came into the room in a quick flood of light. Patrick waited for something to happen, something to occur, a revelation, a great idea perhaps. But all that came was the day, the bird songs, the little rattle the window made when touched by the breeze.

...July the 30th, A.D. 1841. This is Emily's birthday. She has now completed her 23rd year, and is, I believe, at home...' On holiday in Scarborough with the Robinson family, Anne sat writing a diary paper by the desk. She gazed about for a moment, deciding what to write about Charlotte. Fully aware of her unhappiness, she would cut that short. *'... Charlotte is a governess in the family of Mr White. Branwell is a clerk in the railroad station at Luddenden Foot, and I am a governess in the family of Mr Robinson. I dislike the situation and wish to change it for another. I am now at Scarborough. My pupils are gone to bed and I am hastening to finish this before I follow them. We are thinking of setting up a school of our own, but nothing definite is settled about it yet, and we do not know whether we shall be able to or not. I hope we shall. And I wonder what will be our condition and how or where we shall all be on this day four years hence, at which time, if all be well, I shall be 25 years and 6 months old, Emily will be 27 years old, Branwell 28 years and 1 month, and Charlotte 29 years and a quarter. We are all separate and not likely to meet again for many a weary week, but we are none of us ill that I know of, and all are doing something for our own livelihood except Emily, who, however, is as busy as any of us, and in reality earns her food and raiment as much as we do.*

How little know we what we are.
How less what we may be!

Four years ago I was at school. Since then I have been a governess at Blake Hall, left it, come to Thorp Green, and seen the sea and York Minster. Emily has been a teacher at Miss Patchet's school, and left it. Charlotte has left Miss Wooler's, been a governess at Mrs Sidgwick's, left her, and gone to Mrs White's. Branwell has given up painting, been a tutor in Cumberland, left it, and became a clerk on the railroad. Tabby has left us, Martha Brown has come in her place. We have got Keeper, got a sweet little cat and lost it, and also got a hawk. Got a wild goose which has flown away, and three tame ones, one of which has been killed. All these diversities, with many others, are things we did not expect or foresee in the July of 1837. What will the next four years bring forth? Providence only knows. But we ourselves have sustained very little alteration since that time. I have the same faults that I had then, only I have more wisdom and experience, and a little more self-possession than I then enjoyed. How will it be when we open this paper and the one Emily has written? I wonder whether the Gondolians will still be flourishing, and what will be their condition. I am now engaged in writing the fourth volume of Solala Vernon's Life. For some

time I have looked upon 25 as a sort of era in my existence. It may prove a true presentiment, or it may be only a superstitious fancy; the latter seems most likely, but time will show.
Anne Brontë.'

She sighed. How weary she was of Thorp Green. She thought just then she might pack her bags that minute and leave, surprise them all at the parsonage like Branwell did. For the main part, she kept her thoughts to herself, and often just listened to her siblings in the parsonage as they related their worries and disappointments. But she went about her duties at the beck and call of them all in this house: the plight of tutors everywhere! She recalled her brother's lessons with their father at the parsonage. How eager he'd been to please them all with his learning, to please their father especially. He had never shown the least objection to his lessons, their father's ceaseless efforts to deliver him knowledge. He'd tried to imbibe it silent and gentle as the air. Though Anne had often seen the struggle in his eyes, the fear and worry lest he failed. And it still lingered. The door opened behind her.

'I would like to talk to you, Anne,' said Mrs Robinson, entering the room quietly. She found herself a seat. She was wearing red and black silk. Her dark curls shone round her face. Her white pearls glimmered around her smooth, beautiful throat. Lydia Robinson was indeed a beautiful woman, just like those they'd created in their childhood stories. Anne braced herself to listen.

Lydia Robinson talked on about her son's illness; the influenza he'd suffered earlier that month, the way Anne had tended to all his needs. 'I don't always say it,' she said, haughtily. 'But you are very good to him Anne, way beyond what is expected. You make him laugh, and you ...'

Anne's cheeks reddened.

'I want you to have this,' said Lydia. She held out a packet of notepaper.

Anne took it with wonder and opened it carefully. The paper was perfumed and wonderfully smooth to the touch. 'For me?' she murmured. Lydia Robinson appeared by nature self centred. Was she actually capable of gratitude, even generosity? Anne wondered if she suspected she might be leaving. She'd been more reserved than usual, perhaps Lydia had noticed.

'It's very good of you,' said Anne, catching her breath. Lydia, it seemed, was at least attempting to be kind. Recently she'd been outrageous, making impossible demands, and despite what she'd said, expecting

Anne to take care of Edmund in his illness. As a matter of fact there'd been no-one about throughout his fever. Lydia had been out in her carriage all day, and sometimes all night. Her husband had been away.

'I hope you will find it useful,' said Lydia, oddly a little shyly. 'You are often writing to people.'

'Yes,' said Anne. 'Oh, believe me, yes, I shall use it!' She clasped the paper to her breast.

'My pleasure,' said Lydia. 'I'm grateful for your goodness and kindness.' She looked away. 'I do not possess such qualities myself . . .'

Anne looked up slowly, and met Lydia's eyes. She had never said words like that before, and there was a hint of sadness in her tone that was new and strange. Could it be that with all her wealth and beauty, she was actually unhappy? Anne listened as Lydia talked on, in her soft, lisping voice, saying how helpful it was that she didn't need to leave her instructions, that it was wonderful Anne had initiative.

'I am quite overwhelmed,' Anne faltered. It had bothered her that the boy had been alone in his illness. Though he loved his mother enough, and was always eager to see her. Lydia's maternal affections, however, were not of the kind Anne might have felt had the boy been her own, and she sometimes felt angry about it. She put the paper to her face. What a wonderful scent of roses! She intended to pay a brief visit home very soon. Could she write to Willie before she went off to sleep? Could she find the strength to disclose the feelings in her heart? Lost in thought, she didn't hear Lydia open the door and go out.

29

It was now a whole year since he'd visited Hartley Coleridge. Branwell held in his hand his very first poem published in the *Halifax Guardian*! He hoped Hartley might see it. Standing amongst the old trees by his hut, he read it again. Oh, the precise confidence of it, the proudness of it, standing as it did beside such distinguished writers! He felt very encouraged. The newspaper featured important poets and those who were gaining recognition.

He stood listening to the soft breath of a gentle breeze through the trees. The railway line was silent. He read the poem yet again, this time out loud.

> 'On earth we see our own abode,
> A smoky town, a dusty road,
> A neighbouring hill, or grove;
> In Heaven a thousand worlds of light
> Revolving through the gloom of night
> O'er endless pathways rove.
> While daylight shows this little Earth
> It hides the mighty Heaven,
> And, but by night, a visible birch
> To all its stars is given;
> And, vast as fades departing day,
> When silent marsh or moorland grey
> Mid evening's mist declines,
> Then, slowly stealing, star on star,
> As night sweeps forward, from afar,
> More clear and countless shines.'

Yes, it was an excellent poem! How much better he'd have felt though, if he had published it under the name of 'Branwell Brontë' and not 'Northangerland'. Northangerland's name, he realised, was beginning to offend him. Percy wouldn't go away. He returned to the hut and looked through his notebook. He'd polished up a lot of his poems lately and had written some new ones. The great beam of literature still shone on his soul! All was not lost. Indeed, all might be found.

That day he had posted a parcel again to Milly, but he didn't know what became of the things he sent. Nor did he know if the money he sent ever got there. But he continued to send her his gifts of love and affection. Insidiously, though, and without his knowledge something was happening inside him, so that an occasional chill went down his spine that made him feel cold; a sort of shuddering in his blood, as if it might somehow render itself impenetrable and pitiless as rock. He had been to Broughton on several occasions, hanging about near Michael's cottage, or up near Parker's house, hoping to catch a glimpse of Milly, longing to see her, but afraid of seeing her, of suffering the inevitable pain and confusion seeing her would cause him. He sat thinking in his hut. He felt quite lost. He needed to visit the parsonage, to feel the warmth of his home again, the pleasure of being with his family. Anne would be there; she was taking a few days' leave. It would be good to see her and Emily. And he would certainly drop in on Brown.

As he walked up Main Street, the little houses, the faces of the locals, gave him a feeling of contentment. The old place softened and enveloped him. 'Who is this man,' said the afternoon light, 'who has published a poem in the *Halifax Guardian* and returns to us so grandly?' None of his siblings had ever published a poem. But he wouldn't tell them. The poem would remain in his pocket and make him feel good. That alone, was a blessing. He ran up the steps of the parsonage and opened the door.

'Well, I fancied I might find a sister or two in here!' he called. The usual smell of wholesome food greeted him.

'Ah, you are wanting hugs are you?' said Emily, coming from the kitchen. 'Go on then, give me your shoulders.'

She put her arms around his neck and embraced him. He could feel the beat of her heart close to his chest, always louder and stronger than that of the others.

'Anne is out by the currant bush,' she said, in her sagacious way of knowing his thoughts before he spoke them. 'I doubt it will last the summer, poor thing. We've managed some odd little scraps.' She frowned and opened her palm. 'See how miserable they are.'

Branwell gazed at the sad little purple currants in her hand. They looked so hard and dry. The currant bush had been such a prized possession. What could be wrong with it, he wondered. Did it need more water? Had some dreadful fly ravaged it?

'I expect it will recover,' he murmured, picking at the offerings and putting a couple in his mouth. He screwed up his face. The currants were indeed bitter.

'I'll go fetch Anne,' said Emily. 'Then I must finish the baking. I'll make a pot of tea and come through.'

Anne came in from the garden. She ran to him, holding him close and sighing with relief. Just as he'd thought, she was tense. She wouldn't be happy in her post at Thorp Green, she too, would be longing to write. 'How well you look,' he said. 'Is life treating you kindly? I do hope so.'

'Kindly?' she said sardonically. 'I'm not so sure about that. Let's go and sit in the parlour.'

A steady fire blazed in the grate. It was a chilly day for May. Anne's tiny fingers were red with cold. She leaned in towards the warmth. 'Listen to Emily,' she laughed. 'She talks to that hawk as if it were a human being!'

'Martha is terrified of the thing,' Branwell laughed. 'And rightly so. I believe it would peck your eyes out if it were free!'

'Indeed it would,' said Anne rubbing her arms. 'So how is your work with the railway?'

'Well, it isn't going to change,' said Branwell. 'You know what rail tracks are like.' He made a gesture with his hands. 'First they go this way then they go that. Then they go do it all again.' He could see his sister's eyes were waiting. She did not smile. He couldn't invent with Anne. She would not have it. She wouldn't forgive him as Emily did. Nor would she attempt to re-shape his inventions like Charlotte, making them into something different. 'It's work,' he said flatly, dropping into a chair and spreading his legs. 'It pays good money. More than Weightman gets, apparently.'

'So I am told,' said Anne, fingering her curls.

Branwell stared back at her. Weightman shone in her eyes.

'But do you enjoy it?' Anne said quietly. 'I don't like you sitting in that hut, pouring over those ledgers all the time, hurting your eyes with such nonsense.' She couldn't repress the thoughts she had had, she said; she must tell him. 'I don't know how to say it . . .' she went on restlessly. 'My own situation is hardly ideal. And of course you are earning money, but . . .'

'That's right, I am! And whenever was work enjoyable for the Brontës?' he laughed. 'We must earn our bread, one way or another. No-one does it better than you, dear Anne.'

There was silence for a moment. Anne bent her head, pondering. 'I am not so perfect as that,' she sighed softly. 'You wrong me if you think so . . . Allow me my imperfections.' She lifted her head and smiled.

Branwell sat very still, watching her face. Did she and Weightman have something hidden? He certainly had things hidden himself. Was it possible that now they were adults, the whole family might have things hidden from one another, never to be disclosed?

'I wasn't cut out to be a painter,' he said finally.

'You are not cut out to be a railway clerk.' Anne said quietly. Their labours seemed sometimes so heavy, so senseless, so separate from themselves. 'You aren't cut out to be a tutor either, and neither am I.'

Branwell folded his arms and sighed. His eyes were busy with thought, though he did not speak.

'Charlotte is taking a break,' said Anne presently. 'She'll be back at the parsonage soon.'

'This school thing . . . Will it happen?' Branwell began, knowing that Charlotte was probably returning to discuss it.

Anne sighed deeply. 'I don't really know. Sometimes I think she isn't serious. But whenever she talks to Aunt she sounds eager.'

'Don't let the chance of going abroad slip through your fingers, Anne,' said Branwell, smiling. He leaned across and touched her hands in her lap.

'I don't want to go,' she replied, quietly. 'She's taking Emily, I think.'

Branwell laughed, loudly. 'Oh, I doubt it. Emily would rather stay here.'

'Did I hear my name?' said Emily, bringing in tea and cakes.

Try as they would, neither of them could provoke her to discuss the project. 'Luddenden Foot is a very pretty area to work in,' said Anne to Branwell. 'You are getting out to concerts, I believe . . . Tell us about your friends.'

'The good ones, or the bad ones?' he laughed, slapping his thighs.

'That man, Francis Grundy, seems pleasant enough,' said Anne.

Branwell scratched his head. 'Francis? Oh, Francis is fine.' Francis Grundy, a young railway engineer, had befriended him right from the start. 'I have learned a lot from Francis, and he's excellent company, too.' He talked on for a while, trying to shape their time together into something happy. Branwell watched their faces as he spoke, Anne's features busily following his narratives, Emily's still and unbending. 'You know,' he said wistfully, dropping his voice, 'sometimes, when I look in Aunt Branwell's eyes, I search for mother.'

Emily and Anne went silent. The feelings they felt for their dead mother gathered amongst them.

'I search for mother's voice in her speech, her body in her movements,' said Branwell. 'I watch her when she adjusts her curls in the mirror, and I wonder if mother's were like that.' He glanced at them both by turns. 'You know that look she has sometimes? – That look of longing? Do you think she was ever in love?'

'Perhaps she was,' said Anne wistfully. Her voice came shakily as she spoke. 'She was certainly beautiful, and you know how she loved to dance.'

'Do you remember that story Tabby told us about fairies dancing at the beck?' said Emily. `I never saw them, myself.'

'Fairies, dancing at the beck?' laughed Branwell. 'I haven't seen them either. I shall have to keep an eye out for that.' He stretched his arms in the air. 'I want to get some of the moorland air today, if I can.'

'I don't believe in fairies,' Emily added, her grey eyes suddenly serious.

'But believe in demons, you must!' Branwell said firmly. 'I tell you they are alive and well, Emily. Often in human form!' Branwell frowned hard, and finished his tea. 'Well, I think I'll take that walk while the daylight is strong,' he said cheerily, peering out of the window. He took three steps towards the doorway, then turned, standing thoughtful for a moment.

'What is it?' asked Anne. Emily looked at him, preoccupied.

'Nothing,' he said, quietly. 'Nothing.' After that, he went out.

30

It was a warm, white morning. Emily and Anne decided to go out on a picnic. And why, if it came to that, Anne said, shouldn't Branwell come along too? And perhaps even Willie?

William Weightman was drinking tea in the kitchen before setting off on his visits. He'd work to catch up with, he said, but he'd come to find them at noon. Branwell, falteringly, suggested Ponden Kirk. He hadn't been to Ponden Kirk since his baby's burial, though the bond he felt with the people around him helped him feel strong. He longed to return to where his child was laid in the moor. He disciplined himself to show nothing on his face that might cause his sisters to question him. Weightman's nostrils dilated for a moment but his eyes revealed nothing.

Anne and Emily got on with making up the basket. Anne talked on happily; it would be a kind of celebration, she said, a chance to get out in the open air, a chance for Willie to have a rest. She knew he was tired. In the open country they could think and talk freely. She looked at Weightman as he finished his tea. He was sitting in the little corner in the kitchen where nobody wanted to sit, an uncomfortable, awkward space. He appeared relaxed. It was quite an achievement, she thought, like so many other things he managed to do that others found difficult; he could talk to impossible people, he could do impossible things.

Into the basket went apples, freshly baked bread, a large pork pie and a newly boiled ham, along with some cold potatoes and hard-boiled eggs. Branwell added a bottle of wine, some drinking glasses and some plates.

Emily thought Anne and Branwell looked strong and healthy. She was missing Charlotte, and wondered what she'd be doing that day with the White family. How did she pass her time on her own? Who did she talk to? A lot of the women they worked for had wealth without brains. It was difficult not to feel irritated by them. They'd written about such women in their childhood dramas. Was the world paying them back, she wondered. Now they must bow and scrape to such people in an abominably crippling fashion. She felt she was weaker than her sisters; they were kinder, finer women. She had backed away from the world. Charlotte and Anne could live in the world without. She must live in the world within; there was no other way. Charlotte often wrote home to them. It seemed she was contemptuous of their brother's work with the railways, and he seemed to have changed, she'd said; he had lost his laughter and spontaneity. Where did such things go? Emily wondered. Her own letters were brief, her main thoughts committed to poetry. She knew Anne was in love. Matrimony was a favourite conversational topic. They talked about people they might have fallen in love with, men they might have married.

William Weightman got up from his seat. Anne reached for his cloak and passed it across. 'Lunch time,' he whispered. She nodded.

Anne was different when Willie was there, Emily noted; she was all shyness. Emily wondered about the future. Would she, herself, go abroad with Charlotte, to that lonely place, away from the moors she loved, away from her life? Whenever she thought of it, a wild panic entered her. She wondered what would happen to Branwell. Would he always work for the railway? It didn't seem possible. Branwell had pathways denied to the rest of them. His mind could take flights of fancy that stopped her breath. He flew without direction, without a goal, exploring his imagination just as it suited, unfettered and free as a bird.

'Why, my dears,' said the parson, entering the kitchen, passing Weightman as he left. 'I see you are packing for a picnic!'

He'd been a long time coming from his study that morning. Emily suspected he'd been writing a letter to the *Leeds Intelligencer* again. He reached more people that way than he did from his pulpit.

'To be sure,' he said, 'there are some fine apples in there! Where did you get them?'

'I bought them on Main Street,' said Emily. 'They had a fresh delivery this morning.'

'We are lucky to be eating apples,' said the parson sitting down to watch. 'A local tree I'll wager.'

'Anne has been given strict instructions to allow Willie just one,' said Emily. 'You know how he likes his apples.'

'Is Willie to join you, then?' said the parson, looking surprised. 'Hasn't he things to do? I mean, really my dear, he hasn't got time for picnics.'

Anne came quickly to his defence. 'He's done so many burials lately, Papa,' she argued. 'Must he always have such sad reflections? Might he not have some happy ones now and then?'

'What's that?' said Patrick, thinking about something else.

'Willie must have some fun sometimes, Papa,' said Emily quietly. The parson fixed his lips tightly. He would say no more. He was well aware of his curate's heavy workload. He took on more than he should and was an enormous help in the parish. He frowned. Truth be told, he would like to have gone on a picnic himself. He rarely did anything that was fun. Eliza sometimes joined him in a walk on the moor, but they didn't go far. She didn't like wetting her skirts. And she wasn't too steady on the tussock grass either. He saw Emily put a corkscrew into the basket. 'Well then,' he said, with a sigh. 'I'll be off. I've a letter to post and there are one or two people I must see.' So Patrick went out into Haworth, and the girls and Branwell walked out on the moor.

The birds were a riot of song. Blossom everywhere was fast emerging from the trees. Anne was intensely thoughtful. She breathed in deeply the joy and splendour of the moorland. There was something she longed for. It came from a feeling deep in her heart. It stopped her thoughts. It was a great, gnawing need. The need was for William Weightman. Unchaste thoughts filled her mind. Every night when she retired to her bed she could not sleep for wanting him. She had written him several letters, and he'd written back. Did he really care as she did? Or did she simply embarrass him? She often watched him; walking, sitting, moving his beautiful hands in accordance with his words. She loved the look of him, his smile, his kindness, the steady certainty of his manner.

They were all three thoughtful as they walked. Branwell carried the basket, looking about, his dark eyes preoccupied. As they reached Ponden Kirk, he stood silent for a moment, letting the breeze bathe his cheeks. A steady glow from the sun lit up his hair. His boots shone black and sturdy. Just then he seemed strong, far from the dreadful weakness he sometimes knew. 'Do you remember the things we used to say when we were here as children?' he said wistfully. His words mingled with the soft sounds of the breeze and the bird songs, the chatter of stones falling from a nearby cliff.

'How could we ever forget?' said Emily.

'Come to me,' he said. 'Both of you. Put your head here, and here.' He closed his eyes and held them tightly. 'Now listen,' he said, there was a shake in his voice as he spoke. 'I want you to know that I love you. That whatever I say, whatever I become, I am always your loving brother.' Emily hid her face in his shoulder. They were very close to the burial place of his child, but they did not know. Grasses and wild flowers had sprung from the earth above her. All was well. They each sat down in the dry grass and were silent a while, contemplating the moorland.

'Look!' cried Anne, watching a butterfly alighting nearby. 'It's a Painted Lady! How strange it is that some creatures emerge so beautifully from something quite different.' She laughed in wonder. 'How odd to belong in one body, then suddenly be in another. – Perhaps it's like entering heaven.'

'You should write a poem about it,' said Emily.

'Most poetry is either a celebration or a requiem,' said Branwell, thoughtfully.

'Yes, Emily, I might write a poem to celebrate it,' said Anne happily. 'To celebrate metamorphoses!'

'You should,' said Emily.

Branwell took the cloth from the basket, gazing at the contents, moving them about to see what was there.

'All those serried gravestones.' said Emily, gazing down the hills towards the village. 'There's nothing to see through the window of the parsonage except graves.'

'At least you haven't had to bury those people,' said Anne, reproachfully. 'How awful for Papa and Willie to have to lower so many people down into the earth like that, never to be seen again.'

Branwell winced and drew a breath. 'Someone must do it, I suppose,' he said.

A soft haze burned in the valley. The thin dark paths intertwined as they meandered through the moor. The water was high in the little streams, moving on urgently.

'Do you think Ellen Nussey will ever marry?' said Anne.

'Ellen? – Why?' said Emily.

Anne smiled, casually. 'It's just that I wondered. She shares all those letters with Charlotte. I wondered if they talked about men.'

'Oh, they certainly talk about men!' laughed Branwell. 'I'll say.'

'How do you know?' said Emily. She glanced at Anne. 'Branwell and Charlotte are terribly nosy, you know. Don't leave anything about, or they're sure to read it.'

'Would you, Branwell?' said Anne, looking surprised.

'I'll bet? Why not? Wouldn't you?' said Branwell to Emily, raising his eyebrows playfully.

Emily shook her head. 'Not unless I was asked.'

Anne turned to Branwell again. 'You mean you would read my writings if you found them?' She gazed at him in amazement.

'My dear sister, you always act so innocent,' said Branwell, laughing. 'You would do the same yourself. – Why, if I left my writings about, for sure you would read them!'

'Well, perhaps I would.' said Anne, who often had. She'd marvelled at Branwell's work. And was shocked by the way he could discard it so easily, once he became disenchanted. Which was a crime, since there lay his genius. But his genius was lost in the mire of everything else.

'That's more like it,' he whispered. 'You do escape from your piety now and again, thank goodness.'

'So what are you up to?' Weightman called, all of a sudden with them. He was breathless from hurrying and appeared to be limping slightly.

Branwell got up.

'I was seized down there by some tussock grass!' Weightman said, laughing. 'It wanted to bring me down.'

'It would take much more than that,' Anne murmured, watching him as Branwell took his arm and they looked for somewhere to sit.

Willie removed his cloak and rolled up his trouser leg to examine his injury, pressing his fingers into the soft brown hair of his calf.

'That graze looks sore,' said Branwell.

'I'll survive,' said Weightman with a sigh. He looked them all over kindly then took off his boots and socks, showing that he had also managed to bruise his ankle in the bargain. 'I'm sorry I'm late,' he said. 'It's a fault of mine. Once I get talking to people I can't get away. Have you been waiting long?'

'It's only twelve thirty,' said Branwell. 'We've been discussing the philosophy of life!'

'It always happens when we're out on the moors,' laughed Anne. 'The fresh air does it!'

'I hope you'll be alright getting back,' said Emily.

'Oh, let's not worry about my getting back,' said Weightman. 'We must enjoy the here and now, Emily, for we never know how long we have it. – Gosh, that pie looks wonderful!' He gazed into the basket.

Anne cut him a slice of the pie. He lay back in the grass, a hand behind his head, the other holding the pie, which he devoured with careless abandon. The sun, Anne knew, was a dreaded enemy to his skin. He had often said so. Though he lay with it beating down on him now as it came hot through the clouds, so that his brow glistened and his hair lit up with life.

They were all in a sleepy mood for a while, eating and drinking. 'I can't imagine being married,' said Emily, picking up on their earlier conversation. 'The creature summoned to satisfy both parties can often be a monster, its sole purpose to destroy its creators.'

'Oh, that's grim,' laughed Weightman, cringing. He sat up slowly, regarding Emily, curiously. 'You don't really believe it, I hope.'

'Emily's been reading about Frankenstein's monster,' said Branwell, who knew too well the monsters the mind could imagine.

'Marriage should be about honest, undying love,' said Weightman, his eyes wide and innocent. He touched Anne's hand. He was twenty-eight years old, full of hope and fresh for life. He wanted to love. He had so much love in his soul it was bursting out of him.

'I hate the idea of marriage,' said Emily, with a definite edge of anger. 'What starts as love so often ends in despair.'

'You speak as if from experience,' said Weightman, frowning, watching her face while breaking the shell from an egg. The whiteness of the egg shone in the sunlight. The yellow centre crumbled on his lips as he bit it.

'Truth only happens when both sides are open to it,' said Branwell, wistfully. 'So often in marriage the truth is locked out.'

'Did I see some wine in there?' said Weightman, looking into the basket again. 'You've been reading Frankenstein then?' he said, turning to Emily as she poured out the wine. She smiled and answered with silence. 'Mary Shelley wrote a wonderful novel there,' he laughed.

'Hartley said his father had wanted to read Mary Wollstonecraft's letters,' said Branwell.

'Mary Shelley's mother?' said Anne, looking up. 'A wonderful writer.'

'Yes,' said Branwell, thoughtfully. He'd wanted to write to Hartley again, but his life just hadn't been stable enough. He would hardly want to hear about the railways. And he'd only published one poem since last time he'd seen him.

'And did he read the letters?' asked Weightman.

Anne cut slices of ham from the bone and handed it round on thin china plates. 'Hartley wasn't sure,' Branwell continued. 'He told me she put a lot of dramatic scenery into what she wrote, though. Some of it was a bit like Kubla Khan.' He took some forks from the basket and passed them round.

'You think they might have inspired him?' asked Emily, deeply interested.

'Who knows?' said Branwell.

'Her daughter's *Frankenstein* is a powerful story,' said Anne, shuddering. 'I can't imagine writing it myself.'

'Oh, I'd relish it!' said Branwell, narrowing his eyes. 'The story of a monster who is abandoned by the man who has created him? And all because he wasn't perfect. – Oh, a marvellous subject.'

'Doctor Frankenstein is the monster, of course,' laughed Weightman.

'Well, yes,' said Branwell. He put down his drink and began to quote a passage.

"As the minuteness of the parts formed a great hindrance to my speed, I resolved, contrary to my first intention, to make the being of gigantic stature."

They all listened intently, Branwell's ability to recite poetry or a passage from a novel at will astounded his sisters.

'But the being was something of a shock,' said Emily. 'More of a monster than he'd thought.'

'Keeping things in proportion is difficult,' said Branwell, thoughtfully. 'Especially in the mind. That's where our monsters are.' He quoted again, this time from Milton.

"Did I request thee, Maker, from my clay
To mould me Man, did I solicit thee
From darkness to promote me."

'Paradise Lost,' said Weightman. 'Marvellous words.'

Branwell continued, quoting again from Frankenstein.

"I cannot believe that I am the same creature whose thoughts were once filled with sublime and transcendent visions of the beauty and majesty of goodness. But it is even so, the fallen Angel becomes the malignant devil."

'So you think you are Frankenstein's monster, do you?' said Weightman, laughing.

'Those are the monster's words,' said Branwell, gravely. 'I somehow feel an affinity with them.' He quoted again, even more dramatically.

'"Accursed creator! Why did you form a monster so hideous that even you turned from me in disgust?"'

'Did God flee from us, like Victor fled from his monster?' said Anne, bending her head sadly.

Weightman's brow tightened. He was trying to put on his socks. The swelling around his ankle was turning blue. He shook his head and frowned, gazing about at the benign hills, the seemingly eternal rocks, the great expanse of white sky above him. It was all so magnificently beautiful. The terrifying view Branwell had of himself filled him with fear. He knew far more than the rest of the family about Branwell. He knew the secret lying in the earth beneath them. He knew the worst of his pain. Was it possible, he wondered, to get him to see that he could fight his demons, that he could even conquer them? As he listened to him now, hearing the depth of his bitterness, he feared it might fix itself inside him, and even become him.

31

Violet Draper stopped, breathless for a moment. She hated climbing the hill. 'If yer worried about yer sowl, ye should have a word wi' t' parson,' she repeated, linking her husband's arm. 'Go an' knock on t' parsonage door.'

'Nay, I'd never go up tuh t' parsonage,' said Joe Draper, gazing at the shining cobblestones. 'That Emily might come tuh t' door. Ye 'ave t' admit, she's hardly what ye'd call friendly.'

'She's parson's daughter, Joe. Happen she's a bit reserved, but it's nowt more 'an that.'

They set off walking again. The Draper family had seen a few changes in Haworth. Healthwise they knew they'd done well. So far, there had been no horrible deaths, no babies had died, and till recent times they'd enjoyed a happy existence. They walked on silently for a while, quietly dreaming of how things were and the way they were now.

'All three girls are different,' said Violet. 'Charlotte's the one who has most to say though. Emily's quiet.'

'Anne's a quiet one an' all, in a nice sort of way,' Joe mused. 'Ye don't see much of her nowadays.'

Violet frowned, thoughtfully. 'She 'as such inquisitive eyes, don't ye think? Ye never forget those eyes.'

Joe and Violet Draper were generous-hearted, but Joe was frightened of Emily; she moved through the streets like a ghost, he said, a thin dark ghost. He would never have dared to address her, and he thought her face too pale. There was the look of another world about her, he said, as if she belonged somewhere else. The great yellow light of the July afternoon sun shone brightly about them. 'I 'aven't seen Branwell in ages,' said Violet, observing the colours shimmering at the top of the hill. 'The lads round 'ere allus liked him. – He's thinner, they seh.'

'An' madder, an' all!' laughed Joe. 'Ye can't imagine it, can ye, Branwell working for t' railways?'

'Well, he's a man wi' a brain,' Violet asserted. 'An' a brain's needed for a job on t' railways, or else there'd be havoc.'

'Them railways 'll be t' death of us,' Joe Draper grumbled. 'Everythin' that's kept t' poor on their feet 'll be ripped from under 'em.'

Violet Draper thought the look in her husband's eyes too hard. He was angry about the railway trains, and claimed they would take the old ways off in their carriages. Her face creased into a frown. 'Aye, an' t' Chartists dunna do much that's useful, do they?'

'Chartists never did owt for us,' said Joe bitterly. Chartism had grown out of desperation, he said. It had eaten into itself with too many grievances. A poverty movement, born out of poverty, it was bound to collapse. 'It's just a standard to rally round,' he said. 'If summat upsets ye, be a Chartist! I canna see what they've done for anybody. Too many people fightin' for too many causes.'

'People should show their feelings sensibly,' said Violet, frowning. 'Fightin's wrong.'

'Sensibly?' her husband mocked. 'What are ye on about, lass? It doesna get ye anywhere that.' He beat his palm with his fist. 'No, I'm with White! Ye must get what ye can, as ye can!'

'Aye, an' look what happened to him,' said Violet quietly. 'Ye dunna want t' be like him, do ye, in and out o' prison like a Jack-in-a-Box?' This was the general chant of the women in Haworth, their men might change from common sense to barbarism in a matter of seconds. She hated the spirit that stirred in him now, the way he was showing his teeth when he talked. He was getting too old for fist fights, but he'd a riotous tongue when he started. The women in Haworth were eager to keep their men from going on the loose. For when they did, they acted like a pack of wolves. 'Ye should go an' talk to Reverend Brontë,' she said. 'Ye can go an' knock on t' parsonage door whenever ye like.'

'Aye, I know. He's a good 'un,' Joe Draper sniffed. 'But t' parson isna much help these days.'

'He works for God,' said Violet quietly, her brow tightening. 'He'll always help ye.'

Joe coughed loudly. 'Aye, I know, but God ... doesna know what it's like ... bein' ordinary like us.'

'That's blasphemy, Joe,' Violet whispered. 'God knows everythin'.'

'Ah, rubbish,' Joe retorted, wiping his nose with his hand. 'He'll not be listening tuh t' likes o' us, I can tell ye.' He began to falter and mumble. Violet thought he was praying. He went on muttering to himself. 'A man gets sorrowful when his family and friends keep dyin',' he said, his voice low and trembling. 'A man feels shamed.'

Violet shrank away from him now. This sort of talk was usually the prelude to something serious, as if he were asking forgiveness before he started. She knew there was something afoot in Halifax that week, she'd heard people talking. 'Is Anne to marry Mr Weightman?' she said, with a sudden light heartedness.

'Eh? What makes ye think that?' said Joe, his eyes smiling.

'They gaze at each other i' church with the eyes o' lovers. It's a well known fact around 'ere.'

'Hee, hee, ye don't say,' said Joe, stopping for a moment to think about it.

'Oh, but I do,' said Violet. 'Well, t' women do. You men wudna notice.'

'But she's away teachin'. They canna be doin' much courtin'.'

'Ah, but they're not like us are they. They can put their feelin's on 'old. – They all like Reverend Weightman round 'ere. He doesna miss anyone out, not i' prayers nor provisions.'

'A man doesna like it when 'is poverty's staring i' 'is face like that,' growled Joe. 'A man hates that. He doesna want the curate's charity. Let a man say his own prayers to God if he wants. And let 'im feed his own family an' all!'

'Reverend Weightman's just doin' his job,' said Violet, frowning.

'A man likes to feed his own!' said Joe adamantly.

'And if he can't, must they starve?' Violet said, glancing at her husband, angrily.

'No, a man must fight!' cried Joe, taking a deep breath. 'Aye, he must fight!'

They walked on quietly for a while. A dull, silent stillness encompassed the streets. It seemed the place was sleeping, as if the afternoon were poised for a new direction, as if somewhere a council of elders sat in session, debating what would happen next.

32

Patrick battled Dr Scoresby now without flinching. And he watched the papers like a hawk. The enormous unrest, threats of imprisonment, continued bitter disharmony, caused him to wonder if the honour and respect the church had traditionally enjoyed could possibly continue.

'... *it appears to me,*' he had written to the *Bradford Observer*, '*that when a new church is built in a large parish, and has, as it ought to have, a district assigned to it, there should be absolute independency there – so that, in no one instance, the parishioners should be answerable for any rate, but that which should be requisite for the repairs of their own church. As for the laying on two or three rates annually on any one district, to keep in repairs churches it has nothing to do with; this is unreasonable and preposterous, and if there be laws which require it, they should, for the general good, be altered and amended, as soon as possible.*'

'I can't tell if it's the church rates or the Poor Law they're shouting about out there, they shout so loudly,' he said to Emily. He took off his coat and went to join her by the fire. 'Nobody talks any more.'

'Did they ever?' said Emily flatly.

'Oh, there's worse to come,' sighed the parson. – 'Does anyone really read my letters?'

'They'll read them the way they want to,' said Emily, putting down her book and looking at him. She could see what was happening in the village had disturbed him deeply.

'I'd like to get shot of the trouble makers,' he said, stroking his chin and frowning. 'The ones who don't even think and just like commotion.' Patrick could feel a vivid sense of crisis in the area.

Emily drew a quick breath of annoyance. 'Those meetings are nothing but noise.'

'I shall sort something out tomorrow, my dear,' said her father, resignedly. 'See if I don't.' He smiled at his daughter kindly. 'So what about this school then?' He folded his arms and attempted to relax.

'Aunt is lending us some money,' Emily said hesitantly.

'Is she now?' said Patrick, raising his eyebrows. 'She's a generous woman, of course.'

'I shall probably accompany Charlotte to Brussels,' Emily sighed, settling herself more comfortably.

'Brussels, eh?' said Patrick. He sat very still by the fire, his long legs stretched in front of him. He felt uneasy, wondering if his daughters would like living abroad, and what he would do if they needed him. It was coming to the end of August. The parson felt the summer had fled, filled with worries and work. His children still weren't walking their chosen paths. He was somehow waiting for them to start the lives they wanted then he might at last be happy. But maybe it isn't to be, he reflected sadly. Perhaps this is all they will have. Imaginative people could often be disappointed by life, he decided. There was always something infinitely better to imagine. 'And the school?'

Emily shook her head. 'I'm leaving everything to Charlotte.'

'You don't want to go at all, my dear, do you?' Patrick knew from the whispers he'd heard in the parlour, the occasionally raised voices, that the visit abroad wasn't exactly straightforward. Charlotte was keeping her cards close to her chest. 'I shall have to come with you,' he said straightening. 'I can't have my daughters wandering around the continent on their own.'

'Oh you needn't come with us,' said Emily taken aback. 'You have duties to attend to.' His words had drawn her from her thoughts. She suddenly realised she had entered into a new phase of life. It was bound to happen. She would go with Charlotte to Brussels. Could he see she was afraid of the venture?

'Oh, I always have things to attend to,' said Patrick. 'All the same, I shall see you safely there, then return.' He sat with his lips firmly together, gazing at the fire.

Emily began to think about Charlotte's plans. The exaltation her sister was feeling hadn't really touched her. She had no particular interest in starting a school, and no desire to go abroad. The thought filled her with horror. Her father was right, she didn't want to join her at all. And yet Charlotte talked about departing in the spring next year. All her energies were directed towards that end. 'I expect we might get something out of it,' Emily murmured heroically. The perspective before her was grim, however. She had writing to do. She needed the intimacy of the moors for inspiration, its sights and sounds, its air. 'You must stay here at the parsonage, Papa,' she said. 'We must think of Branwell. How will he feel if he returns and we have all deserted him?'

'Oh, I won't be away for long,' he replied, rubbing his nose. 'Branwell is often in Haworth anyway. He doesn't always come to the parsonage. – Did you know that?'

Emily looked downwards. 'He would rather talk to Brown than me,' Patrick murmured, a slight hurt in his tone. 'Anyway,' he said, smiling, 'Anne is happy with the Robinson family, that's something. And you never know, perhaps Branwell enjoys what he does.'

'I doubt I shall ask him about that,' said Emily.

Patrick hoped Branwell was happy, if only intermittently. There were moments that deeply disturbed him, like finding his children suddenly silent around him, as if lost and bewildered for a brief moment in time, throwing the weight of their lives to the wind, to fate, to the parsonage and to him. Times like that made him fearful.

'I think those are mine,' said Emily, seeing her father gathering some papers from the table. 'I ought to have moved them.' Patrick glanced over his spectacles.

'Do let me have them, Papa,' said Emily, shaking her hand before him.

The parson handed them across. Not that it really mattered; he had seen the poems earlier that day and had known to whom they belonged immediately. There was trepidation in Emily's eyes, which he didn't like to see. He could not guess the reason. Her poems were quite extraordinary, strong, unusual and dramatic. But she held them behind her back, shaking her head with annoyance, her lip quivering. 'It would serve you well, my dear, to have time away,' he said quietly. He passed her and went upstairs.

33

Branwell could not sleep. He picked at his food and felt forced into a vile place in his mind, thinking vile thoughts, determined to do vile deeds. Such were the pains his impassioned feelings caused in him. Once or twice he had been on the point of ending his existence, in order to end his suffering. He was caught by something now that he couldn't escape from. He'd allowed himself to succumb to it, to turn it over and look at it in disgust. He'd decided it would have to be his life. He must force his body to respond to the chug of the trains. He must become a machine like them, like a thing without a soul. He wondered if he could do it, and for how long. Time and again, drinking came to his aid, and laudanum whenever he could get it.

'Oh, damn the railways! Damn them!' he cried. Sometimes he walked out into the darkness and walked all night, cold, tired and alone. Since the death of the baby and the loss of Milly's love, his heart had stilled. In his mind, he had come to a place that was neither life nor death. When he went to the parsonage he acted as if he were dreaming, talking and walking in a dream, even laughing with his aunt and his father, acting his dramas. When he felt most dejected, he despised himself for his moanings, and despised also the proud genius that would not leave his mind, turning its nose up at anything less than superior or mighty. When the voice grew dim he longed for its resurrection, deeply afraid for its loss.

Even reading his poem in the *Halifax Guardian* gave him no solace. The joy had been short lived. Leafing through his notebook, he found Brearly Hall, a poem he'd written in August that year. It was now Christmas. Time, it seemed, had somehow left him for dead. Slowly and painfully he read the lines, though the words tormented him.

'When I look back on former life
I scarcely know what I have been
So swift the change from strife to strife
That passes o'er the wildering scene
I only feel that every power –
And thou hadst given much to me
Was spent upon the present hour
Was never turned My God to thee.'

He did not like the poem. It was so defeatist. Some of his poems were much more hopeful, as if amidst his misery there was still hope of happiness. He went through his notebook, reading through poems he had written when he felt better. Might he yet overcome the foul demons that plagued him? How good it would have been to spend Christmas with Milly, he thought, watching the snow fall by the window of his hut. And the poison of jealousy again flooded his blood.

'What time is it?' he murmured, peering out of the window. The snow hit the pane like tiny fluttering moths. 'Is it really only midday? Just one more glass of wine, then I'll go,' he said to himself, resignedly. 'I've had my fill of this miserable dungeon for today!'

He slammed the door of the hut, walking easy as he might, finding his way across the hills, a bottle of whisky in his pocket to keep him company. 'You think you are Gods!' he called to the trees. 'All because you enjoy your dreams without bother. Oh, how I envy your stillness, your silent grandeur, your ecstasy! – Charlotte, is that you? Why are you hanging on my heels? Yes, I am talking to trees. Don't tell me what I can talk to, or what I must do! Go away! I will not war with you, Charlotte! That's what you want isn't it? Well, I won't! – Oh, come back, you fool! – Charlotte, where have you gone?'

He stumbled on through the snow, taking drinks from the whisky as he went. After some time, he saw he was in reach of Haworth. 'Father! Father'! he cried as he stumbled on. 'How I need holiness now!' He peered into the darkness of the night. 'Where is my father? Pray tell me. – My father, you know, has holiness in his pockets.' Tired and weary, he broke suddenly into drunken, delirious laughter. Then fell back quickly into misery. 'How much more can my poor brain take before it breaks!' he cried, walking into a sturdy oak. He beat its trunk with his fists. 'You don't feel it do you?' he shouted furiously. 'You don't feel a thing! If I tell you the sky rejects you, that the grass won't grow round your feet, that the light will forget you, you would wave me away with contempt. Ah, you know nothing of hate, of joy, of love ...You have no heart, so how could you feel unhappy? A heart can only be stirred if there's a heart to stir ... But you have no need of a heart, you see – of a mind.' He touched the soreness on his knuckles. 'Yet, see how your hardness wounds me.'

He stumbled on further, and further, finding himself on Main Street, calling to people as he went. 'Who are you, sir?' he cried, a wildness in his manner. Someone was standing in his way. 'And tell me, if you will, who am I?'

'Yer name is Branwell Brontë,' said the man, taking him by the arm. 'And ye shouldna be drunk like this.'

'Drunk?' Branwell said sottishly. 'You think I am drunk? I am far more likely to be insane. There is a kind of refuge in insanity, you know. I intend to try it!' He went for the bottle of whisky in his pocket. Finding it empty, he cast it away by the roadside so that it rolled down the hill. He pointed up to the parsonage, hidden in mist. 'They want me to rise in the world you know – my father – my sisters.' He laughed and climbed onto a low wall beside them, then fell off. He climbed onto it again, balancing himself with his arms. 'Is this how you do it?' he laughed, his arms cast out at his sides. 'Is this how you rise?' He raised his face to the sun, coming through the clouds. 'Tell me sun, how do you rise? You are the one who knows best!'

'You'll not rise drownin' i' drink,' said the man.

'What are you doing?' said Branwell, as the man reached up and pulled him down by his arms. 'How dare you pull me about, you rogue! Leave me alone I say, or I'll give you a hiding! – I gave him a hiding, you know. Oh, a poet can fight if he wants. Byron was a boxer too. Though I doubt he could box like me.'

'I'm takin' ye home,' said the man. 'I shall stay out here,' said Branwell. 'I am not ungrateful to you, sir, for thinking of my needs, but I am not so deserted as you think. Drink and laudanum are my fellow companions here. And grand companions they are! I am not alone. Laudanum allows me such ro-man-tic wanderings, such pastures, such love as the world denies, an irr-e-futable gift to the mind.'

'It'll kill ye,' said the voice.

'I want to see Milly,' said Branwell, tears in his eyes, as he allowed the man to help him down. 'Will you take me to Milly?'

'I'm takin' ye up tuh t' parsonage,' said the man. 'Ere, put yer arm round me shoulder.'

'What is it? – Is he ill?' cried the parson, opening the door in a hurry.

Joe Draper lifted his eyes calmly, and gazed at the parson in silence.

'Thank you Joe, you are more than kind,' said Patrick. 'Will you let me give you some money?' Patrick fumbled in his pockets and pulled out some coins.

'Oh, I dunna want money, Reverend,' said Joe, ashamed for the parson's embarrassment.

'Please,' said Patrick, holding it out in his palm. 'Please Joe, take it. – How long has he been like this?'

Joe Draper took the coins and put them into his pocket. 'He were like it when I found him, at bottom o' t' hill just now.'

Branwell stood wet and shivering. The parson nodded his head slowly, surveying his son carefully; his unkempt clothes, his damp, dishevelled hair. 'Thank you, Joe. I bid you good-day,' he said quietly.

Joe Draper turned and went through the gate.

Branwell, still at the door, put his hands to his father's cheeks, weeping. 'My poor father,' he said. 'What a worthless son you have sired! Better I had never been born!'

Patrick shook his head.

'Let me tell you a secret, father. The devil is a one-eyed monster ... He plays a very seductive tune. You must close your ears to his music. This one-eyed monster is ubiq ... ubiq ... ubiquitous. He is here! – He is there! – Look! – Look! He is everywhere!' He lowered his voice and whispered in his father's ear, 'I have it in mind to kill him.'

Patrick urged him inside. But Branwell put out his hands. 'I am not fit to walk beneath your roof,' he slurred. 'And anyway, I can't bear the sound of that clock! – Oh Time, Time, the ever constant tyrant!' He glanced backwards at the gravestones, the church tower, stiff against the sky. 'Out here I can be a sort of chimera. I can escape. – In there I am Branwell Brontë. And oh, what an idiot he is!' He covered his face with his hands. 'There is someone I need to kill, Father,' he whispered. 'Will you lend me your pistol?'

Patrick drew a breath. 'Come into the house, will you!' he demanded fiercely. 'I can't imagine what rubbish you have in your head just now, or why you are here. You want to borrow my pistol to kill somebody? What sort of talk is this?'

Branwell sat down on the parsonage steps. His father sat down beside him. 'I feel like an alien on my own planet,' Branwell moaned. 'I feel like a polar bear might in the jungle.' He turned his face to his father. 'What would a polar bear do in the jungle, Father? How would it manage its mind?'

'Oh, this talk about polar bears!' Patrick blustered, waving his hand. 'Why would a polar bear be living in the jungle in the first place? How would it get there? You must stop inventing, Branwell, stay with the truth.'

'Truth?' said Branwell, gazing at his father dreamily. 'If I stayed with the truth, I wouldn't be able to manage that either, it's a dirty hellish mess. I'd be worse than a polar bear in a jungle. I have to forget the truth, Father. It destroys me.'

'Your imagination will destroy you if anything does,' said Patrick wearily. – 'Oh, don't look so grave, my son, I can't stand it.' Patrick stood up quickly, his great height towering above Branwell on the steps. 'You must try to be the best you can, for the sake of the people who love you!'

'This love you are always talking about, Father. Where is it? If I ever had it, someone has stolen it away.'

'You are very much loved, Branwell, and you have no right to deny it!' said the parson adamantly. 'The love people have for you also belongs to them. Love is a sharing, a sacred thing that ties our souls together. And it must not be torn asunder! – My God, Branwell, you do try my nerves!'

'Ah yes,' said Branwell, suddenly solemn. 'The secret about our family, is that we have never torn our souls away from each other. And there's a price to be paid for that.' His voice fell low. 'I need more laudanum.' He struggled up. 'Did you hear me, Father? – I need more laudanum!'

'Silence!' said Patrick. He looked at him straight. 'Go into the house and clean up.'

Branwell went into the hall and stood silent, looking about strangely. He put his hands to his face. 'My dead mother, who I did not know,' he wailed. 'My dear dead sisters who I loved. What has happened to those loves, Father? Are they as dead as the flesh that was once their dwelling? Or are they finally at peace from love, resting in the earth? Oh such happy rest! Or do they still live, sometimes raging in the wind? Do their ecstasies reach from the tender blossoms in spring, their kisses reach us as fragrances?'

'Love continues in our Heavenly Father's sanctuary,' said the parson, sighing and wringing his hands.

Branwell was silent and thoughtful for a moment. 'I need some brandy,' he said, finally.

'You need your bed,' Patrick murmured, abstractedly. 'You must get back to work tomorrow.'

'Work, ah, yes,' Branwell muttered, his eyes closing.

'Take my arm,' said Patrick. He conducted Branwell out of the hall to his bedroom. He watched him wash then helped him into his bed. Within minutes he was sound asleep.

34

Another year. Another March. But it did not feel like March; it felt like December. The skies above Luddenden Foot station were dark that day. The tree opposite the window of his hut had never come into bud; it was dying. Branwell could no longer discern what his thoughts and feelings meant, or where they came from; so much he'd repressed, so much he had tried to forget. But worst of all, he was starting to forget himself, and that was fatal. He could hear the sound of the hooves again, deep, deep in his mind . . . He looked in his file of drawings and poems for comfort, and found a recent poem he'd been trying to finish.

> *'Amid the worlds wide din around*
> *I hear from far a solemn Sound*
> *That says "Remember Me!"* . . .
>
> *I when I heard it say amid*
> *The bustle of a Town like room*
> *Neath skies by smoke stain'd vapours hid,*
> *By windows, made to show their gloom –*
> *The desk that held my Ledger book*
> *Beneath the thundering rattle shook*
> *Of Engines passing by*
> *The bustle of the approaching train*
> *Was all I hoped to rouse the brain*
> *Or startle apathy.'*

It was a plea from his poetry that he would never desert it. He found it strange that he had needed to write it down like that. Poetry stalked him constantly, but he was drowning in apathy now. It had somehow happened again; he had got himself sacked! He sat making drawings of dying, wingless birds, crags without sunlight ... and demons. He had scarcely got through Christmas with a full night's sleep. `*March 1842'*, said his calendar. Everything around him seemed changed. He could see Milly's figure in the dying tree opposite his window. He could see her face in the clouds.

The March winds blasted against his hut, almost as if at any moment they might lift it. He hoped they would take him up to heaven, where life would no longer bother him. 'Do what you will!' he shouted to the silence, and laughed madly. 'Dear God! – Oh, you are indeed bountiful! So bountiful!' He rested his head in his hands, mumbling on, continuing his bitter prayer. After a while he braced himself and found the ledgers again, turning the pages carefully. There had been a discrepancy in the accounts. Money was missing. He had needed money badly, but he had not stolen a penny from the accursed railways! Stealing wasn't something he did. He would beg, he would borrow, but no, he would not steal! – Though he knew he'd been careless. He'd been more than careless; he'd been downright negligent. Now he must suffer, in shame, in agony, in humiliation.

He would have to see Brown. He'd say how it was. He would tell him how he had somehow lost his mind, his thoughts, his intelligence, everything, but had kept on trying to do the ledgers and had somehow ended up writing poems instead. He would have to explain himself now in a sensible way. He felt feverish. How could he convince his father that he hadn't been stealing, that he'd simply been a bit too casual? He knew they said that he drank too much and took drugs. That part was true. He liked a drink when he was miserable. And he did need laudanum for his headaches. But he did not steal. He had seen their agitation, the senior official, thinking the worst, the others frowning. The harassment had been too dreadful. The senior man had gone on and on in a rant. At a half past five earlier that day they finished. It had been like a funeral service. And it was in a way. If money had gone, either in numbers or cash, they would have it back. They intended to deduct it from his wages.

Spring was starting up. Neither his friends in the area pleading his case, nor his own protestations had helped him. He sat shivering, feeling somehow shrunken, like a creature only half-born, like a lame bird struggling from an egg. He felt so ill and tired. He gazed at the rain lashing against the window, then rested his head on the desk. All he could see in his mind just now were Milly's ecstatic eyes, as she'd run to him in that glorious spring of their love. He held the image and would not let it go. He would – not – let – it – go.

35

To calm himself, Michael had gone into The Old King's Head to rest. He didn't feel talkative today. He sat in silence in a corner, staring at space. He had placed himself close to the window, so he could gaze outside and not have to look at the men. He didn't want to face them just now. Neither did he feel like sitting alone in his cottage. And he'd suffered enough of Matthew's woe over the last few days. His own was a hateful kind of grief. He had not known it with any other bereavement.

He had lost dear Milly. She'd been gone five days. Matthew had mounted his horse and gone out searching. He'd known, of course, where to look. He'd found her on her way to Yorkshire. She'd been wandering the moors, looking for Branwell again, just as before, in that state of confusion she'd often found herself in since he'd left. One day she wanted him, the next she was shying away. At such times, Michael had been perplexed. She wanted Matthew. She wanted Branwell. She couldn't live two lives at once. Now it didn't matter. Nothing mattered any more.

Michael rubbed his eyes. He was weary and sick at heart. Milly had told him to discourage Branwell, and that's what he'd done. She'd never have lived in Haworth anyway, he reasoned. And Branwell wouldn't have lived in Broughton, either. He heaved a sigh. He had shouted at her, blamed her for her confusion, told her to sort herself out. And he had made her worse.

And all the while, Matthew had kept her comfortable, tending to all her needs, sitting with her quietly by the fire at night, taking her out walking in the daytime, trying to work things out. And he had asked him constantly if there would ever be a day when she might love him in the way she loved Branwell.

But Michael had known there would never be such a day. Her love with Branwell was a dream kind of love, a memory that she couldn't let go of. It had been a tragedy. She'd been pulled between the dream and the real, caught like a sunbeam that doesn't know which way to shine. And the strain of it had finally killed her. Matthew had brought her home early that morning, strewn across the back of his mare, dead, bedraggled, like a withered, uprooted flower. He'd found her out in the country collapsed by a stream. The trees, the elements, had ravaged her and made her their own. Now she was lying dead at Matthew's house, waiting for a priest, waiting for a coffin. Matthew had taken her straight there before coming to fetch him. 'It was you who loved her best,' he'd said, wringing his hands wretchedly. But Michael had seen he'd been quite immovable in his strength, and had promised to carry out all the necessary arrangements.

Every impulse of self-loathing still churning inside him, Michael had, for the time-being at least, done weeping outwardly. Though he wept profusely inside. And he knew his tears would come until the end of his days. He had done it all wrong. He had wanted Milly close by. He'd actively stopped her from going to live at Haworth. That was the truth of the matter. With a little less selfishness he might have let her follow her heart, instead of allowing Matthew to have her as he had. He felt sick with pain, as if physically wounded, as if he had been in a war. For he had in truth. He had been in a war with himself since Branwell had gone. He could not count the times he had asked himself if he ought to visit Haworth and find him. A fine young gentleman, he was bound to have risen in the world.

But Milly would have been out of place in all that, surely, he reflected. He breathed a little better as he thought of it. Could he find any solace anywhere, he wondered, any whisper at all that said it wasn't his fault? He felt like a murderer now, as if he had killed her, as if all three of them had killed her. 'I loved her best, did I?' he murmured, bending his head. The news had got round quickly. The villagers had flocked from their homes, to see Matthew riding into Broughton on his dark brown mare, his body proud, upright as ever, Milly lying over his horse. All through the night and the morning heavy rainstorms had lashed at the streets, thunder had broken the air, lightning had flashed on the windows.

But a terrible silence had pervaded the place after Matthew had ridden down the street. And it remained. I have known this town all my life, thought Michael, as he raised his head. And yet I suddenly feel an outsider; like a loathsome person who has just walked in through the door, a man despised. He would not meet the eyes of the men around him. It was time to leave. He would walk near Parker's house. He would walk through the trees. He would think. He dare not look on Milly again just yet. He'd do that later.

36

Eliza Branwell rarely walked out so far, especially in the early morning. But she'd been worried. The letter from Branwell had been enigmatic and disturbing. She'd needed to clear her head. She liked to know the children were safe. Anne was still at Thorp Green with the Robinson family, and Emily and Charlotte were in Brussels. But where was Branwell? He hadn't arrived home as he'd promised. The least hint of him going into one of his dark depressions made her panic.

Patrick was working at home that day on a sermon, and would be there if Branwell returned. But Branwell had been due yesterday. 'I hope he hasn't been silly,' she murmured, watching her footing. She'd never liked the tone of his drawings; men hanging from nooses, ugly demons that gaped out of pages with eyes big as saucers. What had happened, she wondered, to her highly creative nephew, once the life and soul of the parsonage? Both she and Patrick had expected he'd rise to his destiny sooner or later, the destiny of a writer, a great writer, or an artist. But it didn't seem to have happened.

But they still hung on to their hopes, wondering how he would cope at the railway, hoping he'd find time for his writing and not let himself down. Lately though, his countenance had lost its energy. He was distant when he visited the parsonage. He was always preoccupied. If only he didn't drink so much, she sighed. And she loathed the laudanum; it made him forget his troubles, but he also forgot who he was. There were deep-rooted issues bothering him. She also knew that not a single one of them knew what those issues were, or the evidence would have shown in their eyes.

Charlotte treated him badly nowadays, she reflected irritably. It was a pity. They'd been close in childhood, doing their Angrian writings and drawings together, shutting themselves off, whispering and laughing.

Didn't anything remain of all that? How could such energy, such creative imagination, be lost, swamped beneath the sea of life? She lifted her skirts and made her way across a muddy part of the path. She realised, pleasantly, she was walking more easily today. She was actually stronger. Last week she hadn't been well, and had started to hear the voices of the dead, a most disagreeable sign.

She adjusted the strings of her grey silk bonnet, and decided to walk on further. She'd had to get away from the parsonage for a while. It was quite disconcerting not knowing where Branwell was. Eliza felt irritable about it as well as concerned. She passed the birches near the foot of the stream then stepped carefully on the large flat stones Branwell had laid in his youth; they were still secure. She breathed heavily, feeling a little tired. Poor, poor Branwell, perhaps he had gone to Brown's? She mused on the past while she walked, the joy in her nephew's eyes, his greedy conversations.

Patrick's eyes were getting worse. That bothered her too. And her own eyesight was weakening; she often got headaches. She ascended to where the rocks began and the dark trees. The freshness of the morning was bracing. Turning to look, she could see she had walked some way. Her eyes wandered across the hills and valleys, the little houses, the dew of early morning on their rooftops. Suddenly she stopped.

Several yards away, beneath a withered hawthorn, she made out the shape of a man. He looked so still. She went towards him slowly. He lay with his back towards her, huddled in a heap. She caught her breath as she looked. Immediately, she recognised Branwell's hair. Moving forward quickly, she almost fell over. Her heart beat fast. He looked so weak and dirty. 'What on earth are you doing here?' she asked, incredulously. She waited afraid, hoping, praying he would move.

'Why, Aunt,' he murmured sleepily, 'am I dreaming?'

'No you are not,' she said flatly. 'I am no apparition, Branwell. And I am angry.'

Branwell rubbed his eyes, and gazed at her wearily.

'Have you been here all night?' She looked on the ground and all about him. The grass was scarcely disturbed. He might have been there for days.

'All night? I'm not sure. I might have been here a day, a week, a year. Does it matter?'

'Well, of course it does. – When did you last eat?'

'Where am I? Have I died?' he asked in a strange low tone.

'Don't be ridiculous,' she whispered, sitting down beside him. 'Have you died, indeed! What a silly question. I hope heaven will offer you more than me sitting here in wet skirts! You are out on the Haworth moors, and it's a good job it hasn't rained.'

'Heaven wouldn't have me, Aunt,' he said, wincing with the pain in his aching limbs. 'You should forget me, Aunt Branwell. I am nothing but a nuisance to you all. I should have died out here on the moor.'

'So you should,' she sighed. 'Then the crows would peck out your eyes. And what a grand sight you'd be when they found you, eh? Something quite splendid for your father to bury, don't you think? Hasn't he enough miseries? – Had you intended to come home?' She straightened her skirts. There was mud on the bottom of her petticoat.

Branwell bit at his nails. 'Home? –You mean to the parsonage?'

'Well, what other home have you? What other home have any of us?'

'I'm finished, Aunt,' he said in a rush. 'They think I've been stealing money from the railways.'

Aunt Branwell's bony hand waved in the air. 'Oh, that they should make such a fuss over what? – A mere couple of shillings?'

'But it isn't true,' he moaned. 'I haven't. – I'm sorry. This isn't how I wanted it to be.' He sat up, resting his head in his hands. 'I wanted things to be so much better than this.'

'Of course you did,' said his aunt. 'We all want things to be better. Do you think I want these bunions? Why it's taken me almost an hour to get to this spot. But I was determined to do it. I had a mission, you see. Though I didn't understand it at the time. Now I do. It was to find my nephew lying on the moor like a wild exhausted animal ready to die. Oh, what a to-do.'

'I have done good things, Aunt,' Branwell protested wearily. 'I have known great sensations. I have been as wild as the wind on the moor. I have shone as hot as the sun, scorching the heather in summer. I . . .'

'Yes, yes,' Aunt Branwell coughed. 'You have done all this and more.'

'. . . I have thrown myself like a great sea against the rocks, again and again, without fear!'

Eliza Branwell shook her head, what grand speeches her nephew came out with sometimes. 'You can't be perfect,' she said flatly. 'Now come on and get up. There's good food back at the parsonage.'

'Human beings are far too complex for them ever to be perfect, Aunt,' he said struggling to his feet.

'We can but try,' said Aunt Branwell. 'Each day we must try. We have to be open to God's revelations, and equal to them.'

'When we have gone and the world is dead, what will it matter what we did or said?' Branwell murmured.

Eliza sighed loudly. 'You shouldn't have been working for the railways anyway. Why, the railways are mad, uncaring things. They make me tetchy like the damp that rises from the parsonage floors in winter.' Branwell's hair hung limp and greasy on his shoulders. His clothes were dirty and his bootlace was undone. 'And tie that bootlace, or you'll trip.'

'I'm not going anywhere,' he said stubbornly.

'You are coming home, I tell you,' she said crossly. 'If you act like a child, I shall treat you like a child.'

'Oh, Aunt Branwell,' he moaned. 'All I have in the world is what I stand up in.'

'You have things at your lodgings, haven't you?'

'One or two things.'

'Well then.'

'But I haven't a penny to my name, Aunt. They've deducted money from my wages.'

'Have they now. Well, let them have it,' she shrugged. 'You don't need their money.' She placed her hand on his back.

'Earlier today, you know,' he said suddenly wistful, 'at dawn, I had a vision.'

They were both silent a moment.

'What sort of vision?' Eliza fixed her eyes on him carefully.

'It was a sort of person ... Yet it wasn't a person. It was me, I think, in another guise. The best part of me. The best I could be. It came to talk to me.'

'Oh my – you have seen your soul!' gasped Eliza.

'It told me things I have always known deep down, but refused to think about.'

Eliza clasped her hands and widened her eyes. 'My dear nephew, what did this being tell you?'

Branwell spoke seriously and solemnly. 'That I need not fear. That I was good. That I might become pure. That there was purity to be had somewhere, away from this world.'

Eliza Branwell could feel her heart beating faster. The weariness in her nephew's face just now was alarming. And he'd seen his soul. Would he die right now, any minute? How terrible if he did. How could she prevent it? She panicked for a moment. The early morning light shone into his eyes from the moor. He was lost and dejected, not a penny in his pocket, not a morsel in his stomach. 'Well, Branwell,' she said firmly. 'I think you should forget it for now. You were probably delirious.'

'How far we are from our dreams,' he said, as if in a trance. 'I have wanted so many things. I have tried so many things. I have walked to the ends of the earth for all of you ... Don't you see? I have wanted to look at the seas from all places at once, to see each hurl of wave as it happened, to hear each roar of wind, to know how the rocks and moonlight speak in the night ...' Milly had made him feel like that. She had filled him with wonder. 'Love stretches the boundaries of wonder, beyond and beyond,' he said softly. 'It enters the bones and is somehow lost in feeling. It becomes something else. It becomes my visitation, Aunt. My visitation understood such things, had experienced them.'

'You're killing yourself,' said Aunt Branwell. He looked at her and sighed.

'Well, what if I am? I might be doing it for the greater good. Wouldn't it be better if I were out of the picture?'

'How can you think such a thing? – You're on laudanum aren't you? You'll kill yourself, I tell you.'

'I am trying to get out of your lives. I've failed to become what you wanted. What all of you wanted.'

'These are very strong words, Branwell!' said Eliza sticking her chin in her neck and frowning. 'Now be silent. – You could have gone to London, you know. You might have been a great artist.' Branwell leaned against the hawthorn, tiredly. 'Ah, London,' he murmured. 'Such big, wide streets, such wonderful crescents, such grand, high buildings ... And the people all elegance, all elegance.' He pointed to himself. 'Me, Wiggins, in London?'

Eliza observed him with some concern. It was ages since he'd used his childhood name. 'Are you coming back to the parsonage with me?' she asked him gently. 'Or will you stay here forever?'

Branwell braced himself and gazed round the moor. His trousers clung damply to the thin muscles of his legs. Slowly they made their way home.

37

If only I could be out and about again! Branwell thought, restlessly pacing around the parlour. He had seen that morning his father's darkest scowl. This new failure was disastrous. Oh, he knew what he really thought, despite his continued kindness. He thought him idle, false, immoral – and perhaps – for he had really begun to believe it now – insane. How had he come to this? He slumped into a chair. It was all too much. He felt reduced to a ghostly presence, thrown on the mercy of his mind. Emily and Charlotte were still at Pensionnet Heger. Anne was still at Thorp Green, which left only his father and Aunt Branwell in the parsonage for company. He searched constantly for the sharp edge of his thinking. He attempted to write, but nothing came to his mind. His father had assured him something was likely to turn up, and that he shouldn't despair. But apart from tutoring and working on the railways, what was there? He was seriously in need of money. He consoled himself with reading for a while, and went to play the cottage piano.

But he wasn't consoled for long. Soon he was pacing the house again, wringing his hands. Might he find work with the railways again, he wondered. They had no proof he'd been stealing, and a discrepancy in the accounts was hardly a criminal offence. Thinking he'd send a letter to Francis Grundy, he braced himself and went to find pen and paper. It was unlikely though, that Francis would know of any work. The railways weren't doing well. But he wrote on anyway, his hand trembling and the ink blotching on the page.

'I cannot avoid the temptation to cheer my spirits by scribbling a few lines to you while I sit here alone – all the household being at church – the sole occupant of an ancient parsonage among lonely hills, which probably will never

hear the whistle of an engine till I am in my grave. After experiencing, since my return, extreme pain and illness, with mental depression worse than either, I have at length acquired health and strength and soundness of mind, far superior, I trust, to anything shown by that miserable wreck you used to know under my name. I can now speak cheerfully and enjoy the company of another without the stimulus of six glasses of whisky; I can write, think and act with some apparent approach to resolution, and I only want a motive for exertion to be happier than I have been in years. But I feel my recovery from <u>almost insanity</u> to be retarded by having nothing to listen to except the wind moaning among old chimneys and older ash trees, nothing to look at except heathery hills walked over when life had all to hope for and nothing to regret with me – no one to speak to except crabbed old Greeks and Romans who have been dust the last five thousand years.'

He couldn't even contemplate entering the church, he told Grundy, he hadn't the least inclination. But if something were available with the railways – anything – he'd take it.

But his mind kept soaring to the lofty realms of literature. Oh, how he longed to write! He needed new inspirations, new themes, new vistas ... What was he? A miserable, failed railway clerk, who had left behind his laughter and fun. Wasn't it time to try again? As he combed his hair by the mirror, the sight of his sunken cheeks and pallor, his wild, intense eyes, stunned him. Hurriedly he left the parsonage and raced down the hill.

In the Black Bull Inn, seated at a table by the fire, he talked with Brown. 'I'm wasting my energies on hope,' he told him. 'I need some useful occupation.'

Brown listened carefully. He hadn't seen Branwell for a week. Branwell spoke in gasps, as if he were out of breath. 'Will you have some of these potatoes, John?' he said. He dug his fork into a potato and passed it across.

'You're doing yourself no good keep leaving your food,' said Brown.

'I'm not very hungry,' Branwell murmured. 'But it's kind of you to buy me a meal.' He leaned back and sighed. 'The question is – is it not? How to find work? I am in the hands of fate!' He laughed weakly.

'A terrible place to be,' said Brown, who was coughing a lot that evening. 'It's all a matter of luck, of course. You need some luck. – So what are your sisters up to in Brussels? It was good of your father to go and help settle them in.'

'Yes, he feels better knowing where they're living,' said Branwell thoughtfully. 'But Emily won't be happy. She makes good progress, however. From the sounds of things though, they don't like their classmates very much.'

They could hear something happening on the high street.

'What's going on?' said Brown. Branwell frowned and went to the door. There was a gathering of twenty or so men, who appeared extremely incensed. Brown followed and stood beside him. 'They're going to join the Chartist activities in Halifax,' he said. 'They've been making arms. There'll be bloodshed, I know it.'

Branwell could feel his skin tightening with tension. Would his father have to join in? Though he doubted they'd listen if he did. Men were often irrational when rowdy. 'It seems there are rumblings of Luddite activities in the area again,' he murmured. Factory workers had been subtly damaging machinery.

'Weightman looks ill,' said Brown, as they returned to their drinks.

'Does he?' said Branwell, surprised. Weightman was normally in perfect health, it was strange to hear different. Though he'd been working way beyond his duty, and often involved himself in political disputes in the village.

'Though it isn't any wonder,' said Brown. 'I've heard he's out visiting, even at dead of night.'

'That's right,' said Branwell, finishing the last of his drink. 'He's as dedicated as Father.' Leaving Brown, he made his way to the parsonage.

Having passed by the commotion, he went to the parlour and sat about brooding for a while. What a ridiculous excuse for a man he'd become. He was nothing apart from his imaginings. He looked curiously at his hands. He had painted with them, he had written with them, he had played the cottage piano with them – and they had touched Milly, so many times. He flexed his fingers. And yes, yes – he had fought Parker with them too! They had served him well.

But his mind was a mess. He could not sort it out properly. It did not serve him as it should. He tried, yet again to turn his back on thoughts that upset him, bracing himself and taking a deep breath. He'd made some progress with his poetry and had been getting into print. Surely it counted for something? He must force his way out of captivity, break out of his chains! He would start things and leave them because he wasn't happy with their standard. On finding them later he'd be pleasantly surprised at what he'd written. How strange it was, he thought curiously, that he judged himself so harshly and inconsistently. It was part of his weakness. He held the sides of his head. Was he finally going mad? Would he actually lose hold of the reins of sanity? He heard his father enter.

'That was a wicked one!' said Patrick, coming to join him. 'Those men out there are their own worst enemies! There's neither sense nor reason amongst them. – Weightman defies me, you know. He will do what he wants. He shares his food with the poor – and that's all well and good. But he walks out into the midst of the rabble whatever I tell him. Oh, those weapons they have, those things.' He hesitated. 'Perhaps I'm growing too old for it all,' he sighed. He sat down on a chair by the fire. 'It takes young men.'

'Young men don't have your wisdom, Father,' said Branwell. 'We are wild and filled with passion. It isn't the way.'

Patrick sighed. 'It is and it isn't,' he said thoughtfully. He rubbed his knees, which were aching. 'You need passion for progress. There is never progress without passion.'

'Doesn't Willie have passion, Father?' asked Branwell frowning.

'To be sure he does,' said Patrick. 'Weightman has passion enough. But he will not use it as he should. He walks into danger.'

Branwell watched his father mumbling a prayer. It amazed him how easily his father could pray, any place, any time. Branwell shuddered at all that praying, all that succumbing to something you could not see.

'Don't be despondent, Branwell,' said his father, opening his eyes. 'Times will get better. There are so many changes afoot. We must all keep praying and hoping.'

This was the nearest his father could get to an answer. So far as Branwell was concerned, the only spiritual forces a man could harness were those in himself. He'd created gods and devils of his own. He knew he had planted good and evil in the characters he'd formed. He'd explored those powers in his stories.

'You must not scorn me,' said Patrick solemnly. 'Oh, I know what you think. You think I need instruction. That there is no God. That it is all pure imagination!' His voice fell to a whisper. 'God will survive, you'll see.'

Branwell stood up slowly and went to the window. 'Can I not wander a little, Father?' he asked. 'Will God not allow it? Let any young man question his God, surely? – Just as he might question his father. And love him the same . . . It's just that I get confused.'

'I know, I know,' said the parson tiredly. 'We are all confused, my son. Consciousness is a very untidy business.'

'I have things to do,' Branwell said, rising to his feet. Everything was so uncertain, but at least he could attempt to write. That much was under his control. One by one his dreams were collapsing about him. He imagined them now, strange wild creatures in the outbacks of his mind, forever lost. He would leave them there and try not to mourn. There was a kind of suspense in his soul, as if it had ceased to breathe. He felt lost to fate. But at the same time he found again that strange creative energy that urged him on, battling the repulsion he so often felt for himself, telling him he might yet succeed.

Fate was all too busy. Too self-willed to listen to Patrick's warnings, William Weightman had been in and out of the houses, up and down the hill, sitting sometimes for hours with people, regardless of how they were afflicted. Shocked and bewildered, he was suddenly taken ill. But he would not accept it. He was weak and delirious, rambling on about what he had to do, where he must go, trying to get out of his bed and having to be restrained.

'I always feared it,' said Patrick distraught by his bedside. 'Life advances fast with its weaponry, Willie! I am so sorry if I . . .'

William Weightman reached for the parson's hand. Whatever else Patrick Brontë did, he wouldn't be allowed to bludgeon himself for this. Some sickness was out to murder him, and it seemed it would have its way. 'I am not a cowardly fellow,' he groaned, 'though I suspect my strength has been misguided. It is now too late to make amends with myself, I fear. I do not know if I am ravaged by innocence or stupidity. However, I am nonetheless ravaged!'

Hearing of Weightman's death, Branwell was stilled to the bone. Had all their visits to his sick bed been in vain? Had all his father's prayers come to nothing? He hated the way his father justified the taking of Willie's life. What good was the man in heaven? He was far more use on earth. His father, visibly weakened, sat about staring at space. The whole of Haworth mourned.

38

'I've news for ye!' Joe Draper laughed to his wife. Violet Draper had been worried that day about her daughter's imminent labour. Every birth always brought the fear of death. The Reverend Brontë had married their daughter Bess last summer to Barry Richards, a twenty-two year old carpenter who lived near the church. 'We've a little grandson!' said Joe. 'An' our Bess is on top o' t' world!'

Violet had been up all night and had gone for a nap. It seemed she'd slept through it all. Joe and a new young doctor from a nearby village had brought the little boy to birth. And what a screaming bundle he was. Violet quickly got up from her chair and rubbed her eyes. 'An me i' t' Land o' Nod an' all! – 'Ere, let me 'ave a see.'

'Well now, I'd best get Barry,' said Joe. 'He'll be waitin'.'

Bess had been living with Barry and his father, but had wanted to be with her mother for the birth of the baby. Violet Draper went to her daughter's bedside, full of smiles and happiness. Her very first grandchild, and they hadn't even thought of a name. The forceful bundle of life kicked and thrust his arms at the air in curious and surprised wonder. 'He's a lot to say for himself,' she said, taking the child in her arms. She imagined herself helping bring him up, hearing his first words, seeing his first little steps. The house was quiet now. Some of her children were out playing in the street, those that were in were shocked into silent awe. 'Look – come and see!' she called. 'His eyes are just like his father's! – Reverend Brontë said he'd pay us a visit today. I must tidy things up a bit 'ere. I hope yer feelin' alright, lass. Ye must let us know if yer not.'

She returned the child to her daughter, and set about cleaning the surfaces and taking soiled linen to the washroom. Violet had been taking in washing for people; she was lucky to be strong. It had brought in the odd shilling. She was fortunate enough to have a little caddy of tea she hadn't opened yet. Someone she worked for had given it to her as a present. She'd make the Reverend a nice cup of tea, and they'd celebrate the birth of the baby. 'So what will ye call him, then?' she asked Bess.

Bess gazed into her baby's face, touching his cheeks. 'We can find a name for him later, Mam,' she said softly. 'Oh, how I love the dear little thing, how I love him!'

The laughter and rushing about that afternoon brought a new spirit to the house. Violet gazed at her children about her, her daughter sitting in bed nursing her baby. How lovely she was, Violet thought, her skin fresh with new motherhood. 'Ye must put 'im to yer breast right now,' she told her. 'Let 'im get used to ye. – See, let me show ye.'

Violet Draper was a gentle, flaxen-haired woman, with a core of steel. The baby suckling, her children watching, the quiet sunlight streaming into the room – it was all so beautiful. She could hear the church bells ringing, and had a sudden vision of skylarks and thrushes about her; she could almost hear a nightingale's song. She felt the surge of the sun, entering her body from the window with an almost blinding light. Going to the kitchen, she searched about in the cupboards. 'I'll make that pot o' tea for Reverend Brontë!' she called. 'An' I'll see if there's a bit o' that cake!'

39

After the death of William Weightman, Haworth was seized by an almost tangible stillness. The villagers went about silently, children were less boisterous, there was a sort of hush in the breeze, a light, careful fall, even in the rain.

And there was further torment in the parsonage.

Branwell went to look at the clock. It was late afternoon. He could hear his aunt groaning again upstairs. She'd been moaning night and day for almost a week. He took her a drink, and made her more comfortable, though he couldn't bear witnessing her misery. He listened in paralysed fear. Did he not love her as a mother? Had he not seen in her talk, her laughter, his mother alive on earth? What kindness she had in her heart! What unselfishness! He could not dare imagine her seriously ill. It didn't seem fair. And he felt so useless. If only his sisters were there at the parsonage to comfort her. She'd been getting worse that week, but had tried to continue with her duties. She had even gone out talking to people in the village. But it wore her out and she came up the hill in pain. Yesterday she'd returned to the house, crawling along the floor like an old brown moth, her silk skirts damp about her.

The parson entered the house and marched upstairs. 'We must get a doctor!' he declared firmly.

Aunt Branwell put out the flat of her hand in front of him.

'No, Eliza,' said Patrick loudly. 'No! I will not listen to your protests a minute longer! We must get the doctor immediately.' He gazed at her wretchedly. She'd constantly protested they were still in mourning for Weightman, that they needed time to recover, that it was all too much too quickly. She'd be better soon, she'd insisted. But in truth, she had grown quite worse. There were various preparations she kept by her bed, which she occasionally drank. But they rarely had much effect. Each night she moaned.

Patrick drew a deep breath of resolve. 'Go bring the doctor right now!' he said to Branwell.

Branwell left the door wide open and ran down the lane.

'She is very stubborn,' Patrick said, as the doctor examined Eliza, a grave look on his face. 'I had wanted you to come before, but she wouldn't allow it.'

Branwell clung to her hand. His aunt felt cold. He watched the doctor's eyes, trying to read his expression. She had developed an obstruction of the bowel, he said. In carefully framed language, that they understood only too well, he said she was dying.

Patrick gazed out at the graveyard woefully. Must the earth take Eliza too? That greedy uncaring earth! Must it have them all so fast? His throat tightened with tears. He had scarcely caught his breath from the death of Willie, now this . . . Eliza had been so good, so strong. Her long straight back seated in church, her steady, reserved manner; even sometimes shivering with cold in her pew, filled him with affection. She had been like a mother to his children. She had given so much. She had done so much. What of the sound of her footsteps on the parsonage floors? What of the sound of her voice? His limbs felt weak at the thought of what was to come. Try as he would, he could not rid his mind of the faces of death.

Sitting by his aunt's bedside again, later that evening, Branwell's thoughts wandered. What a terrible year it had been. He'd a letter to write to Francis Grundy, though he didn't think he'd write it tonight. What would he tell him, anyway? He searched his mind for a single, happy thought. All the gentleness and kindness of his nature was fast disappearing. He wanted to shout. He wanted to scream. Every accusation, every rebuke, every complaint that had ever been made against him thundered his mind. He rested his head in his hands. He ought to have given his aunt more happiness. What a disappointment he had been! What an embarrassment! And now she was dying. The doctor had given her some medicine. She was sleeping soundly; that in itself was a blessing. He gazed round the empty room. He could not feel her spirit; that powerful force he had known his aunt to be. It was as if she had gone already. His father was out. It was dark outside. The dim light of a candle illuminated the room. He needed to speak of how he felt, but who would he talk to? Perhaps he would write that letter to Francis after all; it might just help. He went for his writing materials.

'. . . I have had a long attendance at the death-bed of Rev Mr Weightman, one of my dearest friends, and now I am attending at the death-bed of my aunt, who has been for twenty years as my mother. I expect her to die in a few hours.'

As he scribbled on, suddenly he came to a stop. There was a chilling stillness around him. A dark, aged shadow moved across the room; a woman his aunt's size. It stayed for a moment then disappeared.

His aunt died several days later. Charlotte and Emily, Branwell realised, couldn't attend her funeral. They were too far away. Branwell shivered at the thought. Would his aunt be laid in her grave without their goodbyes? Well, he sighed, at least Anne would be there. The Robinson's had given her leave. He paced the house and the gardens. He was now in a fearful panic. He felt as if a malevolent force was taking away his loved ones; insidiously, ruthlessly, removing them one by one.

40

What a sombre Christmas it had been. The loss of Willie and Aunt Branwell had left a great hole in the lives of the family as they sat round the fire that evening. Charlotte, Emily and Anne, along with a cousin in Penzance, had inherited equal shares of Aunt Branwell's estate. Though it did little to warm the cold space she had left.

'Just a small memento for you, Branwell,' his father had said with a frown. The male in the family, he would have to find his own way through.

Branwell tried constantly to write. But creativity eluded him. Even my muses are dying, he'd thought, as he'd sat with his pen struggling. Was he to stay at home with Emily and his father doing nothing, nothing at all of any value? Is that what his life would amount to? It was bad, very bad.

He glanced at his sisters, they all seemed healthy enough, though Emily's features were tense. 'I won't be returning to Brussels with Charlotte, Papa,' she said suddenly.

Her father lifted his eyebrows, as if surprised, though he had half expected her words. 'You've informed Monsieur Heger I take it?'

'Yes,' replied Emily with a sigh.

The parson looked at Charlotte and Emily by turns. The whole time Emily was speaking, Charlotte sat on a cushion by the fire, gazing at the flames.

'I'm glad,' Branwell yawned. 'You didn't want to go there anyway.' He too was sitting on the floor, his back to the wall, his chin resting on his knees. His mood had been solemn all Christmas.

'What?' said Charlotte, frowning. 'Oh, Emily must do as she wants.' She bit her knuckles broodingly. 'She was never happy in Brussels. It will be good for Papa if she stays.'

'It's a wise decision, don't you think, Papa?' said Anne, always concerned for the best solution all round.

Patrick changed his position in the chair and crossed his legs. 'You must do whatever is best, my dears,' he said. He opened his eyes widely and looked at them all. 'So that's decided then, is it?'

Charlotte sighed and nodded.

'I'll make some tea,' said Branwell getting up. He took the odds and ends of gifts his family had given him for Christmas up to his room, then came down and went into the kitchen. He could hear them talking in the parlour.

'So you've discussed all this with the Hegers then, Emily?' said his father. 'And what about you, Charlotte? You'll be all on your own. It could be miserable you know, all on your own over there …'

Branwell closed his mind to it all and thought about brewing the tea. The kitchen didn't feel the same without Aunt Branwell. People became a part of you, he reflected. They couldn't just die without taking some of you with them. Little by little he was losing himself somewhere. He wiped his hair from his brow and kept his eyes on the water as he poured it in the pot. He would have to concentrate carefully; his hands were shaking again. How conscientious his father was. Nothing prevented him from going about his work. He'd delivered his services as usual. Not one of his parishioners could have seen how he suffered it was so well hidden. By dint of something hardy in him, like a mighty warrior, his father was sound, invincible, unconquerable.

'We shall all of us find it a better situation if I return alone,' Charlotte said, in an oddly formal voice.

'We've lost so much so quickly,' said Anne shakily. 'Oh, the joys we don't appreciate till they've gone!'

Branwell came in with the tea.

'This will pass, my dear,' said Patrick gently. He patted Anne's hand.

Branwell put down the tray, then placed his arm around her shoulder. 'Father's right, Anne,' he murmured. 'It will pass.' Though he felt totally fragmented, as if he were in bits and pieces, scattered around the house, scattered in every nook and cranny on the moor. Each day the dawn light entered his room, searching. Still he was lost.

Anne went to stand by the window, it seemed, deep in thought. After several minutes, she turned. – 'Return with me, Branwell. Come to Thorp Green,' she said, all of a sudden.

Branwell sat stunned. His sister's cheeks were flushed with emotion.

'What are you up to?' he frowned, putting down the slice of cake he was just about to bite into. They all listened intently.

'It's a bit of a rush, I know,' said Anne, pacing the floor, her arms folded tightly. She went to him and knelt beside him. 'Mrs Robinson thought you might like to tutor Edmund. You'll need time to consider it, of course . . .' She watched him carefully, observing his reaction.

'Is it definite?' he asked, thoughtfully.

Anne nodded. 'I've thought about it all Christmas. You are not exactly excited about tutoring any more than I am,' she said, drawing a breath. 'But I think they've been kind. They will need to have your answer quickly.' She lowered her head. 'It would be good to have your company. They will pay you well, and I'm sure Edmund will like you. He is clever and learns very fast.' She looked away for a moment, thoughtful. 'You would like the house, and there are beautiful places to walk. As long as Edmund learns, you can do as you like.'

Charlotte gazed at the ceiling in silence.

Branwell glanced about the company. Anne's words whirled around in his head, though he hardly felt confident about tutoring again. Nor was he madly inflamed. Yet his heart beat fast at the thought. If the boy was bright, he might actually teach him something. Ah, that it happened like that!

Anne rose and went again to the window. 'You could even find time for your writing,' she said to the glass, a serious tone in her voice. 'You're rarely observed. The Reverend Robinson is often in his study, and Lydia goes off to see friends.'

For several moments, they were all absorbed in silence.

Gradually the family came back to itself. Patrick clapped his hands on his knees. 'Good! Very good!' he cried. 'Well then Anne, what a clever little schemer you are! I suspect you have done a lot of work behind the scenes. Posts like this do not come easily, I know.'

'What are you thinking?' asked Emily, turning to Branwell.

'Well I certainly need a job . . .' said Branwell, getting up. He worked his hands together slowly. His palms were sweating with emotion. The thought of earning some money again was tempting. 'I am not the finest of tutors . . . I have found it difficult to teach my charges in the past . . .'

'You mean they won't work,' Emily corrected quickly.

'Well, yes,' said Charlotte, with a sigh. 'Teaching can be fun if children want to learn. A disaster though, if they don't.'

'You must seize it straight away!' said Patrick. 'Before somebody else does.'

'Poor boy,' said Branwell. 'Do his parents know what they are doing?'

'Aye, I'm sure they do!' said Patrick. 'And they should think themselves lucky to get you!'

'The last situation I was in . . .' Branwell went on.

'Was hilarious!' cried Patrick, standing up. He broke into sudden laughter, turning to the others. 'Branwell had them drawing birds, birds, nothing but birds!'

'But what else could he do, Papa?' said Anne, also starting to laugh. 'If they couldn't pay attention and learn what he was trying to teach them, then they must do whatever kept them happy.'

Emily laughed also. 'Aye, perhaps they'll be famous artists one day.'

'Well at least they enjoyed themselves,' Charlotte said, smiling. 'And what's better than drawing birds? Why, I could draw birds all day!'

'An' so they did!' Patrick said, now chortling. 'All day yesterday, all day today, and all day tomorrow! And like Emily says, they might just be famous too! – Much great art is often spawned from absurdity!'

For several minutes the room was a riot of laughter. All their eyes were suddenly bright with hope.

41

It was a damp January day that met them when they reached Thorp Green. But the sun had come out and a glorious double rainbow had stretched itself over the grounds. It was strikingly low, Anne thought, almost touching the trees. It astonished her. And it also disturbed her. Was it a kind of omen? If it was, it had better be a good one. She hoped for a better future for her family this year. She thought about Charlotte in Brussels alone, and Emily with their father at the parsonage without Aunt Branwell. And she wondered how it would be for Branwell, here at Thorp Green.

She walked down the drive towards the house, glancing back to see if Branwell and Edmund were following. Edmund had seen them arriving. Galloping his horse too fast towards them, he had shamefully fallen off. Had he been with his mother he'd have cried. But when Branwell had rushed to his aid, he had pulled himself together quickly, protesting loudly he was fine.

Anne smiled to herself as she went to the house ahead of them. It had all been quite amusing. Branwell had struggled with the horse and finally mastered it. The boy had calmed very fast. There had been a great deal of talking, a lot of questions, many proud answers. Approaching, she saw that the lady's maid, Ann Marshall, was looking from an upstairs window. She had probably been awaiting their arrival. 'Look,' Anne told her pointing as they met at the door. – `It's a double rainbow!' But the colours were fading as she spoke. The sky began to lose its magic, the previous pinkness turned as she watched, into a dull, dark grey. Small drops of rain wet her face. She entered the house quickly.

The rich scents of perfumes and spices came to her strongly on a flood of warm air. And she could smell once more the familiar scent of lemon oil polish the Robinson's used on their furniture. Lydia Robinson liked to collect antiques. She was particularly fond of her dolls. Anne looked out from the doorway to the edge of the grounds. Where were Branwell and Edmund? A chill east wind had started up.

She felt strange today, arriving back at Thorp Green. She felt older. She felt as if she had changed. The house too seemed different, larger and unfamiliar. Even Branwell wasn't the Branwell she'd known; he was stronger and more in control of himself, though oddly less gentle. Unusually, he'd had little to say on the journey and had fixed his eyes on the passing scenery all the way. But they were both still grieving. 'The gardens are always so grand,' she said to Ann Marshall. 'Whatever the season.'

'Yes,' said Ann Marshall, quietly, in a flat and unfriendly tone. She was a woman of medium build, handsome though not beautiful.

'My brother will be with us shortly,' said Anne. Ann Marshall made no reply. It hadn't been a pleasant journey, thought Anne. The horses seemed to have laboured more than normally, and the roads had been wet and slippery.

Lydia Robinson came into the hall to greet them. 'Anne how nice to see you!' she said, casting her eyes down the drive. 'But what a damp afternoon.'

'We called at Branwell's lodgings on the way,' said Anne. 'We're a little bit later than planned. – I'm afraid Branwell's been delayed . . .' She looked downwards, gazing at the pebbles. 'It's nothing serious, but Edmund's had a slight accident.'

'An accident? – Why what happened?' asked Lydia anxiously. She clasped her hands tightly and went to the door. 'He was riding a little fast,' Anne faltered. 'He attempted to dismount too quickly, and well, he sort of fell off . . .'

'Is he hurt?' asked Lydia, looking horrified. The blood had risen to her cheeks. She wandered on to the pebbles, her eyes searching the distance.

'Thankfully, no,' said Anne, 'though he might have one or two bruises. Branwell is giving him some instruction.'

'He shouldn't be riding that animal unattended,' Lydia said irritably. 'I'm forever telling my husband these things, but he never listens! – Ah, there they are! Edmund, what have you been doing?' Her voice rang with concern.

Branwell and Edmund approached them quickly. Lydia rushed to her son, brushing her hands down his clothes. 'So Mr Brontë has given you your first lesson, then?' she laughed, seeing he hadn't been hurt. The boy was tall for his age with busy, turquoise eyes. It was obvious from the state of Branwell's attire that the horse had been difficult, his shirt was soaking with sweat and one of his sleeves had been torn. Her son held Branwell's hat. He handed it to him as they spoke.

Lydia Robinson smiled at Branwell warmly, and shook his hand.

'My horse is in the stables, Mama,' said Edmund. 'We have just taken him. He didn't want to go back though. He fought so hard.'

'I see,' said Lydia. 'I expect he would.'

'I seem to have lost my coat,' said Branwell, frowning

'You threw it off,' said Anne, reaching it from a chair. 'It's here.'

Branwell took it, all the while studying Lydia. He put his arms in the sleeves. Lydia Robinson was just as he'd imagined, a haze of purple silk and soft white skin. Her long dark curls glistened. Her jewelled necklace and jewelled ear-rings sparkled. 'I'm glad you're joining us, Branwell,' she said. She fingered the lace on the scooped neckline of her dress. The marble coolness of her features, her bright blue eyes, told nothing of how she felt. She looked Branwell up and down slowly. 'I have never seen hair so red!' she laughed. 'Anne tells me you are a painter and a poet, a passionate and accomplished man.' She turned her attention to Edmund. 'My poor boy,' she said, attempting to pet him.

'Bah!' he cried, struggling away. 'You worry about nonsense, Mama!' He shrugged hard and moved in closer towards Branwell, stretching up by his side. He was almost up to his shoulder.

Lydia Robinson's striking appearance had stunned Branwell for a moment. 'Well,' he said finally. 'We showed that horse a lesson or two, didn't we Edmund? Life has a habit of throwing us. What matters is that we get up!'

The boy's cheeks were bright from the bracing air. His hair was ruffled. His clothes were dirty. But he didn't appear too upset. On the contrary, his look was one of having achieved an objective. Branwell laid his hand on the boy's shoulder.

'My son is a free spirit,' Lydia murmured.

'And so is his horse,' laughed Branwell.

'Yes,' said Lydia, smiling. 'I can see that you and Edmund will get along fine.'

Branwell glanced into the house. 'Can I smell apple-wood burning?' he said, sniffing the air. 'A wonderful smell for January!'

'The gardener sawed down the apple in the summer last year,' Lydia said sighing. 'It had finally had its day. It makes good firewood though.'

The magical scent of burning apple-wood came to them from the parlour. They went in the house, assembling in the hall. Just then a man with pale and ghostly features joined them. Ann Marshall gazed at him in silence.

'So you finally got here!' the parson exclaimed, putting out his hand. 'Pleased to meet you, Branwell. I heard your conversation from in there. My son, you know, can be very foolish with that horse. He must learn to ride it properly. – You've been shown how to manage your horse, Edmund, and manage it you must!'

The Reverend Edmund Robinson appeared to be stern and alarming to his son. The boy moved about from foot to foot nervously. The parson had silver hair, thinning at the temples. His dark grey, delicate eyes moved across Branwell slowly. He had a proud determined demeanour, Branwell thought, though he appeared to be limping slightly.

'The horse misbehaved, not me,' said the boy sullenly. 'I shall punish it with my whip!'

'You'll do no such thing,' said his father. 'You will learn to ride it better, or you will not have it!'

'Anyway, all is well,' said Lydia, working her fingers together. 'Come and have something to eat.'

A manservant appeared and took Anne's belongings to her room. 'It was quite a grind getting here today,' said Anne as they went to the parlour. There was a lively fire in the grate. 'I am knocked to bits by those roads. I'm sure there's a better lane than that for the coach.' She frowned. 'I never remember it being so rocky before.'

'But there were two of us this time,' said Branwell. 'It's added cargo for the horses and the coachman.'

Lydia Robinson smiled. 'I believe my son is far too young for that horse,' she said quietly.

'I totally disagree, as you know,' said her husband crustily. 'The built up energies in the blood of a youth are often like tightly bound springs. They must find release. He must learn to ride more carefully.'

'I would rather he didn't have the horse just yet,' Lydia insisted. 'Maybe next year.'

'Father is right,' said the boy flatly. 'I do have these energies, Mama. I can feel them right now.' He stretched out his arms and clenched his fists. 'And I like my horse. I shall teach it how to obey me!' He frowned hard and looked at the dragons on the carpet. 'I'm sick of you bossing me about. All of you! – You invite those silly old ladies to tea and they treat me as if I were a baby! What do they know about boys?'

'Now mind your tongue,' his father scolded. 'They are good Christian women. They polish the pews and do the flowers of a Sunday. I doubt we could manage without them.'

'They should keep to polishing the pews,' said the boy with a shrug.

'Shush,' said his mother, touching his hair. 'Not here, Edmund, in front of Branwell. What will he think?'

The boy pushed his mother away and went to climb on the piano stool, then scrambled on top of the piano. He sprawled himself out, resting his head on his arm, his boots still filled with grass and leaves from his fall. Branwell, standing by Anne, fastened the buttons of his coat slowly, watching the boy, watching the parson, watching the parson's wife. Edmund Robinson stood before the fire and directed Branwell to a chair.

'I thought we'd have something light to eat and some tea,' said Lydia. Ann Marshall nodded and went out.

Branwell sat down, doing up the last of his buttons.

Ann Marshall returned and set out the table with a white lace cloth. On it went silver knives and forks, thin China plates and crisp linen napkins. The boy leapt down into the soft silks of his mother's skirts, disturbing them slightly, so that Branwell caught sight of the pink silk slippers she wore and her white silk stockings. Her ankles were slender, more like the ankles of a girl than a woman in her forties. She was youthful looking, as if forgotten by time.

'Is there anything else you require, Ma'am?' said Ann Marshall, after bringing them food and drink. Lydia shook her head.

The display of sandwiches and cakes before them was quite a feast. Branwell sat on a low comfortable chair beside Anne. Lydia offered them refreshments and they ate for a while, talking about the religious conflicts in the area. His father and Edmund Robinson, both parsons, had much in common. 'I have quite an impressive library,' said Robinson. 'Feel free to use it as you will.'

'Thank you,' said Branwell, quietly.

The parson coughed and patted his chest. 'There's a lot of dampness in the air today,' he said. He coughed again. 'I walked too far this morning. I won't be sensible, you see.' He laughed at his words, though half-heartedly. The boy filled his mouth with chocolate eclair and gazed at Branwell. 'My friend, the doctor who lives in these parts,' the parson continued, 'has a lot of sickness to contend with. – Though it's worse in Haworth I believe.' He met Anne's eyes.

'The water supplies are quite contaminated,' said Anne, thinking of Willie's death. 'There is always the danger of typhoid.'

'How awful about the curate,' said Lydia, with a gasp, turning to her. 'And your aunt too. What a dreadful time you've been having.'

Edmund Robinson took a long drink from his tea and nodded. 'Yes.'

They were all subdued for a while. Lydia rose and went to a cabinet nearby.

'Oh, don't get the dolls out, my dear,' moaned Robinson. 'You shouldn't, you know.'

'But I want to show something to Anne. It's new. I think she might like it.' She took out one of her dolls and handed it across. The doll was about a foot in length with a shining porcelain face and thick black hair. Anne took it in her hands. 'The legs are remade, but the rest is original,' said Lydia. 'I believe it was assembled in France.'

Branwell's face grew dark. He rose slowly, clumsily, and stumbled across to the window as if he were ill. Anne watched with concern. Both the parson and his wife frowned, looking at Branwell confused. Branwell stood with his back towards them, gazing outside. Anne tried to smile at Lydia, then at the parson. Her cheeks burned with embarrassment. 'How red the lips are . . .' she murmured, trying to concentrate on the doll. 'And what a beautiful porcelain face.'

The room was silent for a moment. Reverend Robinson watched Branwell with a curious stare.

'Here,' said Anne finally, handing the doll to Lydia. 'Do take her. She is such a fragile creature, I should hate to break her.'

'One of my daughters brought her back from London as a gift,' said Lydia, glancing across at Branwell, still standing with his back towards them. 'That's why they can't be with us. They are there visiting friends.'

Branwell turned to them slowly, his head bent, his hands clasped behind his back, though he looked away. 'You will meet them later,' said Lydia, returning the doll to the cabinet. – 'Is there anything wrong, Branwell?' she gazed at him frowning.

Reverend Robinson braced himself. 'It's those wretched dolls, my dear! He hasn't come to look at your dolls.' His tone was filled with annoyance. 'Take no notice of my wife, Branwell. Lydia collects antique dolls. It's hardly an exhilarating pastime, but she enjoys her little frivolities.'

'I'm sorry,' said Branwell, joining them again. He put his palm to his forehead and frowned. 'I was feeling quite dizzy.'

'The journey perhaps,' said Anne, bending her head. `It was most unpleasant.'

The boy sat tugging leaves from the laces of his boots. Edmund Robinson fixed his eyes on Branwell. 'If anything bothers you,' he said thinly, 'do tell me. We don't stand on ceremony here.' He hesitated, as if he might say something else. Glancing between his wife and the tutor by turns, he murmured, 'I think we understand each other. I will let you know if that alters.'

42

January and February passed. The March winds had been mild that year, but there was often rain. After one or two setbacks, Branwell succeeded in establishing a proper routine with Edmund for his learning. The boy had an inquiring and busy mind, and was easy to teach. It was quite a change from the way things normally went, where he must beg his pupils to listen. Edmund listened to everything he said. He hung on his every word.

Branwell had settled down in his new employment. He enjoyed the parson's library and the good food and drink, as well as his surprising generosity. Robinson was quick to recommend sources from which he might find interesting books and learn about concerts in the area. Anne, too, seemed happier. Various people called on the family for tea, but they rarely stayed long. The house was mostly a silent place, the dark shadows of the tall trees bending about it.

Anne Brontë was amazed at the change in her brother. He appeared a lot more relaxed. The previous anxieties he seemed to have felt had been abandoned now in favour of a quiet composure. He was lodging quite happily at the Old Hall, which had once been part of a farm. Anne had been to investigate, and had liked it. The place was comfortable enough, and Branwell had managed to find time for his writing, and even to draw. He had never looked better. Previous painful memories were beginning to subside. Time had provided him with the opportunity for a better existence, and he'd embraced it wholly.

Anne put the things she was taking home for the weekend into a bag and went to find Edmund in the library. It was just after lunchtime. He was alone. 'You're looking exhausted!' she laughed. 'You write so quickly, Edmund. It is just the way Branwell was at your age. He was so absorbed in his writing he didn't even punctuate.'

'Punctuation is a bore,' Edmund said petulantly. 'It is forever stopping and starting, I shall never bother with it. I like to run the words on the page as they go in my head.' Normally Branwell worked with him in the library, sometimes reading while he wrote, other times instructing him.

Edmund sat frowning, while Anne looked over his work. He sought Branwell's approval in everything he did, adapting conscientiously to whatever new circumstance he presented. For there were times when Branwell made him angry. Like now, when his father was away, and he must sit about working on his own, watching the rain battering against the windows, and wondering how his mother and his tutor kept dry on their walks. What happened to her beautiful clothes? Did they not spoil? Today the house was particularly lonely. His mother and Branwell were so often out of the house that he scarcely saw them. His father was away on business. His sisters had gone to London. Ann Marshall was staying with a friend overnight. And Anne would soon be making her way to Haworth. She said goodbye and left the room.

Though there was talk of ghosts at Thorp Green, he did not fear his home. It was a grand and beautiful place. His sisters were often foolish, and his mother and father sometimes forgot him for a while, lost in their own concerns, but he loved them all. He didn't much like Ann Marshall, with her creeping silent ways, though he could tell his father was fond of her. She and his mother had little to say to each other. But the household business went on smoothly enough, and he was gradually finding a place in the family as a youth instead of a child. Being a youth was a complicated affair in a family of women. It must have been similar for Branwell, he reflected. Yes, they had much in common.

But when the evenings came and darkness fell, he didn't like being alone. Some very strange things had started to happen lately too. His mother no longer asked him to bring her pink silk slippers when she returned from one of her jaunts; Branwell brought them instead. In the grey afternoons he would often see them sitting in the parlour together, talking earnestly when the candles were burning low. Sometimes he would catch his mother smiling at Branwell, giving him those long still looks that he didn't understand. He counted on Branwell coming to teach him regularly. He watched the clock for his times, laying aside the grievances of the previous day. For sometimes Branwell had broken his promises and let him down, going off with his mother instead of teaching him. He wanted an education from Branwell, like Branwell had received himself. He wanted to learn languages, to visit far away places and speak their tongues. He wanted to know what Branwell knew about painters, writers and musicians.

He was beginning to examine his thoughts, trying to assemble them into something that might make sense. It was now getting late. Anne had been left two hours. As he sat at his desk writing, he began to wonder if Branwell would return at all that day, or decide to go on to his lodgings instead. Since Anne's departure he'd been writing furiously and his hand was aching. He had a throbbing pain in his head. And he was bored. – Be sensible! said a little voice in his head. You mustn't bring trouble on the household! Behave and learn! But he kept on feeling disappointed with Branwell and cross.

He looked about at the walls, at the cold uncaring stone. He often felt angry nowadays. The grown-up world was quite an enigma to him. He hadn't seen much of his mother lately, and missed her presence. And he was too often conscious of the loud thud of the door of his father's study, shutting against him. Even his sisters were ignoring him. They were so obsessed with their silly talk about men. As he sat staring at his work, he suddenly took up a handful of essays and flung them down on the floor.

The weather was cold and wet that day and his mother had taken a large umbrella, hurrying away beneath it with Branwell without even saying goodbye. Rain fell fast on the drive. He could see the pebbles shining beneath a dim struggling light. The view of the gardens was obscured by mist. He spent the next half hour repeatedly going to the window and returning to his desk. The most important thing in his life just now was his learning. It excited him, as if he were like a young eagle on a cliff, looking out on the great world about him.

After another half hour, he heard his mother's voice in the hall. Lifting his head from his desk where he had fallen asleep, he went to the door. She was rattling her wet umbrella. Putting it into the stand, she saw him, but didn't acknowledge him straight away. She carried on talking to Branwell instead, lost in that singing voice of hers which said she was happy.

'Edmund, I'm late!' Branwell cried, suddenly catching sight of him. 'And I promised to mark your work. – The time has flown!' He gazed at the boy guiltily.

Edmund saw that his mother touched Branwell's sleeve. 'You can mark it now,' she whispered. She spread her coat on a chair and took off her boots.

Branwell frowned at the clock. 'It won't be possible,' he said, anxiously. 'I have to be back at my lodgings for supper.' But the sight of Edmund's hurt expression disturbed him. His insistence on learning was endearing. And it was something to be applauded too, and nurtured. He'd been selfishly enjoying Lydia's company and had forgotten his commitments. But he would have to leave. He wanted to finish a poem, and it was important he wrote to Brown.

But it wasn't just that. He was beginning to feel submerged beneath Lydia, as if he were drowning in her. He liked the feeling, the excitement of struggling with her currents, gulping her essence in until he could hardly endure it, yet finding himself still strong and surfacing again. It was a game they played together. There were moments he feared her, moments he was filled with desire.

'You don't even care,' said Edmund beneath his breath. 'I've hardly seen you this week.'

'True,' said Branwell going to a chair and sitting down. He shook his head and frowned. The boy's eyes were waiting. Branwell breathed in deeply. 'You have every right to chastise me, Edmund. And I like a boy who stands up for himself.' He had wanted to get back for Edmund, but all the while Lydia had kept him in the summer house, and the time had passed in that easy happy way it did when he was with her. None of the angst of the moment seemed to have bothered her. She had left them and gone upstairs.

'Anyway, it doesn't matter,' said Edmund with a sigh. 'I'm not in the mood any more.'

'If you have to be in a mood for learning, then you won't learn anything,' said Branwell flatly. 'Come on. Let's go to the parlour,' he said, directing him.

Edmund stood still and tense, his books and his essays clasped tightly to his chest. They crossed the hall to the parlour together and went to the table.

'You've done your Latin, I take it?'

'I have done all you asked,' said Edmund.

Branwell felt compromised now. He was delicately poised between gaining his pupil's confidence or else losing him totally. The boy gazed at him suspiciously, then threw his things onto a chair. 'Well done!' said Branwell watching the books and essays scattering about. 'I can't see what sense there is in that.'

The boy frowned resentfully. He was hurt by his mother and

Branwell. He had come to care for Branwell. He copied the way he spoke. He copied his walk. The minute he woke in the mornings he thought about Branwell. Whenever he was out of the house he talked like Branwell. He tried to emulate him. More than anything else, he wanted his tutor to respect him, and it seemed he didn't. 'You haven't apologised yet,' he said. 'You were late and you ought to apologise!'

Branwell scratched his head. 'You are quite right. I ought to have said I'm sorry. And I say it now. – Can we start afresh tomorrow? I'll take your essays to my lodgings.'

'It will not do!' snapped the boy. 'I like to sit beside you when you mark them. I need to know what you are thinking, how you are looking.' The words stumbled from his throat. He was almost weeping. He would not forgive Branwell his neglect. He wanted to distinguish himself, he said, to go to university. He had great hopes for himself, and he knew he could learn. He might report Branwell to his father, he said spitefully; tell him he wasn't teaching him properly, that he didn't turn up on time that he went off with his mother instead.

There was silence for a while. Branwell felt worried.

'Are you sad?' asked the boy suddenly. It seemed the adult world was a place of mystery. You must ask questions, embarrass them if you had to, but discover what was happening, if you could.

Branwell bent his head. 'Sad? – Yes, I suppose I am.'

'Do tell me about it,' said Edmund stretching up tall. His eyes were busy and urgent. 'Perhaps I can help. I know about sadness.' His voice fell low. 'My mother was sad when we lost my baby sister.'

'A baby sister?' Branwell said suddenly curious.

'Yes,' said Edmund. 'It hurt us deeply.'

Branwell watched his eyes, such a still, silent grief. Anne hadn't mentioned a baby.

'It was almost as if Mama had forgotten the rest of us. But my little sister was a baby, you see, just walking. Such tiny footsteps going to Father's library.'

'How old was she?' asked Branwell, waiting a while since he saw that Edmund laboured.

'Just two years old . . .' Edmund's brow tightened. 'It has been difficult here since then. Mama never forgets. She has terrible dreams. Sometimes she walks in the night.'

Branwell put out his hand. The boy's hand felt warm in his own, his face was flushed with emotion. 'You are certainly my friend, dear

Edmund,' he said. Branwell's coat clung damp on his body. He removed it and took it to the hall. Returning he saw that Edmund had picked up his books and found himself a chair. Branwell sat down opposite him. Leaning forward he gazed at Edmund unreservedly, seeing the intensity in his eyes, the frustrations of his youth, the loneliness.

Edmund held his gaze. 'Tell me what hurts you,' said the boy. 'I know that something hurts you – in the deep, silent place where we are all alone.'

For a long moment, Branwell looked at him. 'I wish I could tell you, Edmund, but I can't . . . I'm trying to forget things, you see . . .'

'How many things?' asked Edmund, his eyes searching Branwell's.

Branwell sighed. Just for a couple of seconds, Milly's face came to him again in the candlelight, the last time he had seen her at Parker's house. He saw the love in her eyes. He remembered the baby's funeral at Ponden Kirk, Brown digging so determinedly, Willie's prayers echoing into the night, the Reverend William Weightman, now also deceased. He feared the future. Lydia had protested he was acting coldly towards her. She had made such declarations to him. He was everything to her, she'd said. She loved him. He had taken long walks on his own that week and had been trying to think it through. It was true about him acting coldly. He had hoped to distance himself. He'd treated her politely, as he ought. But over the months, she'd wanted more. He knew she wanted him to love her. It was there in the looks she gave him, the way she touched his hand, the whispered words. 'I'm tormented, Edmund,' he murmured. 'The best way to help me is to leave me alone for a while.' He rested his head on the back of the chaise longue and sighed.

The boy's bright blue eyes fixed themselves on him intently. He remained silent. Branwell covered his face with his hands. It was becoming obvious to him now what Lydia wanted. He had loved Milly with all his heart and soul. It was a pure and innocent love. Thorp Green was a house of games. Nothing was real. Lydia Robinson was exciting. Feelings he couldn't control surged through his blood. 'You should go to bed,' he said. 'You'll feel better tomorrow. And we'll do some Latin together.'

Edmund stood silently before him. 'It makes me think of birds deserted in their nests,' he said presently. 'That's what it's like when I am left in the house on my own. I feel like a deserted fledgling. I shall try to fly very soon, and then you'll see . . .'

'What will I see?' asked Branwell wearily.

'You will see my bones dashed to pieces on the floor.' The boy gazed downwards for a moment, then walked off slowly.

The fire had burned low. Branwell sat quietly for a while. The rain was stopping. He would walk home slowly and think. He felt as if he had somehow betrayed Edmund. It wasn't what he wanted at all. But he couldn't let go of his habits as easily as he'd thought. His eyes focused on the cabinet of dolls and a sharp stab of pain went through him. Each time he looked at them he hated them. The thought of Milly and Parker together was like a knife entering his ribs. He'd seriously intended to change, to harden, to forget the tenderness in his soul; it had done him such harm. The room was dark and warm, dimly lit from the fire. What had Lydia suffered, he wondered, losing her baby girl, and with a cold, uncaring husband? It was doubtful he'd have comforted her much. Some days it seemed Robinson sent an icy wind through the house when he walked through the door.

'You look comfortable there,' Lydia smiled, walking in quietly. 'Will you have a brandy?'

He looked up slowly, as if waking from a dream, and stared at her. In a red silk negligee edged in cream-coloured lace, she looked beautiful. Her arms were bare, her soft smooth breasts slightly revealed above the neckline. She poured them drinks then brought them across, the silk of her negligee sliding and whispering about her. 'Do I embarrass you?' she asked. She handed him the drink, then stood before him smiling softly.

'No,' he said, surprised how easily, how naturally he accepted her like this. 'You look very lovely in red.' He felt as if they were lovers, and yet they were not. It would have been so simple, so easy just then to have held her. He watched her with fascination as she settled into the deep chair opposite, holding her drink, her head thrown back, her lovely throat shining in the firelight. She closed her eyes.

'Do you remember today when we were under the tree, and the man came by with the dog?' she said tenderly. 'And you hid your face in my chest?' She gave a low little laugh. 'I was going to kiss you.'

'You are far too seductive,' he said.

And you are far too decent,' she said with equal seriousness. There was a fearlessness about her, Branwell thought that was deeply dangerous. A piece of her hair had fallen loose on her neck. She settled her drink on a low table and let down the rest, so that it fell long down her shoulders. How much did Robinson love her, he wondered. Sometimes in his mind he saw her with him like that; imagined him touching her. It didn't seem possible. Did he understand her needs? Could those clumsy hands ever have caressed her in the way she ought to be caressed?

For a moment or two they looked at each other in silence. He wanted to hold her, to explore her, but he knew he dared not. She got up slowly from her chair and came towards him. Standing before him, she held his gaze then knelt, resting her head in his lap. 'I need you,' she moaned. She slid her arms around his waist and lifted her face.

Branwell felt full of emotion. 'There is so much happening in those great dark eyes,' he said, caressing her cheeks with his fingers.

'Please . . .' she begged, holding him tighter. 'You want me, I know.'

The stillness of the evening gathered about them softly. There was a special gentleness in her just now that he loved. He ran his finger down the shining skin of her arm. The sweet scent of her hair filled him with longing. It was true, he wanted her. But he knew he could not have her. It was a soft, dark, sinister urgency he felt. It was overwhelming. She was Edmund Robinson's wife, and he was tutoring their son. Today he'd deprived him of his lesson. He was failing yet again! With what seemed like enormous effort, he pulled himself away. 'I'm sorry, Lydia,' he said painfully. 'I must leave.'

'Hush – no!' she protested. She held his hands tightly. 'Is it such a terrible thing for you to love me? For me to love you? Sometimes I wish I hated you, and could dismiss you from the house for something. Oh, anything, rather than feel as I do! Why can't you stay? No-one will miss you at your lodgings. Tell them some tale, tell them whatever you like.' Tears came into her eyes.

'It might be better if I resign,' he said tensely. Her forehead tightened.

'But you can't just leave me – not now!' There was a sort of rebellion in her, some kind of decision she'd made that she wanted him part of.

'What a beautiful woman you are,' he sighed, stroking her hair. 'But nothing can happen for us. I won't disgrace you. You'll . . . You'll . . .'

'I'll what?' she said with mock laughter. 'You'll weary of me. – You will!'

'I won't, I won't! – Listen! It's cold down here. I want you to come upstairs with me where it is warm. Shut your eyes and I'll lead you.'

'No, Lydia, no!' he cried angrily. 'We shall both be destroyed!'

He turned away his face. 'You'd hate me!' he said quietly. 'If we make love tonight, you'll hate me tomorrow.'

She got up wearily. 'Do you think my husband is a saint?' she laughed sardonically. 'Have you any idea how humiliated I am, here in my own house? That woman, she . . .' Branwell frowned curiously. Lydia shivered. She laughed a crazy little laugh, then put her hand to her mouth. 'It's nothing, nothing . . . Forget what I said.'

He rose and went to her, touching her arm gently. 'What is it?' She shook her head. 'Sometimes I feel so ghostly in here . . .'

He smiled gently. 'That's ridiculous.' She laughed again briefly, it seemed with shame.

Branwell felt confused. Something was happening to him now, unconsciously. He was gaining deeper insight into her life. He had drawn a warmth from her, a passion he would never have believed existed in the still dark house, with its pale-faced parson, the giddy daughters who giggled and chattered in the library with Anne, and, of course, young Edmund. Yes, he could see how Edmund was Lydia's son. There was the same passion in his eyes, the exact same energy, a similar speed of thought. They were the thunder and lightning of the place. The others were just fine rain.

Branwell sighed. 'I would enjoy loving you, Lydia. You deserve to be loved. But I . . .' They were both silent again. He could hear her breathing quickly. Her face was wet with tears.

'I've promised Edmund I'll take him to town tomorrow,' she said, suddenly talking quickly. 'I'm always making him promises I never keep. I ought to be more appreciative of him. He's trying so hard to grow up.' She paced the floor agitated. 'I need to be a better mother! I shall start tomorrow. Yes, he will have the mother he deserves tomorrow!'

Branwell glanced through the window into the dark night. The rain had stopped. 'Everything always tomorrow,' he said wistfully. 'Lydia, I must go.' He went for his coat and hat in the hall. 'It's a pity . . .' he said putting on his hat, and stepping out on to the drive.

'What is?' she asked, staring at him and waiting.

'All of it,' he frowned.

Lydia put out her hands.

He turned and stood with his back towards her for a moment. He felt stupid and dull. But nothing had happened tonight that he'd have to be ashamed of. He braced himself defiantly and thrust his hands in his pockets. A fierce battle was on. But he knew it wouldn't last. It would all be over by morning.

43

Time sped by filled with dreams and frustrations. These damned social conventions! Branwell thought vexedly, striding about the garden at Thorp Green, why must they always limit us? Society, Lydia had said, prevented her from properly loving. It stopped her from having her own true feelings; it made her artificial. He imagined how afraid she might feel, about what happened in their secret meetings, the passions they freed. But she always came to find him, again and again. Branwell, when he gazed in the mirror, sometimes feared for himself and his family. But it was all too late. It had happened. She had caused in him the wild wail of love.

He went to the summer house and sat by the table, attempting to finish his letter to Brown. Everywhere about him was silent. He rubbed his face. He was tired. The first spring flowers would be out on the moors. He longed to see them. He hadn't seen the crocuses that year. Their frail trembling lives would have been and gone. He braced himself. Spring was surging through the earth. Flowers burst out of the blue. The grass chased upwards, eager and thick on the lawns. What he was feeling for Lydia made his veins tingle with excitement. The song of a blackbird came through the stillness. He bent his head and wrote on profusely ...

Then he stopped again, thoughtful. Why did Lydia keep on approaching Anne, he wondered. Did she distrust him? He thought for a while, planning what to tell Brown next. Ought he to tell him how flirtatious her daughters were, how he ignored them? He had always told him the truth. But now the truth was distorted; it was blending with fiction in his mind. He went on writing as fast as his pen would go, delivering himself like the early morning light, losing himself in the dull afternoon of his thoughts, declaring his supremacy over all other men, confusing himself, asking for help, weeping. The letter was finished. He sealed it and gathered his thoughts, then walked into the garden. Lydia was standing by the door of the house, still in her dressing gown.

He'd been waiting for Edmund to go to the library at the time they'd decided. He was now on his way to join him. Seeing Lydia like this, like some poor untamed animal, captured, confused and afraid, unnerved him. The soft green leaves of the new thickening foliage trembled about her. 'What are you doing out here?' he asked her, frowning. She pressed herself against a tree, and did not move. She was waiting. This is the way it was. She waited for him daily, even constantly now. She watched for him from the windows. She observed his every movement. Their lives, it seemed, had become an ache of waiting. It was a tense existence. Ann Marshall often appeared before or behind them, silent and aloof as a shadow. The sound of the parson's footsteps would alert them sometimes. The gardener would suddenly alight on them in the gardens.

'You must dress,' Branwell told her.

'I need to sleep,' she moaned. 'I can't seem to sleep, however I try.' She ran her hands through her wild, flying hair. 'So many thoughts run through my mind!' she cried. 'They are all so loud!' She put her hands to her ears. He stood beside her worried, wondering how to console her, glancing towards the open door of the house. 'He came to me again in the night,' she said anxiously. 'He is still coming to my room!'

Branwell hated what he saw in her now, her whole being abandoned to this sobbing woman who had never felt loved. This was the real heart of her, the pained soul he had unearthed.

'It's past ten o'clock, and you didn't come to find me!' she cried. 'You knew he was out with her today. – I told you.'

The light was low against the tree where she stood. She was lost just now in cold white sunlight. 'I don't like coming to your bedroom, Lydia.'

'It's a little too late for propriety, Branwell,' she laughed scornfully.

He sighed confused. 'I have to be careful.'

She laughed again. 'I see. You have to be careful, do you?' She gazed at the ground, her eyes blazing fiercely. 'Remember who pays you here!'

'Ah yes, you employ me, of course,' he said, moving about awkwardly. 'To teach your son, remember.' He spoke with anger. 'That's where I was going just now, until you stopped me, that is.'

'I have not stopped you,' she whispered.

He strained his eyes in the bright light, trying to see her expression.

Catching his gaze, her features softened and she came to him, holding out her arms. 'Branwell!' she cried wretchedly. He began again to argue gently, till the boy appeared in the doorway.

'Branwell!' Edmund called. 'I've been searching for you. I need you to look at my work.'

'Go back into the house!' cried his mother, with a frantic gesture of annoyance. She ran to him, her soft velvet dressing gown scraping on the wall where he stood. 'Branwell saved me from the wasps!' she said. '– Look, can you see them?' She pointed upstairs. 'There by my window? Do you see them? I must tell the gardener about them. I ran out here to escape them, but there were more!'

She went on talking rapidly in that way of hers that Branwell understood as screaming. Branwell nodded at Edmund. 'Go to the library. I'll be with you in less than a minute.' Edmund went back into the house.

Branwell shook his head. 'How clever you are,' he smiled. But she looked exhausted, sitting on the damp grass, the mistress of the house, shivering and weeping. 'Come inside,' he pleaded. 'I'll make you some tea. Did you have breakfast?'

'Don't upbraid me,' she moaned, covering her face with her hands. 'I know it's all wrong. I always do it wrong. It's the way that I am, you see. It isn't because I'm bad. It's just that others have made me so. I hate who I am!'

'I love who you are,' he whispered, offering his hand. She got up slowly.

'Who are you writing to?' she asked, seeing the letter in his hand.

'It's a friend in Haworth. I'm sending him news.'

'News? – What sort of news?' She shivered with cold. 'You mustn't send him news about me like this? You can tell him about Edmund, though. Yes, you can tell him about Edmund. Tell him how fast he is learning, how well he is growing. But you mustn't tell him about me. Oh, I am the worst of wives, the worst of mothers . . .' She grasped his sleeve. 'Nothing will separate us, Branwell, will it? Not now. Not ever. – Not life. Not death. Not anything!' The church bells pealed through the trees. 'Oh what a din!' she cried clapping her hands on her ears.

There was a kind of brutality in her now, Branwell thought, directed towards herself. The emotions of ordinary life had given way to a dangerous heightened feeling. There were moments he felt she absorbed him utterly, everything he was, both real and imaginary. He must feel himself then, pinch his hands, touch his face and know he was still alive. They went through the hall. The boy stood in the doorway of the library waiting.

Some days later, striding across the cobblestones up to the parsonage, Branwell felt somehow disorientated. He had needed to get away for a while. And he wanted also, to see Emily and his father and ensure they were both well. A furious row had broken out between Lydia and Ann Marshall, and he didn't know what it was about. Lydia had refused to tell him. There was a dark area there that he could not fathom. There were a number of servants at Thorp Green who were rarely seen, though Branwell felt they spied on them from unseen places. He imagined sometimes secret corridors in the house, panels that might slide back and forth to allow people through from parts of the house that were hidden. Often, while teaching Edmund, he would stop for a moment and listen as footsteps came up close, then faded away, though he could not trace their origin. The only people who knew of their love were Ann Marshall and Robert, the gardener. They were both discreet, she had said, and he need not worry.

But he feared exposure daily. If Lydia went on a visit to London, she packed her things in a hurry and without care, as if simply carrying out the motions. Hearing of his intention to visit Haworth, she had taken refuge in the company of her daughters, listening to their endless chatter, ignoring him for the whole of Friday afternoon so that he went home lonely. Treading the streets of Haworth just now, he was deep in thought.

'So where did you get the coat?' came a loud voice from around a corner. Brown stood laughing before him, looking him up and down, the bright spring light striking his face so that he appeared white and gleaming.

'Where did you come from?' smiled Branwell, screwing up his eyes.

'I've been waiting about for you,' said Brown, joining him quickly. 'You're looking well, and a new coat too, by Jove!' He ran his finger along the soft, silk collar and laughed.

'You got my letter?' said Branwell.

'Aye,' said Brown shaking his head worriedly.

'She's in love with me, John,' said Branwell, quite overcome by the thought, standing silent for a moment.

Brown sighed and stared at his friend concernedly. 'Ah, Branwell, come on. That woman has money and power. What would she want with love?' He nodded towards the parsonage. 'I know how you're feeling. Where would you be if it wasn't for her? In there, no doubt, dosing yourself on laudanum. She's given you work, lavished you with kindness, bought you a new coat too, by the looks of it! But it's nothing to do with love.' Brown frowned at the cobbles. 'Nah, it's all about her.'

'I'm beginning to regret telling you this,' Branwell said, frowning.

'Hold on,' said Brown. 'You barely know her, yet she's filled your head with gibberish!' Brown had read Branwell's letter carefully. He'd turned it over in his mind, wondering how he might phrase his reply to cause least pain. He feared now as he saw Branwell's face, that Lydia Robinson had passed her being through his blood. And that was that. He went in his pocket and waved the letter before him. 'Now, I can't stop what's cavorting downhill in your head, but I might stop a headlong disaster.'

'Don't say these things,' Branwell pleaded. 'It's possible for her to love me, you know. I am not unattractive to women. – Why, I must drop a portcullis between me and her daughters!' He braced himself and ran his hands through his hair. 'She has a passion for me, John, a real passion!'

Brown observed him carefully. His hair was thick and shining. He looked strong and well. 'She's the parson's wife and seventeen years older than you to boot. – She'll have done this before . . .'

'Done what? You are making a mockery of something that's deeply important to me,' Branwell said vehemently. 'Besides . . .' His voice fell low. 'Robinson's thick with the lady's maid who works there, I think. I fear Lydia knows things.'

'She'll tell you whatever she wants,' Brown said flatly.

They were silent again for a while, staring about. Brown was troubled. He would like to have helped Branwell, but he feared he couldn't. It frightened him to think he'd lost him. Branwell's eyes were closed. Brown could hear him murmuring something.

'I know thee and thou knowest how I love thee. We will not confess what needs no confession but rather let me live an hour of heaven here in the arms of one with whom I sacrifice all hope of it hereafter ...'

Lines written in my youth,' said Branwell. He threw out his hands in a gesture of hopelessness.

'Well, I live a bit of a quiet life up in the graveyard,' said Brown. 'I can understand the need for excitement, but what you're doing is madness.'

'Madness?' said Branwell raising his eyebrows. 'Is love madness? –

Yes, I suppose it is.' He sighed. People were emerging it seemed, from nowhere. The silver afternoon light, chased on the windows of the cottages, cascading on to the cobblestones, pulling out the shadows from ginnels and doorways, dancing on the dry stone walls. 'A quiet life, eh?' he smiled. 'There is nothing quiet about Haworth. – My father's been writing to the *Leeds Intelligencer* again. Something about schooling, I think. He's very concerned about schooling.'

'Weren't your sisters starting a school?' asked Brown. Branwell hadn't mentioned it lately.

'The project's been abandoned for a while. They'll return to it later, I suppose.'

'And how is Charlotte in Brussels?' said Brown.

'The professor's wife annoys her,' said Branwell, biting his lip. 'Though she's easily annoyed nowadays. She's infatuated with Heger, her professor in Brussels, though he's hardly likely to notice her. Apart from her being an intellectual opponent, that is.'

'Opponent? – How's that?'

'They keep on writing these essays to each other, challenging each other's views, on philosophy, art, anything Charlotte comes up with. It's her way of flirting, I think.'

'But what can she hope for?' asked Brown incredulously. 'The sort of attention you've been getting at Thorp Green, perhaps?'

'You shouldn't belittle what you don't understand,' sighed Branwell. 'It's completely different with us.'

'Aye, happen so,' said Brown. For a moment or two he suspended his words. 'Your mind is fixed,' he said finally. 'I know what you want me to say, but you're not going to hear it.'

44

'Emily! Emily!' cried the parson, catching her up on the moor.

She held tightly to the late summer flowers she'd gathered that morning. Her father looked distraught. Patrick stood catching his breath. 'I got this letter,' he gasped, waving it before her.

'Who from?' she asked frowning, seeing it had obviously bothered him. A grouse flew up from the heather: '*Geback-geback-geback!*'

'Do you want to walk on?' he said, offering his arm. 'It's from Anne. There's funny goings on at Thorp Green.'

'What's new?' said Emily, staring at the sky. They'd had such peculiar letters from Anne lately. It was difficult to tell if the boy Edmund was deranged or simply frustrated. He'd been absent for a whole two days earlier that month. His father had sent out a search party. They had finally found him sitting in a derelict farmhouse in a sort of trance. He'd been very resourceful, however, and had taken food and drink.

'None of this has anything to do with Anne,' said Patrick. 'I'm sure she's good as gold at that place. She's simply informed me about it.'

'About what, Papa? You're acting very strange.'

'You know how I feel about fire,' he said, pursing his lips and frowning. They could see the church below, tiny cottages beside it, the white sky hovering, the black specks of birds flying about the rooftops.

'I know you fear it, Papa.' Emily could hear a slight tremor in his voice as he spoke.

Patrick nodded. 'I do indeed. And I'm afraid for Anne.'

Emily considered his words. Her father made a lot of fuss about fire, and they must always be careful with candles. He had the morbid idea that their clothing might be somehow set alight and they would burn to death. Over the years he had buried a lot of his parishioners who had died from burning. He wrote letters to the newspapers about it, he talked about it; it was such an important concern. 'You fear fire at Thorp Green?' Emily asked frowning.

'Aye, I do,' sighed the parson.

'But why?'

Patrick stamped mud from his boots then carried on walking. 'The Robinson boy is a problem.'

'Has Anne told you that?'

'There's something wrong between him and his mother.'

'Doesn't he like her?' Emily thought about the things Anne had told her. She had heard young Edmund was a headstrong youth who had a clever mind. The mother seemed selfish and vain.

'He's been burning his mother's clothes in the garden,' Patrick said tensely. His smooth strong brow gleamed in the sunshine. He shook his head and braced himself, walking with long straight strides. His horror of fire stared out of his eyes.

'I'm sure she'll soon replace them,' Emily said sardonically. They stopped for a moment, gazing down the hills. There was a sort of panic in Emily's heart when her father was disturbed. It was rare his nerves were on edge, but fire could do it. 'They should beat him,' she said flatly. 'It's dangerous to play with fire.'

The parson turned to her quickly. 'You are far too harsh, my dear,' he said smiling, curiously. 'I wonder where you get it.'

'Well, at least he's burning them in the garden,' said Emily thoughtfully.

'Aye,' sighed the parson. 'I'm thinking he might set fire to the curtains next, or himself!'

'He'll know what he's doing,' said Emily. 'It's just a cry for attention.' She tucked her hand through her father's arm.

'I shall speak to Branwell about it next time I see him,' said Patrick firmly.

'Perhaps his mother taunts him,' said Emily.

'To be sure, Emily, you do say the strangest things! How would she taunt him now?' He spoke broad Irish as he often did when upset.

'Oh, I don't know. How might a mother taunt her son? Perhaps she confuses him and makes him angry.'

'Would a mother do that?'

'Some mothers would. It depends what they're trying to achieve. People have strange perversities sometimes.'

'She's his mother, Emily,' said Patrick, shaking his head. 'I would hope she loves him.' He bent his head sadly.

'Love can be very manipulative and selfish,' Emily said quietly.

'She should talk plainly with the boy,' said Patrick resignedly. 'They must get to the bottom of what's happening.' He gazed about him. How fast the summer had flown. A light mist hovered in the distance. It was almost autumn.

'She might prefer things as they are,' said Emily thinking about it. 'Not understanding him, I mean.'

'Aye,' laughed the parson. 'And what if he burns down the house!' He was getting more restless by the minute.

'Papa, you are such a dramatist,' said Emily squeezing his arm. 'The boy is intelligent. Branwell will have his measure. You needn't worry.'

'Then why does Anne tell me? She knows how I am about fire.' There was crossness in his tone.

'Maybe she wants you to speak to the parson next time you see him.'

'Aye, and sooner rather than later, I think.' He stroked his chin. 'But how can I talk to Robinson about that sort of thing? – Do you know, I have heard your son is burning your wife's clothing in the garden? Now what do you think about that?'

Emily smiled. 'You might be more discreet, Papa. Tell him about your fire concerns. He'll have seen what you've written in the papers. He'll have read what you've said.'

'Goodness Emily, do you think so? Do people actually read what I say, then? Now there's a surprise.'

Emily smiled. 'Don't let this bother you, Papa. Branwell is the boy's tutor. If there's anything untoward he'll know.'

'Aye,' sighed Patrick. 'I'm glad you have faith in him, my dear. It's good that he has your support. – Do you still have plans for the school?' His daughters had money enough to start it, and Charlotte would be eminently qualified on returning from Brussels. 'I have a very good feeling about it.' He spoke excitedly now; there was always a special energy in him whenever he talked about education. It was an important interest of his, and it thrilled him to think his daughters might open a school. But Emily didn't answer. And her father pressed her no further.

Back at Thorp Green, Branwell was living a kind of surreal existence. Everyone in the household acted strangely. Few people called on the Robinsons lately. The parson continued to write his sermons. Ann Marshall continued to creep about silent as ever. The gardener got on with his gardening. And Branwell taught Edmund his lessons.

Edmund though, had discovered talents that he had not acquired from Branwell, but rather more acquired from his mother. He made himself felt in a series of mysterious ways. He disarranged his father's books in the library. He disarranged the silver in the cutlery drawer so that Ann Marshall must put it straight. And he hid jewellery from the heart shaped boxes in his sisters' bedrooms. How they loved their jewellery. What desperate tears there were when it was lost! When the house was silent and he was alone, then he would enter his mother's bedroom and open the wardrobe door, breathing in the sweet, soft scents of her perfumes. He would touch her smooth, silk dresses, her velvet cloaks ... And that's when it would happen. He would flood again with the joy of recollection, remembering how he had hauled her prettiest dress downstairs to the garden and had singed the silken frills. What a thrill it had given him to smell her perfume thickening in the fire, to watch the frills spread their silken folds and dissolve into still, grey shadows. He was perfectly safe, of course. Nothing would be said about what he did. For each of them had a secret, and each of them knew he knew. They were all in his power. His sisters had secret men friends. His father and mother held secrets in their long silences. He was quite safe from them all. Branwell came on time nowadays, and taught him well. He extracted from each what he needed: caring and kindness from his mother, fine words from his father, cakes from Ann Marshall, gifts of ink and paper from his sisters, and knowledge from his tutor. His life was fine. Only Anne Brontë disturbed him, watching silently from doorways and windows with her large knowing eyes. Matters had changed somewhat, but it wasn't important. His mother had put a lock on the door of her wardrobe now. His father had locked his library. Branwell must teach him in the parlour instead, though it was warm and cosy. He could still have cakes from Ann Marshall whenever he wanted. And Branwell still came on time.

45

What a time of intense activity the past year had been, Patrick thought as he sat in the parlour that day. And why was Smith, the new curate, so difficult! He was always ready for a fight. His mind turned to Branwell. Did he ever do any boxing these days, he wondered. He appeared to be settling down nicely with the Robinson household, though he hadn't sent many letters. That was odd. He liked writing his letters. But Anne wrote often enough. Perhaps Branwell thought he would only repeat what she'd said so didn't need to bother.

He leaned in closer towards his Bible. His eyesight was terrible today. How was a parson to get through his work without his eyesight? He was glad he knew his Bible. He turned the pages, though he wasn't thinking about all that. He was still thinking about Smith. He glanced at his calendar. The letters were big enough to read, that was a blessing. At least he would know what year it was and what day! '23rd January eighteen forty four!' he said out loud. He sighed. William Smith was such an unpleasant fellow! And conceited too. Yes, conceited, that's what he was. He had much to learn.

It was good having Emily at home. He glanced at Charlotte's letter on the table. What was that all about, he wondered. Emily had read it out to him. It wasn't her normal kind of letter at all, it was far too emotional; full of bits and pieces of unnecessary information, about people who didn't matter, things people had said that were hardly worth bothering about; in a word 'distressed'. Well, whatever the case, it seemed she was coming home.

He closed his Bible and turned his attention to another letter, a different letter, something he was writing to the newspaper that made him chuckle. Emily came into the parlour. 'Have a look at that then, Emily. Tell me how you like it!' he said, handing it across. 'That'll get 'em thinking, won't it?' He sat back folding his arms.

Emily read it through. 'Wonderful Papa,' she smiled. Though it wasn't. Her father's writing was now almost illegible.

'When the *Leeds Intelligencer* publishes that there won't half be a kerfuffle!' he laughed.

Emily bit her lip. She doubted the editor would take it. He would probably want it written again. She knew how her father would feel about that. The deterioration in his eyesight made him bad-tempered. His sermon on Sunday had seemed laboured. How strange it was, she thought, to be separated from the others for such long periods. She wondered about the boy, Edmund, Branwell was trying to teach. According to Anne's letters, he'd become quite awkward lately. Lydia Robinson seemed a petulant kind of woman; one minute happy, the next withdrawn and sullen. No wonder the boy acted badly. It seemed she and Branwell were often out walking together. And for long periods too. Anne said little about the sisters. But Branwell, it appeared, had great sympathy with Lydia, who apparently was often unhappy. Anne's reservations though, had made Emily think. She and her sister, she decided were of the same mind: Lydia Robinson was bored. She feared Branwell was becoming infatuated with her, just as Charlotte was infatuated with Monsieur Heger. Couldn't they see the truth? Did they not see that their worlds were so far apart they could never unite? Just as the dead might rise to life, Charlotte and Branwell believed that blood could be pumped into the veins of their fantasies. Emily was waiting. Very shortly, Charlotte would walk through the door of the parsonage with a dreadful tale of despair. She knew sadly it would happen to Branwell too. Heger and Lydia Robinson would play out their parts, just like those people did. It was pure entertainment to them. And they would not care how hurt her siblings were. She and her father would listen to their cries of protest; how badly Madame Heger treated her husband, how wicked Reverend Robinson was to his wife, how much happier they'd be if they were only free to love them instead.

Her father had returned to his writing, though he had suddenly grown tired. He sighed and closed his eyes. She stirred the fire and added more coals. In a few minutes she would prepare him some lunch and wake him. She removed his pen from his fingers, and saw he had smudged his work. She would help him write the letter more carefully later.

Bright, white January light danced ecstatically on the church tower, flashed on the gravestones, flashed on the stones of the parsonage, then alighted on Charlotte at the window. She was home. And she was thinking about Monsieur Heger, thinking until she had given herself a headache.

Well, at least I got a diploma, she reasoned. Oh, but the misery it has cost me! Yet, she longed to see him. She wanted to hear his voice again, to listen to his wonderful words. Her whole body and soul were absorbed in Heger; he had become her very self.

She had wanted her own school. She had wanted it a lot. But she wondered if she wanted it now. What she wanted was love, and she wanted Heger. But she could not have him; he was married. What might she do with herself now that would make her feel better? What could she make of her life? She had learned some languages. She had taught some children. She had written some poems ... On a sudden impulse she put on her boots and cloak and went out for a walk.

How strange and remote Haworth seemed next to Brussels, she thought, as she went down the path. She marvelled how Emily got by with such little stimulation. She could hear the sound of Brown in the graveyard and went to find him.

'The fact is, John,' she said, adjusting her gloves. 'Branwell isn't telling us much. I wondered if you had any news.'

Brown shook his head, and turned the earth faster with his spade. The content of Branwell's letters nowadays could never have been disclosed to his sister. 'Will you be going to see him?' asked Brown. It seemed Branwell hadn't been back to the parsonage in months. His behaviour was very evasive.

'I doubt it,' said Charlotte tiredly.

Brown saw she was deeply frustrated and worried. Charlotte was rarely happy. In fact, happiness didn't visit the Brontës very often. Branwell was a sort of genie. He could put out his hand and draw happiness out of the air. But when the black times came and he was down, he was down, and down he would stay. The impulse that had taken him now though, was like a tidal wave. He listened to Charlotte, talking about her plans for a school, but she sounded half-hearted. He could tell from her face and from the things Branwell had said, that it wouldn't happen; it was simply a dream.

'How do you like Papa's new curate?' asked Charlotte tentatively.

'Oh, Smith. – What a rogue!' laughed Brown. 'An excellent rogue is

Smith! – Oh, pardon me, not a word will I say against the clergy!' He laughed again.

'You can say all you like for all I care, John,' said Charlotte, adjusting the collar of her coat. 'Apart from Willie and Papa, I wouldn't give tuppence for the lot of them. – Oh, I'll not bite my tongue!'

'Ah, you're a dreamer from start to finish, Charlotte,' laughed Brown. 'But you don't mince your words. No, I never knew you do that. And you must keep on having your dreams. Sometimes they're all we've got.'

'Oh, I'm weary of all that,' she moaned. 'You've touched a raw nerve I'm afraid. I'm always accusing Branwell of too much dreaming. Most of the time he lives in his head. We both do.'

'Aye,' said Brown, looking at Charlotte curiously. He hated seeing her like this. Charlotte was the mainstay in the Brontë family. Just like a mother, she held herself strong and proud. It bothered him to see her upset.

Charlotte looked down into the watery hole Brown had just finished digging. He was already on to his next. Oh always, always, she shuddered, the eternal embrace of the earth! If only she could feel some enthusiasm for something, just anything! How she admired Brown. He was hardworking, he was kind, and he supported Branwell like a brother. She watched him as he raised his face to the sun, letting it beam on his skin. Oh, some muse who mocked you and tore you into shreds would never seduce Brown! No, no! He would seek out decent work to engage his muscles in, and his mind would be freely available to those who needed it. Would she ever do anything that could give her the same content she saw in Brown's incomprehensible features? Could a man gain joy out of simply gouging out the earth to make room for the dead? She glanced around the graveyard. How beautiful his carvings were. Though how many times had he forced his chisel into the stone, writing his sort of prayers, the grit flying in his eyes and entering his lungs? He'd been coughing a lot lately, their father had said. Whatever the weather he must dig, for there were always dead to be buried.

Charlotte felt she was in a hurry, but with nowhere to go. She felt she had lots of time, though she didn't know what to do in it. Never before had she felt so down-hearted. She stared about her, wondering what to do next. The truth was, nothing mattered to her now without Heger. His presence had become indispensable to her. She wasn't complete without him. He had made her feel a terrible sense of her own limitations. She lifted her skirts out of the clay, and with slow, heavy movements walked back up the path to the parsonage, fighting fiercely with the monstrous love that held her. It wounded her. It hurt her. She was gripped by its will. There was no part of her mind that belonged to herself. She loved Heger. And she hated him too. But who would understand?

46

Ann Marshall's eyes had fixed themselves on the gardener. As a matter of fact, during the last hour, they'd been fixed on him several times.

Robert frowned uncomfortably. He rubbed soil from his hands and bent his head. It was a late afternoon in May, a warm sultry day. He knew he should keep his counsel, and he normally did. There was little sense in saying what would do him no good. But it irritated him that in just two years Branwell Brontë had familiarised himself with every inch of the house and land, and every inch of the lady of the house in the bargain. 'I'm glad there's no childer about,' he said gruffly.

'Is Edmund not a child?' said Ann Marshall, turning her attention to the flower bed. She continued to cut the flowers, feigning nonchalance.

'I wudna tret Edmund like a child,' said Robert, a wry smile on his lips. 'There's a price to be paid for that. The lad's canny.'

'Oh,' said Ann Marshall, still without raising her head. 'Why do you say that?'

Robert stayed thoughtful. Ann Marshall was simply grilling him, and he would not have it. Young Edmund was strong and fiery. It was unwise to rile him. And that's what they'd done. It was worrying to find Mrs Robinson's dress in the garden like that, the silk frills singed and ruined, and having to report it to the house. Not to mention the discovery of jewellery hidden in the soil. He didn't want anyone thinking he'd been stealing from the house. Normally he'd wash it at dusk then leave it in the hall.

He put his trowel in the earth again and got on with his planting. There were new bedding plants to put in the ground for the summer. At least his flowers grew strong and true and didn't tell lies. He never quite knew how to act when he walked into the summer house and found the parson's wife in the arms of the tutor. Sooner or later there was bound to be an explosion. The parson would catch them, or her son would. The youth's mind was in as much a mess as her own. She was hardly a good example to her daughters either. They were bound to know of her antics. He'd often seen them whispering together when they were having tea on the lawn.

Today, things were quiet. He'd seen Edmund at the window once or twice. And he'd noted the parson had gone out in a carriage with his daughters. He'd noted too, that Mr Brontë and Mrs Robinson had been in the summer house for well over an hour. It bothered him how easily they embraced nowadays, in full view of the large windows of the house. They'd become quite careless. Oh, yes, there was bound to be a reckoning. It was just a matter of time.

'To my way of thinking,' said Ann Marshall. 'You should best pass by what isn't your concern and get on with what is.' She pointed. 'Those roses are due for dead-heading.'

Robert saw that young Edmund had come to the door.

The boy glanced across the garden, his eyes lighting on the summer house. Standing sullenly in the doorway, he called out, 'Where is my mother?' Then he stood about frowning. He didn't want to upset his mother or cause his father to banish her. Burning her clothes was one thing, exposing her to his father was quite another. He knew how neglectful his father could be, and had also seen him exchanging smiles with Ann Marshall. Time on his hands, he had often wandered the house, hearing his mother and Branwell in the parlour, and sometimes upstairs. He'd ignored them. But he hadn't exactly been passive about it. By various means he'd shown how he felt. Oddly though, the household had adjusted to his tricks, and no longer feared him. The more his mother shut herself off with Branwell, the more his father forgot him, the angrier he got.

Matters were subtly changing. He'd heard Ann Marshall and his father arguing when his mother had gone out. The difference in everyone's behaviour, the excitability of his mother's relationship with Branwell, the strain in the house, that kept on making him anxious so he couldn't do his work; and the way they had all pushed him out, made him furious! And it hurt him that his mother's loneliness had been solved by Branwell, and that he, himself, was of little significance to her now. Did they think he was some sort of dullard? Had they any idea how clever he was, how he burned inside with so many thoughts and feelings, how he felt about being ignored? There were moments when he thought he might vanish again, this time for good. Though he wondered if anyone would care.

'There are jam tarts in the kitchen,' said Ann Marshall as she passed him. The sweet scent of roses wafted through the air. 'Do come through, Edmund.'

'I don't want any jam tarts,' he murmured sourly.

'They're freshly baked this morning,' she said, turning to him. Roses lolled from her basket. She gave him a rare smile. Edmund straightened fiercely. After an interval of several moments where he took deep breaths, he took off across the lawns, fast as his pace would carry him. His way was west to the summer house!

The afternoon sun beamed on him heavily as his determined strides took him closer and closer, and closer. Very soon he was there.

Everything happened at once. Ann Marshall dropped her basket, watching by the door of the house. Robert watched from where he worked. He would never forget those shouts of anger, the youth's mother, her clothes in disarray, pleading for understanding, for forgiveness. – There were such hysterical entreaties – the tutor, his shirt undone to the waist, fighting with the boy as if he were fighting a tiger. What screams and recriminations! The lady of the house looked a picture, running across the garden tying up her bodice.

After something of a struggle, the youth stood with his tutor, both of them breathless. But the saddest sight of all was the face of young Anne Brontë, looking from an upstairs window, every drop of blood drained from her features.

The scuffle had sent the dusty smell of dry earth into the air. Mrs Robinson ran into the house, past Anne Brontë, now standing in the doorway, past Ann Marshall, and right upstairs. From the open window Robert could hear her weeping; blaming the tutor, blaming Ann Marshall, blaming her husband, even blaming her daughters. The only person she did not blame was herself.

Weeks went by. Then it started. Letters were sent from Thorp Green to the parsonage. From early morning till the end of day the parson felt nothing but confusion and heaviness of heart. What had actually happened? He conjured up all manner of scenarios; the letters were so ambiguous. He talked with Emily and Charlotte about it. Branwell had somehow disgraced himself, though no-one knew how. It was simply a matter of fact. He had been given notice again. What sort of conclusions could they reach; they had nothing to go on? Also, Anne had resigned. Both she and Branwell were coming home.

At the top of the parsonage steps, Anne leaned heavily against the door. In a few seconds she would enter her home. What would she say to her family? Soft summer light flooded about her, showing the touch of grey at her temples, the pallor of her cheeks. Her mind was filled with anxiety. Two more wages lost! How could her father support them? Though tireless in his willingness to work, his body was weary and his eyesight grew steadily worse. How could she burden him more? She could not lie to her father, and reproached herself bitterly for what she'd done. She'd known what was happening from the first, and she hadn't given Branwell the least warning about Lydia. She'd shut herself off from it all, hoping he'd gain some insight into his folly, thinking it would run its course, though afraid for him too, and afraid for their family. But she'd prayed hard, determined that his time at Thorp Green would redeem him, ignoring what she saw, what she heard. And silence still held her. Whatever tale ensued, no matter what truth or fiction, it would have to come from her brother. Resolutely she opened the door.

47

Making his footing through the hall that day had been horrendous. His father had listened to his words in silence for quite some time, and had made no reply. The tale gradually emerged. Branwell's own version that was, as he believed it to be. Nothing was entirely clear, but he made a skilled speech, and his father had listened. What a barrage of letters and complaints there had been from Thorp Green! 'It's the end of everything, isn't it?' Branwell had murmured. He felt that what he had done was stupid, unsuited to someone of his station. But he had done it, and he still loved Lydia. It seemed his father had erected a wall around his feelings, and was maintaining a thoughtful silence. Anne had also stayed silent; he was grateful for that. Charlotte had stayed upstairs, and had scarcely acknowledged him when she'd surfaced.

But little by little Branwell began to raise his eyes to them again.

'I am not the only one afflicted by love in this house,' he said wearily that morning after breakfast. He sat in the parlour with Charlotte and Emily. Charlotte sat by the table writing. 'That's another letter to Heger, isn't it? You are always writing to him, Charlotte, yet he never answers.'

'It just goes to prove how foolish you are,' Emily sighed. 'Both of you. You'll tire yourselves out. It's as if you are locked in a box. You'll suffocate in there.' She left them and went to the kitchen to begin her baking.

Branwell sat pale and unshaven, his emotions exhausted. It was just like Emily had said, he felt locked in a box. He looked at Charlotte mindfully.

'Why are you watching me?' she asked, raising her head. 'Must I write this letter upstairs?'

Her words were welcome, whatever she said, they'd scarcely exchanged a sentence since he'd returned. 'You'd be wiser not to write at all,' he sniffed. It annoyed him the way she threw herself at Heger, her endless nonsensical letters. 'You're making a fool of yourself.'

'Not that you would do anything like that . . .'

'The more he ignores you the more you worship him.'

Charlotte bent back to her work, writing quickly.

'You are such a hypocrite,' she whispered.

'It's futile,' he moaned. 'Don't you see?'

She turned to him and narrowed her eyes determinedly.

'Do you ever really open those tiny eyes of yours?' he asked with a sigh. 'I mean open them and actually see?'

'Considering your recent history, I really don't see how you can dare to criticise me.' Her breast swelled as she spoke. She spoke to him in a careless, mocking fashion, as if she cared nothing for him now, had virtually disowned him.

'Ah, but Lydia loves me, remember,' he retorted quickly, determined to hold on to her anger; if nothing else, he would have that. 'This Heger fellow won't be thinking about you like you are thinking about him. You will never enter his mind. He'll . . .'

'Oh, what a devil you are!' Charlotte said through her teeth. 'I wonder if you feel for anyone except yourself!'

'Don't look down,' he smiled. 'You will see my cloven hoof.'

'I've already seen it,' she sighed. 'And more's the pity. – No, why should I pity you. If you wish to become a devil there is nothing I can do to help you!'

'No, Charlotte, there isn't. We become devils on our own. Nobody helps us.'

Charlotte bent her head, trying to return to her writing.

'See, you're ashamed aren't you,' he said, as if triumphant. 'Well, at least I'm not ashamed. Lydia and I have something wonderful.'

Charlotte laughed. 'How you fool yourself!'

Their conversation grew even more intense.

'I am sorry for you, Charlotte,' Branwell said smiling. 'You never actually had him, did you? And wouldn't you like to have had him! Oh how it hurts, this unrequited love . . .'

'Stop it!' she cried. 'Stop it, will you!'

'Perhaps they should stone you for your thoughts,' he murmured, closing his eyes.

'Anyway, how do you know it's unrequited?' she said with angry frustration. She gathered her things from the table and tucked them beneath her arm.

'Think about it, will you,' said Branwell firmly. 'He loves his wife and family, you have simply been a pupil. Well, and a jolly good laugh I expect.' He got up and went to the window. 'There's yellow light outside. How strange for midday.'

Emily came through from the kitchen. It was happening just as she'd expected. Here they were, making their excuses, having their arguments. She wondered how long it would last. It was all so tiring.

'He respects my intellect,' said Charlotte. 'It's good to be taken account of.'

'Well, of course it is,' said Branwell returning to his chair.

'You are a man. You are always taken account of,' Charlotte said fierily. 'The very fact of your manhood makes it so. It isn't like that for a woman. – Do you think because I'm a woman I don't have a mind, that I don't think as you do, feel as you do, long to reach out into the world, leave something behind of what I am?'

'Charlotte, please . . .' said Emily, seeing she was trembling. 'The two of you – why do you do it?'

Charlotte stood with her eyes fixed on Branwell. 'But it's true, Emily! How hard it is for our voices to be heard in the world!'

'You want to be God,' said Branwell in a scarcely audible voice. Emily frowned at him reproachfully. 'But she does, Emily, I'll warrant you. Charlotte would like to sit and dictate what we do, how we feel . . .'

'And you think that God is like that?' said Emily, her features darkening. 'Someone who would set out rules, dull us into obeisance, destroy our capacity to think for ourselves, to feel as we will?'

'To tell the truth, I rarely think about it at all,' said Branwell, rubbing his face. 'Ordinary feeling is all I ask for, just the joy of ordinary feeling.' He threw out his arms.

'When was ordinary feeling good enough for you?' Charlotte retorted with a sneer. 'You have racked this house with your so called ordinary feeling!'

Branwell met her eyes. 'And you have lapped it up like honey,' he smiled, rising from his chair, and coming up close to her. He pointed to the stationary in her hand. 'That man will never love you.'

'You can't be sure . . .' said Charlotte indignantly.

'He doesn't answer your letters,' said Branwell.

'I forgive him for not answering my letters.'

'Forgive him!' laughed Branwell scornfully. 'Oh, we don't feel forgiveness for long. I fancy it has a shorter life span than anger! Anger is what you will feel shortly, mark my words.' He shivered and went to the fire again. 'Oh yes.'

Charlotte stood gazing at the floor, shaking her head. Branwell turned his eyes to the ceiling. 'The air is so hushed today,' he said softly. 'I feel as if something is listening . . . And that odd yellow light out there. What does it mean?'

Charlotte watched him as he talked, his body slacker, losing strength by the day. Even his voice sounded weaker.

'If Robinson dies, I'll be rich,' said Branwell thinly.

She gasped at the shallowness of his words. 'You can't believe she'd marry you?' She lowered herself into a chair. 'And anyway, what if she did? Would you really want a penny of her money?'

Branwell laughed. 'Oh, Charlotte. – You would live in heaven, I know. But heaven and earth are two very different places.'

'And so you write poetry, refine your mind with the glorious music of the masters, read great writers, translate Horace's Odes, and all for what? To service that loathsome woman and enjoy her money?'

Branwell turned on her again, pointing a finger. Words were on the tip of his tongue but they did not come. 'You know nothing of what we have,' he whispered at last.

'Well, if you're prepared to be her servant, to prostrate yourself as you have before her, then you're a fool. – Oh, see how you look! But that's what you've done, isn't it? You've set yourself up as the lover of a rich woman. Why, she isn't even beautiful! And as far as I know . . .'

'You know nothing,' said Branwell quietly. 'She has a fine and beautiful soul.'

Charlotte trembled with emotion. 'Do you think she cares about her soul? Why you are mad if you think it. Women like her live in a world of things.' She broke off quickly. 'She is sending you money to this house. Why is she sending you money?' She spoke sharply, venomously, her eyes holding him.

'Poor Charlotte,' he murmured. 'You are quite jealous, aren't you. I have known the joy of physical love, you see, whilst yours is simply on paper.' He laughed cruelly.

'Papa is going blind,' said Emily. 'He is sinking beneath his cravat. I fear it may smother him soon.'

48

Branwell was getting impatient. He had no idea what was really happening at Thorp Green. Weary of the endless to-ing and fro-ing of letters, secondary communications, that might not have been true, the only way he could get to the root of it all was to see Lydia himself. He sat wondering about it. When would he go? How would he achieve it without causing her greater distress? What if Robinson were keeping her a prisoner in the house, refusing to allow her to come to him, to express the feelings of her heart?

He began to indulge his hopes, imagining how it would be when Robinson died, how he would go to Thorp Green and claim her as his own. Perhaps they would sell it and live somewhere else, away from the gossip. They would buy new clothes. They would furnish the house to their own taste. They would make new friends. He wondered how long it would be before it could happen. He didn't much care for the antiques. But the chaise longue, however hard on the bones, had a special place in his heart. He would have it stuffed with a lighter, more comfortable, material. He had read somewhere it could be done. He didn't have much in the way of possessions of his own. He glanced about the parlour. How hard it had been for their father to get good furniture. Branwell remembered his father's pleasure in opening and shutting the drawers of things. Drawers should be capacious, he said, and slide easily in and out. There was nothing worse than a drawer that wouldn't hold your things, or that stuck and wouldn't open.

Branwell was piling up resentment now against Robinson; anger at how Lydia had been treated, the way they'd been forced to hide and sneak around, as if they were convicts. She'd confided in him on their walks about her husband's ill-health, the hopes she had for her children, the hopes she had for herself and him. He remembered the night she'd invited him into her bed, the fever pitch of their passion . . .

He had grown desperate and eager. And it had taken his strength. He forgot to eat. He forgot to breathe. He was nothing but feeling. Would he have to admit to himself that it had all been nonsense, that he'd simply been involved in a drama, Lydia's drama? He dared to consider that Lydia might have said he was lying even, that he had simply invented their relationship. Was it possible? A stillness brooded in the parsonage just now which seemed to have entered his being. Alone at night by the fire, he heard the hooves pounding, pounding, pounding through his head. He had lost Milly to Parker. Would he lose Lydia too? Beautiful, sweet Milly, her face came into his mind, so that a rush of pain passed through his blood. Then it was the face of Lydia. Then it was the face of Milly again. Then Lydia. The faces merged and merged, so that he could scarcely tell one from the other. He felt tired and dizzy. He needed daily to convince himself that love was alive and strong somewhere, that it had not died within him.

It was Wednesday, a miserable day of the week, neither end, nor beginning nor weekend. Silently, lying in the darkness of his room, he listened to the sounds downstairs, though his family talked in hushed voices and crept about the house, as if there were someone with a terrible sickness amongst them.

The next few weeks were a kind of convalescence. He walked alone on the moor. He couldn't find anything definite to cling to. He tried to find things to do. One morning he carried a woman's baby up the hill, another he cleaned out a midden and burned the refuse. The villagers looked at him strangely.

'We are the talk of Haworth,' said Anne, throwing up her arms on returning from the village. 'What faces they make. Oh, what faces!'

'You may go on thinking the worst of me, if you like,' said Branwell vehemently. 'Lydia would see me if I wanted, if I went to that house, if I . . . Oh, don't look so sad, Father. I implore you. I know how you feel. What else can I expect? But before you come to despise me, I have to tell you, I once had hopes for myself, great hopes, aspirations, just like anyone else. But they have left me for want of luck. I have been sincere, totally sincere, in everything I've done. I have loved her sincerely. I . . .'

The parson covered his face, listening to his son's ravings. Branwell's constant refrains were now familiar. And he chided himself for giving him money to get drunk with. He could not speak. He had nothing further to say. Why, in the space of just a couple of months had such a calamity occurred? It was like the apocalypse. He felt feverish at the thought of what had happened. He prayed each day that he didn't break down and could be there to support his son. He thanked God for Arthur Bell Nicholls, his new curate, who had come to replace Smith. Nicholls was honest and caring. He might help Branwell get better. For he did not feel he had anything else to give. What had happened at Thorp Green was like a dark cloud in his mind. But he did not blame Branwell. He blamed the fate that gripped him, the cruel jaws that were finally tearing him to shreds. Would it go on forever, he asked himself. Anger and injustice surged through his mind, stopping, pointing, questioning. In spite of all he had learned, regardless of all his efforts, in the cold light of day, in the careless eyes of the world, Branwell had failed.

49

Time passed busily enough. The parson went about his duties. And Branwell, in a world of confusion, by starts and turns, wandered down into Haworth like a madman, talking incoherently to the villagers, stumbling into the Black Bull, then stumbling out again filled with despair, only to return to the parsonage.

His outings were usually short, since he rarely wore adequate clothing and often got cold and wet. But his eyes were forever searching, looking around at the idlers hanging about the inn, with that long dark gaze of his, which had somehow become permanent. It was almost as if he were waiting for something, waiting for anything.

Then came the message.

Sitting in the Black Bull Inn that evening, the man who sat waiting for Branwell had a cool dignified appearance and spoke calmly. He had brought news from Thorp Green. The rumours, it seemed, were true; the Reverend Edmund Robinson was dead. Though he had expected them, the words shocked Branwell into silence. And there was something in the man's demeanour that he did not like. His countenance was cold as ice.

'I have come because she wanted you to know,' he said, with a nervous little cough. He was Lydia's coachman, and a dedicated servant of the household. 'She is deeply disturbed by all this. Almost driven to insanity.' He rubbed his nose and sniffed. For a minute he did not speak, but gazed at the ceiling instead rolling his eyes. Then he sighed and said, 'She has suffered so much from her husband's wrath! – Oh, I dare not report it! She sat down and tried to write letters to people for two whole days, without getting up. Her husband was contrite at the end, and good to her too.'

His voice droned on for a while, relating what Lydia had said, what her daughters had said, how the son had behaved. 'Events have been quite catastrophic,' he said, blinking his eyelids constantly.

'I must go to her,' said Branwell, getting up. 'Right now!'

'No, no,' the man entreated him, putting out his hand. 'News of what's happening will be brought to you regularly, I promise. Why, the woman is scared to death by it all!'

'Did she not ask to see me?' Branwell asked, with a firm, suspicious look. He sat looking at the coachman, trying to remember how it was; the way Lydia had loved him, or at least had appeared to love him. He closed his eyes and remembered her words, her laughter. He remembered ... He remembered ...

What did he remember? He remembered her carrying a basket in the bright sunlight, running towards him, making signs with her hands ... His eyes turned to a plant on a stand by the door. It had stood there for several years, and it was still green and strong. Was Milly still strong like that? That very evening he'd been haunted on the way to the inn by her vision, taller it seemed, more willowy, like a thin silver birch, her arms waving into the night, her eyes looking right past him, no longer knowing who he was.

The coachman continued talking.

'Hush,' said Branwell, breathing heavily. 'No more! I don't want to hear any more.'

The man sat now his arms crossed over his chest, looking at Branwell disdainfully. 'Very well then,' he replied. 'It is an extremely complex situation. You do understand? The executors detest you. Why, they declare they will shoot you on sight if you dare to show up!'

'I see,' said Branwell in a quiet voice. He felt as if he were treading familiar ground; old, bloody, tortuous, familiar ground. After a few minutes silence, the man threw on his cloak and strode out of the door. Branwell got up and followed, watching him drive away, shouting at the horses and lashing them with his whip. They reared and whinnied and careered off down the hill.

50

'Best stay silent in 't village,' said Joe Draper to Bess, his daughter. She was struggling to wash her baby from a bowl of warm water, carefully, delicately bathing his head. The child, tender and trustful, opened and closed his eyes as the water trickled down his face. 'Just out o' common decency, lass,' said Joe, sitting beside her. 'There are some out there wi' pretty treacherous minds. They exaggerate, ye see. Away wi' that kind o' dishonesty, I seh. Whatever's happened at Thorp Green, is nowt do wi' us. Some o' them rich uns 'ud drop ye as soon as pick ye up! Branwell probably found summat out as weren't to his good.'

'No-one got a wink o' sleep in here last night, Dad,' said Bess. 'Baby were cryin' all night.'

'Aye, babies don't know t' night from t' day. He'll learn. He's a good little fellah on t' whole.'

Little Harry Richards had fine round limbs and was forever kicking out his legs and throwing out his arms. He was a great delight to them all. Joe Draper stretched out his big worn hands and took the baby from his daughter, talking to him in the only way he knew how, telling him about the problems in the village, and his hopes that they'd all be sorted for when he grew up.

'Ye must dry his neck proper, Dad, or it'll get sore,' said Bess, showing him how it was done. 'And dunna fill his head wi' worries. Ye never know what he's thinkin'.'

Bess was in a brown cotton dress fitted to her comely figure. She was getting more like her mother every day, Joe Draper thought, handsome and womanly. But her sleepless night had given her something of a pallor.

'For all ye seh though, Dad,' she argued softly. 'Branwell Brontë's a mess. He canna keep walkin' out i' t' night, talkin' to imaginary people.

Bobby told me he were sayin' summat about jumpin' out o' t' window at parsonage. He's pinin' for that woman, I think.'

'Ye must keep yer mouth buttoned, lass i' t' village. Ye were bred from yer childhood to only speak t' truth. An' ye dunna know owt about all that stuff at Thorp Green.'

'I feel for him though,' said Bess unhappily, as she put clothes on the baby. 'He's often been kind to our family. An' he's always so friendly. It's a pity he should fling away all his learnin' for some woman who ...'

'Ye dunna know owt,' said Joe, pressing his hand on her own. The plight of Branwell Brontë touched his heart. The last time he'd seen him, he'd been sitting on the Black Bull steps, mending the bridle of a horse for some earnest youth. His hair was long and dirty and hanging about his face. He hadn't lifted his head to greet anyone that day. Some of the villagers claimed he'd be dead the next week. He was a frail and sorry sight. 'There's summat i' the way o' women o' leisure as 'ud destroy a man like Branwell,' he murmured.

'What are ye mumblin' about, Dad,' said Bess, sinking into a chair and lifting out her breast for the baby. 'Ye'd best tell me proper what yer sayin', or ye shouldna seh owt at all.'

Her father watched her, an image of womanly happiness. His mind somehow forgave the world for its shortcomings, for he knew he had little bits of Paradise nobody else had. Even with their struggles they could still find joy. 'That woman'll 'ave a purse full o' gold an' a head full o' sawdust,' he said. 'Branwell's done nowt but comfort her in her loneliness. Women can often get lonely, even wi' a lot o' money. Branwell's naturally trustin', an' that schemin' woman 'll have duped 'im into thinkin' he were special.'

'There are some who think he's after that money. But she'll be keepin' every penny o' that, won't she, Dad. Ye always told me rich folks hang on to their money, or they wudna still 'ave it, would they?'

'Aye, I've filled that head o' yours wi' all sorts, lass. An' am sorry ye remember it like ye do. I dunna allus get things right. Ye should forget a lot o' it.'

'Come an' give us a kiss, Dad,' she said, softly. 'I can see ye intend to be off, or ye wouldna be buttonin' yer coat.'

'Do ye know what I'm going to do this mornin'?' he said, going across to her and kissing her forehead. She looked him full in the face and shook her head. He gazed at her, his face full of devotion. 'I'm goin' to do summat active!' He clasped his hands. 'I'm goin' to go runnin' o' t' moor. An' when I find me a pool I shall swim i' it!'

'Last o' t' summer flowers'll soon be over,' Bess said wistfully.

Joe Draper glanced around the house. 'How long did it take ye to scrub that table, lass?' he laughed. 'It could do wi' some eggs on it an' a bit o' fruit. An' I'll see if I can find some flowers o' t' moor to bring back. – An' if yer mother happens by, tell her I'll not be long. There's summat she wants me to do for 'er. Do ye know what it is?'

The sluggish rays of the midday sun were entering the room.

'I dunna like tellin' ye, Dad. But I think she wants ye to clean out that midden at t' back.'

Joe Draper rubbed his brow and frowned. Like everyone else in Haworth, he'd prefer the streets were clean, and that there wasn't offal all over, or that foul stench sticking in your nose on hot sunny days like today. Perhaps he'd go on the moor later. Though the sun would have gone by then, and he doubted he'd have the energy.

51

Now Branwell was mad with fear. Every movement, every sound, became a threat. He felt the sun would shrivel him. He felt the rain would drown him. I am at last insane, he thought. It has finally happened!

'Someone is coming up the path,' said Anne, looking through the window.

The rest of the family were out. It was early morning, a warm sunlit day. Branwell, on the chaise longue, opened his eyes quickly. 'What? – Where's Father's pistol!' He struggled to his feet.

Anne's voice fell low. 'I think he has a letter.' Once one of life's great pleasures, letters were no longer welcome at the parsonage; they dreaded news from Thorp Green. She put down her needlework and went to the door. A man in shirt sleeves thrust a letter in her hand then left. 'It's for you,' she said, returning and passing it across.

He tore it open quickly. 'It's from Lydia's doctor at Thorp Green,' Branwell said shakily. His mouth fell open with horror. 'He's telling me Lydia is ill, that she's suffered a breakdown! – She's talking of entering a nunnery!' His eyes grew wild and puzzled. 'She can't go into a nunnery! What can I do?'

'You'll do nothing,' said Anne, coolly. 'It is all false. She would no more enter a nunnery than I would. How can you believe such rubbish?'

'He's saying there's no hope . . .'

'No hope for what?'

'For Lydia and me, for us getting back together, for . . .'

'Branwell, there never was,' Anne moaned.

'But she loves me, Anne, I know it.' His voice was tense, his eyes aching with concern. 'Her circumstances won't allow it, that's what it is. I suspect if I try to go to her, it could make things worse. He says she fainted when somebody spoke my name . . .'

'What's the matter with you?' said Anne, gazing at him unhappily. 'Don't you see? She might have loved you for a time. It was a sort of love, of course it was. But it wasn't real.'

Branwell collapsed into the chair again. 'Perhaps I should just go and get her. We could run away. We could . . . She'll have money when everything's settled. She can leave Thorp Green. We . . .'

Anne looked at her brother's wasted limbs, dared to look at his sunken eyes, his broken spirit. It made her angry. She blamed herself for taking him there in the first place. She ought to have realised there was bound to be a disaster. Her beloved brother carried disaster in his blood.

'I must think carefully,' said Branwell, screwing up his face.

'Think?' said Anne, shaking her head. 'That's the last thing you want to be doing. We think too much in this house. – Anyway, what is the use of thinking? It will all come to nothing. Can't you see what she's doing? I know what Lydia is like. You just can't see it. She's worming her way out of it all. She wants to make you think she's sick so you'll leave her in peace.'

He pointed a shaky finger to the letter on the table. 'She is having very little peace. I must go to Thorp Green!'

'She doesn't care about you, Branwell. Please understand.' Anne's colour was up in her cheeks. She was breathing fast.

'You don't know what you are saying, Anne.' He spoke in a low voice and gazed at the letter.

'I do, I do. I have known her longer than you have.'

'In a very different way,' said Branwell, frowning.

'I probably know her better.' Anne was vehement. 'She'll marry someone else. – Oh, one of those men she knows. She'll . . .'

'Please don't,' he begged.

'I will,' she said defiantly. 'I shall say what I feel. She'll marry a Lord, I tell you. Just watch.' Her eyes filled with tears, her breast heaved and fell. She took up her needlework again. 'Oh what will we do with you, Branwell? You are prowling this house moaning and weeping day and night. You walk the streets like a ghost. Why people round here are afraid of you. Don't you see what you're doing to yourself? – What you're doing to us all?'

'Such careful observation of my habits,' he laughed quietly. 'Why it's a wonder the lot of you don't keep notebooks on me! If you had such bad thoughts about Lydia before, then you ought to have voiced them.' He picked up the letter again.

Anne saw that his hands were shaking. 'You're on laudanum aren't you,' she said quietly. 'I can tell. You talk nonsense on laudanum, and you know it. We all have to suffer.'

'Then don't.'

'We have to.'

'Why?'

'Because we love you,' she said, her voice almost a whisper.

He read the letter again then pushed it into his pocket.

Anne went into the kitchen. There was an apple pudding to prepare for supper, she set out the knife and the board and searched for the apples. Their father had gone into Haworth with Charlotte and Emily, perhaps she could finish her writing.

All afternoon Branwell walked the house in a state of frustration and tension. He kept on reading the letter. For supper they had potatoes and lamb and the apple pudding Anne had made for afters. Though Branwell still couldn't eat. He sat for some time, trembling by the window then stumbled out of the parsonage.

The soft evening light quivered on the glistening pavements. He would have gone right there and then to Thorp Green, though he was in no fit state. He couldn't get away from the tormenting thoughts in his head, and he didn't feel well. But at least he was out in the open air, under the stars and free. If only the air would receive him, he thought. Oh, if it would only lift him up and take him away!

'I'm going for your father,' said Brown. 'What are you doing, huddled by the roadside like this? Some carriage will run you over.' Brown put out his hand. 'Get up. There's nothing heroic about this. You're ill.' He'd been following Branwell for the last ten minutes, watching where he was going and how he was behaving. 'They'll be out looking for you soon.'

'They're glad to see the back of me,' he said, his teeth chattering. 'I'm a madman in there.'

'You are worse out here,' Brown sighed. One or two people passed and looked. Branwell no longer cared. 'I need laudanum, John. I need laudanum so badly!'

Brown glanced about. Dusk was falling. The shadows were already lengthening. A thin breeze ruffled the lapel on Branwell's coat. Brown saw it was covered in soil from a fall. 'Are you still refusing to eat?' he asked, seeing how lean he was.

'Ugh! The thought of food sickens me. – John, I need money for laudanum. I can pay you back ... Once Lydia and I have ...' He drew an empty whisky bottle out of his pocket. 'Empty,' he said removing the top and turning it upside down. 'Emptied out to the bottom, just like me.'

Branwell was shrinking to skin and bone, thought Brown. He had never known him so weak. 'Take my arm,' he said. 'I'll take you back to the parsonage.'

'No, not now! – Later. – She loved me, John. She loved me from the first.'

'Aye.'

'And Milly too,' he said, lowering his voice. They were silent a moment. 'You see, they are one and the same woman ...'

Brown widened his eyes. Milly? He hadn't spoken of Milly in ages.

'They are the same person, John.' He gave him a quivering smile. 'If I closed my eyes with Lydia, then Milly was with me. I imagined Milly in her clothes, her jewels. The truth is ...' Brown waited tensely. 'Do you know the truth, John?'

'No, tell me what the truth is, then.'

'The truth is, Father passed me earlier. He didn't see me.' Branwell laughed quietly. 'It's as well he didn't see me, don't you think?' Branwell's voice was slurred, almost incoherent.

'Well I can see you,' said Brown. 'I see you clearly. And you're not staying here.' A gleam of moonlight touched Branwell's hair then fell on the drystone wall opposite, so that it sparkled a dance of stars. 'Best make an effort,' said Brown.

Branwell got up and leaned on Brown's arm. 'Isn't it strange, the things we notice but never speak of,' he said.

'Aye it is,' said Brown, though Branwell's talk was confused.

'Oh, the way Anne picks at her food ... The way Emily eats so quickly ... The way Charlotte eats so slowly and solemnly, just like Father. And the sound of their footsteps, each so different. Yours too, John.' He turned to him frowning. 'We rarely speak from our hearts do we?' He was panting as they went up the hill. They had almost reached the parsonage.

52

'It's two o'clock in the morning, and you're still dressed,' Charlotte said, observing Branwell worriedly. She had just entered the parlour. 'You ought to be in bed.'

He sat reading by the light of a candle. The fire had burned low. She had known instinctively he was up. He rarely went to bed with the others, and if he did he was up and down the stairs all night, restless.

'He had a club foot,' said Branwell, putting his book to one side. He was reading Byron.

'Who?' She riddled the fire and placed logs on the dying embers.

'Byron. He probably limped.' He stretched his arms above his head and yawned. 'There were times I saw Robinson limping. I suspect he had gout.'

Charlotte sat down and faced him. She felt helpless. Her heart was heavy because she knew she could not help him. He looked so thin, and his hair seemed finer. There were deep furrows in his brow. 'Would you like some apple pudding?' she asked him. 'I kept some warm in the oven.'

'Perhaps . . . just a little,' he said tiredly. 'I hope I can hold it down.'

She went to the kitchen and brought back the pudding in a bowl. His hand shook slightly as he took the spoon to his mouth.

'Anne made it. She makes a good apple pudding,' said Charlotte.

'Yes, I know, it's the best.' He ate several mouthfuls then gave it back. His hands were trembling.

'Won't you eat a bit more,' she pleaded. He shook his head. 'That's sufficient. Thank you, Charlotte. I enjoyed it.'

She put the bowl on the table and returned to her seat. He sat like a dark shadow by the fire, as if transfixed. It hurt her to see him as he was, his fine limbs wasted, his hair sticking out thinly, his large appalled eyes. 'Do you remember when Father brought the toy soldiers for my birthday?' he said. He was absorbed just then in thought.

'Your seventh birthday. Of course. How could I forget?'

Branwell went on. 'It was late when he arrived back home. Dark like this. I heard him come in. I remember the sound of my door when he opened it next morning, the sound of his voice when he spoke; that young, powerful voice he had then. We were so excited. You especially, Charlotte. You snatched yours first.'

'Did I?' she said awkwardly. 'How awful, and they were yours.'

'No, no. I was glad you were happy. Whatever belonged to me, belonged to you. That's how it was. – And that's how it is now.'

'I don't recall snatching a soldier.'

'My dear Charlotte,' he whispered. 'It doesn't matter.'

Charlotte listened, though she didn't like talking about the past.

Branwell looked somehow forlorn, as if that was where he had gone, to the past, as if he were retreating, disappearing.

'Wiggins lost, you know,' he said with a sigh. A full great moon was with them, lighting the walls of the parlour. The house was still. 'Oh, the hopes you had for Wiggins, remember? Good old Wiggins, eh? Do you remember what you wrote?

"As a musician he was greater than Bach; as a poet he was greater than Byron; as a painter, Claude Lorrain yielded to him; as a rebel he snatched the palm from Alexander Rogue, as a merchant Edward Percy was his inferior . . ."

'Aye, and you called us idiots, remember?' said Charlotte, folding her arms. 'That's what you called your sisters.'

'Did I?' said Branwell, the words struggling in his throat. 'I'm amazed I should say such a thing.'

She continued to watch him. She was afraid. He seemed so separate, so only half with her, scarce even that. There was a strange tension in him, something new. Something was ready to deliver itself; a final burst of energy held secret in his heart. 'Oh, but Charlotte it was all such fun!' He closed his eyes. 'And yet, you see, it wasn't. Not in the end. It sort of displaced us . . .'

For some minutes the room was silent.

'You were always more interested in Percy than you were in me,' he said quietly.

'That's ridiculous,' said Charlotte, tying the strings of her dressing gown.

'Maybe it is, but it's true,' sighed Branwell. 'Truth is hard to find . . . It's best found at night, like this.'

'Oh you and your truth,' said Charlotte, shaking her head.

Branwell braced himself and pushed back his hair. He gazed at Charlotte strangely. 'Look at me, please,' he said in a low voice. 'I mean, really look at me, Charlotte. There's something I'd like to tell you. It's very important to me. It would please me to tell you.' He laboured over the words, his voice choking with emotion. 'It would put me in heaven.'

Charlotte sat completely motionless and perplexed. 'Put you in heaven?' She shuddered. 'Don't talk about heaven, Branwell, not yet.' Her voice trembled. A cold fear came over her. She moved her chair closer. What was he doing, sitting down here in the middle of the night, talking about heaven? She touched his hand. 'I think you should go to bed. Let me help you upstairs.'

He shrugged his shoulders. 'I'm fine. I feel strong. Talking to you like this is good. Please allow me to continue. I need to talk to you, Charlotte . . .' He lapsed into silence for a moment. Again he found her eyes, holding her gaze. 'I would like to confide in you.'

'Well, only if you really want to,' she said frowning, worriedly. 'Is it real or imaginary?'

'Oh, it's real. Very real. So real it is here in this room.'

'Well, there you go,' she replied irritably. 'You are talking fancifully as usual.'

'No, no.' He shifted about in his chair, still looking at her. 'And nobody knows?'

'Brown knows . . . And Willie knew . . .'

'Willie, and not Papa?' said Charlotte, with a look of hurt surprise. She listened in wonder. 'Tell me then. But you mustn't be sorry after.'

'And you must never speak of it again.'

'You mean you would only tell me?'

'That's right,' he said quietly. He hesitated a moment, then straightened himself. He spoke with unusual authority. 'I once had a child.' The room was suddenly silent again.

'*A child?*' said Charlotte incredulously. Questions flooded her mind.

'She died.'

'But when?' She caught her breath, stunned.

'I don't want to tell you. And I'd rather not say who the mother was either. But I'd like to tell you what I can. That's if you'll let me . . .'

Charlotte nodded slowly, and waited. He sat now with his hands clasped in his lap, his features frenzied with feeling. 'She was lovely,' he began, wistfully. 'A beautiful young girl. A barmaid. – No, not from round here.'

Charlotte's mind raced on. When had it happened? Where? It had to be when he was away. But who could she be? She forced herself not to question him.

He shuddered slightly. 'She is mute. Well, anyway, she was with me ... It is a strange kind of disorder. She is only able to speak to one person; just one privileged person. I asked Father about it. He knew of such a conditon.' He bent his head. 'She didn't speak to me. But she did speak to somebody ...'

'Someone more special than you?' Charlotte said, horrified by the look in his eyes.

He put his hands to his face and talked through his fingers, Milly rising from his dark subconscious, having her being in his home. And he was sharing her now with Charlotte. 'Such a soulful, sensitive girl. She had no education to speak of. She expressed herself through sounds and signs. She made noises with her throat; sounds like the wind through trees, or the sea lapping on a beach.' He stopped for a while, sinking into his thoughts. 'I loved her so much,' he murmured. 'I never thought I was capable of love like that. And she loved me back. – But I didn't cherish it as I should. Another man stole her away; a man who loved her better, who knew what she needed more than I did.'

Charlotte trembled. 'And where is she now?' How could Branwell's imagination do this? It had torn him in two. Was this just another creation, or had it really happened?

'I can't tell you. And you must never ask,' he said firmly.

'And the child? – May I ask about the child?'

'Yes,' he said, his eyes suddenly eager. He spoke tenderly, with love. 'It was a girl. We buried her by Ponden Kirk. Brown dug the grave. Willie conducted the funeral. – Oh, such a sweet little funeral. Such a sad, sad little death.'

For several moments neither of them spoke.

'When did it happen?' asked Charlotte, tears in her eyes.

'I can't tell you that either,' he whispered painfully.

Charlotte shivered, and wrapped her arms around herself. Branwell reached into his pocket and drew something out then offered it across. 'Her uncle made her this bangle to commemorate her pregnancy.'

Charlotte ran her fingers over the glistening, clever carvings. 'He gave you this?'

'No, I took it,' Branwell said flatly.

'Where from?'

'From the house where the baby was delivered.'

She braced herself, searching his eyes. 'Why did you have to steal it? I thought the girl loved you?'

'She did. But she also loved him. It was he who delivered our child. She loved him best. She lives with him now in his cottage.'

Charlotte sat thoughtful for a moment. 'But you say you love Lydia Robinson? How is it possible to love two such different women?'

'Oh, the tricks we must play with our heads at the edge of despair!' Branwell said vehemently. 'The loves we must bargain! It is all so perilous!' He passed his palm across his forehead. The talk had made him perspire. 'Neither of my loves really lived. I expect nothing of Lydia now. I see it's impossible. I'm resigned. I love the memory of them both. Lydia lives with Percy in my mind. My other love lives with the man she chose over me; a love more real for her. I was simply a fiction for both of them.' He shook slightly as he spoke, his eyes tormented.

Charlotte searched her mind, trying to make sense of what he said. 'And now?' she asked despairingly. She felt sick, as if she had somehow betrayed him. All this had been happening, yet not a single one of them had known. They'd all been absorbed in themselves. She denied to herself she'd neglected him. Yet she knew she'd ignored him. Each time he'd failed she'd been contemptuous of him, angry because he had wasted all his chances. So she'd detached herself from him, refused to allow him in, ignored that look in his eye she knew so well. Now she too had become part of his story. She wanted to know where the baby was. She needed to go to the burial place, to see it for herself. And perhaps to pray. She ran her fingers over the bangle again, then handed it back. 'Take me to where she is on the moor,' she said softly.

'What now?' He searched her face, a relief in his eyes that he'd told her, even in his voice. 'You want me to take you tonight?'

'Yes, if you feel you are well enough.' The very thought of it thrilled her. An immense feeling of joy filled her, even though the child was dead. Her brother had fathered a child. There were so many questions in her mind that could never be asked, questions that would remain unanswered perhaps forever.

He stood and straightened, taking a deep breath. 'It's a mild night,' he said, peering through the window. 'If we go slowly, I can do it I think. Get me my coat. You must put on your cloak and boots.' The moor was sufficiently light for them to find their way. It was Branwell's custom to walk slightly ahead; this time they walked together. In her nightdress, her dressing gown and cloak, Charlotte made a strange figure, holding on to her brother's arm as they stumbled over the tussock grass and boulders. The sweet night air was fresh, and the moonlight shone gently, benign, beautiful and beckoning. They went in silence, more intimate than they had been in years, together as they'd been in childhood, together with their secret. Out on the moor a little Brontë was buried. Each footstep brought them closer, and closer, to her grave.

The moor was eerily still. Charlotte stood by Ponden Kirk. The loud cry of a night bird came from the shadows. 'Where are you?' she called. Branwell was lost in the darkness.

'Over here,' he called back, his voice echoing on the dry moorland.

He was kneeling several yards away. She found him quickly and dropped down by his side. As they stirred the grass its sweet scent gathered in the soft night air, heavy with memory. 'She's here,' he said shakily. 'We buried her here.'

Charlotte glanced about. The purple cliffs shone brilliantly. The thin grasses waved slowly in the pale white light. The heather appeared so still. 'This is where we came for the picnic with Willie,' she murmured. She was in a strange reverie as she talked, kneeling by the baby's grave. Tears fell down her cheeks. 'Branwell . . . Branwell . . . My dear, brother,' she said. She felt astounded by his courage, the way he had kept his secret, the sadness he must have felt; the sheer, utter loneliness. 'There is no gravestone,' she said, stroking the grass tenderly. She could hear his breathing labouring beside her. 'What did you call her?' she asked him. 'What did she look like?' Already she was forcing her questions. She stopped abruptly.

After a moment's silence, he said, 'She has no name. But I think she looked like you.'

'Me?' Charlotte smiled, pressing her face on the grass. How she wanted to take this moment in, to have it for her own. But fiction and reality were much the same in her brother's mind; it was hard to believe him. Could it be true? Could it really be true? Did a baby girl, a Brontë baby girl, lie deep down in that earth, to be covered by flowers in spring and summer, heather in autumn, snow in winter? She was filled with strange excitement. 'Does the mother know she's here?'

'No,' he murmured. She asked him no more questions. She watched him bending by the grave, his dark figure strangely at peace. He put out his hand and drew her towards him, holding her tightly then they sat in silence for a while, listening to the sounds of the night. What a lonely man her brother had been, she reflected. She wondered how it might have been had the child lived on. She imagined her running on the moor as they did in childhood, leaping the streams, understanding the whispers and roars of the wind, the passions of the moorland weather. What grace and beauty imagination allowed. Jewelled above them the stars hung heavy in the night. She gazed at them as she had done so long ago with Branwell at that very same spot. And she remembered how it had been and what they had said. Their whole childhood tumbled back into her mind. She rose from the grass. Branwell found his way to his feet. With this strange new peace in their minds, they made their way home.

53

Each expulsion of vomit from Branwell's throat sent a shudder down his father's spine. They were alone together in the back garden at the parsonage. Patrick leaned on the wall. It had been going on at least five minutes. He watched the thin bent figure, crouching over the soil. His son was almost unconscious. 'I can't stand this a minute longer,' he said firmly. 'I must go for the doctor. You're going to have a seizure!'

Branwell turned, observing his father dimly. 'I'm okay,' he said shakily. Despite his aches and sickness, he stood and straightened before him. 'I shall always try to stand strong, Father, best I can.' He lowered his head, his voice a thin murmur. 'Even when I am dying, I shall stand.'

An odd silence embraced them. Branwell wiped his mouth on his hand, and leaned with his father on the cold stone wall. Some time ago he might have felt guilty about his state. Not now. There was no longer anything to hope for. He looked at his hands. They were trembling. What was happening was irrecoverable.

As he stood watching his son, Patrick's heart throbbed with sadness. He clasped his hands and prayed.

'You think I'm dying, Father, don't you,' said Branwell. 'I can tell from your face. You know the signs. You know what Mr Death looks like. You have seen him so many times. – Oh, let me have what's left of my life, will you! Don't come bringing me your prayers!'

'My prayers are all I have left,' said Patrick flatly. 'I have given you everything else.'

'I'm sorry, Father,' said Branwell miserably. 'I love you.'

'Nicholson wrote to me from the Old Cock Inn,' said Patrick. 'I believe you owe him money.'

'He wrote to you, did he?' laughed Branwell weakly. 'Ah, he would.

The man's without pity. He's happy enough for me to fill my belly with his liquor, so long as he can get you to pay him.'

'You'll get no more laudanum from the apothecary,' said his father resolvedly.

There was a strange look in Branwell's eyes. He was trying to remember the past. 'What did I do?' he asked wistfully, 'between leaving Thorp Green and now? Can you remember?'

Patrick sighed. 'I think there's going to be rain,' he said, shrugging with the chill of the evening. He glanced at the vomit on the garden. 'Let's hope it's a torrent. I ought to have done a Christening today. I didn't feel up to it. Nicholls has done it instead.'

'Ah, good old Nicholls. Always these other men for you to admire, Father. They are all so much better than me!'

'That's enough!' said Patrick. 'Grundy is in the Black Bull. He's sent for you. Are you well enough to see him?'

'Grundy? Oh yes, I would like to see Francis. He will want to buy me dinner, no doubt . . . Why are my hands so yellow? . . . Where are my sisters? . . . Father, come closer, will you.' He clasped his father's fingers. 'Why must I always disappoint you?' he groaned.

'My dear son,' said Patrick, 'life has delivered you a pretty miserable deal, that's all. How can you think you disappoint me? I am disappointed that you haven't been repaid for your efforts – your learning, your talents, and the way you have given of your spirit. If only you would let this rubbish go! Let go of the drink and the laudanum. Leave them alone!' Patrick could feel his son drifting away from him. If he did not stop it now, an invisible power he knew too well would take him.

Branwell braced himself. 'I shall wash, and try to be strong,' he said. 'And I'll go and see Francis.'

'Good,' said Patrick. 'I'll boil you some water.'

Branwell forced himself forward and into the house. 'It's getting cold,' said his father. 'And there might be a downpour. Make sure you wrap up. I'll come and fetch you in an hour.'

'Ah, there you are,' said Grundy rising to his feet. 'Come and sit down.' He handed Branwell a stiff hot brandy. 'It's a chilly evening. Warm yourself up with this.'

'I'm not really well enough for that,' said Branwell shakily. 'It's good to see you, Francis. I hadn't expected you. How kind.'

Grundy affected nonchalance, though Branwell's tired demeanour, his glazed and blood-shot eyes upset him deeply. All the words he had hoped to say wouldn't come. He sat in silence, listening to the voices about them, noting the eyes upon them, the fear and horror in their gaze. He felt as if he were sitting beside a ruin, even a mighty ruin, but a ruin nonetheless. For yes, there was something mighty about Branwell Brontë at his best. His potential was immense and frightening. Whenever you were with him you felt it. He sat beside him, blinded by his plight. Neither of them spoke for a while. Branwell trembled, biting his fist. Grundy removed his cloak, draped it about Branwell's shoulders and attempted to relax. Branwell's breathing was failing, his eyes were glassy; strange struggling moans came from his throat.

When they had finished their drinks, Grundy rose from his chair. 'We need some fresh air,' he said, taking a deep breath. He was conscious now of a sinister lurking energy. It was all about them.

'I mustn't go far,' Branwell said, pressing his aching ribs and wincing. 'Father is coming. He will see me safely home. Why, Francis, I hardly know one way from another these days. Direction is a funny thing, if your mind becomes fuzzy, you lose it.'

'Indeed,' said Francis quietly. 'We are driven by direction, dear Branwell. – That way to the door!'

As they went through the door and entered the darkness, Branwell thrust his arm up his sleeve in a strange uncanny movement. Slowly, and with earnest precision he pulled out a knife.

Grundy stood staring at the glinting, shimmering blade.

'See!' said Branwell. 'See how it gleams! I shall drive it into Satan's heart! Just let me find him!' He glanced about nodding. 'He's after me, you know! – Did you see him in there? Oh, he was there in the shadows.' He turned madly to look back at the inn. 'He knew I'd seen him.' Cursing and muttering he stabbed at the air. 'There! Damn you! I'll kill you I will, if it's the last thing I do!'

They stood in the darkness for a while. Grundy wasn't sure what to do. He felt a raw sense of dread. Branwell stood limp in the road, clasping the knife. 'Leave me,' he whispered. 'I need to be alone.'

'Give me that knife,' urged Grundy. He put out his hand.

'No!' screamed Branwell, putting it back in his sleeve. 'I have to kill Satan with it!'

Francis Grundy's eyes grew moist. He could not leave him yet, not until the parson arrived. 'Give me the knife,' said Francis in a low, gentle voice.

'No,' said Branwell. Then louder, 'No, no, no!'
Grundy became silent.

'A lot of erroneous opinions are bandied about out there,' said Patrick after he had brought Branwell back and seen him to bed. Not a scrap of disapprobation for his son would he mix with his tenderness. He had insisted that Branwell sleep in his room so he could comfort him through his nightmares. In the darkness he whispered prayers for him. prayers of terror, prayers of pleading, prayers of despair. The hearts of the sisters were heavy.

'You are right, Papa,' replied Anne. 'But there is also much love for Branwell too from the people who know him. All tongues are not savage.'

'Suppose we make Branwell some toast and tea,' said Patrick. 'Do you think he'd have it?'

'I doubt it,' sighed Emily. 'He's in terrible pain.'

Just then he wandered downstairs. He was in his nightshirt, shivering and sweating. 'Is it still night-time?' he asked, peering about. He screwed up his eyes. 'Ah, Father, you're there. Come here. I need you.' He gazed at his sisters then looked at his father sadly. 'Either me or my father will be dead by morning,' he told them quietly. 'He does what he can, but it's all over with me.'

'Will you have some toast and tea?' asked Patrick.

'I daren't eat it,' said Branwell weakly.

'Even a cup of tea makes him vomit,' said Emily.

'You need to rest,' said his father in a strained voice.

'The thought of food revolts me,' said Branwell stumbling to a chair. 'And lying in bed ... Well, you know how I hate lying in bed.' He clutched his head. 'Oh, these damned heads we must live in! If I sleep I am haunted. When I wake the visions are worse! Where can I go for peace?' He tried to stand quickly then fell to his knees, overcome by weakness.

The sisters looked at each other in turn, their eyes brimming with tears. Twice that morning children had arrived at the house inquiring about Branwell, sending their parents' good wishes then hurrying away. Branwell stood up, his hair dripping with sweat. 'Father, is it not true that I was the best of students?' With a painful deep breath he stretched up to his full height. 'Tell Charlotte, will you. Did I not pass all tests you set me with flying colours! – To be quite specific, Charlotte, had I gone to Cambridge, Father said I'd have ranked with the finest intellects! Is it not true, Father?' He stumbled across the room and fell. Emily hurried over, then Anne, then Charlotte.

'It doesn't sound like his voice,' said Anne weeping.

'My dear, sweet Anne, it's me all right,' came the laboured sound from inside him. He shuddered and came to his senses. 'What's left of me, that is. – Charlotte, help me upstairs, will you? Like it or not, I shall have to go lie in that bed!' He clasped his hand to his chest. 'Oh, how it hurts! The fires of hell, I fear, are already inside me!'

His father stood by his side gazing at the floor.

'Branwell, you should pray!' Anne pleaded. 'God is always there to listen!'

Branwell laughed sharply and painfully. 'To you perhaps, not me ... If only, if only, there had been more time, perhaps I could have known this God, understood Him better.'

As Branwell clambered up the stairs, Charlotte saw to her horror there was blood on his mouth. She could feel the thinness of his flesh, the hardness of his bones through his nightshirt. She held back the tears. She knew she might have been kinder to Branwell, and hoped he'd forgive the wrong words she had often said when the right words had been stubborn and proud. He had never been cruel to her like that. He ought to have been, she thought, angry now at his goodness, his easy kindness over the way he was often ill-used. As she helped him to bed, he clasped her hand tightly. 'Go and bring Brown!' he said urgently. 'I need him now.'

The grey haired sexton from Haworth walked fast up the hill with Charlotte. He was still in the long boots he wore while digging in the graveyard. They were heavy with soil. Charlotte urged him quickly up the stairs.

Brown had never anticipated this. He could scarcely meet Branwell's eyes. The sight of him, so yellow, so hollowed, the shades of death so close beneath his skin horrified him. His throat tightened with grief. He had ached and wept for his friend. And how he had prayed! The family stood by the door in silence. After several minutes they went downstairs and left them.

Brown looked down at his boots. He had brought in graveyard earth. It seemed so strange bringing it here to the parsonage on the bottom of his boots. He had left a trail on the stairs. Unable to help himself, he fell before him weeping softly.

'John! John!' Branwell said weakly. 'What are you doing down there blubbering away? I want to see you. Come here, you fool. Doesn't a sexton know about death? Why so afraid of it, my friend? – Here, look in its face. See it as my father must see it on its way. – Let me tell you how I love you, John, before I go. You see, it's all that matters in the end.'

'My dear friend,' said Brown through his tears. 'If only I could help you.'

Branwell sighed. 'Your chest, John. How is it? Does it hurt? Father tells me it's bad.'

'Ah,' laughed Brown, raising his face. 'What can I expect? I have breathed the stone of all those goodbyes on gravestones, they are indelibly carved inside me.'

'John, come close,' said Branwell, moving his head towards him and trying to smile. 'Tell me again what happened with that girl on your twenty-first birthday! Oh, what a night eh? Go on, tell me again!' He laughed, but it was forced. He started to cough. 'Damn it, John, this dying is a miserable business.' He fell back on the pillow holding his chest. He talked on deliriously. 'Milly, John ... Do you remember Milly? All that beautiful hair. And those eyes, John. Do you remember those eyes!'

'Aye,' said Brown, bending his head. 'I remember her eyes.'

'Wasn't she a beauty, John? And how I loved her. I've known it, you see. I've known what a man searches for eternally. I found it. It's here in my heart. She gave it to me.'

Brown nodded, forcing back the tears.

'You've been like a brother to me, John. And I thank you for that. Yes, it's true, I don't rejoice as I should, given my many blessings; my wonderful sisters, you, and my precious father ... I must write a poem about that. But not tonight ...'

He closed his eyes, mumbling. The sound came like a thin wind from the moor.

'The Lord is my shepherd; I shall not want.
He maketh me to lie down in green pastures: he leadeth me beside the still waters.
He restoreth my soul: he leadeth me in the paths of righteousness for his name's sake ...'

Brown opened up the door and beckoned the parson, who stood

at the foot of the stairs. Patrick came quickly joining Branwell in his words, both their voices mingling in the still room.

'Yea, though I walk through the valley of the shadow of death, I will fear no evil . . .'

They went on until the psalm ended. Then there was silence. The sisters stood behind their father. Branwell opened his eyes. He lifted himself suddenly and shuddered. Reaching for Brown's hand he clutched it and called out loudly, 'Oh, John, I am dying! In all my past life I have done nothing either great or good!' Within seconds he had fallen back on the pillow and was sleeping. Patrick ushered them out.

Only Branwell slept that night in the parsonage. As daybreak came they all sank behind the daylight. Branwell awoke to his father's shape in the doorway and stretched out his hand. 'Pray for me now,' he said, in a calm and restrained voice.

The parson ached tenderly. 'You are repentant, my son,' he whispered shakily. 'I am glad.'

'I am, Father,' said Branwell. 'I'm repentant of all I've done wrong, of all the pain I have caused on this earth. But like a leaf blowing in the wind, a lot of the time I was innocent.' He went on quickly. – 'But now I see it. It's wonderful, Father! I see with such clarity what you have often talked about in your sermons. It's there, Father, it exists. I am in that place where everything is truth and love. And it's all so peaceful and good!'

'Heaven has come for you, thank God!' his father said softly.

All three sisters stood by his bedside, listening to their father's prayer. 'Amen,' they said.

'Amen!' said Branwell loudly. For several seconds he threw his head from side to side convulsively then stopped. The family stared in awe as he struggled to his feet, then fell gasping on his father.

'My son! My son!' cried Patrick, weeping. 'My poor, brilliant son!'

The girls went downstairs, sharing their grief. Their beloved brother lay dead. It had all finished so suddenly. They did not know what they would miss the most; his wit, his frenzied passion, the sound of him playing the cottage piano, or those quiet serious moments, when they listened eagerly for whatever came next from his complex, profound mind. Anne wept alone in the kitchen. Charlotte and Emily sobbed on each other's shoulders. Their father shrieked and railed upstairs behind the closed door.

The house was suddenly silenced. Only Branwell's ghost remained of the man he had once been. Yet he would always be alive in their minds, bringing his laughter and sunshine, his earth shattering ability to hearten the sometimes gloomy days in Haworth. Occasionally they would peep from their windows on hearing a familiar sound, and look out into the graveyard beyond. At 31 years of age, Branwell had left them for eternity. Soon the rest of them would follow, leaving the ageing parson alone with his memories. And he would sometimes whisper, 'Goodnight' as he wound up the clock before retiring to bed. Occasionally he would hear a voice whisper back. Then he would clasp his hands in prayer and plead that his loved ones were well in the world of light.

ACKNOWLEDGEMENTS

First and foremost, I would like to thank Juliet Barker for her eloquent and moving biography, *The Brontës*, Weidenfeld & Nicolson, 1994, an invaluable source of information and pleasure, and for her kind permission to use extracts from Brontë letters and poems in the book.

The poem 'Percy's Last Sonnet' is taken from *The Works of Patrick Branwell Brontë*; edited by Victor A. Neufeldt, Garland Publishing, 1999.

Other books I have reached for again, that have been both helpful and inspiring are, *The Life of Charlotte Brontë*, Elizabeth Gaskell, 1857; *Patrick Branwell Brontë*, Alice Law, A.M. Philpot, London, 1923; *The Brontës Web of Childhood*, Fannie Elizabeth Ratchford, Columbia University Press, New York, 1941; *The Bewitched Parsonage*, William Stanley Braithwaite, Coward-McCann, New York, 1950; *The Infernal World of Patrick Brontë*, Daphne Du Maurier, Victor Gollancz, 1960; *Emily Brontë*, Winifred Gerin, Clarendon Press, Oxford, 1971; *Classics of Brontë Scholarship*, edited by Charles Lemon, The Brontë Society, 1999; *Mary Wollstonecraft, a revolutionary life*, Janet Todd, Weidenfeld & Nicolson, 2000; *The Brontë Myth*, Lucasta Miller, Jonathan Cape, 2001; *The Letters of Reverend Patrick Brontë*, edited by Dudley Green, Nonsuch, 2005; *The Timetables of History*, Bernard Grun, Simon & Schuster, 1991; and *England, A Concise History*, F. E. Halliday, Thames and Hudson Ltd, 1995.

I would also like to thank friends who have encouraged me throughout the writing and given their support. They know who they are. And I must thank John, my son, who despite his busy work schedule, and commitments to his young family, has found time to show interest and involvement.

Special thanks go to Bob Duckett, UK Editor, *Brontë Studies*, who read and commented on the manuscript during development, and was a source of much reassurance and new energy.

Finally I would like to thank the National Gallery for permission to use the Angel, from Leonardo da Vinci's 'Virgin of the Rocks', on the cover of this edition.

Wendy Louise Bardsley 2017

Wendy Louise Bardsley has worked as a teacher in schools, colleges and universities. She has also worked in the Manchester Inspection & Advisory Service for Education as Advisory Teacher for Drama, Special Needs and English, with special responsibilities for matters pertaining to The United Nations Convention for the Rights of The Child when she was interviewed on Radio 4, gave lectures and organised symposiums. A noted poet and anthologist as well as a writer of books for education, she has a B.Ed (Hons) a PGCE and an M.Phil, (Manchester University), and three grown children: a doctor and two pharmacists, from her marriage to William Bardsley, Reader in Biochemistry, (Manchester University).

Her Brontë anthology, *An Enduring Flame*, with poems from around the world and photographs by Simon Warner was greeted with acclaim. She has published non-fiction for Education, four novels, several anthologies and four poetry collections, and has also been a book reviewer for *The Independent on Sunday* and many literary journals.